THE
IMMORTALITY
THIEF

TARAN HUNT

SOLARIS

First published 2022 by Solaris
an imprint of Rebellion Publishing Ltd,
Riverside House, Osney Mead,
Oxford, OX2 0ES, UK

www.solarisbooks.com

ISBN: 978-1-78618-512-9

This is a work of fiction. All the characters and events
portrayed in this book are fictional, and any resemblance
to real people or incidents is purely coincidental.

A CIP catalogue record for this book is available from the
British Library.

Designed & typeset by Rebellion Publishing

Printed in the United Kingdom

CHAPTER ONE:
THE NAMELESS SHIP
AND THE DYING STAR

THE NOTHING-PLACE BETWEEN *leaving* and *arriving* during faster-than-light travel isn't really Hell. Hell is the absence of God, or the absence of other people, or something like that. FTL engines just... I don't know, grabbed space and yanked it forward, rippling like a bedsheet tugged out of place, and our ship caught up in the folds.

But it sure as Hell felt like Hell. In the moment between the kick to faster-than-light speeds, and before the drop out, space *narrowed*. In the pilot's cradle, alone, I blinked away afterimages from the brilliant flash that preceded hyperspeed, like the universe warning me STOP in the seconds before I broke the speed limit. When I blinked those ghosts away, there was nothing through the window except black.

Not for the first time, I wished Benny had chosen a ship with a little more elbow room for the pilot. There was no space in the cockpit for anyone except me. I couldn't see the others; couldn't even turn around to look, because then I might miss the drop-out point; I couldn't call out to them or talk, because then I might lose my concentration, and overshoot our stop.

They weren't saying anything, either. Like I was alone on this ship. What had I said Hell was, again? Absence?

Nothing except darkness outside the front window. Nothing to see, no walls, no floor, no ceiling. But I could *feel* it, the space narrowing in on me like the sod walls of some grave, claustrophobia choking me. I was alone—

The drop-out point. I switched engines and space widened out the window, blooming bright and brilliant. I controlled our drop-out, swinging around, adjusting artificial gravity, and when our speed had slowed enough that light had caught up to us, I looked out that cockpit window and saw a marvel.

We had come out not far from the salvage ship, because I was an amazing pilot whose skills were only matched by his good looks and also I'd received very precise coordinates for this salvage. The salvage ship's ancient, pitted metal revolved before us with slow majesty in the blazing firelight of the bloated nearby star.

A star that was verging on supernova.

It was a shame I was the only one who could see it, due to the aforementioned cramped conditions. I let out my breath and said, "That spaceship really doesn't have a name?"

Nothing but the creaking of stabilizing straps answered me. I craned my head back until I could see the other three in the little room, Benny with his eyes shut and head tipped back against the wall, Quint with her little hands gone white around her stabilizing strap, and Leah with legs braced and gun disassembled, cleaning the pieces on the bench between her thighs.

"Hey," I said, "what's the ship's name?"

"It doesn't have one," Quint said.

"Really?" I turned back to look back out the front window; it was time to accelerate the *Viper* to match the salvage ship's revolution so that we wouldn't crash into spinning metal and be shredded like cheese on a grater. "It must have had a name once. Everything important has a name."

The *Viper* jolted and, yeah, I'd changed our theta direction a little too fast, but flying a ship was like speaking a foreign language. There were all these strict rules to follow to get the grammar right, but so long as you had the gist of it intact, you could make it up on the fly and be pretty well understood.

"I knew a girl who adopted a rock once," I said. "She drew little eyes on it. Do you know what she named it?"

"What did she name it?" Leah asked, her tone anticipating the punchline like a mortar shell.

"Roxanne."

"Would you please shut up about names and pay attention to landing the ship?" Quint said.

Making contact with a salvage ship was the most dangerous part of getting salvage—if I was going a little too slow, or a little too fast, we wouldn't latch: we'd *bounce*, and bounciness in space wasn't the harmless fun it was in a gravity well. In space, it tended to cause hull fractures, atmospheric loss, and inevitably death. I guessed that was why Quint was so nervous. She shouldn't have been: this wasn't like the FTL tunnel. I was flying, so I had control. And I was good at what I did.

I extended the *Viper*'s gripping arms, opening like a claw as we approached the nameless vessel. All I could see out of my window now was a long horizon of scarred hull, thinned and pitted by a thousand years' sunlight and debris so that, in places, I could see straight through to the struts and bones. An old and mighty thing. It had been abandoned for a thousand years; no one alive might remember, but this ship *must* have had a name.

"I'm going to call it the *Nameless*," I decided.

"Call it what it is?" Leah asked.

The *Viper* was close enough now. With a quick command typed into the screen, I closed the gripping arms. They slammed shut, impacts reverberating through the ship as they connected. Success.

"That's what names are," I said, while I ran the program that would heat up the connection and open the far side ship's airlock. "Or what they were, anyway. We—humans, I mean—use a specific set of words as names and names only, taken from the old language. Like Benny or Quint or Leah or Sean." We *could* just punch through the *Nameless*'s hull with the *Viper*'s docking chute, but when there was an airlock in existence, it was easier to use it. "But originally, names were just descriptions, like Pretty, or Willow, or—"

"Sean," Benny said, "shut up."

The *Viper* was no longer rocking about. I shut its engines

off. When I turned around, I found the three of them were gathering up their things, heading for the circular aperture in the ceiling that led to the primary airlock. Benny already stood beneath it, tapping something into the wall computer, handbrace glinting. Benny was an inventor. Necessity was the mother of invention and all that, and he and I had grown up in exile from an occupied homeworld, without supplies or the money to buy anything, so he'd learned the skills to make everything. His one-of-a-kind handbrace was one of his inventions—it contained a small-caliber, single-shot projectile weapon to be used as a last-ditch self-defense.

"Air at close to atmospheric pressure, sufficient oxygen, safe temperature range," Benny read. "We won't need the suits."

He pressed a button, and I heard the airlock aperture hiss open. The air of the two ships began to mix, the breath of the *Nameless* disturbed for the first time in a thousand years. Then Benny, my oldest friend, the closest thing I had to family, and the last of my hometown left alive, stepped onto the ladder in the wall. His heels vanished as he climbed up and out.

Quint was next up the ladder, but she took a long time about it, her face pale as she stared up into the darkness of the other ship. Sympathy panged through me at the sight of her silent fear. Of all of us, I should feel sorry for her the least. But I knew what it was like to be frightened and alone.

"It probably won't bite," I reassured her. "In my experience, spaceships don't. Not usually."

Quint gave me a look like she thought maybe the factory had assembled me wrong, and climbed up after Benny.

"How the hell did someone like you end up here with us, anyway?" Leah asked me, but not in a way that cared. She followed Quint up and out.

That left me alone. The *Viper* was coffin-quiet, like it had been abandoned as surely as the *Nameless* had. I hurried after the others.

Frost limned the rungs of the ladder where they joined at the seam of the *Nameless*'s hull, exposed to the vacuum for hundreds of years and cooled almost to absolute zero before the *Viper* had come along and heated it up by a couple hundred degrees Kelvin. I climbed through the cold and emerged out of the floor and into dim red light. One wall of the room was a floor-to-ceiling window—or it had been, before age and decay had filmed the window over. The result was a semi-opaque piece of plastic through which nothing could be seen except the diffuse firelight of the dying star that the *Nameless* orbited.

That was the only light in the room. The *Nameless*'s computers might be—partly—functional, but the lights had burned out long, long ago. The room itself was long and hushed and dark and empty, like the antechamber to a tomb. The walls were splotched and crumbling, decay creeping dust through the flaws in their build. I coughed.

"Remember," Quint said loudly as I emerged, "we have only a week before the sun goes nova, and we have to search this whole ship first. Our boss will let you take whatever you find on the way, but we *have* to find the data."

Or else consequences, terrible consequences, fatal consequences, etc. We knew the score, Quint. I ignored her, scanning the room for anything useful, and my flashlight beam fell upon something carved into the far wall.

I hurried to the wall and fell to my knees, running my fingers over the uneven, ancient scratchings in the metal. I knew that they were letters, though they were not written in the script that I had learned as a child, nor was it written in any of the languages anyone spoke now—not my native tongue, Kystrene, or the Sister Standard that was the only language I regularly spoke anymore. This language was gone, dead, had been dead for a thousand years: Ameng. Real Ameng, right here in front of me.

I trailed my fingers over the letters, carved here a thousand years ago by someone whose dust I was probably now breathing in. A message undisturbed for a millennium until I'd come along, like it had been left specifically for me. I felt out the letters, pieced together the words.

IT IS TRUE

Something scraped to my right, probably Benny or Leah, trying to pry salvageable metal out of the decay. I bent closer to the wall and those long-forgotten letters.

WE SHALL BE MONSTERS

That scraping sound grew louder.

CUT OFF FROM ALL THE WORLD

A piece of the wall fell off beside me, clanging like a cymbal as it hit the floor. The floor hit my palms hard as I fell backwards, recoiling from the clamor.

Dirty fingers reached out from within the wall, curling

around the edge. The nails were cracked and yellow. A head of thick, dark hair emerged, the locks trailing over shoulders and down the side of the wall.

The creature from inside the ship flipped out onto the floor and rose to her feet, shaking wild hair out of her face. It was a woman, the bones of her face standing out sharply, pale brown eyes large in her hungry face.

All movement in the room ceased. We stared at her as she stared at us, with just as much surprise.

Then she dropped her head back and screamed.

CHAPTER TWO:
THREE CONVICTS AND A
GENEROUS OPPORTUNITY

LET ME BE clear: that ship should have been empty. If that hadn't been the case, we would've never been sent there.

A week before a ghost-woman screamed at me on an abandoned spacecraft, some men in suits arrived near midnight to take me from my cell. I didn't *think* the Republican authorities on the planet Parnasse were prone to 'disappearing' illegal refugees who were accidental thieves and repentant almost-murderers, but it wasn't totally outside the bounds of possibility. Still, I've spent a lot of my life being hauled around by authority figures, so I've learned when kicking up a fuss won't do me any good. I followed them onto some cargo elevator that stopped between floors and emptied out into a hallway without cameras. This was the most interesting thing that had happened since the take-down a week ago, which had been full of police officers shouting orders in Sister Standard so tersely and with such heavy Republican accents that I'd almost had trouble understanding them.

The guns pointed at my head and Benny's had made their meaning clear enough, in the end.

"Where's Benny?" I asked as we started down the hallway. I got no response.

Maybe they couldn't speak, or couldn't understand. I tried my question in Kystrene, and Illenich, and Patrene, and once in what I was pretty sure was the local dialect of sign language, but they gave no sign of understanding, which meant they were probably just ignoring me. Fine, I was used to being ignored. Only a handful of Kystrene had escaped the subjugation of our homeworld, and promptly been absorbed by a Republic that preferred pretending nothing had ever happened to facing the fact that they'd abandoned our planet to its fate. Averted eyes and shut doors were commonplace; a little feigned blindness wasn't about to stop me.

My escorts paused in front of a closed door. It was a perfectly ordinary door, like every other door in the camera-less hallway, but I had some reservations about opening it.

"Did you know there are dialects of sign language?" I asked my escorts, staring at the handle for that door. "There's a standardized version, thanks to the Ministers, but it varies by region anyway. Visual languages follow the same rules as spoken ones—"

One of my escorts turned the handle, opened the door, and shoved me inside. I stumbled into a well-appointed room. And standing in the corner was—

"Benny."

He toyed with the standard hospital-issue hand brace that had replaced his weaponized homemade one, but when he heard my voice he looked up and his lips went thin. Such a look. It stopped me like a brick wall.

There were two other people in the finely-appointed room with us, both strangers to me. The woman sitting backwards on one of the fine leather chairs was wearing the same rough prison clothing as me and Benny. She looked like a dirty knife thrown in with the silver. I liked her immediately. Later, I would learn that her name was Leah.

The other woman was skinny, with a short, fussy haircut. She stood behind a polished wooden desk, beneath blacked-out windows, arms crossed over her narrow chest so that her tailored jacket buckled under the arms. Her name, as I would learn, was Quint.

The three of them had arranged themselves according to the fundamental law of mob bosses meeting for a parlay: each of them with their back to a different wall. Thoughtfully, they'd left the fourth wall—the one with the door— open for me.

There was a chair in front of Quint's desk, near the dead center of the room. I shuffled over to that chair and sat down on its generous leather cushions.

Quint eyed me down the line of her narrow nose, then said, "The three of you have committed very serious crimes. Murder," and for a heart-stopping moment I thought that meant the boy had died, but she nodded at Leah when she said it, "or attempted murder of a very important personage," and this time she glanced at Benny and me.

So I wasn't a murderer. Not now, not ever. I exhaled

relief and glanced at Benny, only to find he wasn't looking at me.

"We haven't committed anything." Leah dug her fingernails into the fine leather back of her chair like she intended to split it. "Haven't been to trial yet."

"But you'll be convicted," Quint said. "The evidence against all of you is overwhelming. After your convictions, you'll be given a choice: life in prison, or sentence commutation through voluntary military service."

So, life in prison or a violent death at the hands of the Ministers on some isolated planetoid. And they said the Republic had eliminated the death penalty. 'Voluntary.'

There was an antique clock on Quint's desk, shiny bronze and ticking audibly and altogether better to contemplate than imagining facing down the Ministers again. I picked it up to hide the way my hands shook.

"This isn't some corrupt Minister court in Maria Nova." Leah's voice was clipped. "Talk to our lawyers."

"Benny and I are stateless citizens. I'm not even sure we get lawyers," I said, and flipped the clock over to examine the back rather than see the way Benny was looking at me. I didn't think I'd ever seen him this mad before.

"My boss is offering you a third option," Quint said. "A full pardon. For all of your crimes."

A full pardon? Not just commute the charges, minimize them, whatever weasel-word way of saying they didn't plan on doing anything, but actually wipe them clean? I could get my translation jobs back without having to bolt every time the police rounded the corner. I could travel again, seek out strange new verbs and look for a place that might feel, in some indefinable and wordless way, like it could be home.

Bullshit. The past didn't just go away, and I didn't want to meet anyone who believed it could.

"Who's your boss?" I asked, at the same time as Leah demanded, "What's the catch?"

"There's an abandoned ship orbiting a star near the end of its lifespan. Our estimates say the star will go nova within the month, likely within the next two weeks. My boss wishes you to retrieve a piece of data from the ship before the supernova destroys it."

A simple enough task. Simple enough, in fact, that I couldn't see the need for three felons and a secret room with no electronics. The antique clock was weighty in my lap, ticking away. I got my nails between the seam of body and back panel and started to pry the clock open.

"All three of you have experience with salvage and... avoiding customs," Quint said, eying me while I disassembled the furniture. "My boss requires competence and discretion."

The inside of the clock was all intermeshed wheels, mysteriously interlocked, ticking steadily. "Why does your boss need us to be discreet?"

"The data is of a sensitive nature."

I pulled one of the gears free. "And who is your boss that he wants sensitive data and discretion?"

"My boss's name doesn't matter. What matters is that he's in a position to help you."

"Where is this dying star?" Leah asked. "If we're stealing something, we'll end up right back in jail. And," she pointed one finger at Quint like the muzzle of a gun, "there's no way we're going to Maria Nova to steal anything from the Ministers."

"A prison cell sounds better than the Ministers," I agreed. So did splinters beneath the nails and any other variety of tortures. The gears I'd taken from the clock carved bright lines of pain against my palm.

"The ship is in unclaimed space, and no one but my boss knows its location. You will be the only salvagers there."

"What exactly do you want us to steal?" I asked.

"Data. More information will be provided to you on your departure, as well as a ship and necessary supplies."

Leah scoffed. "You don't know what supplies we need."

"You can choose them yourself," Quint said. "Your budget is generous."

"We would need a fast ship." I'd pulled a handful of smaller gears from the back of the clock, and it was starting to look a little empty. "If this supernova is in unclaimed space and we have fourteen days or less to explore the ship before the star explodes, we'll need to get there within a few hours. That means cutting-edge FTL." I upturned my handful of gears onto the desk. They fell, glittering and ringing like coins.

Faster-than-light engines, or FTL, and its sister technology of artificial gravity were relatively new inventions, barely a century old. The tech was commonly available in the Republic, where it had been invented, and it was constantly being improved as part of the arms race between the two Sister Systems. No one knew if FTL was a common technology in the other Sister System,

Maria Nova. The Ministers—the deadly alien race that had appeared out of nowhere, subjugated humanity for hundreds of years, and still ruled humanity in the Maria Nova system—kept information about Maria Nova strictly controlled. All we knew was that the Ministers themselves used FTL tech.

Of course, the fastest, newest ships were the most expensive. The price of the most advanced ships could be greater than the total monetary value of an outer colony like my home planet, Kystrom, had been.

"You'll have whatever you need," Quint said.

The clock in my hand was missing too many pieces to tick anymore, and so the silence in the room was absolute. Quint crossed her arms over her chest, but didn't take back her word.

I exchanged a glance with Leah. Benny still avoided looking at me, but we'd worked together for eight years now. I didn't need to meet his eyes to know what he was thinking. I said to Quint, "How much will you pay us?"

"Five hundred thousand terraques."

That was the price of a ship by itself, and she'd offered it without demur.

"A star about to blow sounds dangerous," said Leah. "Is that all you think our lives are worth?" She'd dug her nails through the leather of her chair all right, her arm draped over the back.

"One million terraques, then," Quint said.

I tossed another gear on the table. "Personally, I don't get out of bed for less than two."

A slight hesitation, this time. "Done," Quint said.

"Each."

A longer silence, so long I thought she would refuse.

Quint said, "Deal."

I ran my finger through the pile of gears, separating them out onto the table. How many people in the Republic had that kind of finances? Not very many. "It's an attractive offer. How do we know your boss can pay?"

"My boss is… a significant politician in the Republic. He has the means, and the authority, to enlist your services and pay as promised."

So Quint's boss was a Senator. How many Senators did the Republic have? Twenty-five? Thirty? And how many of those Senators had this much money? I separated out a few gears from the pile: one, two, three.

"So you understand," Quint added, "why discretion is important."

"We understand," I assured her, toying with those three little gears.

"Then you accept the offer?"

"I'm in," Leah said.

Benny spoke for the first time. "So am I."

Quint clasped her hands together. "Very good. I've prepared an overview of what we know of the salvage vessel, and what—"

"Wait, wait, wait." I waved my arm over my head; my hand ended up directly in front of her face. "You never asked me."

I saw Quint suppress a sigh. "Mr. Wren, do you accept the offer?"

I smiled at her. "No," I said.

CHAPTER THREE: THE LOST LANGUAGE

THE SAME GUARDS came back to get me from my cell half a day later.

"Hi," I said, while they took me up in the mysterious freight elevator to another cloak-and-dagger meeting with that asshole Quint. "Long time no see." I repeated myself in a couple new languages and dialects when they didn't answer, just in case it really was all a matter of misunderstanding.

My introduction to the nicely appointed, surveillance-less room was a lot less gentle this time.

Quint sat behind the desk, wearing a different tailored jacket, the antique clock still in glittering pieces on the table in front of her. No one used this office except to make shady deals, I guessed. Benny and Leah weren't there, but there was a set of Raginian crystal glasses on the table beside a bottle of wine with a label that was unintelligible even to me.

"Please sit, Mr. Wren," Quint said, attempting to pretend she was glad to see me. "Would you like a drink?"

"I'm *parched*," I said, just to watch her smile grow stiff, and sat down in the same chair I'd taken before, across from Quint and beside the glittering gears. "Yes, thank you."

She passed me a glass. She held her own glass properly, fingers curled gracefully around the bowl. I deliberately held mine in a fist around the stem. We smiled at each other across the table, Quint's smile a terrible little rictus.

Eventually she seemed to understand what I was waiting for, and took a tiny sip out of her glass. Only then did I take a sip out of mine. It was unlikely that Quint's boss would go through the trouble of ruining some—wow, really expensive—wine, just to poison me when he could have me commit a staged suicide in my cell with bedsheets, but my faith in the Republican government was pretty low, so it couldn't hurt to be sure.

Quint said, "My boss believes that I didn't offer the proper incentives. He says that I misunderstood your fundamental motivations."

"Don't be too hard on yourself," I reassured her. "Most of the time, I'm not even sure what those are."

Quint plowed ahead with admirable determination. "You should know how we found that ship. You see, it's difficult to detect the ship at its current location—the radiation of the dying star masks its signature. You have to already know it's there in order to observe it, or else get very, very lucky. We got lucky. A few weeks ago we picked up a broadcast from that ship. This," and she pulled a handheld out of her pocket, bringing the number of electronics in the room up to one, "is that recording."

She tapped the screen, then held it out towards me, lying flat on her palm. Static welled up, the harsh blurriness of a furiously radiating star, but there was a voice buried in that static.

The rhotic consonant gave it away. The liquid sounds tend to be characteristic in a language; if I wanted to distinguish between Wentrese and Temarian, my best bet was to listen for the sound that, in the archaic alphabet, had been usually represented by the letter *R*. The *R* in this recording was an odd one; it sat sort of in the middle of the tongue and had the smooth shapeless sound of a door creaking open. It didn't tap or growl or roll, like any of the rhotic variants more common in our modern languages.

The uncommon rhotic consonant, combined with the characteristic stress-unstress pattern, made the identity of the language unmistakable. I almost missed the desk with my glass; wine sloshed out over the edge and onto my finger.

"That's Ameng," I said. The person in the recording was speaking Ameng.

A thousand years ago, after the First Ministerial War, when the Ministers had taken control of the Sister Systems, they'd purged the old languages in favor of a standardized single language that both Sister Systems still spoke today as a lingua franca. The most common of these purged languages was Ameng. Only fragments of Ameng remained; a recording here and there, a library's worth of old texts, root words and grammar buried in our modern languages.

But I'd never heard this recording before. I listened

intently as the recording looped, carefully transcribing the syllables in my head. It was a simple message—an SOS, a ship without power, and something unintelligible about someone named Mara Zhu.

Quint tapped the screen, silencing the recording. "It takes a very long time by human standards for a dying star to actually reach supernova," she said, tucking the handheld away despite my instinctive lean forward to follow it. "Our best estimates suggest that the salvage vessel has been in orbit for about a thousand years."

Since before the First Ministerial War. Since before the language reform. That wasn't just Ameng, it was *native-speaker* Ameng.

"My boss has heard of your special talent." Quint fussed with the set of her jacket, tugging it down on her torso. "You run a small freelance translation business in and around the refugee camp outside the city, translating to and from at least four languages. The translations aren't official, of course, because you aren't certified, but the quality of your work is on par with the best AI translation software."

On par with AI? Computers could go to Hell; you need a person to really understand implication and cultural context. I bet Quint was monolingual.

"It is said that one of your languages is Ameng," Quint said.

There were only twenty or thirty people in the Republic who could speak Ameng with any kind of fluency. I was one of them. I pulled the disassembled clock into my lap, leaning comfortably back in my chair. "I don't want to be modest about it," I told her. "I'm really good."

"Our sources said that message was an SOS."

I matched the gear to my memory of how the clock had looked when I'd taken it apart, and slotted it neatly back into place. "Your sources were right."

"My boss and I realize that intellectuals like yourself are not swayed by financial offers—"

"No, I like money," I assured her.

Quint leaned forward, that fussy hair of hers swinging against her temples. "That ship has been left undisturbed for a thousand years. It's a treasure trove of historical and archaeolinguistic knowledge. And you could be the first to discover it. Whatever knowledge you want to bring back, whatever research you wish to do—it's all yours. All my boss wants is this one piece of data."

"And what is this data?"

Quint's eyes brightened with the pure, treasure-gold gleam of avarice. Obviously, she had been authorized to answer that question this time around.

Reverently, she said, "It's the Philosopher Stone."

CHAPTER FOUR:
SEAN WREN AND THE
PHILOSOPHER STONE

ONCE WHEN I was a kid on Kystrom, a Chosen woman stopped me in the street.

Before the Ministers killed everyone in my hometown and took over the rest of the planet, there were a few schools of thought regarding ancient history. Most viewed the arrival of the alien Ministers, a thousand years ago, as a random act of destruction, as unstoppable and meaningless as a natural disaster. That was what I'd been taught in school, how my parents had spoken of it; how I'd thought of it, too. Some radicals had claimed the coming of the Ministers had been a blessing for humanity, pointing out how cleanly and clockwork society allegedly ran in Maria Nova, where the Ministers still had control of the human population. I couldn't think of those radicals, now, without bitterness— traitors that had welcomed the slaughter of my home, the subsequent surrender of my planet.

The Chosen thought differently than both.

"Boy," the Chosen woman had called me, long before a three-foot growth spurt made me tower over everyone I knew. "Are you Chosen?"

The Chosen had nearly been eliminated by the Ministers more than once in their history, a singularly unlucky group. If all it took to count as Chosen by a deity was a run of serious bad luck, I should qualify for membership now.

But then: "No," I'd said.

The real Chosen had stricter bars for entry, of course. Then or now, I would never count as one of them.

My answer had not been the one the woman had wanted. I saw her hesitate. But the road was empty, the sun was going down, and she seemed in a hurry. "Would you help me?" she asked.

I agreed, and she handed me a jar of ash.

"My family is away, and I can't do it for myself," she told me. The jar sat heavy and cold in my palm. "Put some on your finger and mark my head."

I knew then that it was a repentance day for her. The Chosen believed that the Ministers, who had appeared so abruptly and out of nowhere, had been sent by God as his vengeance. The Ministers were not living creatures, the Chosen said, but avatars of divine punishment. Ministers could not go to Heaven or Hell, they had no souls, they existed for nothing but our suffering. The Chosen repented in order to convince God to take the Ministers away. This Chosen woman needed to be marked, but she was not allowed to do it to herself. I was the only one around.

God was punishing humanity, the Chosen believed,

because we had created the Philosopher Stone.

All that humanity could be or ever had been was encapsulated by the Philosopher Stone experiments. Right before the alien Ministers had appeared and subjugated us, our ancestors had been at the peak of their brilliance—a level of technological advancement that we were only beginning to reach again now, with the invention of FTL and art-grav. No one knew precisely what the Philosopher Stone experiments had produced, but it was said that they had revealed the secret of eternal life.

The Chosen believed that the Philosopher Stone had not been the victory of humanity. It had been its downfall. We had reached too far, they said, and God had sent his immortal Ministers to punish us. So now, once a week, they took a day to remind themselves that immortal life was denied to us, and one day we all would die.

I supposed I could believe that the God of the Chosen, or the God Who Shed His Blood For Us that my family worshipped, could have sent the Ministers. The Ministers had swept through my hometown Itaka like a plague of locusts, and left the eerie hollow stillness of stripped fields and burnt-out houses and dead things behind. They were humanoid, but not human. Ancient, but unageing. Alive, but not mortal. It was said they could be killed, even though they did not die of age, but in all the horrible things I had seen while fleeing the massacre in my hometown, I had not seen a Minister die.

The ash was soft and powdery against my thumb. I marked the Chosen woman the way I had seen other Chosen marked, a bar across her brow.

"*Ash to ash and dust to dust*," she murmured as I did, in old dead Ameng; distorted by the years but still recognizably Ameng. *Philosopher Stone* was an Ameng phrase, too. In modern Sister it meant something like Thinker Rock. The Chosen were right that we all died one day, but even dead languages left traces.

"You did a good thing today," the Chosen woman told me as she took the ashes back, dust on her skull like the dust she would become just a few years later, when the Ministers came, just like the Chosen always warned would happen. "May God guide and keep you."

* * *

THERE WAS ONE major problem with Quint's incredible theory.

"The Philosopher Stone experiments were destroyed," I said. They'd gone missing at about the time of the First Ministerial War, destroyed by the Ministers to ensure humanity remained under their control.

"Not destroyed. Only hidden," Quint said.

"Why would anyone hide it? That's the most important knowledge humanity has ever had."

"We don't know. Perhaps ancient humans wanted to hide it from the Ministers to preserve it. Then, when the Ministers won the war, its location was lost."

"How are you even sure the data is there?"

"The limited historical records we have of the ship where the Philosopher Stone experiments took place match what we've been able to observe of the salvage vessel."

I sat back slowly in my fancy chair. The secret of eternal life, and who knew what else. The sum of humanity's best and brightest knowledge, of all that humans could be. Knowledge that had been lost for a thousand years. I finally understood why Quint's boss wanted this done quickly and discreetly.

And yet, this whole situation still reeked of a trap.

"I get that you don't want to draw attention to the ship," I said. "If the Ministers notice it, they'll finish the job and destroy it and you won't get your data. But if this trip were legal, your boss would be sending Republican commandos, not three criminals. This is a set-up."

I pushed the last gear into place on the clock, found the dial, and wound it up. The gears twitched, then, as smoothly as if it had never stopped, the clock resumed ticking.

"I will be travelling with you, if that puts your mind at rest," Quint said. "I'm willing to put my life and future on the line for my boss—in all my dealings with him so far, he has treated me fairly and well."

"Yeah, well, you're not exactly a criminal about to get shipped off to jail forever," I said.

Quint was silent. Meaningfully so.

"Quint," I said, delighted.

"I used to work for my boss in a different capacity," she said. "Moving money around. Some of the money I moved slipped through the cracks and into my own account. A very large sum, in fact. Enough that it would have put me in the same legal situation you're in right now. My boss made me an offer, and I accepted it. Since then I've done a number of smaller jobs for him, and he has treated me fairly for each one—and paid me very well. You can trust him."

She had her hands clasped on the desk before her, fingers tightly entwined. I felt a sudden surge of pity for her. "Not how you thought your life would go, huh?"

"If money and freedom and scientific discovery isn't enough for you, then think of this," Quint said. "The invention of faster-than-light engines allowed us to finally throw off the yoke of Ministerial oppression in the Terra Nova system, allowed the Republic to be born. Imagine what the technology of the Philosopher Stone can do for humanity."

Freedom, greed, curiosity, moral rectitude. They really weren't leaving a stone unturned on this, were they?

"We can finally be secure in our resistance to the Ministers," Quint said. "What happened to Kystrom ten years ago will never happen again. The Republic will be safe."

Ah, she was charming. And so *very* Republican. Did she really think the security of her country was going to motivate a Kystrene like me? "The answer is still no," I told her.

She sat back hard in her chair, her earnest expression washing off her face like the tide off stones. Did she hate me? I wondered, when I saw what that tide revealed, but no: she looked at me like you might look at a dog barking indoors, a little dislike, overall indifference.

I think I would've liked it better if she'd hated me. You have to have feelings for a person to hate them. I don't think she felt anything for me at all.

"If you're concerned about Benjamin," she said, "he can be removed from this equation. My boss can easily substitute a different smuggler for him."

Interesting. "But *my* skills are unique."

"Precisely. Is that what you want, then? To remove your partner from the deal?"

"Benny and I come as a package," I told her.

"That's loyal, for a business partner."

How little she knew.

"What *do* you want, Sean?" Quint asked. I wondered if Quint was her first name, or her last. "If you could have one wish, any wish. Many things are in my boss's power to do, and he's willing to do many things. What do you want?"

"I want to turn back time," I told her. "I want what happened to Kystrom to be undone. I want my family back alive." The honesty of it scraped my throat.

Her expression sent me straight back to my childhood on Kystrom, the teacher looking at me in frustration when I answered the question wrong for the third time because I hadn't been listening.

"I meant a wish for *now*," Quint said. "What do you want *now?*"

CHAPTER FIVE:
LEASHED

THE THIRD TIME strange men in suits arrived to take me from my cell, it had become almost routine.

"Gentlemen," I greeted them. One of them came and grabbed my arm, which was new; I'd never tried to escape so I wasn't sure why they thought they needed to restrain me. "Getting a little friendly," I started to say, but then the other came up beside me, and I felt something prick my neck.

* * *

I WOKE ONCE, cold, face pressed to astringent plastic, and felt something digging into the back of my neck.

Alone, I thought. It was the only thing left in my empty head, the knowledge at the base of all my thoughts, as permanent and pervasive as the beat of my heart. No one here; no one left. Just me.

"He's coming to," someone warned, and I mused dazedly over pronoun and verb and colloquialism, and did not quite put together the sense before another pinprick sent me back into the dark.

* * *

I WOKE FULLY in the elevator. My whole body felt clammy, and I was balanced between my two guards, each of them with a hand beneath my arm. I struggled to find my feet, and as soon as I was balanced enough to pull my arm from their grasp I pressed my fingers against my nape. There was something hard there, solid and beneath the skin, right up against my spine. The elevator doors opened before I could do more than register its presence, and I was dragged into the hall, and tossed, once again, into the well-appointed room.

Benny was there, this time. He stood beside the desk, Quint behind it, and watched me with a cold, resentful gaze.

"My boss," said Quint, while I struggled to find my feet, "believes we have misunderstood your fundamental motivations."

"What is it this time?" I asked, enunciating carefully. "Wine and women?"

"You're charged with *attempted* murder." Quint was rapping her knuckles against the edge of the desk, and not meeting my gaze. "If you had killed that cop, you could've escaped. You wouldn't be here now."

She raised her head. I looked into her eyes, trying to find hatred or pity or something, some connection between the two of us, but I didn't see anything except discomfort.

She said, "You'll tell the Republic to go to Hell, but you won't let someone die right in front of you."

And then Quint looked at Benny.

"If you don't accept, Sean, neither Leah or I can go." Benny had his arms crossed over his chest. When Quint did it, she looked like she was hugging herself; when Benny did it, he seemed to be restraining himself. "Then we'll all be dead. Do you know what he's put inside our heads?"

I halted, words tumbling over each other against the closure of my throat. Only one found its way out: "What?"

"He's put a bomb inside our heads. The damn Senator." Benny shook with anger; I could see the tremor in his shoulders. "Tiny little thing, right at the base of our spines. If it blows it'll take our brains with it. And he'll push the button unless we all agree to go."

CHAPTER SIX:
THE IMP OF THE PERVERSE

MY MOTHER CALLED it the imp of the perverse. By the way she'd told it, she'd spent my childhood stopping me from jumping off cliffs or sticking my hand into fires. I'd been an indifferent student, only working at things that interested me, and talking back to whoever tried to tell me otherwise. I can pick up a new language in a week but I can't do any math past algebra. Detention had been an ordinary part of school.

That was where I'd been, a little over eight years ago, when the Ministers arrived. At school late, not at home with my mother and father and sister. That was why I'd lived and they hadn't. I'd arrived at my parents' home a few hours after the Ministers came to Kystrom and immediately fell upon my hometown Itaka, the largest city on the planet, slaughtering every living thing they found as a show of might.

I'd stumbled out of my parents' house some endless time after I'd arrived, while Minister ships still wheeled overhead, glinting many colors in the slowly sinking sun.

I'd found Benny, covered in ash, the same stricken look in his eyes as I felt in mine.

"They're dead," I'd said to him as we came together like magnets in the street, the last living things from home.

His eyes had been haunted, shockingly white against the ash on his skin. "I know," he'd said.

Somehow, I'd thought he hadn't understood. "*Brigid* is dead," I said. My sister was gone.

Benny's uncle had had a small spaceship—about as small as a spacecraft could be, which made it the only thing nearby that had a chance of escaping notice of the Ministers. He'd taken me to it, hiding from Ministers as they passed. Serene and terrible, they stalked through the streets and killed everything they saw. When we reached his ship, while he fumbled through the unlock code, trying birthdays and family in-jokes, he'd said, "This is the Republic's fault."

I'd barely understood him. Language is the last thing I always have, something wholly mine, but it had felt like even it had left me then. "What?"

The Republic had left the day before. I remembered seeing the ships fly by overhead as I walked to school. The day had been clear and sunny, and the ships had been hazy, blue with atmospheric distance, gleaming like little silver moons as they fled. It was a sight to see, but beyond the majesty of the moment, I hadn't thought about it too much.

"The Ministers only came to Kystrom," Benny had said, as his uncle's spaceship unlocked with a *click*, "because the Republic was here first."

I hadn't paid the Republic's departure much mind. My teachers, though, and my parents, had all been subdued, speaking in harsh whispers that stopped when a student entered the room. Even my little sister, Brigid, had had an unfamiliar shadow over her features, a dim awareness of something not yet seen, like the glow in the sky before the sun rose. I wonder if people can feel it when they're about to die.

I hadn't cared much about politics then. I still didn't care much now, but I understood better what the Republic's presence on Kystrom—and their sudden departure—had caused.

Kystrom was one of the independent planets, settled after the invention of FTL had made it possible to spread human colonies out at vast distances throughout our little section of the galaxy rather than restricting such colonies to the two Sister Systems. As such, Kystrom was not part of the Maria Nova system, which the Ministers controlled; nor was it part of the Terra Nova system, now called the Republic. It had its own little K-type star, its own government. It was not heavily defended, like either of the Sister Systems—we hadn't even had a space fleet. Kystrom survived because it was too insignificant to be a part of the ongoing war between Maria Nova and the Republic, and not worth the effort for either side to antagonize.

At least, until the Republic decided they needed a base in that quadrant of the galactic arm, and did not take a polite 'no' from Kystrom's government for an answer.

The Republic knew the Ministers were coming before we did. But rather than stay and defend the planet they'd made into a target, the Republic had taken their small force and fled. When the Ministers arrived at Kystrom, they found no resistance. They wiped my city, Itaka, off the map, and killed everyone in it save me and Benny. And after its largest city had turned to ashes, the planet had surrendered.

Benny and I escaped Kystrom together in his uncle's ship. After we'd broken through the atmosphere and into the smoother ride of outer space, after it had become clear that we'd escaped what no one else had survived, I'd said, "Do you know what the last thing I said to her was?"

Benny hadn't even turned. "You and your sister were always fighting, and everyone knew it. I don't care what dumb thing you said to her."

"That's not true," I'd said. It had felt unreal, sitting in Benny's uncle's spaceship in the middle of outer space, and behind me everything I'd had was ash. "We were best friends."

"My family's dead too, Sean." Benny was getting angry, worked up in a way that was familiar to me now, but had been alien to me then. "You're not the only one who's alone. Where the hell am I going to go now? My whole family was on Kystrom! Where the hell am I supposed to go?" he shouted suddenly, and the volume of his shout filled the tiny spaceship, ringing like the inside of a bell.

"You're not alone!" I shouted, matching volume for volume, trying to drown out that terrible, terrible shout.

"I'm here."

"So fucking what? You're not my brother. And being on the same ship doesn't make us friends."

I had a stroke of brilliance then, or a stroke of self-preservation at least. Hard to tell for me where the two diverge. Just like the imp of the perverse is strongest at the edge of a cliff, my brain is sharpest when I'm on the verge of an end.

I'd lost my family. There was no replacing that kind of love, or that kind of trust. But two people can trust each other even if they don't like each other. My years with Benny have proved that, over and over.

"Let's make a deal," I'd said to Benny, back then, years ago on his dead uncle's ship, fleeing a massacre. "Let's promise, no matter what, to always have each other's backs. To always protect each other and help each other and always put the other first."

He'd wiped the ash off his skin, exposing the swollen redness around his eyes. He'd been just as alone as me. He'd wanted some companionship and some security as badly as I had.

So he'd agreed. And so we'd kept our deal, ever since.

*　　*　　*

Now, EIGHT YEARS after we'd made our promise, Benny faced me down in Quint's office and told me that we were going to die.

I spoke without thinking, forgetting that Quint was right there, listening to our every word. "We can hack the implant," I said. "So it won't detonate."

"The implant will detonate if any attempt is made to remove it without the unlock key," Quint said. "The unlock key is twenty-nine digits, and only my boss knows it."

Benny gazed at me, contained and furious, over his crossed arms. Benny and I could have parted ways at any point during these past eight years. We'd had enough opportunities. We could've even gone back to Kystrom: only Itaka was destroyed; the rest of the planet was left intact once it submitted to Minister rule. But how could we live under the rule of the monsters who had killed our friends; how could we return to a place that was not quite the same as the home we remembered? We were homeless, family-less, stateless; wherever we went, we'd only had each other. So we hadn't left one another, even after all these years.

Trust worked without fondness, if you had a shared goal; our shared goal had been survival.

"How do we know there even is an implant?" I demanded of Quint.

"It's painless and invisible from external examination and most standard medical scans," Quint agreed. "However, you can feel it if you touch the right part of your skull."

I reached up and pressed my fingers where the ache was. And I *felt* it: a small, hard, solid thing, like a pea beneath my skin.

I lowered my hand. We could run, I thought. As soon as we got our ship, we'd just run and find some doctor/

hacker who could take it out—

"The implant will detonate if its bearer passes outside of a set radius," Quint said, like she knew what I was thinking. There was no sympathy and no remorse in her tone, only vague discomfort. "The implant can be detonated remotely by our boss if he learns that you have sabotaged the mission in some way—sold the data to another buyer, copied it for yourself, exposed the secrecy of the mission to anyone else, et cetera. A supervisor will go with you to the salvage ship to ensure you follow these rules. Namely, me."

They had us well and truly cornered. If I'd just taken the deal earlier, maybe this wouldn't have happened. But how could I know how deep the water was unless I dove in? I couldn't just accept Quint's boss's deal, not when I wanted to know just how hard he was willing to push.

The imp of the perverse: in the face of trouble, I always made it worse.

Benny looked like he was holding himself with his crossed arms, like if he uncrossed them his ribs would curl open and all his old festering anger would explode out like fire.

"I'll do it," I said to Quint.

"Good," said Quint. "The sun will go nova in eleven days, so we will leave immediately."

Benny had turned away from me, his only response to my concession. It dug deeper than Quint's impromptu surgery had done. "It's been a thousand years," I said to her. "You're sure no one else has stolen the data already?"

"Shared knowledge loses its value," Quint said. "If my boss had the slightest doubt, we wouldn't be going."

That's how I knew that the *Nameless* should have been empty.

CHAPTER SEVEN: LANTERN-EYES AND THE MINISTER

THE WOMAN'S SCREAM broke us all from our inaction.

"Where the fuck did she come from?" Benny demanded. Out of the corner of my eye, I saw Leah draw her gun.

"Whoa!" I shouted, but Leah advanced, gun still raised. I stepped between Leah and the strange woman, turned my back on Leah, and set my hands on the woman's shoulders.

The woman stopped screaming abruptly. Her cheeks were dirty, and she was the sort of skinny that came from a long period of malnutrition, her large eyes even larger against the hollows of her cheeks. It was hard to tell how old she was, but she was a grown woman, maybe older than me.

Perhaps if the strange woman were seated, less threatening, Leah would put that gun away. I pressed down on the woman's shoulders. She obeyed after a moment of resistance, sinking towards the floor with me.

She wore some sort of frayed uniform, extensively patched and unrecognizable. Beneath the rough, sturdy material of her clothes, I could feel surprisingly strong muscles move in her shoulders and upper arms.

The woman had huge pale eyes, lighter than her skin, an almost amber color like the jack-o-lanterns we had lit every year on Kystrom. Those jack-o-lantern eyes looked past me once I was seated, tracking the others in the room.

"You said this place was abandoned," Leah said; from the tension in her voice I bet she hadn't lowered her gun.

"It was supposed to be." Quint's voice had gone high. "She's obviously crazy. Shoot her."

I would expect Leah or Benny to be a little trigger-happy, but I hadn't seen that coming from office-worker Quint. "Hey, whoa, no! You can't just shoot her," I said. "She hasn't done anything! Maybe she knows something that could help us."

I turned back to the woman with the jack-o-lantern eyes. "My name is Sean," I said. "What's your name?"

"She's probably some pirate who got stranded here and lost her mind." Quint started pacing the floor behind me, quick nervous steps. I could track her movement by the angle of the strange woman's gaze over my shoulder. "Look at her, she's crazy."

And yet, Lantern-Eyes didn't smell like a crazy person. There was no miasma of ill-keeping, like I'd smelled on the sad, broken people living on the streets after Kystrom— on myself, even. Even the dirt on her cheeks looked like a recent application, not something caked in to the skin.

Yet it was clear she had been on this ship for some time.

And the distress signal was still being broadcast. There had been humans on this ship, a long time ago; this ship, where its inhabitants had been studying how to make a person immortal.

"Why are you so gung-ho?" Leah demanded.

"Isn't that why you were hired?" Quint snapped. "To shoot things?"

"I wasn't hired," Leah said. "And I shoot who I want."

I firmed my grip on the strange woman's shoulders, set my back to the building argument, and smiled at the woman with the jack-o-lantern eyes. "If you don't tell me your name, I'll have to give you one," I told her. "Um... how about Lantern-Eyes?"

Lantern-Eyes frowned.

I switched to the Barcolaine dialect of Sister; it was the second most common dialect in the Sister Systems. "Can you understand what I'm saying?"

"If you know something and you're not telling us," Benny said to Quint behind me, "then it'll be all our asses on the line." He spoke in the same dark way he'd spoken to the cop right before we'd been arrested, the cop he'd been ready to kill.

"I've told you everything I know," Quint said.

Lantern-Eyes' attention darted from place to place over my shoulder, attentive but silent. I wondered how much of what we were saying she could understand. I wondered how long she'd been on this ship.

"I wonder what you know about the Philosopher Stone," I said to Lantern-Eyes in Ameng.

When I said the words *Philosopher Stone* her attention

snapped from the others to me. Her lips parted, like she was on the verge of speaking.

"*Shit*," said Benny, and the tension in his tone snapped my attention away from Lantern-Eyes. "The *Viper* is picking up a Minister ship headed this way."

A Minister ship.

That was how it had begun, on Kystrom; a few ships detected in the distance. Bombs to take out what few spaceships Kystrom had in orbit, explosions flashing like supernovae, rumbling through the atmosphere like far-off thunder. Then the Ministers had landed. Blank-faced and eerily beautiful, lights glowing around their necks, striding through city streets like the angels of the old religion, as absolute and destructive as a solar flare—

Nails dug into my forearm, jolting me back to the present. I found myself nauseous and shaking, like I'd been dunked unexpectedly into a pool of ice-water. Lantern-Eyes watched me closely. She did not look afraid, probably because she couldn't understand a word we were saying.

"This place was supposed to be a secret," Leah said. "Now there's a representative from every major government in the Sister Systems. This mission's fucked, Quint."

Quint said, "How close are they?"

"They're moving fast," Benny said. "Too fast. I've never seen a ship that can move that fast—that is cutting-edge Minister technology. We have to get out of here, now. We'll tell the boss—"

"Tell him *what?*" Leah said. "He'll blow up—"

Something hissed, then cracked. There was a shadow on the glass. And beneath that shadow a blade had stuck through the glass from the outside, gleaming white-hot and dripping melted plastic off its edge.

"*Go!*" Benny bellowed, just as a circle dropped out from the glass.

The whole room gasped, the atmosphere rushing for escape, and then a film pressed over the hole in the hull, thin and iridescent like an oil slick. A figure pushed through the oil-slick and it closed up behind them, keeping the room airtight. The Minister entered the room in a rush of red light and dropped lightly to the floor, landing to the echo of Leah's gun.

The Minister raised one hand and the bullet struck some sort of gauntlet at their wrist. They rose to their feet like a fluid and lashed their arm out at Benny, running for the *Viper*; Benny fell across the ground, his body skidding with momentum.

The Minister moved like a candle-flicker towards Quint, who was trying to pull something out of her bag. Something shot out from under the Minister's wrist. Quint stumbled and dropped to the floor.

They turned to me next. I had a moment to doubt whether they were male or female—the Ministers were androgynous as a rule, strange and sexless—but the glowing light they wore around their neck illuminated enough of their features for me to guess he was male. The flickering collar-lights of the Ministers: they had their own silent language. Their army had advanced through Itaka silently, flashing like lightning.

I stood up, put my body between the Minister and Lantern-Eyes. He raised his arm.

Something slammed into the backs of my knees. I landed hard on the floor, the breath driven from me. Lantern-Eyes had kicked me from behind to knock me over. The Minister, expressionless, took aim at her now, but instead of firing twisted sharply to the side to catch the bullet Leah had fired at him on his gauntlet.

Lantern-Eyes climbed back into the hole in the wall, pulling the fallen panel up behind her. The Minister blew towards me like a dark wind. I pushed myself away, elbows digging into old metal, crawling on my back. He reached the wall just as Lantern-Eyes sealed it, and his fist slammed into the metal with a thunderous echo.

Someone grabbed me under the arm—Leah. She hauled me back, but the Minister's attention turned on us.

Leah moved at my side and I knew, somehow, what she would do, and what he would do in response.

"No—" I said, as Leah drew her gun and shot the Minister for a third time.

He blocked it, as he had the other two times, with the guard strapped to his wrist. Then he lowered his hand, no change in expression, and with his other arm he drew a long knife from its sheath down his back.

"No," I said again, shoving back as if I could push Leah out of the way, but his next step brought the edge of his knife into Leah's neck. Leah made a terrible little interrupted gasp, a wet choke, and I heard it echo in my skull.

I sat, half-upright, and waited for the edge of his knife to continue through me.

CHAPTER EIGHT:
INDIGO AND ULTRAVIOLET

THE CHOSEN WEREN'T the only ones who believed the Ministers had no souls. My family worshipped the God Who Shed His Blood For Us, and our church believed the same thing.

They were all right about the Ministers: the priests, the Chosen, my father. I saw it the day the Ministers came to Kystrom. I'd seen a man injured in the street, helpless, unable to move. I'd hidden behind a hedge and watched between the branches as a Minister came down the empty street alone towards him, beautiful and terrible, shaven head, uncertain gender and a collar-light that glowed a dark and bloody crimson.

The Minister had stood over the dying man, their sword in their hand, the tip of it held a careful inch above the ground. The sword was stained a duller red than their collar-light. The Ministers used guns, explosives, bombs, and any other modern weapon—but they had used those at the start of the assault. Now that they were on the ground, they seemed to prefer the silence of blades.

The dying man gasped something, too quiet for me to hear from my hiding place. And the Minister looked down at him, and I'd imagined I'd seen curiosity in their expression as they looked the dying man over, head to toe.

I'd been wrong. Without a change of expression, the Minister sliced their blade across the man's neck and walked away, leaving him behind to expire in the dirt.

* * *

MY HAND AND elbow were warm and damp. I realized it was Leah's blood at the same time I realized the Minister hadn't killed me.

I blinked, and the blackness receded from my gaze. The Minister had stopped his knife inches from my throat.

His collar-light was set to a dark, dark blue, almost indigo, and the cool light made his pallor even more corpse-grey. The Ministers had two circulatory systems, copper and iron. Copper was more efficient than iron in cold or low-oxygen environments, and the blood ran blue. This indigo Minister had been outside in the vacuum without a suit, and the copper circulatory system must have taken over from the iron. He was a haunting, with his corpse-knife at my neck.

I shut my eyes and swallowed. My neck touched the edge of his blade when I did, lightly enough to draw no blood. When I opened my eyes again he was still watching me, a dark and narrow stare, but some of that primed tension had faded. Without thinking, I tried to turn in the direction of his knife to see what had become of Leah.

The flat of his blade touched the plane of my cheek and turned my head to face forward again.

Quint and Benny were both unconscious, sprawled out across the floor. The indigo Minister left me sitting on the floor and went to Quint first, then Benny. He searched them briefly, disarming them, but leaving Benny's handbrace on. Then he dragged their bodies like they weighed nothing and set them down in the corner beneath the window.

I sat perfectly still until his hand appeared in front of me. I went numbly with him to the corner where he sat me down. Then he reached out one hand and laid the palm over my eyes, blacking out the rest of the room.

I shut my eyes and kept them shut when he pulled his hand away. When I dared open them again, I found that where Leah should be there was nothing but a shadowy shape. The indigo Minister had pulled a blanket from one of our packs and laid it over her body.

Benny and Quint breathed alongside me, slow and even; drugged, not dead. I wrapped my arms around my knees and made myself as small as possible while the red light in the room dimmed. Was the star outside finally dying? No, if the star was in its death throes, this room would get brighter in the seconds before our atoms were annihilated. This was a darkness as if a cloud had come between us and the sun, a cloud that grew larger and larger. Soon there was no light in the airlock room except for the flashlights we'd dropped and the gleam of the indigo Minister's collar light.

The shadow outside struck the hull softly, but the impact rattled my teeth. A moment later, the other Ministers appeared.

There were seven of them, each of them in dark uniforms of a material that could probably have stopped Leah's bullets as efficiently as the indigo Minister's gauntlet had done. They were each as sleek as arrows, as graceful as shadows, and their different-colored collar lights illuminated faces that had the same sort of serene androgynous beauty, like they had all been cast from a single mold.

The seventh and final Minister landed on the floor as silently as an owl finding a perch. Her collar-light was a purple so dark and intense it burned black, a brilliance my eyes felt without seeing. Ultraviolet.

When she had landed among us, the indigo Minister touched his collar light and flashed at her in the same shade of ultraviolet she wore.

The ultraviolet Minister rose from her crouch and turned to us. She had a young woman's face, but hair the color of polished steel. I knew somehow that she was old, old and terrible, like this ancient nameless ship or the star outside on the verge of explosion.

"Wake them up." Her voice was clear and sharp, like metal snapping.

A Minister with a green collar light injected Benny and Quint with something, no sympathy or sentiment in her face, then left.

Benny stirred beside me. Relief jolted through my chest, indistinguishable from pain. The Ministers walked through the room, examining walls, floor, ceiling, an old touchscreen that had gone dark with age. And they flashed their collar-lights, back and forth, bright and silent. The light language, spoken before my eyes. Numbly, I thought: I could learn what they are saying, if I live long enough to learn.

When Benny and Quint were awake enough again to sit up, weak and squinting on either side of me, the ultraviolet Minister spoke.

"I hear one of you fired a gun at number Two," she said. "We do not fire guns on spaceships, especially ones as old as this. The hull is too fragile. A bullet could pierce it and cause a decompression. A Minister would survive that. A human would not."

Benny and Quint were right beside me, but beneath the ultraviolet Minister's cold gaze I felt alone. So what if they were next to me? Nothing could stop a Minister from doing what she liked.

"I have some questions to ask you," the ultraviolet Minister said. "You will answer them honestly. How did you find this ship?"

And yet, if she was talking to us, that meant she wanted something from us.

So long as she wanted something from us—so long as she was willing to talk to us—that meant she was willing to keep us alive.

I said, "We picked up a transmission."

"Who sent that transmission?"

"I... We don't know," I said.

"Who was the woman that Two watched run away into the wall?"

"We don't know that, either."

"Why did you come here?"

I hesitated. Quint was listening in. I didn't know how

Quint could trigger our implants to detonate, or if she even would at this point, but I couldn't risk it. I couldn't let this Minister know about the politician. "To get salvage."

She looked at me with the implacable patience of the immortal. Fear crawled its way up my throat, that she would kill us for knowing nothing.

So I confessed. "We were looking for the Philosopher Stone."

CHAPTER NINE:
THREE LIVES AND ONE

"SEAN!" BENNY HISSED, but I ignored him. I could not tell if the ultraviolet Minister respected or despised me for my honesty, if she felt nothing at all.

"What did you want with the Philosopher Stone?" the ultraviolet Minister asked.

"Uh," I avoided looking at Quint, "to sell it."

"Thieves," the ultraviolet Minister said, mildly, but a shiver went down my spine. "How did you know the Philosopher Stone was here?"

I thought fast. "From the transmission," I said. "It was in Ameng. I translated it." The SOS had said nothing specific about the Philosopher Stone, only something about a stalled ship and someone named Mara Zhu, but parts of it had been unintelligible. Hopefully, if the Ministers had picked up the same transmission, they hadn't heard the whole thing either and would assume the Philosopher Stone mention had been in the inaudible part.

"That language was erased. How could you translate it?"

I hadn't expected that line of questioning, but I was

only too happy to avoid any direction that might lead to discussion of a certain Senator. "There are fragments all over the colonies and the Sisters… if you go looking for them hard enough, you can put together a library. I'm good with languages."

"Prove that you can understand Ameng."

"How? Do you want me to recite a poem, or—"

"Open the central door," she said, and gestured to a panel on the far wall. The buttons were glowing faintly— somehow, the Ministers had restored power to this small patch of the ship.

My legs were unsteady when I stood, but I forced myself to walk away from Benny and Quint. The Ministers were busy on their own tasks; one was examining the panel where Lantern-Eyes had vanished, others were scanning the air and the walls. One had vanished down into the *Viper*. But I felt them all watching me. A particularly tall Minister was standing beside the wall panel, his collar-light glowing softly yellow at his throat.

The machine was labeled, as I'd seen before. For an empty, sinking moment, all the letters were nonsense to me, and I had no plan, no thoughts, no goal, nothing left but the fear. And then I took another breath and memory trickled back in. The labels were simple, mercifully. There were three doors in the room, one on each of the windowless walls. I knew the Ameng word for *door*. I could never keep *left* or *right* straight, but I could reasonably assume the keys were laid out in the same order as the doors. Or so I hoped. I could forgive our ancestors for discovering the secret of immortal life and promptly hiding it in the middle of a supernova just to inconvenience me a thousand years down the line, but putting the *right* button on the left side and the *left* button on the right would be inexcusable.

There were more buttons on the panel than there were doors in the room. I scanned them quickly, reading the Ameng. The lights probably wouldn't work any longer, but the others might.

"Central door," I said, and pressed the button marked so; the door on the center wall groaned and creaked, and then thunks echoed through the wall. The Minister standing nearest the central door, the woman with the green collar-light, drew a long knife into one hand. Then she gripped the handle and pulled. The door slid, reluctantly, into the wall. She checked the hallway, then nodded at the ultraviolet Minister.

"How about the right-side door?" I asked, and pressed that button, too. A dull click sounded from the right.

"And the left-side," I said, and did the same over there.

"I'm going to lock the right again," I said, and the right side door clicked sealed again.

"And for my final trick," I said, "I'm going to close up the airlock," and I pressed the button that I gambled would seal the way to the *Viper*.

The ground trembled, then, slow and sticking, the aperture of the opening between the *Viper* and the *Nameless* began to close like a metal pupil. In the seconds before it sealed, a hand shot up from inside and held the metal in grinding stillness.

Oh, right. There was a Minister inside.

"I'll open it again," I promised the ultraviolet Minister, and hit the switch; the closure of the aperture reversed, the metal vanishing into the floor; a moment later a Minister with a red collar light pulled himself free of the *Viper*, grim-jawed.

The Ultraviolet Minister stared at me with all of her cold immortal attention.

I clasped my hands behind my back, hiding their tremor. "Satisfied?"

* * *

IT HAPPENED THAT a week before the Ministers came to Kystrom, while I was heading home from school, I found a cona lying beside the road, long ears lax, little paws twitching. There was blood on her fur, and her rolling eyes were fixed on a tree overhead. When I looked up I saw an owl perched there, glassy eyes staring down at us, blood on his talons.

There are rabbits in the Republican system, of many and varied different species, but none are quite the same as conas. I picked the cona up and brought it home and gave it to Brigid. My sister had been begging for a kitten for weeks, to no avail; an injured baby cona was a far worse pet. You could buy simulated skin for humans to close up gashes at the grocery store, but sim-skin for a cona was not exactly widely available on the market. My mother had glared daggers at me, but Brigid already had the thing cupped in her palms, and there was no going back from there.

The cona wasn't in my family home when I made it back, on the day the Ministers had come. My parents and Brigid were there, but the cona was not. I didn't know if it had escaped, or if Brigid had set it free; if the Ministers had killed it they would have left its body for me to find, just like they left Brigid's.

It wasn't the cona I thought of now, though, but the owl. For a moment, when I'd stood underneath the tree branch over the baby cona, the owl had looked at me instead of the cona. And even as inhuman as the bird was, I'd read consideration from its body language, the calculation it was doing in its head: the length of its talons, the depth of my neck.

* * *

THE ULTRAVIOLET MINISTER approached. I tightened my fingers behind my back, where she could not see, but somehow I was sure that she knew I was afraid.

She stopped less than a foot away, so that the light that illuminated us was the terrible jewel-dark violet of her collar light, not the downed flashlights or the lanterns the Ministers had placed around the room.

The ultraviolet Minister said, "What is your name, boy?"

"Sean Wren," I said.

"You're Kystrene," she said, as certain as I had named myself.

My accent slipped every time I said my own name. I could have changed it, if I'd liked; I had the ear for phonetics, and I could speak Sister like a native. It had been eight years since Itaka had been destroyed and I'd left Kystrom behind forever. I knew how to mangle the sounds of my own name into a Republican accent, but then it was no longer my name.

The Ultraviolet Minister looked at me like she knew all of this. "You speak Ameng fluently, then?"

"Of course I do," I said, and in that instant, I realized two things.

The first was that none of these Ministers could read or understand Ameng. This was strange. It was a fact that Ministers did not die of old age. New Ministers must be born, to replace the ones who were killed, but their species had appeared in human history at the same time as this ship had been lost—meaning that the oldest of them probably spoke Ameng fluently. I had taken this ancient-eyed Ultraviolet for one of those oldest—and yet, if she could speak Ameng, she would not waste her time testing my knowledge. The Ministers had implied they had received the same transmission the Senator had. They must have known that there would be Ameng aboard the *Nameless*. What it meant that this race of immortals had not sent one of their own who was old enough to speak the language of this ship, I didn't know.

The second thing I realized was that, for whatever reason, the Ministers wanted something on this ship— and that something was, almost certainly, the Philosopher Stone data. If all they had wanted to do was finish the job from a thousand years ago and destroy the data, they could've blown the ship from orbit, not boarded it and shown interest in a translator.

"It's a useful skill," I said to the Ultraviolet, "but I don't do it for free."

She tilted her ancient, ageless head. "And what do you think that skill is worth to me, Mr. Wren?"

I chose a higher price than I'd bargained for from Quint. "Three lives."

Over the Ultraviolet Minister's shoulder, I saw the Indigo Minister look sharply at me.

"Your skills seem to be barely worth your life, let alone two more," the Ultraviolet Minister said.

"Three lives," I repeated.

"I saw your hands. I know how the Kystrene scar their fingers as a funeral custom."

Hidden behind my back, I ran my fingers over the scars that lined the side of my hand from wrist to fingertip.

"You must have lost a great many friends in the reclamation of Kystrom," the Ultraviolet Minister said. "I understand your reluctance to lose any more. But you came through the war physically unscathed, didn't you? Hands, arms, and legs all intact. Is your price worth three lives, and all of your limbs?"

It was not just the dryness of the air in the old spaceship that parched my throat. "If I'm bleeding, I'll slow you down. Three lives—and no amputations. That's my final offer."

She considered me. There were fine lines around her eyes and mouth; how old must an ageless Minister be, to have marks of age?

"Three lives, then," she said. "Seven, disarm the humans."

"Wait," I blurted out, as the ultraviolet Minister turned away. "What should I call you?"

"I am Number One."

One, and Indigo Minister was Two, and Red Minister, who was now patting down Quint and Benny, was Seven. The colors were ranks, and maybe names as well.

The indigo Minister—number Two—approached me. It was difficult to name a creature by a number; even soulless as the Ministers were, it felt wrong. Besides, I would have to count the colors of the rainbow in my head every time. Number One had explicitly told me her name was her number, but the others had said nothing of the kind. I would think of them by their colors, I decided. The Indigo Minister patted me down quickly while I watched One walking away.

It was clear that Quint's boss had sent us here lacking some important information. But if we left now, our deal was off; he might just decide to kill us offhand, to cover up his tracks—and that was assuming we didn't stray outside the safe radius our implants allowed. The only way out of this was to find that data and hope the Ministers didn't kill us after.

Indigo finished patting me down and shoved me, gently, in the direction of my friends. One flashed indigo light at him and, as I made my way to Benny and Quint, the Ministers dispersed through the three doors: Yellow and Blue went through one, Orange and Green through another, and Indigo went alone. Red and One stayed behind. They were a comfortable distance from us, but it would take an incredible idiot to think we could escape.

"We should run, now, while they're gone," Quint whispered.

"Are you crazy?" I exclaimed, barely remembering to keep my voice down. "Any one of them could kill us with their pinky finger!"

"The dark blue one who killed Leah is gone. He's got to be the most dangerous or they wouldn't have sent him in first! We won't get a better chance!"

"We're gonna escape." I leaned in, just in case. "We're definitely going to get away from them, the first chance we get. I mean, we have to, they're looking for a reason to kill us—"

Quint made a kind of funny noise in her throat.

"—though we should be safe for the moment," I added hastily. "But we can't just make a break for it when we don't have a chance of escaping. We need a way out first."

Benny spoke. "I have a way out."

"What way out?"

In answer, Benny lifted his arm, his handbrace shining dimly against his skin. His homemade handbrace, which hid a very rudimentary projectile weapon in the wristband, just a single shot.

The Red Minister hadn't noticed it when he'd patted Benny down, because it was one-of-a-kind.

I followed Benny's gaze across the room to Number One.

CHAPTER TEN:
ROT AND BONE

ONE'S BACK WAS to us, and even Red was looking away, down the hall. Benny's fingers slid over the catch on the brace that would expose the trigger—

A dark blue light glimmered in the left-hand door. I knocked Benny's arm down before the Indigo Minister could see. "We're going to get out of this without anyone dying," I warned him, low, his face inches from mine. "Follow my lead."

Deep violet light flashed out behind me, some complicated message. The Indigo Minister had returned. The other hallways were glowing, too, as the rest of them came back. Our window for idiocy had closed.

"Mr. Wren," said One, when the flashing of lights had ceased. "Walk with me." Then she set off into the left-hand hall, her collar-light glowing dark.

The Ministers were watching us again.

I followed her without a word.

*　　*　　*

FASTER-THAN-LIGHT TRAVEL AND artificial gravity were two effects of the same technology, invented by a cavalier inventor somewhere in the star system known, at the time, as Terra Nova. At the time, Terra Nova had been ruled by the Ministers, the way Maria Nova was now. The story goes that after news of the invention became public, academics and engineers and investors all flocked to the lab, where they found machines propped up with discarded wrenches and held together by twist-ties. Only the insulating properties of an undergrad's scarf, used to hold together two pieces of crucial machinery, had prevented a collision between opposing types of matter that would have produced an explosion powerful enough to destroy half the tiny moon the inventor had been based on.

Once the lab had been hastily disarmed, production of the new technology began in the then-Terra Nova system. In less than a decade, the Terra Novans were able to zip around the local segment of the galaxy, planting the seeds that would become the outer colonies, and hurrying to their Sister System, Maria Nova, to share the good news of their new technology. Both Systems were one government, back then, under control of the Ministers. They thought nothing of sharing technology between.

The *Nameless* was from hundreds of years before the invention of FTL and art-grav. It simulated gravity through centripetal acceleration. The ancient vessel spun around, and we walked on the inside of its vast wheel. Maybe that was why I felt so unsteady, following One down that long, dark hall. My inner ear said we were walking a straight line, but my eye recognized the near-invisible curvature of the floor ahead.

The hallway was pitch-black, without even a filmed-over window to allow in flickering traces of light. The Ministers had all turned down their collar-lights, so as not to blind themselves. The only source of light was their flashlights. We salvagers had no lights; the Ministers had left us nothing in our packs except food and water. The world around us was built of glimpses of walls and ceiling and uneven floor, half-seen shapes of doorframes and molding hanging loose. I knew the size of the space only from the way sound echoed.

One had taken the lead, a slight figure a few steps ahead of me. Unlike Indigo, who kept his one long knife strapped behind his shoulders, One kept her two knives at each hip. The blades hung in her silhouette like flight feathers.

The air here—breathable; I'd seen Green examining a handheld scanner, tracking the quality—was heavy with an unpleasant, musty-oil smell that was somehow familiar.

"Roaches," I realized, then repeated for everyone to hear, "There are roaches on this ship."

From the back of the line, I heard Quint make a small, involuntary noise of disgust. One said, "We appreciate the warning, Mr. Wren."

She'd already known. Still, if there were roaches on this ship—and quite a lot of them, from the smell, though they were probably hiding from our flashlights—then that meant that life *could* survive on the *Nameless*, and had. Like Lantern-Eyes.

"This ship was designed to host generations," One said.

She was having no trouble finding her footing, because *she* had a flashlight to light her way. "It has a robust autorepair. It is likely there are self-perpetuating sources of food and water, deeper in. All the things humans need."

"We don't exactly need generation ships anymore," I said. "We've grown out of them. Like old shoes. Or Ministers."

Number One looked at me like a snow-capped mountain looks at the sun, the ancient frost of her untouchable even by the brightest day. My imp grinned: point one for Sean Wren.

Before the invention of faster-than-light engines, humans had been born, aged, and died on the ships that traveled between star systems. That was why we had needed the Ministers—the past tense being the operative word. Much of the Ministers' control over the Sister Systems had been their ability to make the journey between planets within only a fraction of their lifetime. A few decades was nothing to them.

The invention of FTL had rendered them as obsolete as outdated technology, but the Ministers, used to thinking on timescales of fifty years or more, were slow to recognize the threat this new technology posed. It was the one and only time human technology has outpaced the Ministers', but the effects had been far-reaching. As soon as the Ministers realized the humans had had a breakthrough that put the Ministers at a disadvantage, they took steps to re-assert their authority, not realizing how far the situation had already slipped from their control.

"Was that woman who escaped a member of your crew?" One asked.

"What woman?"

"The one who vanished into the wall before Two could catch her."

"I don't know anything about her."

"Then she wasn't your contact aboard this ship?"

Contact? No one had any contacts aboard the ship; it had been abandoned for a thousand years. Unless my suspicion had been correct, and Lantern-Eyes was one of the original crew, made immortal and lost here since time immemorial.

If that was the case, then she would speak Ameng—which meant I was the only person she would be able to communicate with.

"I don't know anything about that strange lady," I said. "And even if I did, would you trust me to tell you the truth?"

She looked back at me over her shoulder. In the dark, the only light that illuminated her face was the cold violet-black of her collar light. Her eyes were pits in the underlighting, her high stark cheekbones the gleam of a skull. Immortal, undead patience regarded me. There was no telling how far my imp could push her—or what she might do when I pushed her too far. She was frightening in a way Quint's Senator had not been.

My foot went through something in the dark, cracking and closing around my ankle like teeth. I stumbled. Hands caught me and hauled me up. The Indigo Minister had stopped me from falling.

One stopped, and so the rest of the line had halted as well. Indigo crouched down and shone his light at what I had stepped into.

Shattered, jagged yellow gleamed; a cage of old ivory, in a distinct and familiar shape. A ribcage.

I had stepped into a pile of human bones.

CHAPTER ELEVEN: SIGNS IN THE DARK

THE INDIGO MINISTER gripped my foot and pulled it free of the ribcage. The bones had scored the plasti-leather of my boot, but not punctured through.

I tugged my ankle out of his grip, but Indigo was more focused on the bones than on me. They were old, old bones, meatless and yellowed, curved in the precise and subtle fashion of a musical instrument. Indigo turned them with a fingertip.

I bent down to see them better. There was something weird about the shape of the ribs. "What's that?" I asked, and pointed to a gap in the cage of bones not far from where my foot had gone through.

"That's the wound that killed him," Indigo said.

He had a low, soft voice, like he'd grown up in a library. It startled me. I had expected One to answer. "Can you tell what killed him?"

Indigo turned the ribcage this way and that, with one finger hooked around the bone.

I said, "It's not some Minister state secret, is it?"

"Not precisely." Indigo released the ribcage, which rocked against the floor. "Claws."

This time when I looked at the ribs I saw not just the place where bone was missing, but saw the scarring in the ribs around where something had carved through flesh and into bone. I held up my hand over the wound for scale, bending my hand around until it aligned correctly.

Four distinct claw marks, one for each of my four fingers, with my thumb tucked in. But the distribution was too narrow for the width of my hand.

I glanced sideways at Indigo's hand, narrow and long-fingered. His hand would be just about the right size and scale. Whatever had clawed into this man's chest had been human-sized, just with narrower hands than me. What had our ancestors gotten up to, in the final days of this nameless ship?

One flashed an indigo light down at us from her collar-light. The end of her sentence curved up, from a shade at the darker end of indigo to a lighter sort of dark blue. Intonation? A question?

Indigo responded with a full ascending spectrum, from red up to violet. One nodded to herself and said to me, "Get up, Mr. Wren."

"What do you think killed him?"

"Something a thousand years ago," One said, and flashed a white light from her collar light down the line. The Ministers started moving again.

"Wait," I said. Indigo had just let the ribcage fall, rocking on the ground in the dust amidst the pieces of its own shattered bone. I crouched down and gathered up the pieces, setting them to the side, putting the larger chunks of bone near where they should have been, if I had not broken them.

"Is this necessary, Mr. Wren?" One asked.

I swept up a few smaller pieces and set them beside the spine. "I don't want any angry ghosts to follow me around."

"The dead are the least of your concerns on this ship."

The Republicans had a mix of religions, though the Redeemer was the predominant god at the moment; on Kystrom I'd been raised to offer ritual blood to the God Who Shed His Blood For Us, which the Republic in general seemed to think was barbaric. The Chosen were such a small group they were hardly worth mentioning. The Ministers, I'd heard, had no gods at all. I had no idea who these old bones had worshipped a thousand years ago.

I could only offer what I knew. I hoped whoever these bones had belonged to wouldn't be too offended. I touched my forehead, my heart, then crossed my arms over my chest, the way I'd been taught on Kystrom. A proper blessing for the dead required three people, to form the holy triangle around the bones, but I could only offer what I had, and the only thing I had was myself alone—

A palm touched mine where it hung outstretched. I lost the trail of my prayer, opened my eyes to find that the Indigo Minister had crouched down on the other side of the bones, one hand resting on mine, the other outstretched at his side where the third person should be to complete the triangle.

Two was still imbalanced, but not so much as one alone. Indigo met my gaze with dark, alien eyes until I stumbled my way back into the prayer. His hand lifted from mine when I had finished, leaving nothing behind, not even a trace of warmth.

"We have no time for scarification," One told me when I stood up, her tone neutral.

I would only scar my hand for someone I knew personally; these bones were a stranger's. Strange that the Indigo Minister should be so familiar with Kystrene traditions, but not the Ultraviolet.

There were more bones on the floor as we walked, though I managed not to put my foot into any this time. Glimpsing the things underfoot, I could not tell how many bodies were in the hall, how many men or women had died here a thousand years ago.

One halted the line again at an intersection in the hallways. She shone her flashlight down one way, then the other, then on the walls at the fork until the beam rested over faded old Ameng letters engraved into the walls. "Read the signs, Mr. Wren."

I looked up at the nearly-invisible lettering. "What am I looking for?"

"Just read the signs."

"Well, are we going directly to the data, or are we going to sightsee?"

"Mr. Wren." One sounded impatient, if a force of nature could be impatient. "The sun is days away from going nova, which will destroy this ship and everything on it, including us. We are not going to sightsee. We are going directly to Mara Zhu's office. If you continue to waste my time, I will reconsider your limited use to me."

Mara Zhu's office? Is that where the Philosopher Stone data was stored?

"Fine," I said, and squinted up at the sign overhead. I couldn't decide whether one of the letters was an *a* or an *s*. It was an *a*, I was sure of it. Captain's—four? Captain's... "Captain's rooms," I said. "Captain's quarters, that way."

"And this way?" One asked, her flashlight beam steady on the ancient script over her head.

"It would be easier for me to read if I had a flashlight," I said. "When someone holds a flashlight it moves without them noticing, as they breathe or look around, right? That's why it's so hard to look at a flashlight someone else is holding, because it's moving a little all the time."

One's flashlight beam was perfectly steady, preternaturally still. Her violet gaze was expressionless. Then she reached up and tapped something in deep blue on her collar-light.

Movement beside me in shadow; the Indigo Minister placed something hard and cool in my hand. The metal surface of one of the flashlights I'd packed. I flicked it on, head bent to conceal my surprise. I wondered if I could convince One to give Benny and Quint flashlights, too.

"Read it, Mr. Wren," One said, in that ancient cold voice of hers, and I looked at the words my flashlight had revealed.

"A path over water," I said, then, "The bridge. That path leads to the ship's bridge."

"Very good, Mr. Wren," One said, and started down

the hall towards the captain's quarters. For a second I thought I saw something move in the shadows towards the bridge—just a flicker. Just a shadow. When I turned my flashlight back that way, however, there was nothing there.

We followed Number One a long while along the curve of the *Nameless*. I did not know how far we walked—I was preoccupied with the shadows around us, the gaping doors and empty rooms.

And then the path ahead ended.

One called me forward, and I came up to stand next to her. It looked like the hallway had been deliberately blocked off at one point: the metal panels had warped seams, as if from ancient welding. A word had been scratched deep into the makeshift barrier.

The corner of the barrier was broken, the metal bent away, allowing ingress and egress. Whatever this barrier had served to contain was no longer contained.

"What does it say?" One asked, shining her flashlight on that carved word.

I knew that one immediately. "Danger."

CHAPTER TWELVE: DEAD END

QUINT HAD DESCRIBED the *Nameless* as hidden, in her initial sales pitch. Now, staring at the inscription on the ancient barrier, I doubted that claim. Hundreds of years ago, someone had scratched out that word into metal. It would have taken time and effort, but they'd inscribed it, instead of painting it or writing it or making a new sign. They had been desperate to make sure the message stuck around.

A powerful, ancient vessel, just left lying around like a book someone'd gotten bored of reading? Conveniently left in the corona of a violent star, where no one would notice it for hundreds of years? If this ship was not meant to be found, why not destroy it outright? And if it was meant to be found, why not put it someplace easier to do so? It was impossible to predict exactly when a star would go supernova—it was pure luck that we'd found this ship before the star had gone. Pure luck, or a strangely well-timed SOS.

The *Nameless* hadn't been hidden.

It had been abandoned.

One tapped her collar-light, and indigo light flashed out. Indigo knelt down, shone his light into the hole in the barrier, and crawled inside.

"Aren't you worried about what's back there?" I asked One.

"Number Two can take care of himself."

We waited for a long time beside the door marked DANGER. I managed to stop myself from pacing—I doubted One would appreciate it—but I couldn't stop myself from worrying at the hem of my shirt, finding a weak spot in the fabric. The Indigo Minister was gone so long that I wore a hole into it, large enough to fit my finger through. I'd never dealt well with waiting. At least I didn't see anything moving around in the shadows here. If there had actually been anything before.

At long last, a dark blue light shone from the hole in the barrier, and the Indigo Minister crawled back out. Dust streaked his cheeks, but his expression was calm. He flashed a quick, complex sequence of flashes in white light.

White light: addressing the entire group. Telling them what he'd seen inside the passage, I guessed.

One flashed dark blue light at Indigo and he nodded, then turned to the group and spoke aloud, presumably for the benefit of the humans.

"The passage ahead is very small," he said. He was pitching his voice louder, but his voice did not carry well, and Quint and Benny had to come closer to hear. "We will have to crawl through most of it, and get on our bellies for part of it. It goes on like that for ten to twenty yards, but then opens up to a normal hallway again."

I kept worrying at the hole I'd made in the hem of my shirt. "Why is it so cramped?"

The Indigo Minister paused, the same way Quint had done back in the Republican System a million years ago whenever I'd asked a question that was not in her script. Indigo, however, recovered a lot faster. "I believe at some point in the past a bomb was detonated in the hallway beyond this door," he told me. "The ship's self-repair systems closed up any damage to the hull, keeping atmosphere and heat, but did not clear the internal obstructions."

What the hell would drive a group of people to detonate a bomb on their own ship?

"The passage is difficult to traverse," Indigo said. "But to find another way forward would mean doubling back."

"We go forward," One said.

"Wait," Quint said. "How narrow is it in there?"

"Do you think we've got another choice?" Benny snapped.

"No, but... what if we get stuck?"

She'd spoken what I'd been thinking. Indigo was slender and not particularly tall; all of the Ministers were built similarly. I was a head taller than Yellow, the tallest of them, and had broader shoulders than any of them.

"Number Two took your height and breadth into account for his assessment," One said. Disdain dripped off her like water from an icicle.

"Shouldn't we just cut through?" Quint said.

"If we cut through, it may disturb the debris overhead

enough to cause a collapse." Indigo sounded terribly calm for discussing the possibility that we could cause this ship to fall apart around us. "The risk is too great. The passage is passable."

Quint fidgeted. "But—"

"I'll go before you," I said. "I'm bigger than you. That way you know if I can get through, you can get through."

"I—"

I clapped Quint on the shoulder, smiling. "It'll be fine," I said, trying to will calm into her; I could feel One's owl-eyes on us, assessing effort and cost. "Just follow me, okay."

I crouched down next to Indigo before Quint could protest again. "Lead the way," I said. His gaze flickered up and down me once, unreadable. Then he turned away and crawled into the hole.

Indigo hadn't been exaggerating. My shoulders scraped the walls as soon as I crawled in. I slowed down immediately, feeling my way; I only had Indigo's light to guide me, and the walls were uneven. What was almost impassibly narrow at one point was wide enough to roll my shoulders loose a few feet further. In places the passage was only narrow because broken metal bars stuck out like swords, and I had to suck in my breath as I wove through to avoid being stabbed.

I could hear Quint behind me, breathing hard, murmuring some litany to herself I could not hear. There was no airflow in a space this narrow, which made it seem even smaller than it was.

Abruptly, ahead, Indigo was gone. My hand landed on

gritty debris, stacked thick and impassible.

Quint bumped into me from behind. "Sean?" she said, panicked.

"A minute." My flashlight was almost useless at such close quarters; the blinding white of it obscured more than it revealed. It showed nothing ahead of me except metal and dust.

I switched off the flashlight and swallowed, shutting my eyes against the afterimages and the dark. I stretched out one hand to feel for the path, wherever Indigo had gone. My hand landed on ragged, ancient metal and soft dust.

There was no passage ahead. Indigo had vanished, and I was trapped.

CHAPTER THIRTEEN: A WAY OUT

"SEAN!" QUINT SHOUTED.

My heart was pounding so loudly I could hear it in my ears. Trapped.

Quint's hands shoved at my thighs, trying to force me forward. "*Sean*—"

"A second," I said, and opened my eyes again. I turned my head, blindly in the dark, and caught a glimpse of a glow. I reached to the side and found open space.

I took a breath and tried to calm my racing heart. "The path turns sharply to the right up here," I warned Quint, trying to sound calmer than I was. "It's still passable, though."

I twisted my body to make the sharp turn, and found that the path didn't just bend right, it was an uneven S-shape; how Indigo had gotten through this in the first place was incomprehensible. I took a deep breath and deliberately did not think about how there was no backing out now: Quint was behind me, and Benny, and six Ministers all intent on moving forward.

No one had visited this ship in a thousand years, I told myself instead, as I contorted my body to follow the twist in the path, my pounding heart certain that I would become inextricably wedged into this curve and die here like a rat in a trap. This is an archaeological discovery for the ages, etc.

I dug my nails into the uneven floor and pulled my way through the twist. Ahead, I could see a faint indigo glow again. The path straightened out. My arms were not as strong as they had been a minute ago, but I kept crawling.

How far had Indigo said this path went? Ten, twenty yards? It had to be longer than that. The ship pressed down on me overhead, the weight of debris that had not fallen for a thousand years, but hadn't been disturbed for the same thousand years. What if me shoving my way through, bouncing off walls that pressed in so tightly I had to hunch my shoulders together, was enough to disrupt some fragile balance and cause all that old metal and plastic and carbon to fall? I was starting to seriously doubt, too, Indigo's assessment that there was enough breathable air here.

And then suddenly Indigo was gone, and then a bright light was shining in my face. I blinked and found that the light was not shining directly at me, but at a glancing angle into the passage, so that I could see what was ahead. Indigo was on his belly facing me, his collar-light glowing blue; the end of the passage was ahead.

I had a moment of relief before I looked at what his flashlight was revealing and my blood went cold.

Parts of the passage, Indigo had warned us going in,

were so narrow we would need to crawl on our bellies. So far, I had stayed on my hands and knees—hunched and compressed, but still able to crawl.

The passage ahead looked like it was barely six inches in height. There was no way I could fit.

Quint hit my back again. "Sean? Sean, don't stop!" She pushed me again, but I couldn't move, blocking the passage for all of us. Oh, God, I couldn't go back either; how would I ever navigate that S-bend backwards? I was stuck here; we were all stuck here, trapped and powerless.

Light hit me like a splash of water. The Indigo Minister had shone his flashlight full in my face, jolting me out of my state. My breath was coming very fast, but I didn't seem able to slow it.

"Turn your head sideways," Indigo said. I wondered, detachedly, whether the language he thought in was Sister Standard, or flashes of light.

Then the sense of his words trickled into my brain, and, "Are you joking?"

"You move forward or you die."

I was going to die. There was no air in this tiny tunnel anymore. Indigo's expression tensed up, like he was angry, and then he stretched his arm out into the tunnel. I stared at his hand, only a few feet away from my face, and thought: That was the hand that killed Leah.

Quint shoved at my back again, shouting something I didn't listen to. I didn't let myself think anymore. I laid down on my belly, reached out, and grabbed the Indigo Minister's wrist. Then I kicked and squirmed forward, aided by the relentless pull of Indigo's grip on my wrist.

I had to turn my head to the side to fit through the tiny opening. Metal scraped my cheek.

And then my head was free, and my shoulders. I pulled my arm from Indigo's grip so that I could pry myself out, frantic, metal scraping my back and legs. I was shaking and cold where I had been too warm in the closeness of the tunnel before.

"Sit over there," Indigo said, directing me to a mostly-empty corner of the room; it looked like we had come out into the remains of an ancient bathroom. I saw cracked sinks and stall walls fallen over like cards.

Quint was still in the tunnel. I shouldered next to Indigo and lay on my belly, peering into the gap at Quint's white, horrified face.

"Hey, Quint!" I said. My grin felt stiff on my face. "It's gonna feel real familiar coming out of there, okay?"

"What the hell are you talking about?" she whispered, in the distant tones of a woman almost out of her mind with fear.

I wriggled closer, stretching my arm out into the tunnel the way Indigo had done for me. "It's *just* like being born. You remember that, don't you?"

"What are you—"

"I remember," I said cheerfully, giving her no chance to think or react, and reaching my hand in further. "It was on a Tuesday morning. The first thing I did after I was born was mimic what the doctor said. *It's a boy!*" I said, speaking the announcement in Kystrene, my own language a triumph and a declaration, though I knew the words of it would be unintelligible to her. I switched back to Sister before I could lose her: "Give me your hand, okay, I'll pull you out. It scared the doctor out of his mind; newborns don't usually talk on Kystrom, you know?"

Numbly, Quint reached out and set her hand in mine.

"Sometimes they talk on other planets, though. I hear on Serene they actually come out singing. Get on your belly and start kicking with your feet, pushing with your palms against the walls. You know the baby is ready to be born because they start kicking their mother in perfect rhythm. Like a metronome. Turn your head to the side."

She was moving forward, kicking weakly with her feet, mostly being propelled along by my grip on her wrist. It was a good thing she wasn't particularly heavy, but it was hard to pull her at this angle.

Wordlessly, the Indigo Minister reached in, grabbed Quint's collar, and began to pull as well.

"The, uh, doctors sometimes can lure the child out on their own by playing music in the birthing room," I said, pulling. "The mother doesn't have to do anything. Really easy. Here you go."

Quint's head came out, then shoulders, and then she seemed to come to life. She clawed out, stumbled to her feet, fell to her knees, and then ran for the far wall before I could catch her, fetching up alongside the fallen toilet stalls. There she stopped, and vomited.

She was fine. I turned back to the opening and peered in. "Hey, Benny."

"I got it, Sean," Benny said flatly, and made his way out without my help or the Indigo Minister's. As soon as he emerged he joined the shivering Quint by the wall and checked his handbrace over for damage.

I left Indigo to it, joining Benny and Quint where they had gathered beside the ancient toilets. The design of toilets hadn't changed as much in a thousand years as I would've guessed.

Quint was still shaking, arms around her knees, that fussy haircut of hers gone limp with sweat and grey with dust. I didn't like her expression, like she was one surprise away from snapping. "Hey," I said as I came to stand beside her, "anyone have to pee?"

She raised her head but only so that she could stare at me, incredulous and unfriendly.

Benny clicked his handbrace back into place around his wrist, then stood up, turned to face one of the toilets, and unzipped his fly.

"Oh, that was a joke, not a command," I said.

"I'm not going to try to escape with piss in my pants."

"Will those even still flush?"

"No." The echo of liquid on metal punctuated his words. "Sinks won't run, either. This ship has some sort of self-repair systems or it wouldn't be intact, but they don't seem to be working this close to the hull. Deeper in, there's probably running water."

He finished up, shook himself.

"I don't want to smell your piss the whole time we're here," Quint muttered into her knees.

Benny turned around, still tucking himself back into his pants. "If you were smart you'd do the same. How about it, Sean? You wanted the lead on this; when do we escape?"

I glanced back at Indigo, still crouched down beside the little gap in the collapsed wall. Far enough away that he *probably* couldn't hear us.

"There's only one of them here with us now," Quint whispered. "The others are still in the tunnel."

But Indigo was the scariest of them all, except for One. He'd singlehandedly taken the four of us down a few hours ago, and that was when we'd had our weapons on us. "We wait," I said. "If we make a move to leave, he'll just turn around and grab us."

A screaming, grinding noise called my attention back to Indigo. He was crouched at the opening, which seemed smaller than before. His arm was held at an odd angle within the opening, his shoulders stiff. The pile of debris had shifted, I realized—it was about to collapse. While the Ministers were still inside.

And Indigo, holding the opening in place, was pinned down.

CHAPTER FOURTEEN: MISSED CHANCES

INDIGO HELD THE passage open with one arm. He needed help, I thought, and then I realized that he was stuck there holding the passage open. He couldn't move.

If we ran, now, he couldn't chase us.

I reached down to Quint, beckoning her up. She stood, slowly and quietly, and I glanced around for the door. We could get there before Indigo could free himself. He didn't even seem to notice us, too focused on trying to hold the opening up. I could see the strain in his narrow shoulders.

Strain, because he was struggling to save them.

Those were his people in there.

Out of the corner of my eye, I saw Benny raising his braced arm, aiming at Indigo.

It was like right before Leah had died, when I'd seen what would happen before she'd done it, like I had a limited prescience for blood. Except this time, it wasn't Benny's death I foresaw. Indigo had his hands both in the opening. He couldn't block a bullet this time, the way he had with Leah. Benny would shoot him, but such a low-caliber bullet wouldn't kill Indigo instantly, not with Benny's aim. He'd be wounded, die slow. Probably die still trying to hold open that opening for his companions, bleeding out in slow and desperate agony.

I knocked Benny's arm aside before he could fire.

The motion caught Indigo's attention. He moved, fluid and graceful, freeing one gauntleted hand to aim it at us— the same gauntleted hand that, earlier, had shot sedative pellets to subdue us.

"Sit down," he said, quiet but calm.

I pushed Benny's shoulder until he sat down beside me. Quint had not made it up past her knees, eyes gone round.

Indigo moved his gauntleted hand away from its threatening posture at us to tap at his collar light. White light flashed out in a simple pattern: a quick flutter, a longer hold. Then he angled his arm back out to point at us while he felt around inside the tunnel with his free arm, brows drawn down in concentration.

He seemed to find whatever he was looking for. His movements stopped, his arm went still. Then he took his gauntleted hand back to his throat, dialed the collar-light to green, and flashed a solid burst of light.

The Green Minister writhed her way out of the gap under Indigo's arm, curly dark hair snagging on metal as she went. I could feel frustration vibrating through Benny. There were two Ministers free now—our chance was gone for good.

Indigo, ignoring us now that Green was there to keep an eye on us, flashed that first pattern again: a quick flutter, a longer hold. Then he shifted again, shoulders flexing, getting his arm in a better position. He lifted up again and I heard metal groan, and then Indigo tapped out a yellow flash on his collar-light. Yellow emerged a moment later.

Red light, green light, I realized. Indigo was telling them *stop*, quick-flutter-longer-hold, and *go*, single-flash.

"You had better have a plan, Sean," Benny said, so close to my ear I could feel his breath on my cheek.

"I'll make one up," I whispered back, and made my voice as hard as his.

One emerged last, collar light violet-black. She cast her gaze over the room, taking in the broken stall walls, the ancient toilets, Benny and Quint sitting behind me.

The wall of debris shifted and groaned, crashing down with a wash of dust, as Indigo pulled his arm out of the tunnel and let the whole thing collapse.

No way back.

CHAPTER FIFTEEN:
ONE AND TWO

"MR. WREN," ONE said, calm amidst the dust. "A word."

I didn't think of myself as a coward. I had the imp, didn't I, and the one thing that made the imp come running every time was the whiff of fear. Getting burned wouldn't beat the candle flame, my mother had warned me, but I'd rather blister than wonder.

"Mommy's calling," Benny said, when I did not move from my seat.

I left him without rejoinder and followed her.

There was a little room separated out from the main bathroom. Once it had been a changing room, maybe. It was small, with splintered remains of counters still clinging to the walls, and old mirrors facing each other across the floor in infinite reflection. Our flashlights gleamed in the mirrors like a line of diminishing stars.

"Have you come up with a plan for escape yet?" she asked, and set her flashlight down on the sink.

I followed suit with my flashlight, and told the truth extravagantly to make more believable a lie. "Of course

I have. It's flawless. You'll never see it coming."

"Do not mistake my indifference to your survival for complacency, Mr. Wren."

I doubted I could mistake anything about her for complacent. Her face, strangely lit by her collar-light and the faint reflections of her flashlight on the counter, was beautiful and terrible at the same time, inhuman and unearthly in its sexless perfection.

My imp grabbed at my throat with both hands. "The Ministerial council in Maria Nova doesn't know you're here, does it?"

Her silence emboldened me. "There must be some Ministers who speak Ameng as a first language. But none of those Ministers are here. You're the oldest of this group, aren't you? And you aren't old enough to remember the old language. Maria Nova didn't send its oldest Ministers with you, because Maria Nova doesn't know you've come."

One gazed at me with owl-eyes, the violet glow of her light settling like a shroud over her skin. "I've often found," she said, "that in humans who have suffered a great trauma, they become trapped in that moment. Forever seeking to right what went wrong."

"What the hell does that mean?" I started to say, but One was not done speaking, and the moment I saw she meant to continue, my jaw shut of its own accord, biting my own tongue, my imp cowed.

"Provoking me will not give you any kind of control over me," One said, deliberate as a funeral march. "Whoever sent you here did not particularly care whether you and your friends live or die, or he would not have sent you here so ignorant. My mission has been sanctioned by the Ministerial council. I imagine the Republic knows nothing of yours. Who sent you? Some Republican snake, looking to gain an edge over his opponents in the pit of vipers they call a Senate? Do you even know?"

I saw my own arm moving in the mirror over her head, slow, like in a dream, until my fingers could brush against the nape of my neck, the explosive implant hidden beneath my skin. I could see my own face, the stubble growing; could see her faceless back and my wide eyes reflected back and back and back, fading with distance, the two of us stretching into the invisible past.

One watched the motion with attention but no interest. "What have you been blackmailed with? Citizenship? A criminal past?"

I dropped my arm. "What do you want?"

"I am seven hundred years old, Mr. Wren. I have seen terrors you cannot imagine and I have kept them from humanity like a shield in the dark. And what do humans do? Rebel, and resist, and murder. It is a bitter thing when the people you are trying to protect are ungrateful. I want you to stop trying to escape me."

My throat was almost too tight to speak. "You can't really expect me to just sit back and give up."

"Your friends do not respect you," she said plainly. "Any escape plan will fail not just from our attentiveness, but from mistrust from within. The universe teaches us all a lesson, Mr. Wren. Some humans do not live long enough to learn it. And others dig in their heels after the lesson has been taught, and refuse to accept it. Your sacrifices for them will not be returned. And you are alone in this."

Memory shuddered over my skin, the silence of Itaka after the attack, the way the Ministers had not hesitated to slaughter, the way the Republic had left us behind. The way Benny had not come to me that day on Kystrom. I had stumbled across him unexpected, pure indifferent chance. The loneliness of it, a loneliness that lingered, like a dark bell struck and still reverberating through me.

She was a soul seven hundred years old. I was no longer sure whether she was trying to help me or harm me, or if there was a difference to her. I remembered Indigo, suddenly, and the press of his blade to my cheek, turning my face away from my friend's body. Was this what passed for kindness to a Minister?

"I do not have Number Two's sense of mercy, Mr. Wren," One said. "If you, or your friends, try to escape again, I will kill you."

*   *   *

MY SECOND-GRADE TEACHER had scared the hell out of me at the time. The man had been grimly committed to teaching us all times tables, and wanted us to memorize the multiplication table by any means necessary. For me, I didn't see the reason. I had a perfectly good way of doing multiplication. Nine times three was nine plus nine plus nine, and I already knew addition.

It drove the teacher nuts. "What will you do when we start to multiply with bigger numbers?" he'd demanded, his voice a piercing crack of sound that penetrated every corner of the classroom. "Eighty-one times nineteen—you're not going to add eighty-one nineteen times, are you?"

"Sure, if I have to," I'd said.

He'd opened his mouth and I'd known he'd been on the verge of shouting, but he'd swallowed it down and walked away. That restraint, I'd thought, was more frightening than if he'd just yelled.

He'd taken me aside after school that day to talk.

"You're smart enough to memorize the table easily," he'd said. It occurred to me now that I had forgotten his name, sometime in the years that separated me now from him then. "I know abstract methods are difficult for you, but your life will be easier if you're not stubborn about this."

"Right," I'd said, and kept on doing what I'd been doing, which was not memorizing the times table. I'd passed the lesson anyway.

I'd had to learn it eventually, when we did more complex multiplication, but I'd learned it in my own way, which was *not* the way he'd taught it: instead of memorizing the table, I'd memorized the patterns in the table, and then brought those out when I needed a quick solution.

The moral of the story is simple: my second-grade teacher, Number One, the universe, multiplication itself, all of them together—they can go fuck themselves.

If there's a lesson, I'll learn it my own way.

* * *

WE LEFT THE ancient bathroom behind and had not gone far down the adjacent hallway before I became aware of a creaking, rustling noise, like some distant wind.

"What's that sound?" I asked.

"We are near the outer hull." One swept her flashlight over the wall to my left. I saw nothing unusual about it, just decaying old metal. "This is the sun-side of the ship. Radiation has made the hull very, very thin here."

"What happens if the hull doesn't hold?"

"Automatic containment procedures will seal off this part of the ship," One said. "Assuming that aspect of the ship's systems is still functioning. And we will be swept out into space."

I'd seen a man spaced before, watched him choke and gag, the whites of his eyes going red. And we were so close to the furious radiation of the dying sun that we would burn even as we froze. I shuffled to the right, away from the side of the hallway that was thinning and exposed to space.

My shoulder bumped into a ledge in the wall, just barely protruding. I shone my flashlight on it and saw that there was a metal plate inside the ledge, within the wall. Those must be the containment procedures One had mentioned—in case of decompression, they would shoot out of the wall and seal off the section of the hall that had lost atmosphere.

Interesting. If I had a way to trick the ship's computer into thinking we'd lost atmosphere, those ledges would slam shut. Maybe we could use that to separate us from the Ministers. The Ministers would be able to cut through—

after all, the Indigo Minister had cut through the hull to board the ship in the first place—but it might buy us a few minutes. If I could figure out how to do it quickly.

I glanced around, looking to see how frequently those ledges were placed, and in glancing backwards I finally saw whatever had been following us through the dark: fish-white skin, long, long limbs, and hungry, glinting eyes.

CHAPTER SIXTEEN:
THE CHOICE AND THE HULL

I MUST HAVE shouted, or made some sound, because Indigo stopped and the others turned around, flashlights blazing into the hall behind us just quickly enough to catch a glimpse. Whatever that thing was, it was as big as any of the Ministers, maybe even as tall as me. One flashed an order and the Red Minister peeled off from the group, pulling a thick long knife from its sheath at his waist, flashlight wavering as he ran, silent, after that huge spidering monster.

"What was that?" Quint cried out.

I moved towards her but hit the bulk of Indigo's shoulder. Indigo pushed me back with a hand on my sternum. "Don't move," he said.

The Ministers were like gears whirring, shifting position until they formed a circle around us. The hull groaned, and flashlight beams glanced over walls and ceiling and floor.

Then the hallway went dark, all except for my little flashlight, like I'd been tossed into black water, and all my companions swallowed up too. A narrow hand landed on mine, flipped the switch on my flashlight, and threw me into the dark with the rest. "Stay low," Indigo said into my ear.

The Ministers had turned off their lights, both collar and flash. I could hear them moving around, the soft scrape of boot against the ground, the swish of fabric, or a sword coming free. And something from far off to my right snarled.

That wasn't a Minister.

I kept low, like Indigo had said. I curled my fingers around the thin metal of my flashlight and tried to breathe evenly. Could they even see me? Were those even the Ministers, or was whatever else that I'd seen in this hallway moving around me, circling slow, like a buzzard? I'd felt eyes on me earlier, seen movements in the darkness. It seemed like that hadn't just been the cockroaches. Had the Ministers known we were being followed? They must've, but they'd said nothing. Did they know what these creatures were? Could these monsters, whatever they were, have been what killed the crew of the *Nameless*? I remembered the claw marks dug deep into bone.

The Indigo Minister would keep me safe, I consoled myself, and a minute later wondered where the hell that thought had come from. The Indigo Minister had murdered Leah and was holding me captive.

"Benny," I whispered, unable to keep silent, and he said, "Here!" from startlingly close by. I reached out and my fingers landed awkwardly against someone else's hand, pinky striking palm. I shifted my grip in time to find his wrist. I heard Quint whimper, and knew she was nearby too.

Far to my left, a high-pitched shriek. Nails scrabbled against metal. As I turned, a white light flashed, bright and brief as lightning, and an afterimage barely glimpsed burned itself into my retinas: Ultraviolet, with one hand upon her collar and the other holding a narrow blade, facing down some manlike thing, hairless and dead white, with long arms. It looked like the manikins we used to set up during the Holiday of the Dead back on Kystrom, with the unsettling proportions of limb and neck, and the dead white skin. Manikins come alive, and striding through an empty starship voiceless as ghosts, plastic toes tapping.

The flash had been a summoning. Sightless in the dark I felt the other Ministers swooping past us, converging upon the monster all together, the Ministers silent, the manikin crying out shrill and furious like a hawk. My hand gripped Benny's wrist, and this was our chance.

"Up, quick!" I hissed, and tugged on his shirt until he got up. He must've grabbed Quint; I heard her cry out in surprise. I had my flashlight but I didn't dare turn it on; the Ministers were distracted, fighting that thing, but a bright white light was as good as a shout to them, saying "Hey, your captives are trying to escape!" I led Benny and Quint down the hall as fast as I dared to move until I felt, in the air currents by my shoulder, that something was coming towards me.

I recoiled, crashing into Benny behind me, while something ahead of me shrieked. The sound of it vibrated through my bones like metal dragging over concrete. I tried to retreat, but I couldn't see the manikin in the dark. I couldn't even see Benny or Quint, and I tripped over them when I recoiled, the three of us entangled and blind. I heard the air before me hiss, something drawing breath, inches from my face—

Sparks flashed, metal striking metal, and a body shoved me back. My already-unsteady balance collapsed, and I caught myself half on the floor, half on a warm shape that cried out with Quint's voice. Nothing struck me, but something snarled in the darkness ahead, and then the hallway appeared again in a deep underwater blue. I blinked furiously, trying to understand how the opaque blackness had lightened for me, trying to figure out how to escape the silhouette that stood before me. And then I realized that the silhouette was Indigo, the blue glow his collar-light; he stood between us and the empty hallway where, a few seconds earlier, there had been a creature of tooth and claw.

There was nothing ahead of him now, not that I could see in the dark blue glow. What had that thing been? The shadows were deep; the manikin had slipped away, somehow, but Indigo still stood between us and any possible threat—or any possible escape.

The other Ministers were some distance behind us and still under attack, judging from the barely audible whispers of a struggle in the darkness. It was only Indigo here. I saw Benny lift his braced arm, aiming, for the second time, at the Indigo Minister.

I grabbed his arm and shoved it down before he could

fire. The move brought me off Quint and face-to-face with Benny, face deeply shadowed in the blue dark. "He just saved our lives," I said, lowly enough that only Benny could hear.

"He destroyed our lives," Benny hissed back.

"We'll get out of here," I said. "But we'll do it without *anyone* dying."

Benny sat back, expression stony. I looked at Quint to be sure she'd understood and found her looking at me with a blank expression. Indifference. I think I would have preferred if she'd hated me.

Lights were coming back on, some distance down the hall. The other Ministers had defeated their opponents, it seemed, though there were no bodies that I could see left behind. I wondered anew at what sort of creature could fight a full spectrum of Ministers to a draw. Number One had both knives still drawn, held out like razor wings, and a strangely dark liquid dripped off one of her blades. She flashed a sentence in red light with a slight spectrum increase at the end. A question.

Red replied with a descending spectrum, violet to red.

One had asked Red if he'd found anything, I guessed, and he had replied: *No.*

Indigo came to stand over Quint, Benny, and me. I stood up, elbow-to-elbow with the Minister, and said, "Did the Red Minister find anything?"

Indigo shook his head.

Time to face the music. It was pretty obvious that Quint, Benny, and I had made a break for it, but maybe I could spin it another way before Number One executed me—

or worse, executed them. "Really good luck you came when you did," I said to Indigo. "We were pretty lost out here in the dark."

Indigo sighed. He got one hand under my elbow and, using that as leverage, propelled me forward.

"Couldn't see anything," I said to Indigo as he half-dragged me down the hall towards Number One. "If you hadn't showed up those things might have... I don't know, eaten us. Do you think they eat human flesh?" I pressed on before Indigo could reply; it came to me that I didn't actually want to know whether those things were likely to eat us. "We couldn't tell up from down out here. Might've wandered off trying to escape those things, gotten lost somewhere. And you guys were moving too, chasing those things down the hall. I guess we—"

"May I give you some advice," said Indigo.

"Go ahead," I said, intrigued.

"Think in your head," said Indigo, "not with your mouth."

Was that his way of telling me to shut up? I'd saved his life and lost my chance to escape, and he told me to shut up?

I glanced back at Benny and Quint, like a reflex. But when I looked back I saw Benny with his hand on his brace.

Behind me, Benny and Quint sat side-by-side. Ahead of me, the Ministers gathered in a glowing crowd. Beside me, the hull hissed and sighed, so thin it might be pierced even by a single small, low-caliber bullet. And between the humans and the Ministers, Benny and me, jutted one of the decompression ledges in the wall, a panel that would separate us in the event of a sudden decompression.

The pieces fell together.

I pulled myself out of Indigo's grip. "Don't!" I shouted, one hand outstretched.

Benny met my eyes, a flinty look on his face, raised his braced hand and fired.

The world peeled apart.

CHAPTER SEVENTEEN:
THE INDIGO MINISTER AND I

I UNFOLDED LIKE a flower, the air in my lungs exploding out. My internal organs pressed against my skin, trying to spread like oil on water. The side of me facing the exploding sun crisped with heat but my other side was the sort of cold that was dry, ice so frozen your skin clung to it rather than melting. I was an origami bird coming undone, blood through the seams, scorching and charring to ash—

Something slammed into my chest and I slammed into a floor.

Suddenly I could gasp, and there was air to be drawn in. Tears streaked down my cheeks as my dried eyes overcompensated, and I stared up at the ceiling as black spots flashed in my vision.

Indigo crouched over me, a blue cast to his skin like a corpse. He had one hand gripping the back of my neck, my collar pulled painfully tight against my throat. The other hand had drawn his knife, and he held the point of it over my heart.

I struggled to catch my breath enough to speak. Indigo waited, dark eyes merciless. I fought the blackness on the edges of my sight, and tried to tell him without speaking that I had tried to stop it. If I'd had a collar light I would have shone a descending spectrum, *No*, again and again and again. When I finally managed to choke out the word, it came out in Kystrene: "*No*," I said, in the language of my dead people.

Something flickered in his expression, deep behind the eyes, like when he'd cut through Leah's throat and then waited, blade at mine. He lifted his knife away from my chest, released his grip on my collar.

My head slammed back into the floor, lights flashing in my eyes. My eyes were streaming, overcompensating for their scalded dryness, wet trickling down my temples and into my hair.

Indigo grabbed my shoulder and hauled me onto my side. He pulled my shirt up, and my misfiring nerves suddenly got with the program and fired all at once. I cried out in pain. The side of me that had faced the sun was flayed agony.

Something cool and damp misted over my side. Where it touched, the skin went numb. Ministerial burn spray, I thought distantly, was a lot stronger than ours.

The sudden cessation of pain undid the last tether holding me conscious. I was cold all over, frost melting on my skin. My burning eyes shut, and the echoing dark swallowed me like a pit.

*   *   *

"Wake up."

My eyes opened but I could not see. The sun had burned the sight from my eyes. I panicked.

"Hold still and be quiet." It was Indigo speaking. Cold fingers on my face moved something from over my eyes, and then I could see the starkness of dark and light, Indigo's flashlight fighting the dim.

Indigo himself was all contrast too, pale, black brows low over brushstroke eyes. His mouth was set in a line so grim it looked like it had been engraved on his face. He was holding a bandage in his hand, and the medicated smell of it lingered around my face.

My eyes itched, but no longer burned.

"We're not alone," Indigo said, so quietly it was more mouthed than spoken.

I curled my arms around my chest. My jacket was hanging off one shoulder, my shirt rolled up. Where I had been burned on my right side I felt nothing but smooth, painless skin, a little rubbery the way artificial skin tended to be. My chest and stomach ached like someone had kicked me hard, but I could breathe and move. Indigo shifted, slipping a hand under my elbow to guide me up, and I moved with him as quietly as I could, tugging my shirt back down and shrugging my jacket back on.

On my feet, the last traces of unconsciousness dripping from me like water, I heard what he had heard: something large shuffling in the dark.

Indigo shut his flashlight off.

There was still light in the room, very faint, coming from behind us. I craned my neck around and experienced a heart-jolting moment of terror that we would be sucked out to space again, this time without return, before I realized what I was seeing: the hole in the hull behind us was sealed up with that oil-slick surface the Ministers had used to enter the *Nameless* in the first place. Indigo must have grabbed me, cut a hole in the hull, and sealed it up with that substance, and he must have done it in a matter of seconds. Faint orange light filtered through the warping rainbows of the oil slick, and there was no way to tell where in the *Nameless* we had landed.

Indigo's collar light was dialed so low it was nothing more than a suggestion of glow out of the corner of my eye. He was inching backward, guiding me with him. Whatever else was in the room with us shuffled closer.

Something hard pressed into my hand, and I closed my fingers around it. Indigo had passed me his flashlight. I'd lost my own in the explosion. I heard the sound of metal against hardened leather. He was drawing his long knife.

The flashlight weighed in my hand. It would bludgeon, in a pinch, but if I broke the flashlight on something's skull we would have no source of light except Indigo's collar.

Indigo shoved me, hard, and I landed with bone-jarring heaviness atop something that broke beneath me—old furniture, long-forgotten. Something growled, not like a dog did but like a man did, between animal and language. Someone slammed into a wall, and something crashed and shattered in the room. There was the wet thud of splitting flesh, and a cry of pain that could easily have been Indigo or the... whatever was in the room with us. I grabbed for the flashlight, jarred from my hand by the fall, and flickered it on.

The beam of light caught Indigo leaning forward, keen, and the flash of a pale and long-limbed figure retreating from the light, leaving dark blood behind.

Indigo said, "*Run.*"

He was already moving with that slippery inhuman speed of his. I had to scramble up to keep him in sight.

The flashlight bounced as we ran, and did fuck-all to illuminate the path, showing floor and door and wall in isolated useless pictures like camera flashes. Indigo led and I didn't know how, darting this way and that, through rooms upon rooms upon rooms of unknown purpose. And through it all I heard them chasing us, the manikins with their plastic skin and their black blood, nails scraping on metal.

We crashed into them once, in the dark. Indigo's arm arched, sword in hand; I saw a spine, a back, a splayed limb at odd angles. Something came up behind me and I swung around at it wildly with the flashlight, felt it impact the manikin with a force that jarred my arm straight to my shoulder, and the light went out.

I heard a harsh intake of breath behind me that I knew in my bones was Indigo in pain, and reached out, stupidly, blindly, to find where he had gone. He caught my arm instead. "*Run!*" he said again, and pulled me along in the dark, the useless flashlight still in my hand.

We stumbled, slammed into walls, but the sound of harsh breathing and nails scrabbling faded until I heard nothing but my breath and Indigo's, our boots thudding against the ground, until Indigo hauled me to the left so sharply he nearly pulled my arm from its socket and shoved me to the floor.

A door slammed and light ignited in the room; I shielded my eyes but saw Indigo with his hand on his collar light, touching the hidden dials on the side. He was bringing it up to its full brightness, blazing white like a star and illuminating the room we were hunkered in. It chased all the ancient shadows from their rotten corners, and filled the rotting tomb of a ship with brilliance.

The room we were in had been a nursery. The paint-flaked plastic bars of a crib had fallen off not far from where I sat, like a cage split open from inside. I stared in mute horror at a rotting mobile of a smiling sun.

"Is the flashlight working?" Indigo asked. He leaned against the shut door. His hand was bloody, red blood, his physical exertion favoring the iron-based circulatory system over the copper. He'd left little smears on the surface of his collar-light that glowed violet.

To my relief, the flashlight head had simply been jostled loose; when I screwed it back on the flashlight flickered back to life.

Indigo reached up to his collar-light and dialed it back down to a faint glow, wiping away the stains as he did. I said, "How much power does this thing have?"

"It's kinetic." He left the door to walk back towards me at the wall. "If it runs low, shake it."

"And your collar-light?"

He sat down next to me and began to empty the pouches strapped to his belt. His short sword rested across his knees.

It was only then that I realized we had both lost our packs of supplies.

"Metabolic," he said. "It recharges from body heat, electrical impulses across my skin. So long as someone is wearing it, it will work indefinitely. If I die, it will glow for seven days at lowest luminosity, just under two hours at highest."

So we wouldn't immediately run out of light. I set the flashlight down, facing the shut door; there was enough spillover glow to see Indigo's face as he began to set out medical supplies from his pockets. "Do you know where we are?"

"No."

"How are we going to get back?"

"We aren't going back," Indigo said, examining the cut on his hand. It was still bleeding. "We're going forward, to Mara Zhu's office."

"Both of us?"

He set a first-aid machine down on the floor with a clatter. "Would you rather I had let you suffocate?"

"I'm glad you're not leaving me to be eaten by manikins," I said.

"Mani—? Those creatures are alive."

"I know, but they look like manikins."

"Regardless of what they are or what you have named them," Indigo said, "you are too dangerous to be left unsupervised. If you try anything else, I will kill you."

"I didn't try anything last time!"

"Were you aware of the escape attempt?"

"They improvised."

"Were you aware of the concealed weapon?"

Benny's hand-brace. "Yes."

"You attempted escape. Try it again, try anything again, and I will kill you."

Yet he'd saved me, when the hull had blown out. I watched him hold the first-aid machine over the cut on his hand. His fingers were trembling.

I said, "Do you think the others survived?"

The first-aid machine sprayed artificial skin over the wound on Indigo's hand; the bleeding stopped. "Five was closest to the wall. He may not have been able to reach the hull in time. The others likely survived, and probably are together. I can't speak for your companions."

Five was the Yellow Minister. I could see his face in my mind's eye, clearly, drifting through space unable to moor himself to the relative safety of the *Nameless*. Suffocating as slowly as he burned.

It was not a death I would wish on my worst enemy. I watched Indigo wrap bandages around his injured hand. Artificial skin did not always hold up well under repeated stresses, and it was clear that Indigo expected to need his hands.

I wondered how sure Indigo was that the other Ministers had survived. He was insisting on pushing on, going to Mara Zhu's office, even alone, so maybe a part of him suspected that he was the only survivor. I wondered how long he'd known the Yellow Minister.

I said, "What about food? Water?"

"I have a flask of water and a few packets of dehydrated food," Indigo said, still wrapping his hand. "I have some basic medical supplies. But that is all."

So we had one knife, a single flashlight, a single flask of water, and a few packets of food that needed water to be edible. "There should be water deeper in on the ship," I said. "Benny thought so. And the cockroaches. They don't need a lot of water, but they do need something."

Indigo split the bandage with his sword and began to tuck in the edges. The claw marks on his arm terminated abruptly at his gauntlet, where the hardened material had stopped whatever had lacerated his hand. I didn't know what kind of claws these creatures had, but I was relieved that they weren't so impossibly sharp they could carve through Ministerial body armor.

"Don't worry, Indigo," I said, while he tucked away the first-aid machine. "We'll find supplies somewhere."

"Why are you calling me Indigo?"

I hadn't even thought he'd been listening to me. "It's your name," I said. "Well. It's the name I gave you. It's better than Number Two."

His dark gaze cut at me sideways, skeptical.

"Indigo," I insisted, and then the imp took a hold of me again. I reached out to his collar light and found the dials on the side. It took me a moment, but I figured out how to shift the color, and spun the wheel until it roughly matched the shade that had seemed to correspond to Indigo's 'name'. "See? Indigo."

His lips thinned out. "Do you speak our language?"

I dialed his collar light a descending spectrum, violet to red: *No.* His eyes went narrow.

I released his collar light sharpish. "I just picked up a

few things watching you. I wasn't listening in."

"How many languages do you speak?"

"Fluently? Kystrene and Sister. But I know a handful of others, enough to get around. I'm good at languages. I really can read Ameng, more or less. You need me to get through this ship."

"We never needed you," Indigo said flatly. "We could have hacked the computers or carved through the walls. Your speaking the language was simply convenient, not necessary. One wanted to find out what else you knew."

Giving me enough rope to hang myself with, I supposed. And hanged myself I had. "Is that why you didn't bring an expert from your own people along with?"

Indigo said, "Do you have any concealed weapons on you?"

"Like Benny? Uh, no."

"Would you know how to use a weapon, if you were handed one?"

"I broke something's skull with the flashlight," I offered.

"Do not break the flashlight. If you see something, stay behind me. I will—" He cut off so abruptly it alarmed me; I looked at him only to see him staring into a darkened corner of the room, his fingers curling around the hilt of his knife.

"Get behind me," he said.

I got up and stood behind him, grabbing the flashlight as I did. I held it so the beam illuminated the space in front of him. There was nothing in front of us that I could see, but there were cribs between us and the far wall, the bars casting concealing shadows.

A thought struck me. "Can you use that oil-slick as a barrier?" I whispered.

He was silent a moment, parsing what I had said. "The hull seal? It's impermeable to air and heat, but sufficient kinetic force passes through. It's a seal, not a shield."

I wanted to ask what the threshold for kinetic force was—if the room was hot enough, or pressurized enough, would the air be able to pass through? If I touched the oil-slick lightly, would my finger go through, or did I have to punch through?—but before I could give voice to my questions, something struck my hand hard enough to knock the flashlight from it. It hit the floor and went dark.

Indigo moved like a whisper or a breeze, and something slammed into the floor with a bone-breaking sound.

I dropped to my knees and fumbled for the flashlight while Indigo darted around. Whatever was attacking him was human-sized, human-shaped. Something swung through the air with a hiss and I heard metal strike metal.

My hand hit the flashlight and I grabbed it, screwed the cap back on, and shone the light on the attacker.

A human shape, arms and legs and head—thick dark hair and a ragged uniform and wide-set brown eyes.

"Hey!" I shouted, and ran at them though it made Indigo flinch with a hiss that might have been a curse, long knife in his hands. Lantern-Eyes checked her swing abruptly, slamming her weapon into the ground instead of me. It was—God—a homemade mace, or morning star, or something; a club with spikes on the end.

"Hey, Lantern-Eyes," I said, putting myself between her and Indigo. She'd saved me, back when the Ministers had first arrived. "It's all right. Shh, it's okay."

She looked at me like I was the dumbest creature she'd ever had the misfortune to meet and said, in perfect Sister Standard, "Don't be stupid, he's a Minister."

CHAPTER EIGHTEEN: THE MINISTER AND THE LIEUTENANT

LANTERN-EYES GLARED AT me, her enormous bludgeon still clutched in her hands.

I felt slow and stupid, my brain realigning itself in the disparity between what I'd grown to believe of the strange woman living on the ship, and the reality that stood before me. "You're from the Republic."

"She's a Republican soldier." Indigo did not sound impressed.

Now that he mentioned it, I could just recognize the silhouette of Lantern-Eyes' tattered uniform. The stiff shoulders had softened with wear, and beneath the fade and rough patching I could see that the jacket had once been a very dark red. The characteristic broad shoulder and crimson of a Republican officer's uniform. I'd been detained by police officers in the non-military version of that uniform about a week ago.

Lantern-Eyes—the soldier—narrowed her big amber eyes

at Indigo over my shoulder, then said abruptly to me, "He's going to kill you after he uses you to find the data."

"Well, he's gonna have to get in line," I said.

"I won't," Lantern-Eyes said.

Several things happened all at once. I heard Indigo move behind me. Lantern-Eyes pressed one hand to a rough-looking mess of wires tied to her hip. Indigo's fingers brushed my shoulder just as the world split in thunder and lightning.

I blinked myself aware on the floor of the room, the rotting sun mobile inches from my face. Afterimages of brilliance were scoured on my retinas for the second time that day, and the room was filling with some sort of funny-smelling gas, metallic and sour.

Lantern-Eyes dropped to her hands and knees directly in front of me, her bludgeon clattering against the floor. She didn't look as stunned as I felt. "Let's go," she said.

A flash bomb and a smoke bomb, I realized, my thoughts like a laggy computer connection. She'd set them off.

Indigo. He'd been right behind me.

"He's only stunned," Lantern-Eyes warned when I found him, on his knees behind me and breathing in sharp hard breaths, eyes wide and glassy. The gas. The funny-smelling gas.

Indigo swung his head around, his androgyne features even eerier with his glassy eyes staring sightlessly at me.

Minister or Republican soldier; like choosing between ground glass or rancid meat for dinner. Neither sounded great but at least one was less likely to kill me later on. I rolled up onto unsteady feet and followed Lantern-Eyes across the room, stumbling into broken metal cribs.

Behind me I heard Indigo getting to his feet. If getting spaced hadn't stopped him, I wasn't sure Lantern-Eyes' smoke bomb was going to do the job. She led me to a rat-hole in the wall, hidden behind the broken cribs, and shoved me down.

"Go!" she barked, the ear-splitting command of a trained soldier, and I looked past her at Indigo striding towards us through the thick mist, collar-light gleaming.

Lantern-Eyes' hands landed on my back and collar and she shoved me further into the rat-hole. I scrambled, Indigo's flashlight clicking against the floor—somehow I'd kept a hold of it—and crawled through the wall and out into a different part of the ship. It was a room, I thought. The walls were in long ragged tears, like someone had clawed at them until the metal had given way. That was all I could see in my little beam of light

Lantern-Eyes rolled out of the tunnel after me, reached up and tugged a nail out of the wall. A torn-up section of wall slid down to slam against the floor, totally covering the little rat-hole we'd crawled through. She moved like clockwork, sure and steadily paced. This wasn't a spur-of-the-moment rescue: she'd planned it.

"Up now," she said to me, and strode off into the dark as soon as she'd spoken.

I scrambled up, flashlight swinging wildly. "Who are you? Are you really a Republican soldier?"

"I'm a lieutenant. Keep your voice down."

I couldn't see the path in the dark; Lieutenant Lantern-Eyes might have been creating the path herself, guiding me into formless dark. She was a quick walker, sure of herself and familiar with the ground. I hurried to keep up.

"I thought you were one of the original crew," I admitted, obligingly lowering my voice. "You just showed up out of nowhere, and there wasn't supposed to be anyone on this ship. They were studying how to make themselves immortal here, right? But you're from the Republic, so you can't have been here long. Are there more Republican soldiers on the way? Is it because of the Ministers?" Another thought struck me. "What's your name?"

"Reinforcements will arrive in a few days; the Republic sent me here five years ago to find the Philosopher Stone data, which I know you know something about," Lantern-Eyes said, "and if you don't *shut up soon*, we will both be torn apart by the native species."

"Wait," I said. "They sent you here *alone*?"

From far off behind us, invisible in the dark, I heard a sudden *CLANG*—as if, say, an angry Minister had been crawling through a tunnel and hit a slab of metal some Republican lieutenant had put there to block his way.

"That won't hold him long," Lantern-Eyes said, and when I glanced back over at her, I saw her reach underneath her oversized uniform jacket and draw out a pragmatic-looking black handgun. "We've got to move—and shut up while we do."

CHAPTER NINETEEN: LIEUTENANT LANTERN-EYES

LANTERN-EYES HELD THAT handgun comfortably, correctly, one-handed and with her finger resting outside the trigger-guard. What the hell else was she hiding underneath that jacket?

The wall *clanged* again behind me, suggesting that Indigo was attempting to beat his way through with fists alone. I wasn't sure he wouldn't succeed. Lantern-Eyes was already walking away again, at a faster clip than before, apparently expecting I would follow.

Typical Republican. Assuming I'd just do what she told me. I should walk off now, while Indigo was locked up and she wasn't looking. Strike out on my own. Find the Philosopher Stone and get Benny and get gone. It wasn't like I could trust her, after all. The Republic had gotten me into this mess in the first place.

But there were monsters on this ship, and right now I didn't have any way to defend myself. Lantern-Eyes was just on the edge of my flashlight's glow, a few more steps from disappearing entirely.

I hurried in her wake.

Why would the Republic send someone to this ship alone? *Had* she been sent alone? I had absolutely no idea how army ranks worked—was it normal to send a lieutenant somewhere alone? Or maybe she wasn't army, maybe she was in the astromarines? I had only a vague idea of the differences between armed forces. Were there more Republican soldiers stationed on this ship, in the dark, watching and waiting for... what? The Philosopher Stone was on this ship; if the Republic had been here, in some form, for five years, why hadn't they gotten the Stone and left?

For that matter, why had the Republican Senator sent us here if the Republic were already aboard?

Whoever she was and whyever she'd been sent here and wherever her back-up was, if she had any, the lieutenant seemed to know a lot about the ship. She led me through unseen rooms, passing under broken doorframes, turning sharply this way and that in the dark and following some route she seemed to have mapped out perfectly in her head. I was tense at first, worried that Indigo's clanging had summoned some of the monsters that had been chasing us, but nothing appeared as I followed Lantern-Eyes. Maybe we were lucky, or maybe she knew some way that avoided the monsters. Just in case, I tried to keep my steps quiet.

What if the Senator hadn't known the lieutenant was aboard? If her mission had been classified at a high enough level, it was possible only the President had known. Or if the Senator knew that Lantern-Eyes had been sent here, maybe he thought that she was dead. Otherwise why send us, and why not warn us of a military presence already here? Not even Quint had mentioned it.

The only person right now who could answer any of these questions was Lantern-Eyes herself, walking only a few steps in front of me. Curiosity burned, but I kept quiet. Not only was I worried that sound might summon a manikin, but I had to watch what I said to her. If I told her something about the Senator that she didn't already know and got the Senator in trouble, and if the Senator found out it was me... boom, pop, bye-bye Sean Wren's intact skull.

Fuck the Republic, seriously. They weren't content with screwing over the independent planets, they had to go around screwing over each other—which got us independent planets screwed over too, in the end.

I followed Lantern-Eyes through a doorway and stopped, because she had disappeared. I swung my light across the room and found it a dead end, a small closet of a room that might've been an office once. There was a pile of dust and splinters that had maybe been a desk, with iron fittings discolored in the pile. A shattered mound of plastic and crystal might have been a computer, once—in the old days, data had been stored in quartz.

I jumped at movement behind me, ready to brain my attacker with my stolen flashlight, but it was just Lantern-Eyes. She set her hands on my shoulders, turning me to face the direction she wanted, and then pushed me inexorably that way, out of the room and into an adjacent room. I hadn't seen that there were two doorways, side-by-side. She stopped me in front of a closed door inside this second room, maneuvering me like a doll.

She bent down, messing with something hidden from my flashlight beam by her oversized jacket, and this new door swung open. Dim light emitted from inside the room beyond, but it was more light than I'd seen since Indigo had turned his collar-light up high. I squinted against it.

"In," she said, and I stepped in, flicking off my flashlight as I did. The room she'd led me to was boxy, large enough to lie down in, and not much more. The floor and walls had been swept clean—*very* clean. You could eat off that floor, and there weren't tables, so maybe she did. Against one wall was a neatly done-up pallet of patched blankets; the wall opposite the bed had very precise stacks of rations, all at exact right angles to the wall and floor, all grouped by type. The light in the room was coming from a bar set into the wall all around at about waist level—ancient emergency lighting, I guessed. Whether by luck or Lantern-Eyes' rigorous repairs, the lights in this room still functioned, bathing everything in a pale soft glow that flickered gently at uneven intervals, like a butterfly's wings.

On the third wall, between bed and rations and opposite the door I'd entered through, a small army's worth of weapons had been mounted. I saw hand grenades, smoke bombs, knives of every conceivable size, and rather more clubs and bludgeoning instruments than I could name. I saw what I guessed were the smoke and light bombs she'd used to take down Indigo and me. They looked small and lightweight, easy to slip into my jacket pockets. They'd been very effective against me and Indigo, and nonlethal, too.

While I was window-shopping through the lieutenant's weapons collection, I realized something else. Her vast and terrifying array of weapons, like her store of rations, had been arranged very precisely by type.

This lieutenant had all but alphabetized her knife collection. I was starting to suspect she was a little bit neurotic.

A solid-sounding thud behind me caught my attention; Lantern-Eyes had closed the door we'd come through and was now locking it. There were locks all up and down the door, and locks on the top and bottom, plus a long bent pipe that seemed to function as a bar. There had to be like twenty locks, and the hinges were on the inside. The apocalypse couldn't break down that door.

"Where's the rest of your team?" I asked. "Or *did* the Republic send you alone?"

Lantern-Eyes slid another bolt into place. "Dead."

The little room we were in with its one cot felt suddenly a lot lonelier. "I'm sorry."

"You didn't kill them. Monsters did."

"Yeah, those manikin things," I said. "They were chasing us before."

Lantern-Eyes closed the last lock and squinted at me, a judgmental little look. That was the Republic for you, though: judgmental. And condescending. "'Manikin things'? Species 019? Those are only one of the things living on this ship that will kill you."

She headed for the back corner behind the tidy stacks of rations. Her gun had vanished again, probably back in the holster she had hidden beneath her jacket. There was a massive black square in the corner, which I recognized as a particularly powerful relativistic radio, strong enough to make it through the hull of the ship and past the interference of the dying star. It would send messages in packets faster than the speed of light, too. Otherwise it would take longer to send messages between planets than it would to fly between them. You usually only saw radios that powerful in the engine rooms of starships. "How long ago did your team die?"

"Not quite two years."

And she'd been alone all that time. "Why didn't you radio for reinforcements earlier?" That superpowered radio of hers would definitely get a message back to Terra Nova, easy.

Lantern-Eyes ignored me. She bent down beside the massive black transmitter, picked something up, and extended it towards me.

It was a computer tablet—a few years' old technology, but definitely modern, unlike the crystal-based decaying things that filled the *Nameless*.

"Translate that," Lantern-Eyes said, and I looked down at the tablet to see that the screen was full of Ameng.

CHAPTER TWENTY:
MARA ZHU'S EXPERIMENT

"I APPRECIATE THE rescue, but I was sort of hoping you could answer me a few more questions before I got put to work," I said, the pad in my hand. That was a lot of Ameng. I loved a good translation, and you wouldn't get a better translator in either of the Sister Systems or any of the independent colonies, but translating that much Ameng would take hours and was guaranteed to give me a headache.

"That wasn't a rescue, it was a requisition," Lantern-Eyes said. "You do speak Ameng?"

"I speak a little of everything."

She got two fingers beneath the pad and tipped it up, pushing it towards my face. "Then I need you to translate that."

Outside of running or fighting for our lives, she was oddly reluctant to meet my eyes directly. It was a bit weird after spending time with Indigo, who tended to hold my gaze for a few beats longer than was customary or comfortable. "What am I translating?"

"If I knew, I wouldn't need you." She left me to it, though, going to the far wall and starting to fuss with the weapons, hanging her club back up and exchanging one knife strapped to her thigh for another. I hadn't even *seen* that knife until she was drawing it.

"The data comes from the bridge computers," the lieutenant continued, sliding a few smaller knives up her sleeves. "One of my late colleagues spoke Ameng, but she didn't finish translating before she died."

Another Ameng-speaker? There weren't many of us around. "What was her name?"

"Whose?"

"Your translator's. I might know her."

"I don't care if you're her brother. What I need is for you to translate that data, and find out where the Philosopher Stone is."

"I don't even need to translate for that." I lowered the pad. "It's in the head scientist's office. Mara Zhu's office."

"It's not," said the lieutenant. "We looked."

We looked. Five years, she'd said. She had been here for five years, and with colleagues for three of those years. Of course they'd looked—Mara Zhu's office had probably been the first place they checked.

Much like it was the first place the Ministers intended to look.

Which meant that Number One and the rest of the Ministers were looking in the wrong place.

Lantern-Eyes seemed to have finished messing around with her weaponry. She leaned back against the wall, beside the terrifying array of clubs, and folded her arms across her chest. The pale and flickering light washed the pumpkin-orange out of her eyes, made them ordinary and brown.

"What have you been doing since you realized it wasn't there?" I asked. "Sitting around, waiting for a translator to fall out of the sky?"

The angle her eyebrows made was dangerous. "This ship is huge. There are about fifty different labs on this ship, give or take, as well as living quarters, supplies, storage, machinery. My team mapped out over fifty percent of this ship in detail. On my own, I've mapped out maybe another twenty percent. That still leaves about a quarter of this ship unmapped and unexplored—and it's the most dangerous part of the ship. It took me almost two years to explore that same amount of space, with a lot fewer dangers. Now the sun will go nova in just a few days. We don't have time to search room by room anymore. I know the Philosopher Stone must be hidden in that last quarter of the ship, but I need a more detailed location than that, so that when my reinforcements arrive, we can go in and extract it."

Before the Ministers could. "So you do have reinforcements coming," I said.

"I radioed them before I retrieved you. They'll be here in a few days."

Something about that timeline was strange to me, but the tablet in my hands was more immediately interesting. Lantern-Eyes had left one particular document open— perhaps she'd been trying to translate the Ameng herself— but that was only one file out of many. Some were text, some visual, some video. I poked through the folders, examining the huge chunk of text she seemingly expected me to translate on the spot.

"Why do the Ministers want the data, anyway?" I asked, poking through a folder full of ancient videos. Fascinating. Even if we didn't find the Philosopher Stone, there was enough linguistic data here to thrill the whole Republic's worth of academics. "They tried to destroy it a thousand years ago. Why not just blow the *Nameless* from orbit?"

"The *Nameless*? Do you give everything a stupid name?"

"Why, what do you call it?"

"I call it 'the ship'," said Lantern-Eyes.

Her voice was milder than I expected, but I'd finally reached the end of all the videos she'd downloaded from the ancient computer, and the last file caught my eye. I opened it without playing it. An oddly familiar woman's face filled the screen, high dark eyes and narrow angled cheekbones.

I couldn't shake the feeling like I'd met her before. I held the screen out to show Lantern-Eyes. "Who is this?"

She glanced over without moving from her spot against the wall. "That's Mara Zhu."

Then I'd definitely never seen her before—she was a thousand years dead. The only person on this ship who could've met her would've been one of the Ministers.

Speaking of, Lantern-Eyes hadn't answered my question. I said, "Why *do* you think the Ministers want the data?"

"I have no idea why they want the data exactly, but I imagine it's personal."

"Personal? What, like their mother's phone number?"

For the first time since we'd arrived in her safe-room, Lantern-Eyes looked at me directly. "You came all the way to this ship, and you don't even know what the Philosopher Stone experiment was?"

"It's not a very smart rock?" I joked.

"The Philosopher Stone experiment was the experiment that created the Ministers."

CHAPTER TWENTY ONE:
FORTY LOCKS

THE MINISTERS WERE immortal. That is, they could be killed, but they did not age.

The Ministers were humanoid. The way they dressed and moved accentuated their differences, but they looked human enough that they could be mistaken for human, albeit a small-statured and androgynous human.

The Ministers had appeared in human history out of nowhere, with no known origin or home planet. And they had appeared at the same time that the Philosopher Stone experiments had occurred—at the same time the Philosopher Stone data had gone missing.

"A thousand years ago we didn't have faster-than-light travel," I realized, thinking aloud. Lantern-Eyes' gaze held on me, steady. "It took more than one human lifetime to travel between star systems. Our ancestors couldn't make the distances shorter, so they tried to make human lives longer."

All the differences between the Ministers and humans were things that made them better suited for interstellar travel. The longer lives. The smaller bodies—better for the confined spaces of a starship. Even the dual circulatory systems—I'd seen that one personally, with Indigo. He'd lasted much longer in the vacuum than me, and had adapted quickly to our return to regular atmospheric heat and pressure.

I'd thought them aliens, come from some other planet. Or the wrath of an angry god, like the Chosen said.

"They're human," I said.

I didn't know how humans could do what the Ministers had done. I'd been on Kystrom when it had fallen and I had seen what they'd done. But if the Ministers were humans, altered to be improved for life in space, that meant they had human DNA.

"Humans have genetically modified crops for millions of years," Lantern-Eyes said. "We turned maize into its most useful form, but corn isn't human. You can buy bottles of human cells at convenience stores to use on wounds, but sim-skin isn't human. It doesn't matter what they're made of. They're monsters. And if they want that data, they might want to make more Ministers. As if the Ministers we have already aren't enough."

I hesitated. "Make more? Can't they..."

Lantern-Eyes gave me a look that dared me to finish the sentence.

It wasn't like I was gonna just not ask. "Can't they, uh, make more Ministers in the... usual way?"

"I haven't asked one," Lantern-Eyes said.

"Right," I said. "Of course not—"

"Intelligence reports suggest not. They seem to reproduce

solely by cloning. But intelligence reports also say that the Ministers are capable of cloning their own anyway, so why they want the original Philosopher Stone data, I can't say." The lieutenant exhaled, a little too edged to be called a sigh. "But I know Ministers. Whatever they want that data for, it will be bad for humanity. So I'm going to find it first."

"We will," I agreed, already thinking of ways to hide the data on my person where the lieutenant and her Republican reinforcements wouldn't think to look.

"How could you even find this ship without knowing anything about what's aboard?" Lantern-Eyes asked.

"I had a burst of good fortune," I said, lifting the tablet again; I flicked away from Mara Zhu's haunted expression to open the next text document and look at it like I was reading it. "Or really bad fortune. I heard the SOS. You know the SOS."

"It would've been difficult to pick up that SOS. Almost impossible, if you weren't already looking in this area for something."

"Well," I said, "the Ministers noticed it."

"The Ministers have been looking for this ship for hundreds of years. They had a general idea of where it had gone, and they were looking," Lieutenant Lantern-Eyes said. "Why were you looking here?"

"Just my usual run of luck," I said.

"Kystrom was conquered by the Ministers a decade ago," she said.

Realization struck me hard with disbelief. "Do you think I'm a Minister spy?"

The lieutenant's lambent eyes were piercing. "Who sent you here?"

Answering that question honestly would mean my death and Benny's, now or later, once the Senator realized we'd betrayed him. "If you think I'm a Minister spy," I said, "why the hell did you rescue me from Indigo?"

Something slammed against the door, interrupting our stand-off. The forty locks bent, buckled, and when that something slammed into the door again, this time it gave way.

The forty locks on Lieutenant Lantern-Eyes' door were enough to withstand most apocalypses, but apparently not a furious Minister. As soon as the door fell in I saw Indigo standing behind it, collar light glowing darkly and his human-inhuman face as expressionless as stone.

CHAPTER TWENTY TWO:
OH, SHIT!

"BEHIND THE RADIO!" Lantern-Eyes shouted, and ran at Indigo with her club. He moved, smooth as water, and blocked her blow with his long knife. The look he gave her terrified me, but the lieutenant only brought her club around to swing again.

"Behind the *fucking radio*!" she shouted, tripping back as Indigo moved forward, just in time to dodge the slash of his knife. I dropped to my knees beside the huge black box that was the radio and shoved it aside.

Hidden by its bulk was another little rat hole. It was smaller than the first one had been, barely big enough for me, and I couldn't see to the other side.

"Sean, get in!" Lantern-Eyes shrieked, and reached blindly behind herself to grab one of her explosive canisters and launch it at Indigo. He knocked it aside with his sword, splitting it, and the air began to fill with thick white smoke again.

Indigo looked from the smoke to Lantern-Eyes, a dark expression taking shape on his usually impassive face. I made a split-second decision, reached up to the lieutenant's wall of alphabetized murder weapons, and blindly grabbed for the same smoke/light bombs she'd just used. I caught four of them in my spread fingers, and I didn't dare linger to get more, not with Indigo's expression like that. Stuffing the bombs in my pocket, I got on my knees and crawled into the rat hole in the wall. Something crashed behind me.

I scrambled forward, scraping my palms on the uneven floor. The walls pressed in on me. I reached the end of the rat hole like a man surfacing from underwater and moved as far from the narrow passage as I dared, panting hard. My fingers dug into my side but the touch was only faint comfort, holding myself together on the floor.

I was out. I was out now, and who knew what was following me from the lieutenant's safe room, but at least I was no longer trapped in a coffin-like tunnel. I took a less desperate breath and started to push myself up—whatever came out of that tunnel, Lantern-Eyes or Indigo, I would have to be prepared.

It was only then that I realized I was not alone.

I was still holding the tablet. The flashlight I'd shoved into my pocket, and by some miracle it hadn't fallen out in my frantic journey through the rat hole. I could not see anything by the faint glow of the tablet, but I could hear something breathing.

I raised my gaze slowly and saw the shine of eyes watching me across the room.

My hands were shaking still from the tunnel. I reached for my pocket as I pushed myself to my feet, moving slowly, carefully, as smoothly as I could. The eyes rose with me, nothing more than a gleam in the dark, paired with heavy, steady breathing.

I clicked on the flashlight at my side, but didn't turn it on the creature just yet, afraid of setting it off.

A crash from the bolt-hole, frantic movement, harsh breaths. The lieutenant tumbled out, a cut leaking blood from her scalp, and landed hard on the floor.

Out the corner of my eye, I saw the creature move.

"Oh, shit!" Lantern-Eyes said, and lunged to grab the creature by the legs.

It crashed into me anyway, and we three fell to the floor. The creature landed heavily on me, cold weight and a fetid, unclean smell. It panted into my ear and pushed against me, putting itself upright. Something sharp dug into my shoulder.

I kicked, punched, pushed, losing track of the flashlight in the process. The beam bounced wildly around the room. I could only feel it, cold and rubbery skin; could only smell it, growling into my face. Something cold touched my jugular, small and sharp.

A wet *crack* sounded over my head, and suddenly thick dark heat splattered onto my face, reeking of blood and meat. The cold press at my throat slackened, and when I shoved the monster this time it fell off me. Something closed around my forearm and I shoved wildly at it, thinking the manikin had grabbed me.

"It's dead, Sean, come on!" Lantern-Eyes said, and hauled me with her wrist clasped in mine.

I didn't dare to look back. I was pretty sure she'd

shattered its skull with her club, but if it were still alive—
my legs were unsteady beneath me and my forward
motion was mostly the lieutenant, dragging me forward
through the dark. She knew her way around here really
well. She didn't even use a flashlight.

Then, abruptly, she stopped.

In the room before us, which we had been about to run
into, half a dozen pairs of eyes gleamed.

CHAPTER TWENTY THREE: BETA VERSION

USELESS TO HOPE they hadn't seen us, with my flashlight beam blazing like a beacon. Useless to hope they hadn't heard us crashing through the rooms like the devil himself was at our heels.

"Should we back up?" I whispered.

Fear was grey in the lieutenant's face, even in the faint glow of my reflected light. She swallowed. "No use. They're too quick."

I remembered that pragmatic little handgun of hers. "Can't you shoot them?"

"My gun only has one bullet."

"Then what—"

"We fight," Lantern-Eyes said, and something extraordinary happened. All the fear crumbled from her expression, and left nothing but determination behind. It was horrible and hopeless. Like watching flesh peel away from bone.

We were going to die here. I reached towards my side, where my four stolen bombs weighted down my pocket, just as the manikins lunged.

They moved like Indigo, almost too fast to see. My flashlight beam caught one full in the face and it recoiled like the brightness pained it, stumbling back into the shadows, but the others moved low and fast. Lantern-Eyes swung her club furiously at the manikins. But they dodged her blow as fluidly as currents of the air, circling around her, around me.

I turned to follow the motion of the monsters, bomb in one hand, flashlight in the other, trying to find a good target to aim at. The manikins evaded my flashlight beam like the cockroaches had, and it was so much more unnerving to hear them and know they were there but not be able to see them when I looked. My back bumped Lantern-Eyes', the two of us pressed close by the circling monsters.

I had to just throw the bomb, pick a place and trust that there would be manikins nearby. I opened my mouth to warn Lantern-Eyes that a flash was coming, then a manikin slammed into my side like a battering ram.

My head bounced off the floor with a flash of light like I'd accidentally set off my stolen bomb. The weight of the monster pressed down on me, and something dug into my ribs, right about where the wound had been on that ribcage I'd stepped into a few hours back. My hand clenched on empty air—flashlight and bomb had been knocked from my grip.

Blue light flared up suddenly out of the dark, and the manikin shrieked, rearing back. Metal rang against metal and I realized it was scrabbling frantically at a sword embedded into its back—a sword with Indigo on the other end, face expressionless in the storm-blue glow.

He'd turned his collar-light off for stealth, but they knew he was there now, and mobbed him. They weren't stupid, I thought; the manikins knew he was the biggest threat. I stumbled back, out of the way, fumbling for my weapons. I couldn't find the dropped bomb in the dark, but I found the heavy flashlight, still shining brightly from the floor. The lieutenant took advantage of the manikin's distraction to catch one of them with the edge of her club, knocking it aside. She advanced on the fallen manikin, snarling at her from the floor, and slammed her club into it again and again.

Indigo moved like lightning through clouds, dodging between the creatures. I saw one fall, then another, not dead but bloodied. Lantern-Eyes, her single opponent put down, reached into the fray surrounding Indigo and wrapped her forearm around the throat of one of the surviving creatures, dragging it heavily to the floor.

Indigo had a bad angle for the uninjured manikin; it was behind him, he was facing the wrong way. I shone my light full on the creature's face before it could complete its lunge, and the bright light stopped it in its tracks. Creatures of darkness; the light had blinded it. Indigo turned around fully to face it and then, for the very first time, I saw a manikin clearly.

Length of arm and leg and neck, unearthly androgynous features somewhere between appealing and unsettling. Each of the subtly inhuman things that distinguished the Ministers was visible in the manikin, exaggerated from beauty into terror. Indigo cocked his head at the manikin, and she—standing up, I could see she was female—cocked her head back, face-to-face with their own reflection.

The manikins were Ministers.

CHAPTER TWENTY FOUR:
SOME REALLY ANGRY ROCKS

THE MANIKIN BARED her blunt, human teeth and lunged at Indigo. He swung his blade and it clashed against her arm, drawing a howl of pain from her. The only reason his blade hadn't taken her arm off at the elbow was because she had a piece of metal lashed to her forearm, and metal on her hands. Makeshift armor—that had been the rattling, clicking noise I'd heard from them following us.

To my right, Lantern-Eyes was still straddling a writhing, thrashing manikin, slamming her club down wildly and without finesse. The twin light sources of Indigo's collar and my flashlight illuminated a hairless human face, mouth wide in a snarl.

Not quite Ministers, I realized, taking a slow step back. There was something unrefined about the manikins that was not so in Indigo. The Ministers had been created on the *Nameless*. It stood to reason that they were not the first of their kind. The manikins were rough-draft Ministers.

Indigo's collar-light flashed as he spun around, the glow of him eclipsed by one of the wounded manikins as it rose from the floor to lunge, fingers crooked like claws, hatred in the line of its spine driving it forward despite the threat of his blade. The manikin beneath Lantern-Eyes shoved her up and off him. Black blood slicked over his chalk-white skin.

I had the bombs I'd lifted from Lantern-Eyes, but if I used them now, they'd take out my allies as well as my enemies—the smoke would knock out Indigo, and the light would blind them both.

My next step backwards landed my heel on uneven ground, debris beneath my feet. I stumbled, caught myself. My palm landed on a chunk of old pipe.

*   *   *

KYSTROM WAS A garden world, verdant and new. The native flora and fauna were harmless to humans, though the pitka fruit was so sour we used to dare each other to eat it. I knew from experience that to eat more than a bite or two was to spend the rest of the afternoon vomiting and desperately thirsty, but even so, whenever I was dared I would eat the whole fruit just to show I could.

Left uneaten, pitka fruit would eventually unfold into a gauzy globe, just large enough that I could not quite encircle one in my arms. The wind would pull them free of the vines and for a month or so in early summer they would float through the fields and cities, carried along by the breeze, like giant dandelion seeds or flying jellyfish. When the pitka orbs burst they would rain tiny shimmering seeds down onto the soil. The bursting would happen naturally, or it could be triggered by impact.

We used to line up after school, myself and the neighborhood boys, Gan and Peter. Brigid didn't have an eye for it and so she didn't like to play. We would take rocks or sticks or whatever was around and see who could pop the furthest orb. The field would glitter with the raining seeds, and the next season whoever owned the field would have to pull out half a hundred baby pitka vines.

My memory of it glitters like the pitka seeds, the three of us lined up together, laughing, shouting, competing towards the same goal. I got very good at throwing rocks.

* * *

THE CHUNK OF old pipe hit the manikin facing Lantern-Eyes squarely in the temple, staggering it for the instant it took the lieutenant to pull herself up off the floor.

Crouching, I groped around behind me for another bit of pipe or thing to throw.

Indigo was all rippling blue light, moving quick, but the three manikins around him had him constrained. If they got inside his reach he wouldn't be able to use his knife effectively, and then it would be their strength against his. He slammed his elbow into one manikin's face, staggering it; the other two took this opportunity to surge in like tal vipers closing in on a grounded bird.

My fingers touched something else, oblong; I whipped it out and it slammed into the ribs of the manikin between me and Indigo. The manikin lost balance long enough for Indigo to turn, calm, and ram his knife through the throat of the one still coming at him, then on the outswing sever the spine of the manikin I'd struck. I'd say I was glad Indigo was on my side, if I thought Indigo was actually on my side.

There was a new sound from down the hallway, barely audible over the crack of bone and clash of metal. I shone my flashlight past Indigo and Lantern-Eyes to see what fresh hell was headed towards us. There was something down there, low to the ground, moving.

It looked like... I wasn't sure. It had no arms, no legs, no head. But it moved, almost like a slug would move, spreading out and then hitching up. It had an oddly rough texture, like stone come to life.

When it shifted, something poked up through its surface, breaching like a whale. I saw the distinct ivory curve of a meatless bone.

"Hey, Lantern-Eyes?" I said, fascinated but very ready to vomit, too.

Her opponent was downed for the moment. She looked back the way my flashlight shone, and when she saw what I was shining at, she screamed, "*RUN!*"

"What? What is it?" But she was already running, stopping only to grab at my shoulder and haul at my jacket. Indigo was retreating, too, more slowly than Lantern-Eyes. The surviving manikins, all bloodied, gathered in a line of pale corpse-figures snarling after us. And then one by one they seemed to notice the thing down the hall, and they went still and quiet, backing away.

I didn't know what triggered it. If I was honest, it

was probably me; Lantern-Eyes and Indigo were both warriors, light on their feet. I was, at absolute best, an amateur linguist. Or I could blame it on the manikins— it's always nice to have a convenient monster around to take the blame. But regardless, one of us made some sound we shouldn't have, or moved some way that wasn't wise, because the stony rolling mass stopped rolling, went very still.

And then slender yellow tendrils shot out of the mass, shooting towards walls, ceiling, floor, crawling along the surface they landed on, moving with incredible speed directly towards us.

It reached the manikins first—they were nearer. My flashlight beam saw a tendril of yellow land on pale dead flesh, and start to sizzle. The manikin shrieked, a high and piercing sound I wouldn't have thought it capable of making, and tried to run or roll away but the tendril was spreading over its skin like water through a cloth. Wherever it touched, the flesh sizzled.

The hallway was live with shrieking, the manikins were running or falling, skin melting, being dragged in towards that still mass of stone, and the yellow tendrils were coming down the hall towards us.

Lantern-Eyes yanked on my jacket again. "Run, Sean!" she shouted, and I hadn't even realized I'd stopped, staring in horror. Indigo was still between me and the monsters, his sword out and his shoulders set.

A tendril shot out from the mass of stone and Indigo swiped his sword through the air, slicing it in half. When the severed piece hit the ground it spilled a clear gel that hissed upon contact with the metal.

Even running, the tendrils had almost caught up to us. I stomped on one that had slid past Indigo, lightning-fast, to reach me. It popped underneath my boot. Lantern-Eyes slammed her club against the ground to crush a particularly thick branch of yellow tendrils before it could reach her feet.

I shone my flashlight back the way we had come and saw that yellow threads covered the ceiling, the walls, the floor. They were dripping down, quivering. The slow-rolling rock down at the end of the hall rolled towards us again with bones carried along in its bulk. Where the manikins had been, there was nothing but sizzling yellow masses, dripping a dark liquid onto the floor, smelling like melted fat.

"Move," Indigo told me, and then swiped his blade over my head. I ducked as severed tendrils rained down on me.

Lantern-Eyes was still on her own, crushing the tendrils that got too close. But the tendrils on the walls and ceiling had traveled past her, and were dangling down behind her—she was trapped.

Indigo sliced at the tendrils on the wall by the lieutenant, his blade shrieking as it scraped down the wall. The tendrils behind Lantern-Eyes went suddenly limp. I smacked aside a tendril heading for my face with the lieutenant's tablet and kept backing up.

"Work with me!" Indigo barked at Lantern-Eyes. I hadn't even imagined he could raise his voice.

The lieutenant's eyes went wide, then narrowed, determination set in place. She swung her club hard into the wall. It clanged like a gong, the reverberations powerful enough I could feel them.

The movement of the yellow tendrils shifted, lightning-quick, heading for the place where her club had impacted the wall. She pulled her club up over her shoulder, and swung again like a batter. The same percussion echoed out, too deep to be heard, only to be felt.

There were no more tendrils around me. Lantern-Eyes backed up, banging her club against the wall, luring the tendrils to the side. Indigo sliced at the tendrils when they got near, leaving piles of severed, smoking yellow on the floor.

We were quite far from the stone thing by now, and it seemed to be losing interest in us—some of the tendrils were retreating, pulled back into the lumpy mass, and the mass itself was roll-hitching itself towards the dead manikins on the floor.

Lantern-Eyes was halfway down one branch of the hall, still luring the last few tendrils away; Indigo was closest to the stone creature, slicing the last few tendrils apart so that they could bubble and sizzle on the floor. They'd drawn quite far away from me in the process.

Which meant that when one of the surviving manikins crept out from where she had been hiding, I was the only target left.

"Uh," I said, and then my tongue tangled on itself, wanting to call for Indigo, to call for Lantern-Eyes, to call for both, either, *neither*. I faced down the bloodied manikin crouched down on the acid-scarred floor. Humanoid, but not quite human. The torso too narrow, the neck too long.

The manikin was a nightmare of a man, like and not like. She bared her bloodied teeth at me, hatred in her weirdly human eyes.

She was between me and Indigo, me and Lantern-Eyes.

I ran.

CHAPTER TWENTY FIVE: THE TRAP

(Featuring: Sean Wren's Inability to Use a Grenade)

I'D READ THAT humans had evolved on savannahs, running through wide-open fields beneath a blue bowl of a sky; in an open terrain, with nothing to do but run straight ahead, I might have outpaced the thing chasing me. But the *Nameless* was all narrow halls and broken doors, sharp turns and uncertain footing. This creature had been bred for the close darkness of space; I belonged on an open planet. I stumbled and fell, scrambled up and turned sharply around a corner, losing speed as I did; it followed, nails on metal, nails.

One-handed, already winded, I fumbled at my jacket pocket for the smoke bombs I'd borrowed from the lieutenant. There were only three of them, but one should be enough, right? The smoke affected a Minister, so theoretically it would affect a manikin. Even if the smoke didn't do anything to the manikin, the light certainly would. I'd blinded one with my flashlight before.

I fumbled with the little ring doohickey on the bomb. I wasn't actually positive how these things worked. I pulled the ring loose, right?

The ring came loose in my hand. I had no idea how long before it blew up, or if it would blow up, and what it would do to my hand, so I tossed it away wildly behind me. I heard something clatter on the floor, not quite in time with the clatter of manikin's claws, and then nothing happened.

A dud, or I'd screwed up. I was just reaching for the second bomb when the first went off.

Light flashed through the hall as brilliant and as swift as lightning. It was lucky I had my back to the bomb, and that my running speed had taken me some distance away, or I would've been blinded. I heard the manikin let out a shrill cry of outrage, but when I glanced back, in my wavering flashlight beam I saw her still gaining. The bomb hadn't taken her out.

She'd probably been too far from it to have any effect. I reached for the second grenade.

This time I knew how to work it, though I wished I'd thought to count the seconds on the last one. I wasn't sure if my timing was right, and when I lobbed it back at her, the metal struck her in the shoulder. She knocked it aside and it crashed harmlessly against a far wall. I was already running again by the time it went off; we were too far, again.

I slipped the third bomb into my hand. This one was my last chance: if I failed to knock the manikin out with this grenade, then I'd have no defense against it, and it would tear me apart with its weird metal nails. No pressure, right?

I couldn't quite figure out how long I should give the bomb to detonate. I couldn't be quite sure how far behind me the manikin was. I clutched the grenade in my hand, not daring to pull the pin, and counted, and counted, and ran. The space was too dark for me to plan a path before one opened up before me; I went where the gleam of my flashlight reached the furthest, deeper into the labyrinth, but no matter how fast I ran that thing was always at my heels.

And then the beam of my flashlight struck the solid denial of a bare wall.

It came on me suddenly. I didn't have time to stop, but crashed into the wall. The grenade dropped from my hands, pin and all. I caught myself upright, turned left, turned right. My flashlight beam bounced off unbroken metal to my right and my left.

Trapped like a rat. I swung the flashlight over the floor, looking for the brown oval of the grenade, and saw that that thing was in the doorframe. It had stopped running when I had, and it stood there in the doorframe, a shadow in the dark.

I took a step back, felt my heel hit the wall. My chest was heaving. In the room around me, I heard something hiss, like gas through ventilation. The shadow lunged.

I swung the flashlight up and the beam hit the manikin full in the face. It recoiled like the blow had been physical, skidding to a stop in the center of the room and raising its arms to shield its face. While it was stunned I dropped to the ground and groped around for the fallen grenade.

My palm landed on the rough surface of the grenade. I scrambled, pulling it out of the debris-strewn floor. The hissing sound in the room seemed to grow louder, and a strange, metallic scent struck my senses like a ruler slap. I fumbled for the pin, my shaking fingers too clumsy to grip it, going through useless counts in my head. The manikin stepped forward—and fell.

The metallic scent was growing stronger, unpleasant. I watched dumbly as the manikin tried to push herself up on an elbow, climbing for the door, and failed. The hissing sound ceased abruptly, but the metallic scent remained, and the manikin was utterly still on the floor.

CHAPTER TWENTY SIX:
MADE OF MAN

I EXPECTED THE manikin to lunge up like a striking snake until she didn't. The hissing of some sort of gas being pumped into the room slowed into silence, but the metallic stench lingered, overwhelming. I wasn't feeling anything except the urge to cover my nose, but whatever had been released into the air had knocked out the manikin. The same gas as was in Lantern-Eyes' bombs, perhaps?

Moving carefully—I didn't know how deeply she was out—I went over and crouched beside her. She was breathing with the metronome regularity of the deeply unconscious. I pressed two fingers to the point under her jaw where, on a human, the carotid would beat. The unsynchronized throbs of two circulatory systems battered against my hand.

Unconscious, but not dead. This gas smelled the same as whatever white smoke the lieutenant had released to stun Indigo. Maybe Lantern-Eyes had found a stash of the canisters on the ship, or she'd taken the gas from traps like this room. It made sense; the ancient scientists must've had some way of managing the manikins. This room was obviously a trap; the gas had only released once the manikin had crossed the threshold. It was a remarkably resilient trap if it was a thousand years old, but if it was one of the lieutenant's traps, I couldn't imagine why she would use a gas that would only knock out a manikin rather than kill one.

Whatever the source of the trap, I was lucky I'd stumbled across it. It had saved my life—and given me a chance to see, up close, one of the mysteries of this ship.

I bent lower over the manikin, beaming my flashlight into her face. She was hairless, without even the very fine, colorless body hair that even the most hairless of humans had. She didn't even have eyelashes. Her skin was utterly without pigment; not the pinkish-pale of a light-skinned person, but chalk-white. I could trace the intertwined veins and capillaries across the narrow width of her back. I wondered how else she might be different from a human; what was she made of inside, where heart and lungs and liver lived.

Metal gleamed in the beam of my flashlight, and I carefully turned her hand over. Scraps of metal, old scalpels, had been tied and wired together to make something like a set of brass knuckles, but bladed. She wore those old, mismatched blades on both hands, and both feet. I thought of birds weaving nests from strands of hair and yarn and pieces of newspaper.

I caught myself on that thought like a hook. The manikin was not a bird. Her ancestors had been human. The creature in front of me now—how human was she?

Human enough to make tools; human enough to use them. She and I were cousins, so to speak. Why had she attacked me? Had it been because I was a stranger? If I'd lived someplace for a thousand years and then a bunch of noisy strangers had burst in and started cutting up the walls, I'd be annoyed, too.

I wondered if she could speak Ameng.

There was only one way to find out, of course. I hesitated over the unconscious manikin. These creatures had attacked me—attacked the Ministers, too, but that was just common sense. Ministers were intelligent: they could be reasoned with. Weren't the manikins just Ministers that hadn't committed genocide? If I could convince this manikin that I was an ally, then perhaps she could lead me to the Philosopher Stone.

My imp stirred in me. What was I going to do, leave without ever knowing for sure?

I sat down beside the unconscious manikin, cross-legged, and waited for her to wake up.

She woke slowly. Whatever was in that metallic-smelling gas wasn't lethal, but it was potent. The manikin's fingers started to twitch, first, little restless sleeping-animal trembles. I turned my flashlight at an angle so that it wouldn't shine directly in her eyes, and was rewarded with her lids slitting open, irises glassy behind. She had, I marveled to see, grey eyes. As monochrome as the rest of her.

Slowly, those eyes focused on me.

"Hello," I said in Ameng.

She snarled, heaving herself up and at me. She was still

too deeply drugged to do more than flop on the ground, but the motion was unmistakable; if she'd been just a little more awake, I would've had her claws in my jugular.

I retreated to a more prudent distance. "Sorry," I said in Ameng, and again she snarled, bloody spittle flying between her slackened lips. Her manufactured claws scraped against the ground like nails on slate, clenching and clawing like she imagined my skin beneath her talons.

I swallowed. I could still run, I reminded myself, and then firmed my resolve. Trust was not built on a few words. Trust was built on actions, on the other person making themselves vulnerable. She was vulnerable right now. I had to show her that I could be near her, and still not hurt her.

"I'm not going to hurt you," I promised the manikin, while she shoved herself across the floor, away from me, snarling all along like a beaten dog. I felt a surge of pity for her when she stopped, her back against the far wall, pushing herself to sit with shaking arms.

And then she stared at me, trembling lightly, silent.

"You can understand me, can't you?" I said. "You know this language, even if it's been a long time since you've heard it. Can you speak it? Can you even speak?" It could be that there were physiological differences between her throat and mine. She might not even be capable of human speech.

The Ministers had the Light language, though, didn't they? Could it be that the Light language had an older origin than I'd assumed? Maybe it originated here, aboard the *Nameless*. I fumbled for my flashlight, aimed it at her knees, and flashed out one of the few words I knew: GO.

The manikin squinted at me. The light hurt her eyes, I supposed, so I lowered the beam further. And then she stood up.

My slowing heart panicked again, pounding hard against my ribs. I held myself still from sheer stubbornness as the manikin crossed the room, step by careful step, and crouched down in front of me.

She had a peculiar scent. Not dirty, but an odor that my brain did not know what to make of, somewhere between animal and human. If I had to put a name to the expression on her face, I would have called it thoughtful.

Elation surged through me, beating in time with my rabbit heart. I'd done it: I'd communicated with her. I'd shown myself vulnerable, trustworthy; and so she was returning it with trust of her own. These creatures on the ship were not creatures at all, but a type of human, and they could be reasoned with the way every creature could be except for Ministers and Republican soldiers—

The manikin's expression changed, and this time I had no trouble putting words to it. She looked at me the way a person might look at a child, that in their naivety has done something very, very stupid.

And then the manikin's hand closed around my throat.

CHAPTER TWENTY SEVEN: THE MOMENT

HER CLAWS SCRAPED at the side of my neck, but the manikin wasn't trying to cut my throat: she was trying to choke me.

"Stop," I tried to say, in Ameng, "Why?" but she only squeezed harder. The manikin gazed down at me with cold indifference while I grabbed at her slender wrist, useless, struggling for air that would not come.

I stopped trying to break her grip and groped around on the floor instead. The manikin barely glanced at my grasping hands, her expression fixed on my face, like she wanted to watch the moment the light died in my eyes—

My palm touched the grenade. Black spots swam in front of my eyes, blurring the manikin's monstrous face, and I didn't hesitate before pulling the pin.

Time left me, and I came to on the floor in the aftermath of a flash. The manikin was rolling around on the floor, hands twitching over her eyes. This time I did not wait for her to recover. I got up, and I ran.

I could have attempted to retrace my steps to where

I had last seen Lantern-Eyes and the Minister. I chose against it: after they'd defeated the rock-monster, they would remember that they were trying to slaughter each other, and I had no desire to get in the middle of that fight. Besides, although they had each kept me alive before, it had been for their own purposes. I didn't want to help either of them find the Philosopher Stone—nor did I want to end with one of their hands around my throat.

I hurried through the halls, twisting and turning at random, until I felt certain that I had left the manikin far behind. I'd ended up in a moderately sized, empty room. And it was empty: there was nothing in there with me that I could see, or hear, or smell.

I still could've been followed, no matter how far I'd run. Lantern-Eyes or Indigo would be inconvenient, but the manikin or that rock monster would be worse. I flicked off my flashlight and shoved myself into a dark alcove, hidden and out of the way. I sat there, flashlight in one hand, straining to listen and see in the dark, waiting to find out what might follow me.

*   *   *

I REMEMBER MY sister sitting at the kitchen table, her back to me and the sunlight facing her. The memory had the timeless feeling that memories from childhood have, when hours of the day and days of the week meant less. My sister was a silhouette at the kitchen table, sunlight glinting gold through her hair and turning her glass of water into a glass of light.

I realized how thirsty I was when I saw that glass. So thirsty my tongue was dry, so thirsty I couldn't think of anything but drinking. I snuck up behind my sister and reached around her, stealing her water glass from her side and taking a sip from it. The water tasted like nothing, felt like air.

She didn't react. Her hair curtained her face from the side, hiding her features from me, and she was working on a simple circuit-board. I knew this memory. Brigid had liked puzzles and circuits. I'd always been bad at them, but Brigid was patient and logical like that.

The water glass in my hand felt oddly out-of-place, like its texture didn't quite match the world around. "Let me help you," I said to Brigid.

I couldn't see her expression past the wall of her hair. "No," she said, like I remembered her saying. "I'll do it myself."

I was still thirsty, horribly, distractingly thirsty. I took another deep drink from the water glass. The water tasted as weightless and dry as light.

"Let me help you," I said again, from a dry mouth, but Brigid wasn't connecting capacitors and resistors anymore. She had a doll head and doll arms and legs that she was wiring all together, and the battery was pulsing like a heartbeat. When she moved her hands—small, child's hands—her pale fingers were smeared with pulpy red.

Terrible thirst seized me by the throat again, distracting me from the horror under Brigid's fingertips. I lifted the glass to my mouth for a third time, and for a third time, although I drank, no water slid into my mouth. When I lowered the glass I found it was not full of water, but full of light; I was holding a Minister collar-stone in my hand, glowing faintly.

Under Brigid's red-stained fingertips, plastic-white limbs took form, a manikin shape brutally rendered in red.

The light in the room had changed from warm gold to chilling silver, as if a cloud had come over the sun. Brigid's hair concealed her face. I remember pieces of Brigid's face: the pout on her baby-full cheeks, that her eyes had been blue, like mine. But no matter how I try now I cannot remember how she looked. All I have left of my sister's face are jumbled, separate pieces I don't know how to reassemble.

I set the collar-light down on the table beside the crucified cona my sister was building into a manikin-shape, and leaned around to see Brigid's face, just this one more time. She turned as I bent over. Her hair moved aside, exposing her face.

Blood and bone, cartilage, split skin and brain and teeth—

I woke with a jolt in the dark on the *Nameless*, shaking, heart pounding, and horribly, horribly thirsty. I'd fallen asleep waiting for pursuit, and in my sleep, I'd dreamt.

Memories lose their vividness, after a while. Like trying to catch a scent off dried flowers. But a dream is always vivid. Sometimes when I dreamt I saw things that had happened, sometimes I saw things that never did. But no matter what I dreamt, it always came back to the same moment in the end.

I found Brigid last of my family, the day the Ministers came. She'd been thrown on the floor, and there was blood leaking out from beneath her head, soaked in her hair. The next thing I remembered was staggering out onto the empty street, and my hands were red. Even in dreams, I couldn't clearly remember what I saw.

I've forgotten my sister's face. Not just as she looked when she was alive, but how she looked after she had died.

I was gasping on the floor of the *Nameless*, heavy chest-shaking sobs. The air scraped my throat painfully. I shut my jaw and swallowed, and swallowing hurt just as badly. There was very little spit in my mouth, not nearly enough to moisten my throat.

I'd run off from Indigo and Lantern-Eyes without any supplies. If I didn't find a source of water somewhere soon, I'd be in trouble.

The room beyond my hiding spot was still eerily quiet, filled only by my gasping breaths. I swallowed and deliberately slowed my breathing, listening hard, but heard nothing in the silence. When I flicked on my flashlight, I saw nothing, either.

I crawled out of my hiding place, limbs still unsteady, and picked a new direction to walk.

I found myself in a hallway, open doors leading off every few yards on either side. I stepped carefully but I heard nothing except my own footsteps padding softly against the ground. The dust seemed thicker here, and I could see no tracks in it but my own. When I shone my flashlight into the rooms around me, hoping for a bathroom or a kitchen or maybe just a broken water-pipe, I found that the rooms were eerily, totally empty—not that everything in the rooms had decayed, but as if everything in the rooms had been removed, or else broken down uniformly to dust.

It seemed almost deliberate.

One of the rooms unsettled me more than the rest. A roughly-shaped mound in the center of the room implied a desk of some kind, and the wall facing the exit was lined with three massive doors. These three doors were in perfect repair, as if they were too massive to be destroyed—or as if whatever had systematically destroyed the contents of the other rooms in this part of the ship had not dared to approach these three massive doors.

If none of the monsters on this ship had dared to touch those massive doors over the thousand years they'd lived on this ship, it was probably a bad idea for me to do it.

And yet, what else did I have to lose? If I was lucky, those doors led to the showers.

Flashlight in one hand, I left the hallway and walked over to the three doors.

CHAPTER TWENTY EIGHT:
THREE DOORS

I CHOSE THE door in the center. The handle was long enough to wrap both my hands around, and Benny's too, and Indigo and Lantern-Eyes if they'd wanted to join in on my mission to open the mystery door. It scraped against my palm when I grabbed it, and I couldn't tell whether that was because the handle was rough, or my skin was dry.

The door didn't budge. I tugged one-handed, then gave up and set the flashlight down to grab the handle with both hands and lean my full weight against the door. Inch by inch, it groaned open. The door was at least a foot thick.

Moving the door stirred up the ancient dust, which was particularly ashy here. It settled on my skin, pulled into my lungs with the air. I started coughing and couldn't stop; there wasn't enough moisture in my throat to expel the dust, and I hacked dryly into my hands.

When I finally cleared my lungs enough to breathe, I was sitting beside the half-open door, light-headed and aching. I stared into the darkness of the half-open door, the beam of my fallen flashlight crossing it at an oblique angle, and strained to listen. I'd been making a lot of noise. Had anything heard me?

Nothing sounded from the halls and rooms behind me; nothing emerged out of the black. I pushed myself up unsteadily, careful not to disturb any more dust, and dragged my flashlight up and through the heavy door.

It was empty behind. There were shattered slabs of some sort of metal, blackened in places by what looked like a great heat. They looked like they'd been shelves once, before age and destruction had knocked them out of their slots in the walls. Now, they lay sunken in the very fine, ashy dust that covered the ground. The room, or closet, or whatever, was very deep—I could lie down in the room, on one of the shelves maybe, with my head towards the door and my feet would just barely graze the far wall.

At the far wall was a grate, blackened old metal. It looked like the grates in church for confessional. All that was missing was a priest.

My head was pounding so hard I couldn't be sure whether there were motes of dust in the room, or my vision had gone spotty. I tried to swallow again, and could not.

What was the confessional liturgy, again? It had been years since I'd gone to a church. The God Who Shed His Blood For Us wasn't worshipped often outside of Kystrom. I thought it began: *The darkness of sin surrounds us all.*

The God Who Shed His Blood did so for us, that we may come to the light. Do you believe in Light and Blood?

"I do," I said. The ash and dust absorbed my words.

Despair is the false Word the Darkness tries to teach us. Do you turn your back on Darkness and Despair?

"I do," I said, though it hurt my throat to shape the words.

Do you swear to do good and bring light as He did, regardless of the cost of your own blood?

"I do." What I wouldn't do for a glass of water, even if that water was made of light, like my dream.

What sins do you have to confess?

"I was mean to my sister," I said aloud, and this time the words fell heavy into the silence of the ash, like a thick snowfall.

There was no water in this strange closet, and I was wasting time lingering here. I noticed, as I left the closet behind, that there was no handle or latch on the inside. If the door shut on you, you wouldn't be able to get out.

The three doors were sepulchral as I left the room, silent and heavy as tombstones.

*   *   *

I CHASED BRIGID across half the park on her thirteenth birthday. She hadn't wanted me to join her and her friends for the party, though half her friends had been my friends too. She'd wanted them to herself, the sovereignty of not having her big brother around. With stupid mean impish spite, as soon as she'd said I couldn't come, I'd gone and chased her.

Brigid was fast. Some of her friends were fast, too—Liza, for instance, had a leggy stride that could outpace just about anyone over a distance. But none of them wanted rid of me quite as vigorously as Brigid, and so they'd trailed off, falling to the sidelines, clustering together between the flowerbeds and watching as I'd chased my sister. Brigid was running flat-out, but her legs were shorter than mine, and I had quickly caught up.

She'd rounded on me when I reached her and shoved me, flat-palmed, both against my chest. "Why won't you stay the hell away?" she'd shouted.

"Can't make me," I'd said.

"I'll tell Mom!"

My mother's name had been Callie. Her maiden name had been Peterson, and she'd kept her name after the marriage. Our last name had not been Wren, it had been Hart, but there had been a family of wrens in the backyard that we coddled and wooed into hanging around summer after summer in a faded little birdhouse. I'd gone by Wren after I left Kystrom behind. My father's name had been David, but my mother had called him Red, because of the shade of his hair. Brigid and I had both inherited my mother's blonde hair, but the shapes of our faces, I was told, were dead-on copies of my father's. I had no pictures of them left. I'd taken nothing with me from Kystrom except pale and fading memories.

I remember Brigid and I shouted for a while after that, a vicious fight that only my father had broken up, but the rest of my memory falls oddly short. I don't remember what we said. I remember her face gone red and blotchy, streaked with tears. I'd ruined her birthday.

Oh, right. I remembered now. Brigid had told me she

wished I was dead. And I'd told her I wished she'd never been born.

*   *   *

THERE WAS A lump in my throat I couldn't swallow away. I reached up on blind instinct to wipe my eyes, but touched only dry skin.

My head was an ache so solid it no longer registered as pain. Pain requires change. This was just a new state of being. My lip had split sometime after walking away from the tomb doors, but my blood tasted salty, not refreshing at all. I'd lost track of where I was walking.

Going off on my own had been a mistake. Sure, I had the bombs to defend myself, but I had no supplies and no idea of where I was going. If I'd stopped and thought about it at all, I would've realized that. Instead, I'd just run. Imp of the perverse. Benny'd always said it would one day get me killed.

Something skittered out of my flashlight beam. My reflexes were so dulled that I flinched back belatedly and stumbled, nearly falling. I lifted the flashlight, ready to swing it at whatever attacked me.

Which was nothing. I wavered, waiting, then turned the beam ahead of me, crossing over the empty floor. Something skittered out of the light again, but this time I recognized it—a cockroach.

It was the first sign of life I'd seen since I'd left Lantern-Eyes and Indigo to finish murdering manikins. I stared blankly after the wall where the cockroach had vanished until it clicked in my head: Even cockroaches needed water to survive.

I turned on my heel and set off in the direction the cockroach had gone.

CHAPTER TWENTY NINE: THE ROACH

INSTEAD OF LOOKING for water, I looked for roaches. When I found one I followed it until it vanished, and slowly I found more and more, tracking them by light and the chitinous sound of their skittering.

At long last I heard it, faint and unearthly in the silence of the *Nameless*: the dribble and burble of water. I left off following cockroaches and strode straight for that sound, no longer caring if I stumbled across a manikin along the way, and finally, finally, I found it: an old sink with a broken faucet, and water dribbling out of that hole to splatter on the floor and stain the ancient tile and metal with minerals. I knelt beneath that faucet, dropping the flashlight at my side, and cupped my hands beneath the water to drink until I was breathless. Then I sat back on my heels and looked at where I had ended up.

It was a lab, or a kitchen. I could tell by the broken mounds of tiled islands, an oven hood still clinging to the wall by its nails. Judging from what else I'd seen in this part of the *Nameless*, I was willing to bet lab over kitchen. I drank deeply again, then patted myself down for something to carry water in. The contents of my pockets hadn't changed since last I checked. All I had was this flashlight and the lieutenant's tablet. Oh, and a very small notebook and pen that were zipped up in an inner pocket of my jacket where I'd forgotten they existed for who knew how long. The notebook had a stiff plastic cover and was full of scribbled notes even I couldn't interpret. I could fold a little origami cup out of the paper, but it wouldn't exactly work as intended.

I started rummaging through the debris of old counters and old cabinets. There were some clouded old shards of glass that might have once been cups or containers but did me no good now. Every time I disturbed a dark corner of the room, roaches ran out of it with frantic abandon. Eventually I turned up a battered old tin. I didn't know what it had been used to hold once, but although the metal was soft and discolored, it hadn't corroded through. I tested the strength and found I could bend it but not poke my finger through. I washed the tin out carefully in the flowing water and, when it was as clean as I could get it, filled it up halfway. Then I carefully bent the top edges of the tin closed, forming an imperfect seal. It would probably leak, but that was the best I was going to do.

Just as I finished sealing the leaky little tin, a cockroach skittered through the light of my flashlight and took shelter in the shadow of my foot, trusting and stupid. My stomach growled.

* * *

"YOU'VE GOT TO eat it," Liza had said, implacable. The centipede dangled from her hand, legs curling and uncurling as it vainly tried to escape.

"No, he doesn't," Brigid had replied, lying on her back in the dirt. Liza had been the neighbor's child. When we had been little children together, she had been like another sister to me. As we'd gotten older, she and Brigid had become closer, and she'd distanced herself from me.

I hadn't seen her body after Kystrom, but her parents' house had been half-caved in, hollowed out by fire.

"It's the rules of dare," Liza had told Brigid.

"It's a stupid dare," Brigid had said, and the beady way she looked at me meant *and you were stupid for taking it.*

"It's the rules." Liza had possessed an air of finality. She'd held out the centipede towards me, and a wicked little grin had taken up residence on a face that was starting to transition from girl to woman.

Something about that little grin had woken the imp inside me. "No problem," I'd told her, and taken the centipede from her hand. It had squirmed between my fingers.

"Better eat it quick, before Mom notices," Brigid had said, taunting, because in those days I was never alone. I was surrounded by friends and by family, and someone I loved was never more than a room away.

The centipede had squirmed on my tongue until my teeth had come down on it, splitting the exoskeleton, and a burst of oddly salty liquid had splashed over my tongue. I'm pretty sure it was still squirming when I swallowed it.

"That's *disgusting!*" Brigid had shouted, laughing

and repulsed. Liza had looked at me with an odd half a smile. That was the expression I remembered best of her, condescending and admiring both, respect from a girl long dead.

* * *

I GRABBED THE roach.

Or at least, I *tried* to grab the roach. They're quick little fuckers, and there's really nothing to grab on their carapaces, and the roach sitting comfortably next to my foot was gone in a flash.

The motion disturbed the other roaches nearby, though, and I turned to the roiling mass of fleeing insects that had been gathered near the water source. I reached in, intending to just grab one from the writhing pile, but they avoided my hand like the sea parting. Annoyed now, I snatched at the nearest one, and came away for my efforts with a single detached leg.

That was disgusting. I dropped the leg, but its owner was already fled, not in the least hindered by losing one of its limbs. The initial rush of fleeing cockroaches had slowed as they all found new hiding spots, so I identified their direction—an overturned piece of debris that might once have been part of a table.

Stepping carefully, I got my fingers under the debris, and flipped it.

They scattered. This time I was ready, and I corralled a few of them into an open portion of floor, startling them with stomping and grabbing. There was a particularly fat one that I had my eye on, and because of its size it couldn't move as skittishly as the little ones did, and so I chased it round and round in circles until I had it firmly in my palm.

I lifted it up to look it in the eye and shook the roach, scolding it in silence. It waved its little legs around wildly in protest. The carapace was dented under the force of my grip, on the verge of cracking, and I could see all the little ridges in its reddish legs. I swallowed a sudden wave of nausea. It would be disgusting, I knew, but better to eat a bug than starve to death. I'd put worse things in my mouth before, anyway.

The little red legs waved around, frantic, helpless. Roaches have no brain, really. I'm not even sure if they can feel pain. They're gross, but they're helpless creatures; not like ants or wasps, which could bite or sting; not like spiders, with their venom. They're not even predators. Roaches scuttled around and ate trash, nothing more.

Those little legs waved helplessly, desperate, even now, to live. I lowered my hand. The roach writhed free, its legs needle-fine and weirdly sticky against my skin, and then in a flash, it was gone.

They all were gone, actually. While I'd been staring down my presumptive meal, somehow, all the other roaches had vanished. I swept my flashlight beam over the floor and found it as clean and empty as any fine restaurant in the Republic.

Peculiar. Even when the roaches had been hiding before, I'd seen traces of them—little legs sticking out from under debris, the occasional commando-roll between hiding places. But now—I lifted the same broken piece of table to check—there were no roaches at all.

If I had not spent so long—hours? How long had I been wandering?—in total silence, I might not have noticed the peculiar sound, or I might have dismissed it as the latent hum of electronics. But I heard it now: a humming, or a buzzing, like a hive full of bees. And it—whatever it was—was approaching.

I shut off my flashlight, ducked low and tried to quiet my breathing, lying flat beside the fountain. The buzzing grew louder, louder in the dark, almost as if it were directly overhead. It receded towards the doorway on the other side of the room, opposite the one I had entered from.

Then a light from inside that room turned on.

CHAPTER THIRTY: FAMILY PHOTO

THE GLOW FROM the other room was faint, bluish. Had Indigo found me? No, Indigo wouldn't telegraph his presence like that, and even I would've noticed a full-grown Minister walking past my hiding place. Unless Indigo could transform himself into a swarm of bees, that wasn't my Minister.

I wouldn't have noticed the glittering cloud that emerged from the back room if it not for the reflected light. It was easier to track by the hum of its movement than by watching it. A very primal part of me took control over my curiosity, and I flattened myself low to the floor. The hum of the swarm—or whatever it was—moved across the room, overhead, and out the far door. I listened to it recede until I could no longer hear it at all.

The light in the far room was still on, even though it was silent now. A cockroach skittered past my nose.

If the bugs weren't afraid anymore, I shouldn't be, either. I pushed myself up, spent a few seconds deliberating with my good sense, and then the imp won out over caution and

I walked into that room where the light was coming out.

The far room was a little office, confirming my suspicions that the room with the water had been a lab and not a kitchen. Most of the furniture had been destroyed, though not as systematically as in the rooms I'd passed through earlier. It was, mercifully, empty.

The source of the light was on the walls all around me. Electronic picture frames. How they were still working after all this time—ah, the autorepair. Had that humming swarm been the ship's autorepair in action? It had been unnerving, if so. The insectoid hum, and the way the cockroaches had vanished as soon as it had appeared. Cockroaches were stupid bugs, surviving only by pure dumb instinct—and their supposed ability to withstand a nuclear bomb. But as soon as the autorepair had appeared, they'd fled. What scared a creature that couldn't be killed?

I was letting my imagination get the better of me. Cockroaches were very stupid. Just because they'd led me to water didn't mean I should read meaning into their movements like an oracle studying animal intestines. For all I knew, the ship's autorepair had a pest control function.

I went over to the walls, lowering my flashlight so that I could see the photographs better. Age and decaying electronics had blurred some of them into static, and warped others until I was looking at weird repeating patterns that had maybe once been a coherent photograph but now showed nothing but dreamlike abstraction. But in some of them I could see what the photograph had been.

Family and friends covered the walls of this office. One man occurred over and over again, a tall man with very round, deep set eyes, like an owl's. When he smiled, the skin around his eyes crinkled up and almost hid them. There was something vaguely familiar about him, like there had been about Mara Zhu, though I was certain I had never seen him before.

The man stood with his arm around a woman, his other arm around two little girls. The man stood side-by-side with a man who looked like him but a few years younger. The man stood on a beach overlooking the sea. The man stood in a lab coat in a crowd of other similarly-dressed people, all smiling with the sort of stiffness that came of the lengthy corralling that was necessary to take a group photo.

In the center of that group, still clearly recognizable despite the decay of data, I saw Mara Zhu. She was smiling, and looked ten years younger and much less oddly familiar.

I stood surrounded by a dead man's friends and family, all the love he'd had, left here on this tomb of a ship. A lump sat in my throat, as thick and painful as it had been twenty minutes ago, before I'd gotten my fill of water.

Slowly, mesmerized by the memories of happiness left eternal on the walls of this ruined ship, I reached into my pocket and pulled out Lantern-Eyes' tablet. I needed to know what had happened here, in the final days of the ship. I needed, at last, to find out how this ship had ended up hidden beside a dying star, why the creatures inside were so full of hatred, what had happened to these smiling scientists—and what had become of the Philosopher Stone.

Mara Zhu's face filled the little tablet screen, starkly lit and terrible. I let the video play.

CHAPTER THIRTY ONE:
THE LAST WORDS OF MARA ZHU

Part one

IT TOOK ME a while to translate the video Mara Zhu had made, the last recording on the *Nameless*'s logs. Listening to a native speaker talk was a lot harder than reading an official text, especially when that native speaker was as emotional as Mara Zhu was in her video. I did not dare to turn the sound up particularly loud, either—there were many things on this ship, and I was afraid that some of them might hear.

And so I translated Mara Zhu's final words slowly, piece by piece, like putting together that old clock in Quint's office.

She began, "The only excuse I can offer future generations is that the human race was going extinct. The harsh environments of the new planets [*scientific choice of word; not homeworlds, but planets. She was scientific, Mara Zhu*], the hostile alien species—they were killing us. [*Alternate translation: they were murdering us. They were slaughtering us.*] They might still kill us, but I don't think so. Those four billion embryos we sent out will take care of the threats, just like they were designed [*built, made, constructed*] to do."

She looked even more oddly familiar in motion. Something about the shape of her cheek. A horrible grief kept dragging her mouth down like she wished to cry out with it, face frozen like a tragedy mask, but she would swallow and straighten her head and look at me with dark and solemn eyes.

"They were volunteers," she said, "at first. Then they were volunteered [*willing, then made willing*]. We'd stopped thinking of them as people long before then. I don't know when I—I didn't know—

"What happened here was evil. It must be forgotten, it can never happen again. I've done what I can. I've sabotaged [*broken, ruined, poisoned*] the embryos. I took this ship as close to a supernova as I could before the others stalled the engine—I can't fly us into the sun, but they can't fly us out. Sooner or later the sun will explode and turn all this to dust."

Later, as it turned out. Here I sat, a thousand years later, listening to Mara Zhu yearning for the star to explode and atomize her and all her works.

"The others are holed up in Lab 17 with the data," she said. "I can't get in to them, but they can't get out with it. I've made sure of that [*guaranteed it*]. If you find this ship, if the star doesn't go nova soon and you find this log, please. [*I beg you.*] Leave the ghosts here in peace. The final log of Doctor Mara Zhu."

The screen went black with finality, absolute and

unrelenting. No one on this ship had ever spoken again, at least not that the computers had recorded.

So, then. I had my answer. The truth, the secret that everyone aboard this ship wanted so desperately:

The Philosopher Stone was in Lab number 17.

CHAPTER THIRTY TWO: SINS OF THE FATHER

I SAT IN that darkness for a while, the screen black on my lap. There was a hollow-eyed horror on Mara Zhu's face that I knew well, that I'd seen on Benny and in the mirror after Kystrom. For a fierce and lonely moment I wanted to reach out for her, across the thousand years, because she had addressed this video to me a thousand years later, and I wanted to reach back. I'd seen something horrible, too, like her.

But what *had* Mara Zhu seen? Her final message had been cryptic, alluding to things she assumed I already knew. But the implications of what she'd said made me uneasy.

I had a source of water now, and a dubious source of food if I got truly desperate, and there didn't seem to be many monsters in this part of the ship. The *smart* thing to do would be to look through the tablet for some sort of map, or a clue to where Lab 17 might be from my current location, not squander my apparent safety sifting through extraneous data out of curiosity.

So, obviously, I went to the personnel files first.

Mara Zhu had said something about *volunteers*.

Nothing caught my eye in the personnel files, and I nearly gave up there, but an uneasy impulse took a hold of me. It was a weird suspicion, too awful to look at directly, but born out of the horror and anguish in Mara Zhu's face, out of the strange tomblike doors I'd seen, the ones long enough to lay down inside, and with shelves so that you could stack person atop person... Instead of looking for floorplans, I checked the cargo lists.

From there, the whole story unfurled with horrific clarity.

An impossible number of people were brought onto the *Nameless* during its days of operation—more people than a ship this size could sustain, and yet each document showed more and more coming aboard, and none leaving. I tracked these 'volunteers' progress from the cargo hold to the labs, where scientists' notes assigned them colors and numbers and charted their progress from their arrival to their deaths in neat, tidy script. The Philosopher Stone experiments had been conducted on living humans.

Nausea pressed at the back of my throat as I grimly deciphered what the experiments had entailed, and how these humans had been altered, augmented, and died. The scientists had had several different theories on how to produce immortal life. None of the theories seemed to extend the lives of their test subjects. Actually, quite the opposite.

The first breakthrough had occurred not with any of the volunteers, but with embryos, genetically engineered from the scientists' own DNA. Using the knowledge they'd gained from experimenting on their human subjects, the scientists had developed several strains of immortal or semi-immortal creatures, some more successful than others.

The project's success was a race of semi-humans, intelligent, quick, deadly, and immortal. It was this species the scientists had made a few billion embryos of and shipped off to the other planets. Those embryos—the shipment Mara Zhu had mentioned…

With a jolt, I realized why the man whose office I was hiding in, the one with the deep set owl eyes, looked so familiar. In her strange inhuman way, Number One looked like her father. Which meant that, for Indigo…

I looked down at the image of Mara Zhu still on the tablet screen, anguish around her mouth, dark and solemn eyes. At least now I knew why she seemed so familiar.

Horrifying things had happened on this ship. The Ministers had been born out of those horrors, and their own creator had tried to destroy them as a belated attempt to atone for what she'd done. What kind of awful existence was that?

It's a bitter thing when the people you're meant to protect are ungrateful, One had said. Humans had forgotten this history—even Mara Zhu's mention of violent native species in the Terra Nova and Maria Nova systems giving humans trouble was news to me. Humanity had not been native to the Sister Systems, but it hadn't occurred to me that there had been creatures already living here when we'd arrived. The Ministers, perhaps, had never forgotten.

Sitting alone in the dark, surrounded by the images of

dead monsters and dead men, I felt something I'd never thought I was capable of feeling: pity for the Ministers.

And then I heard something scrape outside. A footstep on dusty metal.

Something much larger than a cockroach approached.

I scrambled up, tablet in one hand, grabbing for my flashlight with the other. I'd bludgeoned a manikin once with this flashlight, and hadn't broken it; if I had to, I could do it again, even though the sound and feeling that the skull had made when it broke under the force of my arm was horrific and I—

A figure stepped through the doorway and I brought the flashlight down, flinching all the while, towards its skull. A hand caught mine easily, arresting the flashlight, and while I waited for death to disembowel me with its makeshift claws a second flashlight flicked on.

Lieutenant Lantern-Eyes stood in the doorway, my flashlight caught in one hand, her flashlight lit in the other, and her club tucked under her arm. She gave me a baleful look.

"Done running?" she asked.

CHAPTER THIRTY THREE: THE LIEUTENANT

(again)

"OH, HI," I said. "I was just thinking about you."

"I'm sure you were. I hope you're done trying to get yourself killed, because you're coming with me."

I had a good four inches height and seventy pounds weight on Lantern-Eyes, but the way she gripped my flashlight suggested those pitiful advantages wouldn't count for much. I'd left her armed, but I'd run out of ammunition; I'd found a source of water, but food, not so much.

I said, "Got any crackers?"

The shell of Republican Military Might cracked a little. The lieutenant said, "What?"

"I'll come with you if you give me food," I said. "Like a stray cat."

She regarded me a moment longer, her hand still gripping my flashlight over her head, suspicion a fading light in her eyes.

"Easily bought," she said, "aren't you?"

*   *   *

LANTERN-EYES MOVED WITH confidence through the darkened halls, flashlight off and club swinging in one hand. She led me to a space that echoed, and I trained my flashlight beam over the walls and ceiling. It was the bottom flight of a stairwell.

For the first time since she'd found me, Lantern-Eyes flicked her flashlight on. The steps past her were half-collapsed; a gap of three feet separated the lower stairs from the upper, and metal poles thrust into the empty space, bent and rusted. Not an easy climb.

"So you do use a flashlight," I said.

She flicked the penlight off. "I'm not exactly flush with power sources. Besides, a light makes it easier for things to see me."

I glanced down at my own stolen flashlight, blazing white. "Should I turn mine off?"

"And trip over your own feet? Sound travels further than light on this ship. Come up here."

I had a horrible image of climbing up these broken stairs, up and straight out to the choking emptiness of vacuum. "Won't those stairs go into the hull?"

"No, they go deeper into the ship. The ship is a wheel, these steps lead closer to the inner circumference. Let's go, Wren. Species 019 is probably on your trail again."

"Oh-one-nine?"

She sighed. "The 'manikin'."

The stairs creaked beneath my weight, bending ominously, but they held. I had to stretch out to bridge the gap where stairs had collapsed, but I made it, stepping where Lantern-Eyes stepped. There was no difference between the upper level and the lower that I could see, but Lantern-Eyes seemed a little more at ease. Thirty feet or so down the hall she stopped, and opened up a door. "There are some places in this ship where species 019 and the other monsters don't go," she told me lowly. "This room will be safe, as long as we're quiet."

Other monsters. "Like that rock thing?"

"I'm more worried about the Dreamer," she muttered, then added, with a glance at my expression, "The AI. Sit down."

The door led to some office-sized space. It had received the same treatment as some of the rooms I had seen downstairs: every item of furniture in the room had been systematically reduced to dust. The difference here was that Lantern-Eyes had swept that dust aside and placed caches of food and water stacked neatly against the wall, just as she had done downstairs.

There was nowhere to sit, so I took a place on the floor, leaning my back against the wall. It was easy, once I was there, to shut my eyes, too.

Something grabbed my wrist, lifted it, and shoved something against my palm until my fingers closed reflexively around it. I looked up to see that Lantern-Eyes had handed me a bottle of water. She sat back once I held it and began to unfold some complicated little device.

"What's that?" I asked.

"Campstove, for your promised food. Drink the water."

I was still holding the bottle in the air in front of me,

where she'd dragged my hand. I lifted my dented little tin. "I have a water bottle."

"What the hell is that?" she asked.

"Uh, canteen?"

"Did that work?"

"It worked okay. I had to improvise," I said.

"How did you end up on an expedition without a water bottle?" the lieutenant asked.

"I had one. I just wasn't expecting to be attacked by Ministers, then spaced."

She shook her head. "Drink your water," she said. "And throw out that thing."

Just to annoy her, I put the dented tin back in my jacket pocket. Then I uncapped the bottle she'd handed me and downed it in one go.

When I had caught my breath, the water bottle braced against one thigh, I looked at the lieutenant. The little campstove was glowing gently with heat, and she was setting a battered bowl at the top of it and pouring some rations in.

I said, "The scientists on this ship made the manikins and the Ministers from their own DNA. They're human."

"They're not." Lantern-Eyes replied with a calm that made me suspect she had sat here in the darkness before, pondering the very same questions I was asking now. "They can't interbreed with humans, for one."

"They can't interbreed with themselves," I pointed out. "They make and use tools. Isn't that human?"

"Crows and dolphins make and use tools."

"Crows and dolphins are intelligent," I said. There was

a certain exhilaration to debating with Lantern-Eyes, like what I imagined crossing swords was like. I wouldn't have suspected from our wordless introduction that she would be so quick in conversation. "The Ministers—"

"No one is debating that Ministers aren't intelligent," Lantern-Eyes said. "Unfortunately."

"And the manikins?"

"They're no more intelligent than the average crow. They understand cause and effect and they can hold a grudge for centuries, but they don't have a concept of 'the other'—they can't extend their empathy to see from my point of view. They can only react to me; they can't plan ahead or take my actions into account. Which is very different from human or Minister consciousness. Besides, both Ministers and manikins have got a lot more chromosomes, an entirely different circulatory system, they... No matter how you define human, they're not it."

That was too many large technical words in sequence. She'd left me behind. "You sound like you know what you're talking about."

"I have some medical training." The lieutenant carefully picked up the bowl by the rim, blowing on the liquid inside. "You can't communicate with those things. They don't have any logic or reason, just instinct."

I remembered that manikin in the gas-trapped room, the expression on her face before she'd curled around my throat. That hadn't been mindless instinct. That had been deliberation—and hatred.

Perhaps Lantern-Eyes was partially correct, anyway. The manikins couldn't be communicated with. She was just wrong about the reasons.

I took the bowl she handed me, unthinking, by its base, and pulled my hand away sharply with a hiss. She held it, waiting, while I shook the excess heat from my hand and sheepishly took the bowl by the rim the way she had held it. The food inside was a thick, chunky brown sludge.

"What is this?" I asked, accepting the fork as an afterthought.

"Never ask," Lantern-Eyes said, and set another bowl onto the campstove, pouring another box of rations inside, followed by a bit of water. I wondered how many of these battered little bowls she had. Had her team brought extra, or had there been only one per person? Did she have a set of bowls like tombstones, each one belonging to a different dead soldier? Whose bowl was I using now?

As foul as the food looked, it was better than a cockroach would've been. The first slippery forkful of unidentifiable meat-paste sent a surge of endorphins through my body. I shuffled up my legs to rest the bowl on my knees and took another forkful. "Hey, Lantern-Eyes. You said—"

"My name is Tamara Gupta."

It was a nice name. There were a lot of ways you could say *Tamara*, in anger or fear or affection or exasperation. Not like the one or two ways to pronounce *lieutenant*. It was the kind of name a real person would have, not a faceless Republican soldier.

"So you can stop calling me by that ridiculous nickname," she added.

"Sure thing, Lantern-Eyes," I said. "Are you a doctor?"

She snorted. "I studied medical ethics."

"Ah," I said, around another mouthful. "That's why they sent you here."

"That's why they sent me here." She pressed some button on the side of the campstove, turning it off. The heat radiating against my shin immediately decreased.

"How much did the Republic know about what they would find on this ship, before they sent you here?" I was actually going to kill that Senator if it turned out he'd known all this and sent us here anyway.

"Nothing," Lantern-Eyes said. "Just that the Philosopher Stone should be here, and the Philosopher Stone experiments were about unlocking the secret to immortality. It wasn't a hard leap from there to assuming there'd be some ethical concerns surrounding the data. We just assumed the ethical concerns would be hypothetical, not alive and tearing people apart."

Like Lantern-Eyes' team. I watched as she scraped her fork around the sides of the bowl, gathering up the residue, and licked it off her fork. Then she reached over for a water bottle and poured some of it into the bowl, swirling it around with the fork to clean it. Solitary little gestures, well-practiced.

Over a year, she'd said. She'd been alone on this ship for over a year. I'd only been separated from Benny for, what, two days? The image of the last time I'd seen him, facing me across the hall, expression closed and grim, seared its way across my mind.

What was it One had said? *You're alone in this.* Well, I wasn't alone right now; I had Lantern-Eyes across from me.

"How many people were on your team, Tamara?" I asked.

Her fork paused, stirring through the water. "Twelve," Tamara said at last.

I had lost far more people than twelve when Kystrom had fallen. I'd lost mother and father and sister, friends, neighbors, classmates, people I'd seen on television or heard on the radio or read about on a screen. And when those people were gone I lost the things that existed between them, knowledge or secrets shared, memories, gratitudes, resentments. I had lost a whole world, except for Benny.

But twelve people, on a ship as isolated and terrible as this, were a world of their own just as completely as Kystrom had been. I said, "What were their names?"

"I don't remember."

It was my turn to falter, dropping my fork back into my half-full bowl. "What do you mean you don't remember?"

"I mean I forgot."

"How can you forget something like that?"

"It's been twenty months," Lantern-Eyes said, in a voice as unbreakable as the rest of her, and she tilted her bowl back to drink the water out of it and leave it spotlessly clean.

* * *

A FEW HOURS after Benny and I left Kystrom behind, I sat down in the back of his stolen ship and brought out the knife he'd used to fight his way through. He was up front, flying the ship. A few years older than me, he'd already gotten his flight license. At the time that had mattered to me.

I'd taken the knife and washed it, then pulled out the lighter I'd borrowed from my father that morning without permission, and held the fire to the blade until it was hot and gleaming. Then I sat down and tried my best to remember the liturgy of grief. Like most over-familiar things, it existed in the subconscious; deeply ingrained, but difficult to consciously recall. The less I thought, the more clearly it came. Alone in the back of the ship, I'd murmured all the words I could remember, and then made my offering to the God Who Had Shed His Blood For Us.

The first cut, near the tip of my pinky finger, had been for Brigid. It hadn't hurt, even though it had bled, so I'd cut it again a little deeper, afraid it wouldn't scar. I'd somehow felt like the God of Blood wouldn't accept mine if I didn't do it properly. The second cut was for my father, the third for my mother. After that I froze, because there were many more people I had lost, too many to pick out one immediately from the crowd.

I'd had four cousins on my mother's side, and two aunts; I marked them down below my parents. One uncle on my father's side with no spouse or children; I marked him, too. My friends—seven marks for them, my closest friends. Neighbors, too; my former babysitter who had gone off to school and come back for the summer, an old lady a block down who always gave me fruit from her garden. I murmured a name each time I cut, and it felt like I was carving those names into me, into my flesh and blood, where I could never fail to remember.

I was halfway down my forearm by the time Benny found me.

The first I knew he had come into the room was when he tore the knife from my hand. "What the fuck?" he demanded, and the knife punctuated with a clatter in the corner. I wavered on my knees, lightheaded, in retrospect, from loss of blood. It had dripped down to my elbow, onto my knees. "What the fuck are you doing?"

"Scarification," I started to explain, because Benny had gone to our church, too, and so he should know.

"You're not going to bleed to death on my ship!" he'd shouted at me, wild, eyes red; he'd been crying himself. I'd stared at him. I don't think I had been crying, and maybe that was why he'd looked at me with such terror in his anger.

"Fuck," he'd said again, in a voice that wobbled and cracked, and shoved some fabric at me; his sweatshirt, I think. His sweatshirt, to mop up the blood.

"I didn't ask for this, Sean," he'd said. I remember clearly the way he said it. "I didn't ask for this."

I held the sweatshirt to my arm. My hand was stiff and aching.

"Clean it up," he'd said, and left.

I couldn't remember all the names I'd said anymore. I couldn't even remember all the faces. I'd spent so long trying to remember, bringing up those faces and those names at every moment, that the memories themselves had gotten worn through. It was like sticking your nose in a flower; the smell that was so strong at first faded with overexposure.

But that had been eight years ago now, not twenty months, and I still tried, with everything I had or ever could have, to hold those names in my head, my heart.

* * *

"YOU'VE READ ENOUGH off that tablet to know the scientists made the manikins out of their own DNA," Lieutenant Gupta said once I had finished, tidying up the bowl and campstove and wrappers until the place looked as if we had not been there at all. "Have you found out where the Philosopher Stone is yet?"

So that I could tell her where it was and she could ditch me, discard me in the dark and then forget me like she'd forgotten the names of all the people she'd lived and died beside? Lieutenant Gupta wasn't taking care of me out of the goodness of her heart. I had precisely one piece of leverage to use to keep myself alive. I wasn't giving it up that easily.

Not to mention, it was hard to tell how old Lantern-Eyes was, in the dark and malnourished as she was—but she was old enough to have been in the service at the time when the Republic had abandoned Kystrom.

I told the lieutenant, "Not yet."

CHAPTER THIRTY FOUR: FIELD AND FOREST

"WE CAN'T SIT around and wait," Lieutenant Gupta said. "I know what quadrant of the ship the Philosopher Stone data must be in—the part of the ship with the most traps and monsters, the only part of the ship I haven't searched thoroughly. We can head there while you translate."

"But you've been there before?" I asked.

"Once," she said briefly. "And we didn't get far. You have to do exactly as I say while we go there. Most of my team died trying to get through those labs."

That would be the team whose names you don't remember anymore, right, lieutenant? "Understood," I said.

"Take these," she added, and passed me a few rations, a real water bottle. "And let's get moving."

She led me through the hallways, confusing labyrinths of blackened rooms. It was a good thing Lantern-Eyes knew where she was going, because I couldn't have found my way back to the room we'd just left. Flashlight beams were bad at picking out distinguishable landmarks, and everything looked the same in the dark.

Our journey across the ship came to an unfortunate pause in front of another of Lieutenant Gupta's little rat-holes.

"How have you survived this long?" Lantern-Eyes demanded, from inside a tunnel that would not have fit a mouse.

I knelt outside her little tunnel, staring at the fragile broken edges of an ancient starship wall. "If I get stuck, I'll die in there."

"It's much bigger on the other side."

"What's on the other side?"

A calculating expression formed on her thin, hungry face. "Come through and find out," Lantern-Eyes said, and turned herself around in the miniscule space, crawling off.

It was a bold assumption that I wouldn't take my chance for escape now that she'd turned her back on me. I lingered in the hallway, contemplating an easy escape.

What could be behind the wall?

I climbed in after Lantern-Eyes.

She was waiting for me on the other side, crouched in weeds of green and sickly brown. When I emerged from the rat-hole she grabbed my forearm and dragged me to the ground with her.

I landed on soil, rich and clumping with moisture. A vast field opened up before me, and a brilliant sun shone down upon tall grasses and twisted fruit trees. I blinked my half- blinded eyes. "Wow," I breathed.

"The ship was supposed to support a crew for decades,

if not longer." Lantern-Eyes was speaking quickly and quietly. "It had to produce its own renewable supply of food. The solar lighting is on its own closed system; the Dreamer repairs it aggressively. When the last of the ship's power finally fails, that sun will be the last thing to go out."

"This is incredible," I breathed. I wondered if there were any species here that were extinct in the Sisters now, or if species had evolved here that never existed anywhere in the Sisters or on the far-distant mythical Earth.

Lieutenant Gupta's mouth tipped, crooked. She patted my arm with one hand.

"Because there's food here, this place is full of creatures," she said, the almost-smile gone like it never had been. "It's the fastest way to the other side of the ship, but we have to be very quiet."

There had been a pattern to this place once, I realized as I followed Lantern-Eyes through the wavering wheat, around the copse of gnarled fruit trees. Once upon a time, a thousand years ago, this place had been laid out in a grid. The traces of it could be seen in the blurred edges between types of brush and tree, like the echoes of Ameng grammar in modern Sister.

But it was nothing more than echoes. The fields grew choked and thick, rotting in places, stripped bare of edible parts in others, torn apart by indifferent hands, untended by the farmers that had first planted it. The trees were gnarled and thick with age, and the dead trees had rotted where they stood once they became too large for their root systems to be supported by the fragile farmland.

The old dead wood was held up in place by the arms of its children.

The place was weirdly silent, no birdsong. Once I heard a hum like bees and Lieutenant Gupta went tense, throwing me to the ground and crouching beside me, shadows from the wheat wavering across her face.

The humming receded, and yet Lantern-Eyes held me down still, her lips moving in some silent count. At some signal I didn't know, she moved again, weaving her way through the wheat on stick-skinny legs like an antelope.

In spite of the atmosphere of danger, the farmlands had a certain beauty. I paused to turn my face up towards the warmth of the simulated sun and saw that the sky had cracks running through. When I lowered my head and looked over the fields, I saw two children in the woods.

It was impossible, but there they were. Two children crouching in the loam, side-by-side. They looked to be only about seven or eight, *children*, kneeling beneath the looming specter of a rotting tree and digging through the soil. They had their backs to me, so they had not seen me standing amidst the tangled wheat.

Brigid, I thought, painful and irrational, and then with a memory so sudden and complete it was painful, Brigid and Liza, because both little girls had light hair. Even dirtied and tangled, the two of them had pale hair. The two heads bent together as if in conspiracy, digging through the dirt; I could see it on Kystrom, a memory I'd thought I'd lost, Brigid and Liza in the backyard digging through the mud with a space beside them for me to join—

A lance hit me in the gut and drove me to the ground. I

rolled out from the weight of whatever had knocked me over, breathless from the blow, but Lantern-Eyes sat her hips on mine and one elbow across my neck and the other hand clasped over my mouth, immobilizing me with a soldier's rough efficiency.

"I wish you had *one* survival skill," she hissed into my face from inches away.

I tried to speak against her palm but didn't have enough air. A frown furrowed her brows and she lifted her hand away, but kept it near my face.

"Sorry," I whispered, still gasping for breath under her weight on my bruised diaphragm.

Lantern-Eyes looked over my head, towards the unseen edge of the forest. Strands of her hair dangled down onto my face, and almost obscured the fear on hers. She pressed her palm to my mouth again, a hard look in her eyes warning me, then rolled off my torso so carefully that the grass barely swayed. Flat on her belly, she stared ahead, chin above the soil.

I rolled over carefully and looked where she looked.

The two little girls had stood up suddenly, attracted, probably, by the sound of the lieutenant taking me down. First I saw nothing but two children standing there, and almost shouted at Lantern-Eyes for hauling me down when there were kids out there, kids who might need help. But there was something not right about the two children in the woods.

One girl had a scar on her face, bisecting her cheek, exposing the inside of her mouth. The scar dragged down, thick and gnarled, from her jaw to her shoulder.

A twisted, ropy thing, and old—an older scar than a child should have. Both children had oddly misshapen cheeks, like they had something in their mouths. And, perhaps it was a trick of the light, but between their sandy lashes I saw nothing but liquid black.

Their heads swiveled this way and that, predatory, sharp. The scarless one inhaled on her palate, like a snake. Through her parted lips I could see bulging ivory, teeth stacked on teeth, warping the natural shape of her mouth. Then she shut her jaw. The two children turned away from us and clambered into the forest, vanishing beneath the looming bulk of the rotting tree.

The sunlight had been warm before, but all I felt now was cold. "Why do they have so many teeth?" I whispered.

There were stress lines around Lieutenant Gupta's jack-o-lantern eyes; deeper now than before, and highlighted by the unrelenting sun. "I think sometimes the old teeth don't fall out fast enough. Baby teeth, you know? They're stuck at that age. The teeth just keep growing."

"Stuck at that age?"

"Yeah." Lantern-Eyes pushed herself up onto her hands and knees. "Species 048. An attempt at eternal youth, I think."

I couldn't seem to stop shaking. "Why do they look like children?" Eternal youth should mean eternal young adulthood. Eternal post-puberty. Someone old enough to—to— Not a child, an adult. An adult. Not children.

"Just one of the techniques the scientists tried, I think," Lantern-Eyes said. "Permanent juvenile states. There are some insects that are functionally immortal because they never mature."

"So those children are insects?" That was worse than I'd imagined.

"No, the scientists just used an analogous technique to keep them young. Come on. Species 048 are just scavengers, but if they're here, there might be manikins nearby."

She kept herself lower than before, bent almost in half. The stained and faded color of her uniform was more visible in the sunlight, a deep rich crimson gone dull with dust. I followed her, mimicking her crouching stance.

I could just see, over the tops of the grain, the far wall of the farmlands approaching. We had almost crossed them.

The sunlight dimmed.

I grabbed at the back of Lantern-Eyes' too-large jacket to stop her. "What's that?" I whispered, peering up at the sky. The cluster of lights in the sky simulating the sun were growing darker. Were they failing?

"Scheduled rainstorm," Lantern-Eyes whispered back, freeing my hand from her coattail. "Come on—" And then she, too, stopped short.

I could hear nothing but a soft shushing in the grass around us, like a wind. "What?"

"That son of a bitch," the lieutenant breathed. I twisted to see what she saw, and there, across the fields: a dark figure with a star at its throat, glowing a dark and brilliant blue.

Somehow, the Indigo Minister had tracked us here.

"Son of a bitch," I echoed.

Lantern-Eyes' hand latched onto my elbow. "Let's go.

The Minister isn't our biggest problem right now."

I wished I'd recorded that, if only so I could play back Lantern-Eyes' words and make sure she'd said what I thought she had. Indigo had his sword drawn, but his attention was on the field where the breeze bent the grass towards him, not on us. I found this strange until I remembered, with a sickening jolt, that there was no breeze in the farmlands.

Then I looked around myself and Lantern-Eyes and saw that the grass by us was moving, too, bending with the motion of something beneath, heading for us as straight and sure as an arrow.

"Sean, *run*," Lantern-Eyes said, just as the first of the manikins burst out of the grass.

CHAPTER THIRTY FIVE:
THE MINISTER, THE LIEUTENANT,
AND I

THE LIEUTENANT'S CLUB slammed into the manikin's skull, cracking bone, black blood flying. The manikin collapsed back into the grass, twitching with the last firings of its crushed nerves. "Go!"

Overhead, the light dimmed further, and the ship moaned. A thousand small ports in the ceiling opening up at once, I realized, as the first drops of rain began to fall. I glanced back through the dim and found Indigo easily, a gleaming figure surrounded by pale, snarling shapes.

I saw, too, a manikin standing upright in the field, pale, dripping with water. It watched Lantern-Eyes and I run, then dropped down to hands and knees and vanished beneath the surface of the grass. The wheat where it had been now rippled, heading towards us.

There were at least five of the things heading towards us through the field now, splashing through the puddles that were rapidly forming underfoot. The flash storm was turning dirt to mud. My footing was less certain, my boots sliding. The far wall of the farmlands was getting closer, but it was still quite distant.

"We're not going to make it," I warned Lantern-Eyes.

She didn't falter, her expression determined, and water streaming over her face while the storm roared down on us like a vengeance.

I could just make out the outline of a door in its surface, the door Lantern-Eyes was leading me towards. But even here, the manikins were catching up.

Meanwhile, in the distance, Indigo turned as gracefully as a dancer, the raindrops turned to crystals in the glow of his collar-light. He wasn't having any trouble fighting off the monsters.

Claws and pale flesh and snarling; rain glistened and mud splattered as something hit Lantern-Eyes full in the side and took her down. I shouted and threw myself, without thinking, at the tangle of Lantern-Eyes and manikin; hairless flesh slid beneath my grasping fingers and something sharp bit into my leg. I kicked and rolled, grabbing at the monster, feeling it squirm beneath me. I had to get it off Tamara. When it turned around in my grip, it would disembowel me.

A loud *crack* right beside my head, more piercing than thunder. I blinked past the suddenly still corpse in my arms to find Tamara Gupta, rain sticking her hair to her hollowed cheeks, breathing hard and holding her bloodied club. The manikin was dead. "Take this," she gasped, and produced an improbably large knife out of, apparently, thin air.

I took it. "Where were you keeping this?"

"Do you ever shut up?" she demanded, and hauled me to my feet without letting go of her club.

We ran again, full-out for the far wall and the little door. The other four manikins were closer. We'd barely survived one; Lantern-Eyes had given me a knife but that didn't mean I could actually use it.

"We have to call for Indigo," I gasped.

"Are you insane?" Lantern-Eyes snapped. "He's a few hundred years old; he's known you for a few days. If he comes over here, it'll be to kill us, too!"

That might be true. He'd promised to kill me often enough, especially if I tried to escape—which I had. And yet he'd saved me when the hull decompressed. He'd stepped between me and the weird rock thing. He'd offered me his hand when I'd been paralyzed with fear in the tiny tunnel.

Tamara and I slammed into the far wall together, right beside the little door. Before I could push myself up she was moving, grasping the handle, water streaming down the wall and over her hands. She turned the handle—and the door did not move.

Locked, or simply rusted shut. I looked back at the field and found four pale figures emerging from the grass, long limbs rising rain-slick, metal glinting at their nails. And, far off behind them, the flickering blue glow of Indigo defeating his opponents single-handed.

"Call your Minister," Tamara said.

"I... What? Really?"

"Call your Minister," she said again, and advanced to

meet the manikins, her club upraised like a bat.

I didn't waste time. I turned to face that distant blue glow, cupped my hands around my mouth, and bellowed, "INDIGO!"

The light turned. I raised my flashlight and turned it on, flashing one of the few words I knew in the Light language at him: *Go!*

Tamara let out a cry, the sound weirdly muted by the rain; the manikins had converged around her. Indigo knew where we were; he'd come or he wouldn't. I drew the ridiculously long knife Tamara had given me and waded over to help her.

Or so I tried. I'd barely gone two steps before another creature emerged from the rain, its snarls lost to the roar of the water. The mud underfoot was all that saved me; I slipped when I turned, and fell, and the manikin overshot me. It spun around on the ground, trampling the long grass, eyes glinting. I lifted the knife between it and me like I knew how to use it, like I could stand to use it even if I had. God of Blood, forgive me.

And then a dark blue light filled the air above me like a sweet smell, and Indigo's blade swept down and through the manikin's neck.

I scrambled back up, mud clumping to my side. Indigo's dark hair was sleeked down with water, and his glance was cool. He left me in the mud to join Tamara, shrieking furiously beneath the weight of a bloodied manikin. Indigo's blade sliced through its ribs, black blood bubbling viscous in its wake, and Lantern-Eyes got to her feet, grabbed her club, and bludgeoned the skull of a manikin that was creeping around to flank Indigo.

There was nothing I could do to help them with that battle. I fumbled with the hilt of Tamara's massive knife, and hurried back to the little door. If it were rusted shut, maybe I could break through. If it were locked—

It was locked; the seams of the door were free of rust, though dripping with wet. There was a keypad beside the door, electronics long since shorted out. I glanced behind me to the field of battle. The manikins were *fast*, as fast as Indigo, almost too quick for me to track. I saw Indigo slice at one, catch another's teeth on his wrist gauntlet. Lantern-Eyes' club caught a third in the gut when it came up on Indigo from behind, slowing it long enough for Indigo to move smoothly out of its way. Indigo moved quickly, keeping himself between Lantern-Eyes and the main force of them, while the lieutenant crouched low and swung at any that tried to flank him.

There was more than one way to open a door. I felt along the edges of the door by the knob, found a gap between door and jam. I pulled out my notebook, hunching over to protect the paper from the rain, and slid the stiff plastic cover between door and jam, jerking it down.

The ancient lock was pushed aside; the door clicked open.

I turned back to the battle in the field. "Lantern-Eyes! Indigo!" I shouted, but my voice was almost lost beneath the roar of the rain. "TAMARA! INDIGO!"

Lantern-Eyes ran towards me first, limping through the rain, blood on her club, blood on her face. She wiped hair and rainwater out of her eyes and smeared black blood there instead.

"Come on," I said, and held open the door. She started to step through, then hesitated, looking back.

Indigo was retreating towards us backwards, not daring to turn away from the manikins.

"Go," Lantern-Eyes said to me, and shoved my shoulder, pushing me through the door first. I stumbled into dryness, shocking in its suddenness.

And shone my flashlight on half a dozen gleaming eyes.

There were more manikins in here—outwaiting the storm, perhaps. I tried to turn back and ran into Lantern-Eyes. "Go back," I urged.

She looked past me and swore. "We can't."

Everything happened very quickly after that. Perhaps the whole encounter lasted no longer than a few moments. I saw things in images like camera flashes, my flashlight jerking over Lantern-Eyes with her club, Indigo surrounded, and hating, hating eyes.

And then my beam fell upon a thick pipe directly above me, the surface of it brown and flaking with corrosion. Moisture dripped from it at the seam.

The rain had to get to the ceiling somehow, I reasoned.

That would do.

"Watch out!" I warned my companions, shouting loudly enough to be heard over the roar of battle, and then I slammed the pommel of Lantern-Eyes' fuck-you knife into the fragile old pipe.

It burst.

Water sprayed out with enough force to knock me over. It was impossible to hear anything over the roar of the water, and impossible to see much through the spray. I pushed myself up, gasping, and felt something sharp close around my ankle. The manikins—their lives were in danger from the water as much as ours, but they were still trying to kill us. That didn't seem like hunger, or territorial possessiveness. That seemed like hate.

The room was full of water, echoing, roaring. I pulled my ankle free of the monster, found my feet, and looked around for someone: Indigo or Tamara, or both. I thought I saw the glow of Indigo's collar light and moved towards it, but an ominous rumble traveled through the wall. The ground underfoot, weakened by a millennium of decay, bent from the weight of the flood—and then collapsed, taking us all down with it.

CHAPTER THIRTY SIX:
THE DEER AND THE RIVER

THERE WAS A creek behind my friend Kenny's house back on Kystrom. It wasn't the most extraordinary water to look at; there were bigger rivers nearby, or prettier ones; there were waterfalls and whitewater and long lazy shallows darting with emerald fish. Kenny's creek was so narrow that, with a running start, you could jump clean across it.

But the creek was deeper than it was wide, maybe deeper than it was long. Some crack in the earth had been opened, and the water had come to fill it: you could not see the bottom looking in, only dark water. My mother and father had forbidden me and Brigid to swim in it, because although the water looked slow and still on the surface, we had all heard rumors of dark currents deeper down, of things going into the water and never coming back up. I swam in it anyway. The water was slow and lazy at the top of the river, and I could drift without my feet scraping sand.

I wasn't content just to drift.

I dived in for the extra momentum, to get a little deeper. The rope around my waist tugged, then slackened as Kenny fed me extra length. I'd decided that I wasn't disobeying the spirit of my parents' order if I was being careful while I swam, and with boyish reasoning, Kenny and I had decided that a tether would make the whole endeavor perfectly safe.

The water got darker the deeper I went. There was an aching pressure against my ears and in my head. The walls of the creek on either side of me were spotted with underwater plants, clinging to outcroppings in rock. This deep underwater it was more like flying than swimming. I dove deeper and deeper, until I could see a marvel below me.

The creek was not narrow all the way down. It opened up into a vast cavern, so deep I could barely see the bottom, so wide I could not see the sides. This little creek was bigger than any of the others in my part of Kystrom, but only a little of the dark water showed on the surface.

Then, as I hovered there with a rope around my waist and the marvel of the river visible beneath me, a dark current came. Fast and inescapable, the river coiled around me and dragged me down.

* * *

I BURST FREE of the surface, coughing and gasping. The river was colder than I remembered, the field darker. And it was arms, not a rope, that gripped me around my waist.

"Be quiet," a familiar voice said in my ear. Indigo. I was

not on Kystrom; I was on the *Nameless*.

We floundered together towards higher ground, huddled on wet, rotting floors. Somehow, I'd managed to keep a hold of Tamara's enormous knife. I put it into my belt while I did a quick accounting of myself. I still had my notebook (waterlogged and ruined), the flashlight and the tablet (both waterproof and still functional, to my relief), along with the bottle of water and ration packets I'd taken from Tamara (wet), and the knife she'd given me (wet and bloody).

My flashlight was off, making the only light in the room Indigo's collar light. I didn't recognize the space we'd been washed into. I didn't see Lantern-Eyes.

Something crackled from a room away, followed by a loud POP and a white flash.

"The water is shorting out electronics," Indigo told me quietly.

"Where's Lantern-Eyes?"

"I don't know. We have to be quiet. The damage to the ship may attract the autorepair. We need to get to Zhu's office before it does."

My head was still spinning from my near-drowning experience. Then Indigo's words caught up to me: Mara Zhu's office.

He didn't know.

I coughed. "Have you found the other Ministers yet?"

Indigo shook his head. Amazing how he could be nonverbal, yet still terse. "They are outside the range of my communicator."

"Communicator?"

He touched his collar-light.

Of course. Why make a communications device that could do only one thing? They might as well carry around flashlights. Indigo's collar-light looked a little small to contain a short-range radio as well as a power source and a light source, but Minister tech was centuries ahead of humanity's. That was why humanity's breakthrough on FTL engines had taken them so much by surprise.

"The range is only a few hundred yards, less with the interference from the walls and the solar radiation." Indigo lowered his hand.

"So unless we happen to wander within a hundred yards of them, you don't know what happened to them," I said. Indigo was alone, then, too. Just as alone as Lantern-Eyes. Or me. "Do you even know how to get to Zhu's office?"

Indigo rose to his feet. "We should move," he said.

He didn't know. He probably didn't even know where we were right now—I didn't either, I realized, though if Lantern-Eyes had been here I was certain she'd know. My heart clenched painfully, an unfamiliar sentiment in the face of a Minister. Here was Indigo, surrounded by the horrors of his own creation, lost, alone, and going the wrong way.

Maybe it was pity that made me say it. Maybe it was gratitude. Maybe it was simply the imp. I said, "It's not even there, Indigo."

"What isn't?" Indigo said tersely, in a *Shut the fuck up, Sean, there are monsters around* sort of tone.

"The data isn't in Zhu's office. Lantern-Eyes already checked."

That got his attention. He turned sharply to look down at me, his collar-light reflected palely in his dark eyes. "Where is it?"

"Ah," I said. "Well, that—that I can't tell you."

"Can't?"

"Won't," I admitted.

*   *   *

I SAW A frightening thing when the current dragged me deep into that underwater cavern.

The rope worked as it was intended—at least, as well as such an ill-conceived safety measure could work under the circumstances. It arrested me only a few feet deeper, digging painfully into my stomach, until I could get my fingers in the algae-slick wall and out of the immediate pressure of the current.

I was almost out of breath. I pushed myself upwards, off the wall, ascending back towards the sunlight, and below I caught a glimpse of something pale jolting back and forth in some invisible deep current. Something that had been caught, as I nearly had.

And as I ascended, I saw it tear free of whatever bound it, and began to rise as well.

I emerged into the afternoon with popping, aching ears, gasping wildly for breath. Kenny was hauling on the rope and calling my name, saying something else that was lost to my ringing ears and the irregularities of memory. I hauled myself onto the shore, feeling the rope bite into my gut, and gasped and gagged until I had enough air that

I could bend over the surface of the water again.

That pale shape breached the surface of the river a few feet from where I had surfaced, and caught in an eddy where the current turned aside from stone. It was as big as we were, pale but matted, with branches sticking out of it, bent to the side. Kenny gagged from the stench and I covered my nose while the current turned it slowly around. It was brown on the other side, and a mat of seaweed was tangled around the smooth arch of a branch. A pile of wood and debris, I thought at first, and then I saw the base of the branches was attached to waterlogged brown fur, a narrow muzzle, hollows where rot had eaten out the eyes. The deer's long neck bent gracefully out into the water as the current caught the crown of seaweed it had tangled in its antlers; the rest of its body turned in the river to float white belly-up again, slender legs sticking like broken branches out of its bloated corpse.

Kenny and I said not another word. We watched the body of the drowned deer as it was carried away, slow and peaceful, on the calm still surface of the little creek.

*　　*　　*

THE WHITE BELLY of a deer rose from the depths of Indigo's eyes.

"You won't tell me," he said.

I swallowed, remembering all too clearly Lantern-Eyes' warning: Indigo was hundreds of years old. He didn't care about me. "I won't. And if you want to find the Stone, you have to keep me alive."

"Lives depend on the Stone."

"Yeah," I said, thinking of Benny, thinking of the little bomb nestled up against my skull. "Mine."

"You…" Indigo began, and then fell silent all abrupt, his head turning sharply to the side.

I was about to speak up, question his odd stance, but then my less-acute hearing picked up the same sound that had distracted him: a buzzing hum, like a swarm of bees, growing louder as it approached. The *Nameless*'s autorepair.

I clapped a hand over my own mouth to muffle my still-harsh breathing. Indigo wordlessly touched the light at his throat and dialed it down, down, down, into darkness.

We sat there in the invisible black. I was more keenly aware of the sounds: the ragged edge to my breathing, the buzz and hum growing louder, nearer. Indigo was a faint warmth beside me.

Something landed on my shoulder. I felt its slight weight through my jacket. The buzzing was all around my head.

"Indigo," I whispered, and Indigo's collar light glowed back to life.

They were small, very small robots. Nanotech. They must be controlled by the ship's computer—the AI that ran the autorepair. Lantern-Eyes had had an uncharacteristically evocative name for the AI, hadn't she? She'd called the computer the Dreamer.

The Dreamer-bots were each the size of my fingernail, or smaller. They hung in the air, surrounded by a blurry halo that I knew must be their little wings moving so rapidly my eyes could not make them out. They darted back and forth with the quick, steady movements of bumblebees.

I glanced over at Indigo and found that while I had a few of the Dreamer-bots hovering around me, he had a veritable cloud surrounding him. For whatever reason, they found him more interesting.

Something touched my hand. I flinched, but five little sharp pinpricks latched onto my skin, and the Dreamer-bot did not shake free.

I would have made Lantern-Eyes proud: I lifted the hand that had the Dreamer-bot clinging to the skin, and slammed hand and bot into the ground. The fragile metal shattered like chiton, and I felt it scratch my skin, but at least when I lifted my hand there was nothing clinging there anymore.

The Dreamer-bots around me hummed, all in unison, like a song or a war-cry. Then, as one, they rushed my face.

Maybe Lantern-Eyes wouldn't be all that proud of me, after all.

"Sean!" I thought I heard Indigo say, which was obviously me hearing things, because even if Indigo were willing to address me informally he certainly wouldn't pronounce my name in the correct, Kystrene way. I couldn't trust my ears, anyway—solid and wriggling, the Dreamer-bots crawled inside my skull.

CHAPTER THIRTY SEVEN: SOME FRESH BULLSHIT

DREAMER-BOTS SWARMED MY tongue, climbed between my teeth. I choked and tried to cough them out, but I didn't dare to crush them, for fear I would swallow jagged metal or toxic substances. Dreamer-bots stabbed needle-sharp feet between my eyelids. I scratched at my face but there were too many of them; they crawled between my fingers. The ones that ended up on my hands dug their feet into the soft skin beneath my nails.

A force much stronger than me wrenched my hands away from my face and I shouted out in wordless denial, still struggling to claw the bots off me. What would happen if they got into my throat, my eyes, my skull?

Something cool and dry pressed against my face, flattening the bots gently against my skin. An unknown weight pinned me down. I was going to die here, choking on nanotech, robots crawling through my gut—

I gasped, and realized that my mouth was empty. The last one clawed over my lip as it retreated and I closed my jaw so that nothing could claw its way back in. My ears itched, but then the itching ceased.

The pressure over my face released, and I took in two desperate breaths through my nose before I dared to open my eyes.

Indigo sat on his heels beside me, hand extended before him. In the dim glow of his collar-light, his hand was misshapen, distorted. I reached out blindly for the flashlight and shone it on him.

The Dreamer-bots coated his hand like bees on their keeper, swarming, humming. Indigo stared with unnerving intensity at his living glove, his hand held stiffly out.

Then he hissed through his teeth and shook his hand. A few Dreamer-bots shook free and hummed lazily through the air to land on his skin again. In the bright beam of my flashlight I caught a glimpse of red between the swarming creatures.

My heart thudded unevenly in my chest. I set the flashlight down and tugged off my jacket. "Cover your hand with this," I said, and Indigo stuck his hand out in front of him, on the ground, and I covered it with my jacket. I kneeled on the sides of the jacket to seal it, while underneath, the bots buzzed angrily. With both hands I pressed down on the fabric on either side of Indigo's wrist.

"Okay," I said.

He pulled his hand out through the tunnel of fabric I'd created, scraping Dreamer-bots off against the fabric. My jacket buzzed furiously and moved beneath me, lumpy and living. I swallowed my nausea.

A few bots escaped free with Indigo's hand before I could close the opening under the jacket. He caught them and crushed them, one-handed, expression grim. There were a hundred small cuts on his hands, each beading a tiny drop of red.

My jacket fought me. "Okay," I said, mostly to myself, trying to hold the struggling jacket shut, "I didn't have a part two to the plan."

Indigo stood up. He stepped into me—I got a knee to the face—and slammed his heel down hard on my jacket.

His toes came dangerously close to stepping on a fragile part of me. I shifted back as far as I could without losing my seal on the jacket, and let this fearsome immortal warrior, this god-like killer of planets, stomp a swarm of mechanical bees to death between my legs.

When my jacket ceased moving on its own, Indigo took a step back. He nodded at me like two warriors meeting over a battlefield. I tried to picture Number One hopping up and down on nanomachines until they shattered, and failed.

Distantly, like it was coming from several rooms away, I heard an ominous buzzing start up.

More Dreamer-bots. It had to be. "You've got to be kidding," I said. "This ship is *bullshit*."

"How much of my language did you pick up, traveling with my people?" Indigo asked, low and quick. He was good; he almost didn't sound recriminatory.

I briefly debated playing either dumb or smart. The low, threatening hum of an approaching murder swarm tipped me in favor of honesty. "I can say yes and no, stop and go, but that's about it. I have some ideas about honorifics and question-phrasing, though."

"Show me," Indigo said.

I used my flashlight to speak to him: a quick flutter, a longer hold. *Stop*. And then a bright held flash: *Go*. "I can't say yes and no without colors."

"If you dim the brightness, the meaning will come across. Twist the ring around the head of the flashlight to brighten or dim the light. I would translate that first light as *wait* and that second light as *come*, but you're essentially correct, though off in the," he paused like he was thinking, "accent. We may need to communicate silently. Use those signals if we do, and follow me."

He rose to his feet but remained hunched down, offering me his arm, black gauntlet, hand curled into a fist. I grabbed my jacket with one hand and used Indigo to pull myself up, glittering shards of broken nanobots snowing down onto the floor.

The humming swelled, rising to a threatening pitch. Getting close. Something told me that while Indigo might be able to lure a handful of the Dreamer-bots away from me, we'd be in real trouble if a proper swarm found us. I picked up the flashlight, checked to make sure I had tablet and water bottle and knife in the pockets of the jacket I held, and followed Indigo as quietly as I could away from the crushed Dreamer-bots. I only hoped Indigo knew where he was going; every room on the *Nameless* was starting to look pretty much the same.

I bet Lantern-Eyes could find her way around no problem, though.

Indigo paused right before the next room, where a dim red glow permeated the air, and drew his sword.

From behind us, I heard that soft, susurrating hum, our whispering pursuit. I grabbed Indigo's arm in question. He touched his collar, seemingly without thinking about it, and flashed a word at me that I didn't know: a slow brighten, a slow dim.

"It's okay," he translated softly, when I tugged his arm again, and guided me to the side, through a different passage.

We had not gone far from the heavy footsteps before I smelled something acrid. The air was heavy, and the space in front of my flashlight swirled with particles. "What's going on?" I whispered to Indigo.

He spoke just as quietly as me. "The water from the burst pipe flowed mostly this way. I believe it damaged the electronics."

Which meant even more Dreamer-bots ahead of us. I could only hope that if there were any ahead, they were wandering around independently, not swarming for a taste of my blood.

A few steps further and Indigo reached back, found the switch on my flashlight, and shut it off. I opened my mouth to object but then I saw what he had seen: there was a faint and intermittent glow coming from up ahead, lightening the air.

We walked around the edges of that glow. More and more of the space around us was illuminated as we advanced, and I realized that we had ended up in some sort of server room, quite large, and full of old server towers striping the room like bookshelves. Most of them were dark, no longer functional; others were so much rubble on the floor.

Suddenly I was airborne, and then landing on the ground with surprising gentleness, braced by pressure at my shoulders and hips. I was too startled to speak, but tried to push myself up. A hand landed heavily between my shoulder blades. "Be still," Indigo murmured.

He'd knocked me down, presumably to stop me from being seen by something. From my vantage point on the floor, I could see nothing except broken metal and plastic, illuminated palely by Indigo's collar-light and whatever other light source was flickering so sharply out of sight.

Something hummed. The humming swelled, then ebbed, moving away.

I pushed myself up; this time Indigo let me, though he kept his hand on the back of my neck anyway, uncomfortably close to the implant. If he moved his palm up a little bit, he'd be able to feel it, and then I'd be facing potentially deadly questions. I opened my mouth to say something, but his thumb and forefinger dug hard into my skin.

Not safe, then—not altogether. I swallowed, and followed when he moved, creeping across the debris. Between the piled shelves of servers, I glimpsed a source of brilliant light.

The lights I'd seen, it turned out, were electrical fires. A cloud came between me and the fire and then the fire went out as the Dreamer-bots repaired it. These bots seemed more interested in repairing the overt damage to the ship than investigating us, but there was no telling how long that would last.

Indigo stood up. I followed suit. Upright, we stepped

over the debris-ridden floor, crossing through the narrow alley of partially-destroyed servers. Indigo paused at the end of one. I peered over his shoulder and watched a swarm of Dreamer-bots pass, humming softly, hunting fires in a mechanical library.

When they were past, Indigo stepped so quietly he might have been a breeze drifting over the floor. We were almost at the door when I glanced to my right.

There was an open area on the other side of the room, visible between the bookshelf-like servers. Perhaps there had once been a seating area there, couches, a table— perhaps this room had been a library, of some sort, with all the books made electronic. There was nothing there now except empty space, meticulously tidied of debris by the ship's relentless self-repair. Some of the ship's décor had survived its decay: massive metal statues of men and women were set into alcoves in the wall, looming like watchers. A swarm of Dreamer-bots hummed through the clearing, targeting a fire at the feet of one of the statues, the flashing light of it rendering the figure's mask oddly animate.

And in the midst of all of this, on her knees with one arm swollen and cradled to her chest, was Lieutenant Tamara Gupta.

CHAPTER THIRTY EIGHT: ENEMY OF THE ENEMY

"SEAN," INDIGO SAID, still pronouncing my name the Kystrene way. His hand under my arm pulled, but I dug in my heels. Lantern-Eyes was surrounded by enemies. None of them had noticed her yet, but how long before they did? She didn't seem to see them. Her face was turned my way, barely visible in the uneven light. I tugged my arm out of Indigo's grip, pulled out my flashlight, and flickered it onto her face.

Indigo hissed out his breath next to me, but this room was full of flashing light and the Dreamer-bots didn't pay much attention. As soon as the light fell on Lantern-Eyes' face, I saw why she wasn't moving.

Her face was crawling with Dreamer-bots.

She must have had her eyes screwed shut, but they were swarming over her skin, tiny, so densely packed it looked like her face had become a swarming mask. Her arm broken and blinded, she was trapped, helpless.

For all her knowledge of the ship, for all her careful, precise planning, Tamara Gupta was screwed if something changed in those plans. And she had no back-up to support her in the event of a change, because all her back-up had died on this ship a year ago. Lieutenant Gupta's lack of back-up was going to get her killed, right in front of me, just like it likely would get me and Indigo killed eventually, each separately.

Between the server walls, I watched Lantern-Eyes bend down, unbroken arm extended, sweeping her palm over the floor. Behind her and a little to the right, far outside the reach of her arm, I saw her bloodied club lying in the detritus; beside that, her battered flashlight. She was looking for her light or her weapon: blinded, maimed, and alone, and she was still moving forward with iron determination.

"Sean, we have to leave," Indigo said in my ear.

"What? No," I hissed. I flicked off my light. "We've got to get her out of there."

"She's already dead. If they realize we are here, they will kill us also."

"She's not dead." I shook his arm; he rocked back and forth with the motion, dark brows jolting up in surprise. "She's right there; she's fine. We just have to get her attention."

"How? The soldier—"

"Tamara," I said, and Indigo paused, like he thought I'd said a word in Sister that he was unfamiliar with, and was working to translate it in his head. "Her name's Tamara Gupta."

"Tamara Gupta cannot see." Indigo spoke her name like he was handling a grenade. "If you shout out to her, the computer will hear you."

"Then we go over to her and get her out of there," I said. "You saved me from those things."

"There is no point. If we go over there, the machines will attack us all."

"Then you can fight them off!"

"I am not invulnerable," Indigo said, another dark-water current surfacing, low and harsh. "I can and will be overwhelmed. I can't die yet. I need the Philosopher Stone first."

"So leave," I said. "Go find the Philosopher Stone. Good luck without me."

"I can find it without your information. You've told me it's in a lab."

"But not which lab. Feeling lucky?"

"I prefer a gamble to certain failure," Indigo said.

He was supposed to be partly human, genetically speaking. I thought I'd seen something like humanity in him before. "You fought alongside her before," I said.

"When the alternative was certain death," Indigo said. "If our places were exchanged, she would make the same choice I am making now."

He didn't know that, I wanted to say, but the truth was he did know that, and so did I. I knew, too, that if I died here it would probably screw over Benny, wherever he was, and that whatever Indigo might do with the data would probably screw over every living human in the Republic and the free colonies and all sorts of other distant, intangible possibilities. I looked at the real and tangible Tamara Gupta on her hands and knees in the midst of certain death, shaking with terror, but still determinedly searching for a weapon and a way out.

I said, "So would I."

When I looked at Indigo again he was watching me with an expression I could not name. "I could knock you unconscious and drag you away," he said, with absolutely no sentiment in his voice.

"Please don't," I said. "It's not too late to save her."

He watched me, as impassive as one of the metal statues ringing the blinded Lantern-Eyes like spectators to an execution. Then he sighed. "Step quietly," he bade me, and stalked down the path between the servers, moving towards Tamara. I hurried to follow.

Lantern-Eyes' search for her weapon and flashlight had taken her a little bit away from us. Indigo stopped at the end of the shelves and crouched there. If we kept going forward, we would lose the scant shelter of the shelves, and be out in the open for the computer of the *Nameless* to catch. Dreamer-bots hummed on the other side of the room, busily repairing a server fire that made the whole empty area glow. Lantern-Eyes' good hand, bloody-knuckled, groped along the ground.

She was too far off to reach. I crouched beside Indigo and looked around at the Dreamer-bots, humming busily between the fires and twining around the glinting metal sculptures. Lantern-Eyes was crawling in their direction, still searching for her club. Dreamer-bots swarmed lazily over her face.

I groped around for something to throw. It did not take me long to find a fingernail-sized bit of metal—an old washer, or something. I picked it up and tossed it at her. My aim was perfect: it landed precisely on the curve of her shoulder and bounced off.

Tamara went very still.

I reached for another washer, but Indigo put his hand on my arm. The Dreamer-bots swirling over Tamara's face had been unsettled by the motion, but as I watched, they calmed back down, spreading sickly over Tamara's face, crawling through her long dark hair.

I took careful aim, and threw the second washer.

It struck Tamara in precisely the same place and this time she turned her head around as if to look. The motion nauseated me, because she, of course, could not see— the thick layer of Dreamer-bots climbing over her skin rendered her features unrecognizable; there was no seeing through them. But she turned her face in our direction, broken arm tucked up against her chest, and trembled.

Then she started to shuffle towards us, an awkward, slow, one-handed crawl, as quiet as possible. Even without seeing, she knew she was in enemy territory.

Her aim was slightly off—she would end up not quite at the right spot between the shelves, but a little to the right. When she was near enough I whispered, "Lantern-Eyes!"

She stilled again, though the Dreamer-bots on her face buzzed angrily, a few surfacing from the thick, swarming layer to drift around her skull.

Indigo was very tense beside me. I glanced past Tamara at the other swarms of humming Dreamer-bots. The way the statues stood, firelight glinting, it was very hard not to imagine they were watching us.

"Over here," I whispered again, as quietly as I could make it, and Tamara changed direction slightly, shuffling towards us.

When she was near enough I put a hand on her shoulder, stilling her. She was all bones and muscles so taut they felt like stone beneath the worn fabric of her oversized uniform jacket. She said nothing—could say nothing, beneath the nanomachines covering her mouth—and up close, the sight of the creatures climbing over her skin like tiny insects, obscuring her features, made me sick.

Indigo reached out one hand and laid it over her face. As soon as his skin came near the Dreamer-bots, they reacted—flying off of Tamara's skin to swarm over his, humming excitedly, landing on his hand until they coated his skin as closely as they'd coated hers.

I shrugged my jacket off as quickly and as quietly as I was able, preparing to get rid of the bugs the way we'd done before. Tamara knelt very still, her eyes and mouth tightly shut, even though the Dreamer-bots had left her skin. There were a hundred tiny cuts over her face.

I watched her swallow then crack her eyes open. Then those big jack-o-lantern eyes went wide as she looked at the Indigo Minister, kneeling before her with the Dreamer-bots swarming over his hand.

I swung my jacket over Indigo's hand, trapping the nanomachines; he pulled his hand out as we had done before, and I pressed the jacket to the ground and put my weight on it. Several things snapped and crunched beneath my hand.

The sound of humming that had pervaded the room

abruptly ceased. It was not just the swarm attacking Tamara that went silent—all sound, all movement, in the room went silent.

"Ah, shit," I sighed.

The humming started up again, fierce and loud, a war-cry at static pitch, coming from every direction at once as every Dreamer-bot in the room rushed down upon us.

CHAPTER THIRTY NINE:
IMPROMPTU ELECTRODYNAMICS

THERE AREN'T ANY swarming insects on Kystrom; what wasps and bees exist there had been domesticated into passivity over the years. Beekeepers had to keep their hives under tight guard, otherwise—speaking purely hypothetically, of course—badly behaved teenage boys could walk right up to a hive and come away with a handful of delicious, delicious honeycomb at zero cost. I'd only ever been stung once, but I'd thoroughly deserved it.

I'd never seen insects swarm. But I had, once, stood atop a hill while the weather changed. It was sunny where Brigid and I had stood, but I'd seen a veil of glittering shadow rush across the distant fields: the front of the oncoming storm.

"We need to take cover," Brigid had said to me, because she was always attuned to the changes in the wind. I'd wanted to linger, fascinated by the ominous speed of that grey veil. By the time I agreed to run, it was far too late to escape. The rain fell upon our shoulders like a curtain dropping, driving us towards the ground, engulfing us at once.

Kneeling in the middle of the trashed library with Indigo and Tamara and hearing the humming of the swarms surrounding us felt like standing upon that hill and seeing the rain approach over the fields below. Knowing, deep down, that even with our little bit of warning, there was not enough time to escape before it hit.

Even so, I wasn't just going to stand around and wait.

"Okay, we've got to fight," I said. "I need a big flyswatter, or something."

"We can't fight them," Tamara said. Her voice was hoarse, probably because of all the metal insects that had been trying to crawl down her throat.

"Sure we can; Indigo and I just killed a bunch!"

"There's too many," Tamara said.

Indigo stood up. For one stupid moment I thought he was going to run and leave us to our fates, but instead, he spun on his heel and swept his sword through the base of the nearest set of shelves. And his sword did go through: the metal parted, sizzling, as his blade passed by.

Right, I'd forgotten. Indigo's sword could, if necessary, cut through metal: he'd cut through the outer hull of the *Nameless* twice already. The blade must be more than a simple alloy. It was, in fact, glowing faintly reddish in his hands with heat, a fact I would not have noticed had the *Nameless* not been so damn dark. Glowing blue at his throat and red at his hands, Indigo said, "Grab that shelf."

It was a peculiar sentence to sound so ominous, but I supposed any sentence spoken by a Minister holding a burning sword was liable to sound threatening. "So I can use it as a flyswatter?" The shelf was wide and flat, but it looked a little heavy to swing.

"Just grab it!"

And then Indigo was off, moving like lightning across the floor—not towards the door or any sort of escape, but, oddly, towards the lifelike statues standing in alcoves behind where Tamara had been trapped.

The humming that came from all sides became abruptly louder, as if the Dreamer-bots had reached the edge of the stacks, and there wasn't anything between us and them anymore. I stopped thinking and did as Indigo said, wrenching the shelving unit from its ancient position with a scream of metal.

A crash from behind me, even louder than the removal of the shelf. Indigo had swung his superheated blade through the feet of one of the statues and the statue itself had fallen, smoking, the acrid stench of plastic biting the air. On its side, the statue's oddly animate face seemed to stare at me, as agonized as a theatre mask. With the statue fallen, the alcove behind the statue was exposed— an indent in the wall, enclosed on three sides, and just about big enough for a Minister and two humans.

So Indigo didn't want to fight, either.

Tamara looked a little wild about the eyes, but she strode across the floor towards the alcove where Indigo waited, her broken arm tucked against her chest. She paused only once, stooping down alongside her club and flashlight. I expected her to snag the club, but her bloody knuckles closed around the flashlight.

I was only a step behind, the metal of the shelf shrieking against the floor as I dragged it without a care for caution or stealth. It was discolored by age, but the metal seemed solid, and it was heavy enough. I made the mistake of glancing back, over the shelves I carried, and saw the Dreamer swarm approaching like the line of rain across the hills: glittering and shadowy, massive and all-engulfing, approaching me faster than I could run.

And then Tamara's good hand was yanking me back by my jacket, and Indigo deftly took the shelf from my grip, shifting it so that it completely covered the entrance to the alcove. He lifted his sword and ran the blade over the edges of the metal. It was so narrow in the alcove that I felt the heat of the blade as he reached past me. The metal edges of the bookcase sizzled and melted to the walls of the alcove, and, for the moment, sealed us into an airtight tomb.

My shoulders brushed the walls on either side, and I had Tamara pressed against my spine and Indigo against my chest. The only light source was Indigo's collar-light, but that was more than enough to show how tiny our hiding place was. I tried both to stand very still and to find some more space by shifting, my heart pounding hard against my too-tightly-compressed ribs. We should've just run; that would be better than sealing ourselves up in our own little coffin. I cleared my throat, but my voice came out several pitches too high nonetheless. "Uh, how are we going to get out?"

The deep bluc light from Indigo's collar flickered with invisible motion, and then his sword slammed into the wall near my ear, carving straight through and slicing down. I gasped, overwhelmed by the heat and the stench of burning metal and plastic, and by the time I exhaled the wall behind Tamara and I gave way.

I landed half atop her, half on a metal floor. There was already significantly more space around me than there had been before Indigo had carved a hole in the wall, but I groped around for the flashlight I'd shoved into my pocket and flipped it on to confirm. We'd cut our way back into the hall.

A successful escape. I cleared my throat and said, "I think we could've taken them."

Indigo stepped elegantly out of the alcove on his own, upright and glowing blue. The effect was only a little bit ruined by the exasperated look he cast me.

"We couldn't have taken them," Tamara said. She looked like crap—aside from the broken arm, there was blood trickling down from her hairline—but she was sitting up under her own power, a grim set to her mouth. "There's no beating the Dreamer."

"You saw us crush a handful of bots," I reminded her.

"A *handful*. There are more nanomachines on this ship than you can imagine, and they're self-repairing. The ones you crushed are probably reassembling themselves right now, and manufacturing more to meet their needs. You could fight them, but nothing you could do would stick. You'd be overwhelmed in minutes."

"So we ran," Indigo agreed.

Tamara shook her head. "In another few seconds, they'll eat through the metal."

As if to confirm Lantern-Eyes' ominous prediction, a screeching crack echoed from the barrier Indigo had made of a shelf in the alcove—like metal splinters dragged across metal. I grabbed for Indigo, as if he hadn't heard it, and we all turned to look back inside the alcove just as a tiny, coin-sized hole opened up in the shelf. At first it admitted only the warm glow of the electrical fires beyond. And then a line of Dreamer-bots fed themselves through that hole. So narrow was the hole, so tightly compressed were the nanomachines, that they looked like nothing so much as a ghostly, silver finger sticking itself through the wall.

Indigo shook me off, then reached into the alcove to set his palm over the small opening. His expression twisted, as if with pain. "I need something to close off this opening," he said.

Something to close it off. Okay. He needed a barrier of some kind. I swept my flashlight around the floor, looking desperately for a piece of debris large enough to use.

"Here." Tamara handed Indigo a sheet of metal from inside the wall that he'd cut open. He tore his hand back—I saw red on his palm—and slapped the sheet over the coin-sized hole in the wall, crushing the Dreamer-bots that had already come through. They rained delicately down, glinting silver shards in my flashlight. Indigo ran his heated blade over the edges of his metal patch, melting it into the back of the shelves, and snatched his hand back quickly.

My heart was pounding unsteadily. "God of Blood, don't tell me they actually eat metal," I said. This ship already had people-eating children and spectral, vengeful manikins; not to mention the acid-spitting rocks. That was a full deck of horrors. I didn't need the eye-eating bees to start chowing down on solid metal, too.

For some reason, Tamara was rummaging around inside the wall that Indigo had cut open. "I don't know if they eat it," she told me tersely, "but they can certainly get through."

Indigo was breathing harshly to my right, and leaning against the wall. He looked more exhausted by the past ten minutes than he had during the entirety of our struggle with the manikins. Fear spiked through me. "What's wrong with you?" I asked.

He took a breath. "This sword uses metabolic energy to reach a heated state."

So making the blade hot enough to carve metal was exhausting him? Kind of a design flaw. "Didn't they put that through beta testing?"

"It's meant to be a backup system, but the primary batteries ran out several hours ago."

And there weren't exactly any places to pick up fresh batteries on the *Nameless*. Also, was I imagining it, or was the sound of the buzzing behind the shelf growing louder?

"So we can't fight," I said. "Let's pick up and run!"

"No good." Tamara's voice was muffled, head and shoulders inside the wall. "They'll break through that before we can get more than a few feet away."

"So we put up a stronger barrier first!"

"They won't just stop chasing us!" Tamara emerged from the wall clutching what looked like a pipe and a length of wire. "The bots are in hunting mode. They detected a threat to the ship—us—and they'll chase the threat until it's eliminated."

The humming of the Dreamer-bots on the other side of our barrier seemed louder than it had before, whether because they were chewing their way through the metal, or because of the profound silence that had fallen on our side.

"So what are you saying?" I asked. "Those things are going to follow us until they kill us?"

"Until they kill *something*." Tamara was—incomprehensibly—wrapping the wire around the little pipe or screw or whatever it was. "They're not that sophisticated. They know there was a threat; they know they need to kill it, and they won't stop until they do. They don't remember exactly who or what the threat is."

Indigo said, "So if one of us remains behind, the other two can escape."

"None of us are dying to those things!" I snapped.

An audible crack, and part of the bookshelf split open, admitting a sheet of Dreamer-bots like a slice of light through a gap in a curtain. I scrambled in the wall for another sheet of metal while Indigo swept his sword through the swarm. No effect: they moved around his blade like leaves on a current, and advanced all the faster.

Nothing. There was nothing in the wall. I felt something very light settle against my shoulder. "Indigo—"

"Move," Indigo gritted out, and I flinched back just as he carved through the wall overhead, and a large sheet of metal crashed down where I had been leaning. I grabbed it and, using it as a shield against the Dreamer-bots, shoved it up against the deteriorating metal shelf. Even as I did, I felt more nanomachines crawling on my back, on the shell of my ear. I tried not to shudder or flinch, and I didn't dare to let go of the metal sheet that was the only thing holding back the rest of the storm. Indigo leaned in past me, his face pale and drawn, and sealed this sheet of metal the way he'd sealed the others; I fell back onto the hallway floor and grabbed at my collar and head. Indigo's fingers were narrow in my hair, drawing the machines away; he threw them onto the floor and stomped on them before they could rise. I knelt, panting, trying to decide if the creeping feeling on my spine was a Dreamer-bot or my own trembling.

Indigo said, sounding very calm, "If not one of us, then we need to find one of those creatures—manikins—and seal it up with the nanomachines."

Tamara made a thoughtful noise. "Could work," she said, speaking around the now wire-wrapped pipe she'd pulled from the wall, and disassembling her own flashlight one-handed.

"Or we could find a solution that *doesn't* involve sacrificing another living creature!" I said, just as the Dreamer-bots broke through the barrier at the bottom left corner.

Indigo carved off a piece of the wall overhead immediately, and I slapped it over the weak spot, my heart pounding. No sooner had he sealed it than our first patch broke, the Dreamer-bots drifting in lazily, like the first tendrils of smoke preceding a house fire. We sealed that, too, but it didn't matter, because the shelf split open down the center.

I could swear that, right after the shelf split open, in the instant before the Dreamer swarm burst through, everything was frozen. The cloud of Dreamer-bots glittered and revolved, in some subtle and incomprehensible way; I could not have traced the paths it made. The longer I looked at the movement of the glimmering nanomachines, the more convinced I became that the paths were untraceable—and that through the million glittering eyes of the nanomachines, a single eye, a single mind, alien and incomprehensible, watched.

The manikins hated me, but the Dreamer felt nothing for me at all.

And then the swarm of nanomachines rushed down upon us.

Tamara had been right. I knew it as soon as they descended. We had no chance of fighting them: there were simply too many. I swung my arms, but they evaded my clumsy swings as deftly as they'd dodged the blows of Indigo's sword. No matter how I twisted or writhed, I could not stop them from settling on me. They were all so light individually, so weighty all at once; I felt little feet pricking their way across my face. Would it hurt when they dug through my skin, through my eardrum, down my throat and past the membrane of my eyes? They prickled against my skin, but I could only imagine how much more they would hurt when they finally crawled and ate and dug their way inside me—

And then they all fell off me like dust. I blinked open my eyes and found the floor around us was covered in a glittering snow of knocked-out nanomachines. Indigo had reached out one arm over my shoulders, for all the good that had done; he blinked, looking just as surprised as me.

In the midst of the fallen nanomachines, Tamara Gupta crouched and panted, a pile of wires and metal on the floor in front of her. It reminded me of the messy circuit projects Brigid had liked to make.

"What's that?" I asked, swallowing sour fear around an unwanted spike of aching grief.

"EMP device," Tamara said.

She'd made an electromagnetic pulse weapon out of scrap metal and a flashlight. That was... well, unreasonably impressive, except that I kind of wanted to kill her. "Why didn't you say so before?" I demanded.

"It wasn't done and I needed to focus. This will only knock them out for a moment. Get up and follow me if you want to stay alive."

She got up, leaving her disassembled flashlight on the floor, her broken arm grimly tucked into her shirt. Indigo and I hurried down the hallway after Tamara while she ran, lightless, with the certainty of one who knew these passages like the back of her hand. We ran through hallways, taking quick turns, until finally she led us into an empty room, where she pulled a grate off the wall overhead and exposed a very narrow ventilation shaft.

"Give me a boost," she said.

"You want to go in there?" I asked, horrified. The shaft was too narrow for hands-and-knees; it was another belly crawl.

"Yes, and I can't get up there one-handed. *Hurry*, or we're all dead!"

Indigo had shut the door behind us, for whatever good that would do. I knelt beside the wall and offered Tamara a stirrup of my hands, hoisting her up into the ventilation shaft like an acrobat. Her heels disappeared seconds later.

Was I imagining the distant sound of buzzing? Maybe I was, maybe I wasn't. That ventilation shaft looked incredibly narrow—I'd already been in enough tiny places in this ship; twenty minutes ago, even, I'd been in that little alcove. "Maybe I should take my chances out here," I said. "I don't think—"

Tamara Gupta's hand emerged from the wall like a horror movie and clamped down on my jacket like she intended to pull me in there with her, willing or not. I grabbed the ledge with both hands and pulled myself up and in. I was stuck as soon as I got into the vent, absolutely stuck, head and shoulders in a tiny space and the rest of me exposed and helpless for the Dreamer-bots to land on and burrow into my skin with their tiny, metal-eating mouths. Tamara pulled relentlessly on my shoulder, but I was stuck—

The ground struck me hard and unexpected. I pulled my legs out from the vent to curl up on the ground, gasping for breath in this new, open space.

I could see in here somehow. On the floor beneath me were large flat pieces of metal like the blades of some giant fan. This had been some sort of nexus for the airflow, when the ship had been perfectly functional. Emergency lighting strips were set into the wall at even intervals, and it was that light I could see by, a faintly bluish white that reminded me of Indigo—who at that very moment hurtled through the narrow vent, landing hard next to me, his blade still drawn.

I was sure of it now: in the distance, echoing through

the empty halls that separated us, I heard the Dreamer humming.

My heartbeat jolted in my chest. "We're safe in here now, right?" I said. "We can't fight them, we can't run from them, but this is a good place to hide? They can't find us?"

"They can find us," Tamara said grimly. "But there's a manikin nest not far from here. We have to hope that they find the nest first."

"That's your grand plan? Maybe sacrifice a manikin?"

Tamara flipped down a cover over the open vent, which she latched into place over the opening, sealing it shut. "I told you. There's no beating the Dreamer. All you can do is hope they kill someone else instead. Now shut up, or they'll find us."

Then she raised the index finger of her good hand to her lips, forbidding as a librarian.

Indigo, braced on his elbows, held his breath. I wrapped my clammy hands around my knees. Muffled through the wall, I heard the quiet, ominous hum of the swarm.

The buzzing grew near by slow and terrible degrees. I heard the sound grow louder. I heard the door that Indigo had shut become unlatched. I heard the sound of the swarm filling the room just beyond Tamara's hideout, humming as deliberate and unstoppable as the rain.

Tamara pressed her back to the wall, blood trickling down her cheek, a grim and ready set to her mouth despite the broken arm tucked into her shirt. Indigo's chest was still—Ministers, I remembered, could last without air longer than humans. He gazed down his own body at the vent cover, a narrow dark stare that promised whatever came through the passage would have to contend with him.

The humming sound approached, louder and louder, like static swelling.

I heard a sound like raindrops on glass as first one, and then another, of the nanomachines landed against the sheet of metal concealing the entrance to our vent.

CHAPTER FORTY:
BABEL

THE HUMMING CONTINUED for a long time outside the entrance to Tamara's hideaway. At some point after the end of the first hour, the unremitting terror remitted, transitioning into a weary dullness. Indigo sat facing the covered opening with his sword in his lap. Tamara sat in mirror of him beside the covered opening. She'd lost her club back in the server room, but she had yet another improbably large knife, which she'd also drawn from someplace unseen on her person.

I didn't like waiting. I did like to cut waiting short by doing immediately whatever it was I was waiting to do, whether friends, family, and strangers liked it or not; barring that, it was a solid time for a nap. If those things somehow managed to figure out where we were hiding, it might even be therapeutic for Lantern-Eyes to swing that knife around.

In short order, I fell asleep.

* . * . *

I DREAMT I was back on Kystrom. That by itself was not unusual; I often dreamt I was on Kystrom. But though this place had the clarity of a memory, I could not recall when I had been here before. It was a field in the early spring. It was warm out, but there was still snow mixed in with the grass, melting in the sun.

Brigid, I remembered suddenly. I'd had a fight with Brigid—a bad one. I'd imagined she would never speak to me again. Stupid of me to think that. I couldn't even remember anymore what we'd fought about. I'd been standing out in this field, alone and self-pitying, and Brigid had come to find me to apologize.

I was in the field now, but my best friend and sister wasn't here with me.

"The Philosopher Stone," someone said.

I turned in the field. Mara Zhu was standing uphill, staring over my head. She said something in another language, too fast for my sleeping brain to understand, but I knew it was Ameng.

"Slow down," I told her, because the only words I could recognize with her talking at that speed were *death* and *sorry*.

"What the hell is she saying?" a more familiar voice asked from nearby. Lantern-Eyes was sitting in the grass a few feet away. She looked even sorrier in the sunlight than she did in the dark; pared down to bone, no more flesh to wound. Five hundred pounds of stress and anger packed into a hundred-pound bag.

"I can't tell, she's talking too fast," I explained.

Tamara Gupta looked at me oddly. "What?"

I always dreamt in Kystrene. It seemed in the dream I'd spoken in Kystrene as well. Lieutenant Gupta, of course, spoke Sister. "I can't translate it," I said, trying for Sister, but somehow all I could get out of my mouth was Kystrene.

"I can't understand you," Tamara said.

Light flashed over my shoulder, a familiar dark blue. Indigo stood downhill of me, staring over me at Mara Zhu. She babbled on in Ameng, something pleading, and Indigo flashed light at her urgently, quickly.

"Can you understand her?" I asked Indigo, who flashed *no* at me.

"What are you telling her?" I asked, but he only flashed blue light at me, and the grammar was too complex for me to understand.

There were too many languages being spoken. My brain was struggling to translate them all, even in the dream, and the effort was bringing me closer to waking.

"You can understand me, though," I said to Indigo, and wondered why a Minister would speak Kystrene.

"I can't tell what you're saying," Tamara Gupta complained.

"Typical Republican," said a familiar voice, in merciful Kystrene. "Doesn't bother to learn any other languages."

Benny stood a little distant from the rest, opposite Tamara.

"Oh, thank God," I said when I saw him. "Someone to talk to."

He shook his head, resentful. "You don't understand at all."

Mara Zhu was suddenly speaking louder than the rest. She had something important to say. Lantern-Eyes fell silent; Indigo's light went dark. When I looked for Benny, he was gone. Mara Zhu's voice got louder and louder, the Ameng shouted, but it was a dream, the words weren't real words, but I struggled to translate them anyway, and the struggle of strange phonemes and foreign syntax drove me awake.

*   *   *

I WOKE WITH a jolt in blue-lit dark. My shoulders ached, my neck stiff. There was no longer a humming sound coming from the other side of the vent door. I could no longer hear any buzzing noises at all, in fact.

A pang of pity struck me. Unable to find us, the Dreamer-bots, it seemed, had come across a different victim. Whether that had been a manikin, or a Child, or something else I hadn't yet seen, I would never know.

Tamara and Indigo sat exactly where they had been when last I saw them, their weapons in their laps. Neither of them was dead. Some sort of miracle, I thought, sleep-fuzzy.

Tamara said, "I can't believe you slept through that."

She would be too high-strung to sleep. "I knew you'd protect me," I said.

Lantern-Eyes' one functional hand had gone white around the hilt of her knife. Indigo had his impassive expression back in place but not quite concealing the currents I'd learned how to recognize in his dark-water eyes.

No one was moving, no one attacking. No one was speaking.

Well. It wasn't like the imp was going to let me stay silent for long.

I cleared my throat. "Maybe," I said, "the three of us could come to an arrangement."

CHAPTER FORTY ONE: THREE STRANGERS AND A DESPERATE OFFER

EIGHT YEARS AGO, Benny and I had met on the streets of a dying city. We'd been relative strangers, but we'd fought to survive and escape together. And after we'd escaped, we relative strangers had made each other a promise—a promise to keep each other safe. And that promise had held through all these years.

I didn't expect to have what I had with Benny with Lantern-Eyes and Indigo. The idea was absurd. Benny was basically family to me; we had Kystrom in common, we had *Itaka* in common. We'd known the same people in our childhood, spoke the same language in the same way. That kind of shared experience was something a Republican lieutenant and a Minister could never equal. They could never even come *close*. Lantern-Eyes, Indigo, and I would always be enemies, unlike me and Benny. But my arrangement with Benny, way back when, had proven one thing: when you're alone in the middle of danger, you don't need to know each other, or even like each other, to make an effective alliance.

Lantern-Eyes gave me a look that was part irritation, part weariness, and all hard determination. "What do you expect from this, Sean? You know he and I can't let the other walk away."

The sweep of her good hand marked out Indigo where he sat beneath a strip of emergency lighting, his sword on the ground at his side.

"Whether we like it or not, we have a truce in this room." Indigo spoke with the authority of a man who knew that, should the discussion go south, he was the only person with a proper weapon. "I'm willing to let the truce last long enough to hear the terms of Mr. Wren's arrangement."

So I was back to Mr. Wren now.

"And if I'm not willing?" Tamara said, and by the time I'd turned away from Indigo, she had drawn her gun.

The gun. I'd forgotten about Tamara's one-bullet gun.

She trained that gun on Indigo, one-handed, steady as a rock. Indigo sat against the wall, no discernable tension in his frame, four feet away from a bullet in the heart.

The way they stared at each other suggested they'd briefly forgotten I existed. I tensed, shifted onto my heels. Like I could do anything; what, jump in front of the bullet? "Hey, guys," I said, and laughed a little, nerves jangling. "We don't need—"

"Could you really outrun my bullet?" Tamara asked.

Curiosity shaded her tone, like color revealed by the fading of shadow. I bit the inside of my cheek against the imp that urged me to speak.

"I have no need to outrun a bullet that won't be fired," Indigo said.

For four or five more beats of my rapid heart, Tamara stared at him, jack-o-lantern eyes intent; then she snorted and lowered her gun.

"All right, all right," I said; the words leapt from me, driven by anxiety demons. "Can you two stop trying to kill each other and just talk for like five minutes, please?"

"Convince me," Lantern-Eyes said, but she was tucking her gun back into her holster.

Annoyance hit me like a surge. "Convince you? Come on," I said. "If you didn't already know what I'm about to suggest, you wouldn't have let me start talking. We're all fucked. You," I gestured at Tamara, unrelentingly determined and absolutely unbreakable in her oversized uniform jacket, broken arm notwithstanding, "have been here for years, and you can't find the Philosopher Stone—and even if you did, you wouldn't be able to fight those things off long enough to get to it. You," I gestured to Indigo, still and calm in the same way as thunderclouds at night that have yet to break, "don't know where the Philosopher Stone is, or how to get there, and if you keep wandering around aimlessly those things are going to tear you apart. That's assuming," I added, to them both, "that the sun doesn't go and do us all in before any of us can get the Philosopher Stone."

"And you?" Tamara said.

"And me, I'd be dead in five minutes without one of you to look out for me," I said. "But I know where the

Philosopher Stone is."

"*Fucker*," Tamara said, not quite under her breath.

"I can find the Stone without either of you," Indigo said.

"No, you can't," I said. "My friends and your people are somewhere on this ship, but we don't know where they are or if they're alive. Tamara, your people won't arrive for a couple of days, if they can even find you after they do. We're all alone," I said, "and we're all fucked."

Tamara shrugged her broken arm more firmly against her chest. "Even if I agree with this picture you're drawing for us, you're forgetting one important thing."

"What thing?"

"I'd have to rely on you."

"You already have," I said.

"When I had no other choice," Tamara said. "When he had no other choice. Look at the Minister, Sean. You, *Indigo*—do you trust us?"

I needed no dictionary, no language at all, to understand the meaning of his expression.

"It doesn't matter whether we trust each other," I said. "This is the only way we're going to get out of here alive."

"Trust matters," Tamara said. "Trust is the only thing that matters, and the only person I trust to keep me alive on this ship is me. I've been here for five years to complete a mission. I'm not going to fail it in the last five days."

"If you're alone, you've already failed," I said. "Indigo, help me out."

"My purpose is too important to put in the hands of humans," Indigo said calmly, "especially humans with a vested interest in my failure."

"So you're just gonna let the manikins cut you to pieces, and fail alone? Didn't you tell me you'd prefer to gamble?"

I made myself stop, take in a deep, deep breath. I'd almost been shouting. I didn't like getting worked up; life was a lot nicer without shouting. Besides that, if I started shouting, something with teeth and claws and a murderous disposition might hear me.

"I'm not suggesting this out of some sort of grand, cross-species altruistic peace project," I said, when I was sure I could speak levelly again. "I've got a vested interest in staying alive. And I need that data as much as either of you. But none of us will reach it unless all of us work together."

Tamara sighed. "Say I agree to this arrangement. Say it works out without one of us killing the other two, and we make it across the ship before the sun blows. Eventually we will reach the Philosopher Stone. What happens to our arrangement then?"

"We'll have to decide when we get there," I said, and watched her grimace. She liked her plans and strategies, Lantern-Eyes did. "The point is we'll never get there unless we work together first. Or we can try to kill each other in this room here and now, and whoever survives dies a day or two later, and nobody gets the Philosopher Stone. What do you say?"

Silence fell in the old ventilation shaft. Tamara watched Indigo, her injured arm tucked to her chest and her uninjured hand resting near the holster of her one-bullet gun. Indigo sat against the wall with blood drying on his cheek and his sword at his side, looking at no one in particular. I started to worry that the two of them would call my bluff and take me up on the offer of a three-way melee to the death here in this tiny room.

Then Indigo raised his head, looked at Tamara, and then at me. I couldn't name the expression on his face, but it made me uncomfortable.

"I agree," Indigo said.

"I agree," Tamara said, immediately.

The rapidity and ease of her response jolted my attention from the strange sad way Indigo watched me. "I had to drag you kicking and screaming through that conversation, but that's it, you agree, just like that?"

"I wasn't the one you had to convince," Tamara said ominously. Then she ruined the sobering effect by adding, snippily, "Would you prefer if I didn't agree? And you didn't say yet, Sean. Do you agree to your own arrangement?"

"Wholeheartedly," I said.

An odd little smile found a bitter place on her mouth. I saw her glance up and aside, at Indigo. Indigo, who had pulled his sword into his lap and was wiping blood off it with his palm, smooth strokes showing off the blade's sharp edge.

Once we reached the Philosopher Stone, I knew, the two of them would try to kill each other. Indigo had the physical advantage: stronger, faster, and more experienced. But Lantern-Eyes knew the terrain, and I had no doubt that even as the three of us sat there in that old ventilation shaft, her analytical mind was putting together a plan. I didn't know who would win, but I knew they would try to kill each other and pay no mind to unthreatening little me.

Whoever won, I'd trade my translation services for my life. And they'd take me up on it, because they'd have no other choice. The Philosopher Stone data would be written in Ameng, and I was the only person on this ship who could read Ameng.

For the very same reason, no one but me would be able to tell if the wrong data got sent out—if, for instance, the unthreatening and kindhearted translator made a private copy of the correct data for his own use, to save his life and his friend's, and gave his captor something that looked correct, but wasn't really.

I'd made a promise, and I would keep my promise. Like with Benny. But after we reached the Stone, our truce would fall apart. And no matter who survived, the only person on this ship who would walk away with a copy of the Philosopher Stone data was me.

CHAPTER FORTY TWO:
ANOTHER LENGTHY DÉTENTE WITH
SOME STUBBORN ASSHOLES

"I NEED YOU to confirm something about the location of the data," Lantern-Eyes said.

"Oh." Perhaps I'd been too optimistic about this arrangement. Or her level of intelligence. "See, if I tell you that, then I lose my leverage, and—"

"I understand how this arrangement works," Tamara said, with very forced politeness. "But if I'm going to guide you to the Philosopher Stone, I need to know that I'm leading you to the right general area. I'm guessing that the Philosopher Stone is in one of the odd-numbered labs."

Lab 17, in fact. "Good guess," I said.

Tamara grimaced, whether at my answer or at the way her broken arm jostled as she shifted her weight. "We will have to go through the engine, then."

"Explain." Indigo set his knife aside.

"Have you still got that pathetic water bottle?" Tamara asked me.

"Do you mean the innovative creation of a man in peril, valiantly making do with limited resources? No, I lost it," I said. "Why?"

"Then have you got your notebook and pen?"

"In a useless, waterlogged form."

"Tell me you still have my tablet."

"That I've got." I pulled it out of my jacket pocket and passed it over to her. She took it one-handed, careful with her injured arm. "Can we, I don't know, do something about your arm?"

"If you still had your dented tin, I was going to shape it into a cast," Tamara said. "I'll find some old strips of metal and splint it before we leave."

"There's no need." Indigo shifted onto his knees, leaving his sword on the floor. He pulled something out of the pockets strapped to his hips—the portable medical device he'd used to save me from radiation burns, and to close up the claw wounds on his hand.

"Isn't that just for surface wounds?" I asked.

Indigo pressed some buttons on the screen, and from the nozzle a long, thick needle slowly extended. "It does many things."

"I'll splint it, thanks," Lantern-Eyes said.

"It takes six to eight weeks on a human to heal a broken bone," Indigo said. "It will take two hours before your arm is at its prior strength, using this device. Would you like a working arm, Lieutenant Gupta?"

Tamara chewed her cracked bottom lip. Then she said, "Let me see it."

Indigo leaned forward, the medical device extended out,

needle facing him. Tamara reached out and grabbed it by the other end, avoiding his hand. She set it in her lap and examined it for a minute with an expression that suggested she was getting a lot more out of her examination of the alien device than I'd gotten out of my brief glance.

"Do you know what you're looking at?" I asked her.

"Some of this is strange—it's set to Minister baselines, not human?"

Indigo did not reply. Tamara cradled the device in her good hand and looked down on it like a poor man handed a palmful of gold.

Indigo said, "It will work on a human bone."

"It's very impressive," Tamara said, and offered it back to Indigo. I wondered if I were imagining the reluctance in her expression. "Yes, Minister. I would like a usable arm."

Indigo took the medical device back. "Sean," he said, and I saw Tamara's brows lift at the casual address, "I will need you to hold her arm in place after I set the bone."

Tamara braced her arm with one hand and held it out to Indigo. He came forward and slid the fabric of her overlarge uniform jacket up, exposing her forearm. She watched his hands on her arm, not his face. I shifted closer until I was at Tamara's other side, knees digging into her hip, and smiled reassuringly at her.

Some emotion disturbed the rigidity of her expression, like a stone thrown into water, and before I could find out whether she would face me with dislike or welcome, Indigo moved the bones of her arm sharply back into position.

"Ow, fuck," Tamara said through her teeth, impassiveness gone.

"Sean, put one hand here, and the other hand here," Indigo said. "Make sure not to move your hands or her arm."

I did as he said, leaning over Tamara to hold her arm steady in front of Indigo. I could feel her slightly rapid breaths against the side of my neck. Indigo reached down and picked up the medical device with the huge needle.

"You probably don't want to look for this part," I told Tamara.

"Why wouldn't I want to look?"

"Because I don't want to look." The needle was significantly wider and longer than anything I willingly stuck into my arm.

"At what, the big needle he's about to stick into my bone? You didn't see this comi—ow, FUCK."

Indigo, one hand holding the medical device steady with the needle jammed deeply into Tamara's forearm, tapped a few keys on the screen. "Wait," he told us, "and don't move," and he reached into the same pocket and pulled out a small square of gauze. Red was trickling over the curve of Tamara's arm from around the needle, and he dabbed at it with the gauze, staining a quick bright red.

Tamara breathed through her teeth into my ear for another minute, until Indigo set the gauze aside and carefully pulled the device out of Tamara's arm. The needle was bloody all the way down.

"Keep that arm still for about fifteen minutes, and use it lightly for the next two hours," Indigo said, cleaning the blood off the needle with the same indifference as he'd cleaned blood off his sword. "After that, you should be fine."

Tamara was still breathing unsteadily as I set her arm down in her lap and leaned away. "I'd love a closer look at that machine," she said to Indigo.

Indigo retracted the now-clean needle. "No."

"Aren't you going to fix your hands?" I asked him. Indigo was putting the device back in his pocket, but he still had cuts on his palms.

"The device has supplies for only a few more injuries," Indigo said. "Fewer than that, if the injury is severe. My hand does not need fixing. Explain your plan to go through the engine, lieutenant."

Tamara nodded. She grabbed for her tablet, so I passed it over. Cradling it in her lap alongside her injured arm, she tapped a few screens and then began to draw. "Here," she said. "This is the ship."

She'd drawn a shape like a wagon-wheel, immediately recognizable as the *Nameless*. It was even a little lopsided on one side, like the *Nameless*. I couldn't tell whether that was intentional, or Lantern-Eyes was a bad artist.

"The airlock where you both landed is here." Tamara marked an X on the outer part of the ship, which sort of answered my question about whether she was a good artist or not. "You wandered around, blew out the hull, ran from species 019, et cetera," she drew a squiggly, tortured line in the same general area of the ship, zigging and zagging and looping in on itself, "and ended up here."

She terminated the path in another little X, depressingly

close to the first X.

"We did all right," I said.

"The even-numbered labs are here," she said, and circled an area that we had already passed through, in the midst of all that squiggly back and forth. "The odd-numbered labs are here."

She moved her finger across the ship, on the opposite side of the wheel, far, far away from our current X, and drew another circle, bigger than the first. Right: she'd said she and her crew hadn't fully explored that section of the ship.

"Mara Zhu's office is over here," she added, as an aside, and drew another little circle with MA inscribed about halfway between our landing point and the odd-numbered labs.

"This ship is huge," Tamara said. "You know how far you've travelled these past few days, and you haven't gotten out of the same quadrant. You were doubling back a lot, but still. We can travel through the ship the way it was built to be traveled, along the wheel," and she drew a dotted line following the curve of the wheel around to the opposite side, "but that will be slow, long, and dangerous. If species 019 or the Dreamer don't kill us, the supernova probably will."

Indigo said, "Why do you call the computer the Dreamer?"

"It's an Autorepair AI. Deep learning. You know, dream-logic."

"Obsolete technology," Indigo observed.

"It functions," Tamara said, but there was a darkness

to her tone. "It's repairing what it can, but it's been a thousand years. It's running out of resources and its idea of what needs fixing can be a little irrational. Mostly, it leaves everyone alone, unless it decides that they threaten the ship."

I remembered miniscule buzzing crawling things with razor edges, trying to crawl into my eyes, the seam of my shut mouth. "The Dreamer didn't leave *us* alone. Does it know we're not supposed to be here?"

"I believe that the Dreamer's code was altered to identify humans as a threat to the ship."

My heartbeat faltered. *The others won't be able to get away with the data,* Mara Zhu had said. *I made sure of that.*

But, "Wait, they attack Indigo, too," I said. "They're really interested in Indigo. They attacked him like you and me, they just took longer about it."

Indigo said nothing beside me. Impossible to tell from his expression if he cared at all about the answer.

"I think they don't know what to make of him," Tamara said, with a brief glance Indigo's way. "He's not a human, but he's not a maniki... *species 019,* either. Maybe they decided he was close enough to human."

"Their method of killing their victims is unusual," Indigo said calmly, as if Tamara had not just called him *close enough to human.* "Is their intention to climb through the orifices to gain access to the inner organs?"

That was wonderfully revolting. "Burrow their way inside?" I said.

"I don't know exactly how they kill," Tamara said.

"I couldn't get close enough to any of their victims to examine them as it happened, not without becoming infected myself. But my observations suggest that they're looking for access to the brain, and only the brain. Once enough of the nanomachines have gained access to the skull, the victim stops struggling. Comatose, or simply paralyzed. The remaining nanomachines remain perched on the body, guarding it, maybe. Periodically one or two of them will join the others inside the victim's skull, usually through the eyes, sometimes through the ears. The victim lies unmoving for a period of time between thirty minutes to twelve hours. Then they begin seizing. After death, the nanomachines leave the corpse. Post-mortem examination suggests that the brain has been burrowed through and partially liquified. Currently there are no theories as to what determines the length of time the victim will spend dying."

She sounded clinical, as cool and impenetrable as the metal around us, but the sparse horror of her report carried through. How many of your team did you watch die that way, I wanted to ask, but even my imp right now was silent.

I cleared my throat to break the oppressive silence. "Exactly how many different dangerous species are present on this ship?"

"There are four to really look out for. Species 019, the ones you call the manikins, are the worst—fast, smart, and deadly. Then there's species 048, the ones who look like... like children. There's the Dreamer, which controls the repair bots. Species 082 is the least common one—the

Dreamer's trying to wipe it out. It's a mutated form of coral, as near as my team and I could tell."

The mutated coral must be that rock thing that spat acid at us. The one with bones sticking out of it. I really hoped that there were bones in it because the coral was eating them, and not because the scientists had, like, fused their own DNA with coral in a terrible bid for immortality. Honestly, with this ship, it could have gone either way.

"So you intend to go through the center of the ship to avoid as many of these creatures as possible," Indigo said.

Tamara nodded, dark hair swinging. "This," she tapped the center of the wagon-wheel, where the spokes all intersected, "is the main engine. It doesn't work anymore. The Dreamer AI has been keeping the rotational engines functional over the centuries, which is why the wheel is still turning and we still have gravity. But someone broke the propulsive engine a thousand years ago, and the autorepair can't or won't fix it. That's why the ship is stranded. There are access tunnels in the spokes that are still passable, and since the engine isn't on, we shouldn't have any problem going through. It's a faster route, and there are fewer creatures in the spokes."

"If there is an obstruction in the spoke we will have no way of going around," Indigo said. "We would have to backtrack, and potentially lose a day or days of travel."

Tamara sat back. "Who's new here, and who has survived here alone for half a decade? This is the only way we can get to the labs in time, and alive. If there's an obstruction, we can use your sword to cut through. Unless you'd rather let species 019 tear you apart out here alone while Sean and I go through the center."

Indigo studied the hand-drawn map. "I trust your expertise in this matter, lieutenant," he said, and then I would swear I saw something like spite in his expression as he added, "And I would prefer not to get torn apart by *manikins*."

"Okay, where to, then?" I asked loudly, interrupting the stare-down.

Tamara set the tablet back down then, with a sigh, handed it back to me. "Luckily, it's not too far from here. What kind of supplies do the two of you have?"

"A few packages of dehydrated food, half a flask of water, a medical scanner, my sword, and a few more hull seals depending on size," Indigo said.

Tamara looked at me.

"Uh, my pen," I said, "my notebook, the flashlight, the tablet, and your knife. Oh! And my wits."

"Really?" said Lantern-Eyes.

"We got blown through the hull," I felt compelled to point out.

She was levering herself to her feet, still favoring her injured arm, but not so much as before. "Follow me," she said, resigned. "Let's get some supplies."

* * *

LIEUTENANT GUPTA'S NEAREST supply cache was behind four different barriers, each sealed in a different, creative way. I watched her untie the cords attaching a large sheet of corroded plastic to the wall, revealing the final door, which had two different deadbolts in it.

"Do you think it's secure?" I asked, while Tamara slid the stiff bolts open.

"Watch the hall, Sean." She shoved the door open—it slid into the wall, like most of the doors on the *Nameless*, but the door was so old and stiff it barely opened wide enough for her to sidle through.

"Indigo's already watching it," I reminded her. Indigo stood a few feet away, gazing back the way we had come.

"Sean." Tamara's face reappeared at the crack between door and wall. "I want you to look in the other direction from Indigo. Count to ten in your head, then look away. After another count of ten, look back. Do that four times."

Intrigued, I glanced in the other direction down the hall. My flashlight showed nothing but the gaping mouths of old doorways.

"Why?" I asked, once I had reached my count of ten. "Does the counting mean something?"

I heard her rustling and moving around out of sight behind the door. "It means that if you don't notice something the first three times," Tamara said, "you'll notice it the fourth. Take this. Keep counting."

She passed me a ragged bag through the crack in the door. It had the Republican military insignia on it, but where the owner's surname should have been embroidered, the fabric had been cut out. The cut was very neat and precise, even though I knew Tamara must have done it with a knife.

Tamara wove her way out, two more bags on her arms. She clicked her tongue to get Indigo's attention and he came towards us without any sign that he resented being called like a dog.

"Here," Tamara said, holding out a bag to Indigo at the absolute extremum of her reach. "I had enough trouble getting supplies on this ship in the first place, you'd better not lose them."

I poked through the bag she'd given me. Everything had been packed together very tightly for maximum compression. Inside I found the same kind of ration packets I'd stolen from her before, alongside bottles of water, a box of matches, another flashlight, rope, and a knife.

"Where's the salt and pepper shakers?" I asked Tamara.

"What?"

"Well, you've got everything else in here," I said.

"If only. I'd kill a man for a packet of salt."

"Just for salt? What would you do for some sugar?"

"You don't want to know," Tamara said.

I flicked on the flashlight she'd given me. It wasn't as bright as the one I'd taken from Indigo, but it worked. I held out Indigo's flashlight to him.

He shook his head. "Keep it," he said, and to Tamara, "How many of these caches do you have in the ship?"

"Some twenty, twenty-five. My team left caches throughout the ship," Tamara explained. She'd zipped open her own bag of supplies, checking over the contents. She probably had some strict system for checking that, too, like maybe she had to count all the water bottles three times. It didn't escape my notice that she'd acquired a new club to beat up monsters with, too. I wondered if she'd restocked the hidden caches of huge knives about her person. "After it was only me left, I tried to survive on what I could steal from the farmlands so I had these for emergency."

"That was wise," Indigo said, and it might have been a compliment, but for the absolute neutrality of his tone.

"Done," Tamara said, and swung her bag up over her shoulder. "Now, both of you, follow me."

She led us to a door, not far from her supply cache. It was a fairly large door, and heavily rusted. It groaned and complained when Lantern-Eyes tried to haul it open, and only really came free when I got my hands in next to her and added my weight to hers.

As soon as it had opened, Lantern-Eyes stepped through, peering up towards the ceiling.

"Here we are, gentlemen," she said, her voice echoing. "The passage to the far side."

I looked past Tamara and my jaw dropped.

The *Nameless* was a massive ship. I'd known that from the start—hell, I had been the one to fly the *Viper* to the *Nameless* to begin with. I had a very clear understanding of the size of this ship.

It was one thing, though, to see a ship the size of some moons through the glass of the *Viper*'s front windows. And it was another thing entirely to see the size of the ship as a small, squishy human, standing small and exposed beneath a space so massive it constricted my lungs, made my heart pound harder with awe and wonder.

The strut was perfectly straight, piercing directly through to the other side of the ship. It was so tall that I could not see the end of it, the staircase spiraling upward vanishing into a single point in the hazy diffusion of my flashlight's beam. People had built this monster of a ship, had constructed something so vast and incredible it rivaled planets, something so strong and wonderful it would only be destroyed not by age and decay, but by the nearby supernova. It was awe-inspiring. It was unbelievable. It was *immortal*.

We had a lot of climbing ahead of us.

CHAPTER FORTY THREE:
THE WORST CAMPING TRIP OF MY LIFE

THE JOURNEY UPWARD started out all right. The way up was a mix of mesh stairs and narrow ladders, platforms and levels and layers, spiraling up.

Oh, no, sorry. What I should have said was that the journey upward *would* have started out all right, if not for the Children.

Apparently, we were not the only creatures on the *Nameless* to have realized that the central struts were a faster way of crossing the ship, and a relative safe haven from the more dangerous creatures like the manikins. I wasn't positive I was seeing the Children at first—the walls of the strut were heavily reinforced, but the layers of reinforcement had decayed over the millennium; there were alcoves and holes in the walls around us from which little faces could peep, black eyes shining like ink.

It was only when Indigo said, "Should we do anything about them, lieutenant?" that my ability to pretend I hadn't seen tiny fingers poking out between pipes was totally destroyed.

Tamara's shoulders were high beneath the stiff shoulders of her uniform jacket, tense. "Not yet," she said. "There's too few of them; they shouldn't attack."

I didn't like that verb, *shouldn't*. It was a particular verb tense in Sister that implied *they very well might*. "You told me they were scavengers."

"And vultures will eat live meat, if there's no dead around. Nothing on this ship is harmless."

"Precisely how dangerous are they?" Indigo inquired. He might have been asking about the price of a glass of wine he wasn't sure he'd like. Over his shoulder, I saw a small shape curled up in an alcove in the wall, gumming its teeth on the metal edges, its attention fixed on the back of Indigo's neck.

"They fight like manikins, teeth and nail. They're not as strong, or as fast, or as smart, and they don't have any... weapons, like the manikins do." Tamara flexed her hand like she could feel the makeshift brass knuckles on her own skin. "I don't know if they're smart enough to use tools at all. But they have a bite like you wouldn't believe. They're too skittish to attack on their own, so they'll only attack in crowds, but when they do they mob their victims. Like rats. Because they're skittish they'll back off if you scare them enough, but in groups, they're bold. Trust me... if they attack, don't hesitate. No matter what they look like."

A little face looked up at me from the lower platform of the spiraling mesh steps, full baby cheeks and pouting mouth. Doll-like, with empty doll's eyes.

"The best way to get rid of them is to scare them off," Tamara said. "Bright light, or a sudden loud noise. The sound might attract species 019 but if you find yourself unexpectedly in the middle of a crowd of 048s, that's the best way to get out."

Or if you unexpectedly find yourself in the middle of a group of scavengers on a ship that should be abandoned. I remembered Tamara shrieking suddenly after she'd found me, Benny, Leah, and Quint. The sad thing was, her ploy had worked on us, too.

"Should we scream now?" I wondered. "Scare them off?"

"The strut is too long and narrow. There's nowhere for them to run to. If we scare them off, they'll come right back. Better to save it for if they actually decide to attack. We should rest for a bit," Tamara said.

She'd stopped on the next platform, dropping her bag heavily enough to loudly rattle the ancient metal stairs. I saw a childish head flinch back deeper into the wall.

"What, here?" Did she expect me to sleep with ghost children staring at me like they were wondering what my fingers tasted like?

Tamara sat down, back to the wall—as far from the edge of the platform, and the precipitous four-story drop down to where we'd entered, as she could get. "We've been travelling for hours," she told me. "We've been running and fighting for a good portion of that time. If you sit down, you'll realize you're exhausted."

"I don't know if there's room for anything but crippling

terror," I said, looking back down the way we'd come to find a tiny figure standing at the base of the steps, wavering back and forth on its feet, eyes like pits directly into the skull.

Indigo stepped past me, turning his shoulders to avoid knocking mine, and set his pack down too. The ancient stairs rattled, wobbling beneath my feet.

Fine, if it was gonna be two against one. I set my bag down beside theirs and sat down too, gingerly, craning my neck around as I did. The wavering Child at the base of the steps had vanished, like he'd never been there.

Tamara pulled out her little campstove and set it down on the platform in the midst of our rough circle, switching it on at the side. The heating unit began to glow.

"Anyone bring any marshmallows?" I asked, deliberately not looking back to see whether that Child had reappeared, several stairs closer, maybe showing a few more teeth.

"They must have been in my other pack," Tamara said.

"Wouldn't work anyway. There's no open flame on the campstove." I couldn't resist glancing back anyway, down the stairs. There was no Child standing there, but there was one lying flat on his belly on one of the steps, his fixed unblinking stare on me, like he thought if he lay very still I might not notice him there, and he could creep a little bit closer and tear out my throat with his excess of teeth.

I turned away. "We should play a camp game," I said. "Like I Spy. I Spy, with my little eye, a lot of evil Children. No, that's no fun."

"There are rather a lot of Children here, lieutenant,"

Indigo agreed.

"By all means," Tamara said. "Do something about it."

Indigo's head tilted. "I know you're looking forward to using me as a human shield, but perhaps you could strain yourself to find a better solution."

"Do you think I want to climb this hellish staircase?" Tamara snapped. From the corner of my eye, I saw some of the Children retreat, skittish. "This is our only chance of getting across the ship fast enough. Are you going to trust me on that, or not?"

Maybe it was the way she described the staircase, or the expression on her face when she did, but the clues I'd missed before all of a sudden connected themselves in my head.

"You don't like heights much, do you?" I asked, curious. It seemed antithetical to the lieutenant to have something as illogical as a phobia.

She looked at me with a hard expression: the same expression she'd had when we'd been surrounded by manikins, back when Indigo had been chasing us; certain death, no way out, but she'd lifted her club anyway. Her fear was radiative, palpable, but she wasn't warped by it. As solid as the hood of a car in the hot sun. You might burn your hand touching it, but the car wasn't changed at all.

"What's the alternative?" Lantern-Eyes asked.

"Picking a route is supposed to be your department," I pointed out, but then another idea struck me. "Hey, Indigo. You were born on this ship, right? Maybe? Do you remember anything you saw from inside your test tube?"

Indigo looked at me. I waited, pinned down by the currents in his dark-water eyes, and then he took in a breath... and said nothing. He stood up and headed for the staircase behind me. I think I'd have preferred if he'd told me off. It was like Quint's indifference; it just made me feel more alone.

There was a high-pitched, whistling shriek, and the sound of pattering footsteps retreating. Indigo returned, impassive, and sat back where he had been earlier.

"Uh, we could play a different game," I said. I dared a glimpse over my shoulder and didn't see any tiny corpses huddled on the lower platform, so he'd probably just scared it off. "Maybe... Does anyone have a deck of cards?"

Tamara stirred the bowl on the campstove. "Why would I have a deck of cards?"

"I don't know. For fun?"

She just gave me an incredulous look. There was such an absolute void of anything whimsical or light in Lantern-Eyes that I suspected she'd never been a child. She'd probably sprung fully formed from a mass of Republican weaponry, wearing a Republican flag. I knew about the Republican officers' families. They started training their kids early, in their big Terra Novan houses; reciting the anthem every morning and writing essays on how the Republic is the best and most important because they are the only truly free humans in the universe. That was how you got the Senator; that was how you got the Republican ships flying away from Kystrom one bright sunny morning and abandoning us lesser people to our fate.

The bowl was steaming now. Tamara pulled it off the heat and offered it to her right without looking; Indigo took it in silence. The second bowl appeared in front of me. "Eat," Lantern-Eyes said.

"This is the most boring treasure hunt I've ever been on," I said, taking the bowl and spoon.

"Have you been on very many?" she asked, and I knew a leading question from a cop when I heard one, thank you sir. "This isn't a fun trip, Sean. Did you expect to come here and have a fun time, and leave a couple billion terraques richer?"

More like I'd been forced here at gunpoint, knowing failure was my death and the death of the only other human alive who had known me before everyone I'd loved had died. "Something like that," I said. The bowl Lantern-Eyes had handed me was full of a lumpy brown mass that was probably some kind of oatmeal but reminded me, horrifyingly, of the flesh-eating coral I'd seen not so long ago on this very ship.

"Why *are* you here?" Lantern-Eyes asked.

Definitely a cop starting an interrogation. "Money? And fun."

"Someone must have given you these coordinates."

"I heard the SOS," I said.

"Someone must have pointed you where to look to find the SOS," Lantern-Eyes said.

"Just got lucky," I said. Indigo was still staring into space, eating mechanically. "You have anything you want to add, Indigo? You can be good cop."

"He doesn't care," Lantern-Eyes said.

"Maybe he's sick of your voice," I suggested, in the weaselly tone that had never failed to piss Brigid off.

"Do you even hear yourself?" she demanded. "What are you talking to me like?"

Indigo set his bowl aside suddenly. "I will take first watch," he said. "Who would prefer to take second?"

If I translated that from immortal Minister into mortal human, I think it turned out to mean that Indigo was sick of our shit. "I don't care," I said.

"I'll take second," Lantern-Eyes said, and conversation ceased while we finished eating. It had been easier to talk to them when we'd been in immediate danger of dying. I curled up on the ancient platform, head pillowed on my borrowed bag. The only light was the pale glow of Indigo's collar-light, and I felt as alone as I'd been before I'd allied with them, sleeping alone in the dark, lost in a lab with only the ghost of Mara Zhu for company.

*   *   *

LANTERN-EYES WOKE ME what felt like five minutes after I'd shut my eyes, shaking me hard enough to make me dizzy. "You sleep like the *dead*," she said.

I yawned hugely at her and she got that weird look on her face again, like a cat that's been picked up and is too startled by the liberty taken to decide whether or not it wants to be held. My whole body, I discovered, *hurt*. My hands were the worst, painful along the palms where I had scraped them, but my feet were sore, and my legs, and my shoulders. Even my ass hurt. I hadn't realized there were muscles involved in self-preservation that were located in the ass.

Lieutenant Gupta was already settling down in her own chosen sleeping spot, pressed up against the wall and far from the ledge, by the time I persuaded my resentful abs to let me sit upright. "Just smack them if they get too close," she said as she settled in. "There aren't enough that they'll dare attack yet."

"Sorry, what?" I said, still mostly asleep and preoccupied with the resentment of every overused sinew in my body, and then I finally looked around.

Lantern-Eyes had left a flashlight on and set it down beside me, so that there was more light on the platform than just the dreamy glow of Indigo's collar-light, which he'd dialed down anyway, presumably at the same time as he'd gone to sleep. The flashlight's beam terminated, several feet away, on a pair of small, dirty feet, toes curling and uncurling and nails so long they'd gone yellow.

The feet were standing on the upwards staircase, on the very lowest step, closest to us. I picked up the flashlight carefully and shone it around. There was a Child standing there, leaning forward a little, staring. There was another Child behind that one, a few steps up, clinging to the railing and watching us just as intently.

A soft sound behind me made me flinch. I turned, flashlight raised, and found a Child crouched at the base of the steps we'd come by, squatting knees to ears, hands flat on the rusting mesh, watching.

Something shifted in the walls. I turned the flashlight on that and found something peering at us through a tiny gap in the walls, nothing but ink-gleaming eyes.

The Children had gathered while I'd slept, and surrounded the camp.

CHAPTER FORTY FOUR:
SISTERS, STATE SECRETS, AND
JUST SO MANY CREEPY CHILDREN

LANTERN-EYES WAS *ASLEEP*. She'd actually gone and, knowing the Children had surrounded the camp, laid down and fallen asleep. Incredible.

Indigo, I wasn't convinced was asleep. He lay on his side and was breathing evenly, but it wasn't precisely a sleeping kind of evenness. I'd believe he was dozing, but not anything deeper than that. He probably didn't trust us enough to really pass out.

Or maybe he was having trouble sleeping, knowing that the Children were eying us like sandwiches behind locked glass. I certainly would understand.

I sat myself down where I'd slept, roughly between the up staircase and the down staircase, and tapped my flashlight against my knee. What exactly did being 'on watch' entail? Was I supposed to stare at these things while they stared at me? Should I chase them off? At what point in accumulating monsters did I wake up my companions so that they could kill them and we could run away?

Not that I particularly wanted to watch any of the Children die. Lantern-Eyes had warned us not to hesitate, and they were frightening to look at. I couldn't mistake them for actual children. But they were close enough that the thought of the lieutenant's club crushing one's face in made me shudder.

Something shifted to my right. I turned sharply and caught a glimpse of a skinny naked back scampering down the stairs. The Child crouched in the corner of the lower platform, huddled small, and stared up at me.

It had gotten pretty close to me before I'd noticed it. I turned to look at the upper stairs, but the Children there hadn't moved at all, just standing, like they were waiting. They were all looking at me, though.

A few minutes later I looked back at the down stairs and caught the Child there frozen in the act of crawling up the steps, pale face upturned and eyes wide, wide, wide and black, black, black.

If I looked at them, they looked back at me, but if I wasn't looking at them I could *feel* them watching me. I couldn't decide which was worse. I also couldn't decide whether the one higher up on the stairs had come closer since last I looked, or if I'd miscounted how many steps were between me and it. I stared at it for quite a long time, trying to figure out, before I abruptly remembered the ones behind me and looked back to find that they were—still—watching me.

They didn't move, for the most part, which was almost as unsettling as if they had. I don't like waiting.

Indigo had scared one off earlier. I shifted up onto my knees, intending to... I don't know, shake my fist at the one closest to us, but as soon as I moved they scattered. I was a lot bigger than them, I supposed, sitting back down. I almost felt a little bad about it.

I waited for a while longer, fiddling with the flashlight, wondering when Indigo and Tamara would wait up, when I heard the scrape of a bare foot against metal to my left.

I swung the flashlight around sharply and the light blazed on the face of a Child that had been creeping into our camp. It froze when the light touched it, staring at me, mouth parted just enough to show the blunt edges of baby teeth.

I swung around quickly and found that three more Children had gathered on the upper staircase. They crouched down when my flashlight beam swept over them, hunched like frogs on the metal, watching me in eerie unison.

The one to my left was still frozen where I'd left him, far closer than I liked.

Okay. I wasn't going to let them creep closer and closer until one climbed into my lap, all small cold limbs, soft and corpse-like. How had Lantern-Eyes gotten rid of them, again? Ah, yes.

I gathered myself, seated on the floor, taking one deep breath after another. In the darkness, with my flashlight averted, I heard the one to my left take a tiny, creeping step closer.

I filled my lungs, braced my legs, and then lunged to my feet and *roared*.

The Children scattered. I lunged at them so that they ran faster, shrieking, scrabbling on the ancient metal. I shone the flashlight after them and they ran like the Devil was after them, grabbing at their scabbed ankles, ready to bite their tiny little necks.

When I turned back around, Indigo and Tamara were both sitting up and staring at me. Tamara looked like a teacher on the verge of demanding a five-hundred-word essay detailing the choices I had made and why they were wrong. Indigo looked at me like he had never expected much of humans, and yet somehow we kept disappointing him anyway.

"Sorry," I said, and my own voice sounded quiet after the screams I'd used to scatter the scavengers. "They were—I just—I think what really threw me off was that every time I looked back, they were a little bit closer."

"We should keep moving," Indigo said.

"Maybe they wanted to play cards," Lantern-Eyes suggested, and slung her bag over her shoulder.

*   *   *

"I DON'T LIKE them either," Lantern-Eyes said as we rounded the spiral of the platforms-and-stairs, climbing up another story towards the center of the ship, "but there were four or five of them and three of us. They weren't going to attack with those odds."

I was slowly realizing that I had been a victim of tricky perspective. The strut was massive, it was true, just as awe-inspiringly huge as it looked from the outside. But it wasn't so long that it vanished away to a point in the distance, the way I'd thought at the base of the strut. Instead, the strut narrowed as it went, more of a cone than a tube.

On one hand, this was good, because it meant Indigo, Lantern-Eyes and I didn't have to travel up impossible miles of stairs. On the other, each round further up the stairs was a tighter turn, the platforms briefer. The strut was getting narrower. When we got high enough, there wouldn't be any more platforms, just a spiral staircase.

I wasn't looking forward to that.

"They were looking at me, Tamara," I said. The other thing was that with each foot we gained in altitude, the simulated gravity grew a little bit weaker; the *Nameless* didn't have modern art-grav, but old-fashioned centripetal gravity. The closer we got to the center of the ship, the faster we were spinning, the less simulated gravity was exerted on us. At the center of the ship there wouldn't be any gravity at all, but the whatever-it-was-called, the spinny force, that would be stronger than ever. I was already wobbling a little on the stairs, my body and my eyes disagreeing mildly on the definition of a straight line. I couldn't imagine how dizzying it would get once we reached the center of the ship.

"They're looking at you right now," Tamara said.

"Don't remind me." The Children weren't limited to the stairs, platforms and walkways. Oh, no. They were climbing in and out of the walls like cockroaches weaving through rotting wood. My flashlight glanced over a little body hanging upside-down by its ankles, face red and swollen with blood.

"There do seem to be more of them as we go along," Indigo said, which was absolutely the last thing I wanted to hear at that moment.

"Hopefully it will thin out," Lantern-Eyes said, her airy tone not quite hiding the unsettled edge. "Another thing to remember if they do attack is that they bounce. They've got the elasticity of children. You know how you can just hurl a toddler at a wall and it'll bounce back up?"

I didn't like that she sounded a little shaken. "How many toddlers have you thrown at walls?"

"I have six younger sisters, Sean."

"*Six?*" I said. "I could barely manage one. We fought like cats and dogs, I mean—"

I clamped my jaw shut, painfully, spasmodically. A dull sense of panic threaded through me. I hadn't been paying attention, and the words had slipped out, slurs on a memory, graffiti on a gravestone.

"You have a sister?" Indigo asked me, quietly.

"Had," I said. "What about you, Indigo? Any siblings?"

"I was born from a test tube," he reminded me.

Maybe that hadn't been my kindest comment. "Yeah, but," I said, and then I realized I didn't know if he knew that his genes had come from the scientists aboard the *Nameless*, that Mara Zhu had been, after a fashion, his mother as well as his creator. "You must know... I mean... who shares your genes," I finished lamely.

He didn't reply. Figures.

"Who was that other Kystrene you came with?" Tamara asked abruptly. "Your cousin?"

"Benny? We're not related. He's just a friend."

"I see," said Lantern-Eyes, in a tone I didn't understand and was afraid to question.

"What's that?" Indigo asked suddenly, and when I looked where he was pointing, I saw something growing in the wall, all twigs and leaves.

No, not growing. There were twigs there, meshed together with tubes of plastic and metal, but the 'leaves' were scraps of fabric knotted through to create a sort of raft-like object.

"Damn," Tamara said. "It's a nest."

CHAPTER FORTY FIVE: NESTS?!

"I DIDN'T REALIZE the Children were nesting up here," Lantern-Eyes said. "They must've moved here after my team came through."

"The Children make nests?" I tried to picture one of them sitting there, squatting like a pigeon, grinning too many teeth. "That's a bird thing, though, right? Did they make the Children out of birds too? Are there immortal birds?"

"Humans make nests," Indigo said. "What do you think you sleep in?"

"Beds? What do Ministers sleep in?"

"They're not birds and this is a bad sign," Tamara said. "There's about to be a lot of Children ahead, maybe enough that they'll come at us. We have to be quick."

"We can fight them off," Indigo said.

"I'd prefer not to crush a kid's skull in, Indigo."

"I thought they didn't bother you," I said.

"They bother me, Sean," Tamara said, and started climbing the steps again, more quickly than before.

The padded lattices of metal and sticks grew more densely packed as we travelled up. I remembered seeing those little girls in the farmlands, the ones who had looked so like Brigid and Liza, and wondered if those Children had been gathering twigs there to bring them back here and make nests with. Now that Indigo had pointed it out, those nests did kind of look like woven mattresses.

I wasn't giving up on the bird angle, though. "There was this cliff right outside the city where I grew up," I said. "Sheer rock, but one of the first colonists built stairs right into the cliff. He put his house up top."

Every step I got a little bit lighter. Like I was floating up. Or my head was floating off. I kept leaning to one side without realizing, and catching myself wobbling only when my shoulder bumped the wall or my hip hit the railing. That would be the spinny-force.

I shouldn't be fooled by the light gravity up here; if I fell over that edge, the gravity would get heavy again further down.

"Made it a national park after he died," I said. The metal mesh underfoot was sparser here, wires missing. I wondered if the Children had taken pieces from the stairs to make their mattress-nests. It hardly mattered to me: I could leap right over those gaps, no trouble at all. "You could climb up all those stairs and see the ernes nesting on the cliffside. I climbed over the railing once with my sister and made it into an erne's nest. It was huge. We could sit in the middle and be comfortable and have space to spare. The ernes had already left the nest so we weren't bothering their babies."

"Sean," said Tamara, "the Children already know we're here, so there's no reason to be quiet. That said, shouldn't you save your breath for climbing?"

"I'm climbing," I said. It *was* getting a little hard to catch my breath; with the dizzy nausea and the fact that the strut had narrowed to the point that there were no more platforms, only a spiral staircase turning ever more and more tightly in on itself. I bet you felt weightless when you were buried, too. No falling. Just dirt packed in tight against every inch of you. Maybe a little bit of a lean to one side, like I was leaning now, the spinny-force pushing me inexorably to one side.

It wasn't like I was going to let Lantern-Eyes know she was right, though. It's bad to let cops know when they're right. Inflates their egos. "Anyway, someone called the city when they saw us out there; they wouldn't let us walk back along the cliff-edge to the staircase and we had to wait while someone got ropes and nets and carried us back over." Brigid, I think, had been a little relieved that the fire brigade had shown up with their protective equipment; as thrilled as she'd been by sitting in the eyrie, she'd been nervous about scooting back down the tiny ledge of rock to the safety of the stairs. I could've talked her into it, but I hadn't wanted to; I could've left on my own, but there wasn't a chance I'd leave her behind. So I'd stayed with her in the nest. I could picture a moment from that day clearly in my head, as clearly as if I were there again; a sunlit day, so different from the darkness of the *Nameless*; a sunlit day and the fields and the far-off sea and two of Kystrom's moons pale beside the sun, and Brigid on a nest of twigs and colored string, staring out into the gasp of air over the cliff's edge, the wind tearing her golden hair forward and obscuring her face.

Always obscuring her face.

"Darrington's Aerie?" Indigo said suddenly.

I missed my next step on the tightly spiraling stairs, which on examination was not entirely my fault; part of the metal mesh was entirely missing. At least the gravity was so light that I could catch myself before I fell. "Yeah, that's what it was called," I said. "How'd you know that?"

"Darrington's Aerie is outside of Itaka."

"Yeah, Itaka, the town I grew up in on Kystrom."

Tamara's exhaustingly rapid climb stuttered. "So you were *there*," she said to me, and I had to pull up quick so I didn't run into her back. "I mean you were at ground zero when the Ministers attacked."

I couldn't figure out why they both seemed shocked. "You knew I was from Kystrom."

"Itaka was the only city the Ministers attacked," Indigo said. His tone was flat, but aggressively flat, tamping down on emotions like trying to close the lid of an overflowing box. "The rest of the planet fell without resistance, after Itaka. But Itaka was totally destroyed."

Itaka was totally destroyed.

I heard Lantern-Eyes' voice through a weird warping, like a bubble closed over my head. "I didn't think there were any survivors."

Itaka was totally destroyed. Fire in the streets, and a distant screaming, but mostly quiet, horribly quiet. It had been loud in the first hour, when I was hiding, halfway between school and home; it had been quiet after that, quiet with pockets of shrieking terror, but mostly *quiet*, like I was the only thing still living in the streets—

"There were very few." Indigo's voice was very quiet. "For the most part, they were brought back to Maria Nova."

"Were the other Kystrene relocated?" Lantern-Eyes wanted to know.

"No. They were allowed to stay on the planet with their current property, which is where they remain, under Minister administration. There were no other battles on the planet, so the only damage was to Itaka. The survivors we found—"

"Stop," I said. I could barely hear myself over the sound of my own breathing echoing in my ears, but I must have spoken loud enough for the other two to hear me, because they fell silent.

It really was hard to breathe here. Maybe the air was getting thinner too; that made sense, didn't it? I mean when you climbed a mountain there was less air at the top. I was climbing a spiral staircase in a spinning wheel; spirals upon spirals meant my head hardly knew which way was up anymore, which was bad when my feet didn't feel thoroughly tethered to the ground. And the strut was narrowing further; if it kept this up, I'd be able to span the whole width of it with my arms outstretched, and then it would get too small for me to do even that.

There was a Child sitting in one of the nests. Squatting, it barely fit on the narrow mattress platform. Not like the spacious nests the ernes had made.

There were Children behind us, on the stairs. There were Children in the walls, watching. "Has anyone noticed," I said, and my voice sounded weird to my own ears, "that there seem to be a lot more kids around?"

"Just keep walking," Tamara said, from far, far away.

We climbed. We climbed and climbed, and the stairs turned tighter and tighter, until I could trail my fingers on the steps of the opposite side while I climbed, reaching right over the many stories of empty space. And still we climbed, even as our heels got so light we hardly had to touch the stairs, pulling ourselves along with the railings, and Children barely more than an arm's length away.

Tamara stopped. I almost bumped into her, so focused was I on the way the staircase was narrowing, on my spinning skull. I opened my mouth to ask why she'd stopped, when I saw, instead of a staircase, the ascent changed to a single ladder, stretching up too high for me to see the end.

And, worst of all, the strut itself had narrowed to a tube, as narrow and close as a coffin.

CHAPTER FORTY SIX:
MY MOTHER'S WARDROBE

I GOT LOCKED in my mother's wardrobe as a kid. Not for very long, and it was my fault really. My mother didn't like to throw things out. She kept a lot of mementos. I understood it now better than I used to. Her mementos were all lost now, gone on Kystrom. I wished I'd taken a box with me, but even if I had, they would've been someone else's memories.

I hadn't liked narrow spaces before that, either, but I liked them even less afterwards. All those boxes of my mother's memories pressed against me on all sides, almost too tight for me to turn around. I did turn around, somehow, and banged on the door, first yelling, then begging, for Brigid to let me out. For someone to let me out.

It was close and dark, and though I was standing upright I wondered if this was what a coffin felt like. Confined and dark. Perhaps it was a coffin, I'd thought, and I'd banged and banged as much as I could until finally someone unlocked the door and I came tumbling out.

*   *   *

I STOOD ON the stair below Tamara, the wall hitting my shoulder on one side and the railing hitting my hip on the other, already too small a space, already too tight. How tall was the ladder? It was one thing climbing a long staircase in a big empty space like the lower part of the strut; it was one thing going through a tiny hole in the wall when it was only a foot or two long, like some of Lantern-Eyes' boltholes. But a space as narrow as that, longer than I was tall? *Fuck*.

She frowned up the ladder in its narrow tube, shining her own flashlight up to examine the inside. "Just in time," she said. "The gravity's almost too weak to walk in already. Ladders are better for microgravity. You know how to hook your ankles in the rungs to keep yourself in place, right?" she asked, and then she saw me. "Are you okay?"

"I'm fine," I said.

"You don't look fine." She assessed me like a mechanic looking over a faulty car. That was me, faulty and pathetic, stuck here. I knew there was no going back. It would take too long; there were too many monsters behind us.

"Can you make this?" Tamara asked.

She was afraid of heights, but she'd climbed without hesitation, because that had been her only option. This was like crawling through that tunnel Indigo had found when I'd still been travelling with the Ministers: Go forward or die.

Except that the tunnel with the Ministers hadn't been as

long as this one. And I'd had Benny with me, and there was Quint to be brave for.

I was the only one scared now. And my companions weren't Benny. If I refused to go in, they'd have to force me through, or force me to tell them the location of the Philosopher Stone before leaving me behind. We couldn't go back, not with the Children and whatever else blocking the way.

"What other choice do I have?" I said.

Tamara's frown deepened. "I'll go first," she said. "Keep up. After this, we'll be in the engine; we'll be halfway across."

Only halfway across. Maybe the Senator would pull the trigger on the implant now and put me out of my misery before I had to climb up there.

I watched Tamara's back ascend into the tube, her calves, her heels. Then she was gone, but for the ringing of her feet. My own breathing sounded very loud again, the same way it had after Tamara and Indigo had started talking about Itaka. And thinking about Itaka only made me feel worse.

Maybe my breath didn't just sound loud in my head. Maybe it was because the tunnel was so small, my breathing was echoing. I could *feel* the spinning this close to the center of the ship, and I had to swallow down the pasty dinner of Tamara's rations.

I couldn't seem to make my legs move. "Hey," I said, trying to joke with Indigo, a silent presence behind me. "Maybe you could turn your collar purple and make a veiled threat."

"Was fear of Number One what got you into the tunnel last time?" Indigo asked. His quiet voice seemed louder in the smallness of the strut.

Not so much fear of Number One as fear of what Number One was about to do to Quint, if Quint had refused to enter the tunnel. Somehow, knowing that Indigo would probably kill me if I refused to continue wasn't as strong a motivator as One threatening Quint.

I stepped under the ladder and stared up after Tamara. It was even smaller than I'd expected. When she reached up for the next rung, her elbow bumped the wall; when she leaned back to glance up, her hair, floating in the microgravity, brushed against the tunnel beside her head.

There was no way I could do this. There was no *air* in there. I was breathing as quickly as I could down here and even then I couldn't get enough air.

Indigo said something to me in Sister.

"What?" I said, the one word in Sister I remembered, and all I had breath to speak.

He spoke in Kystrene. "Number One raised me."

CHAPTER FORTY SEVEN: I'M SUSCEPTIBLE TO BRIBES, BUT ONLY IN THE FORM OF GRAMMAR

"SHE—WHAT? ONE? The Ultraviolet Minister is your mother?" Another thought struck me. "Wait, did you just speak Kystrene?"

Indigo ignored my last question. "She is not my mother," he said, in Sister. "Ministers do not have families. Place your hand on the first rung."

"I—what?"

"Your hand," Indigo repeated, patient and somehow gentle, though his expression had barely changed. "Place it on the first rung."

I stood a moment, baffled. Then I reached out and put my right hand on the rung at eye level, the first step towards ascending the ladder. I glanced up as I did—a mistake; the impossible length of the tunnel dizzied me. Tamara had stopped, obviously wondering where we were; the tunnel was too tight for her to even turn her head around properly—

"Ministers do not have families," Indigo repeated behind me, calm as a deep, deep pool. "I know my genetics, who shares them and how far removed we are, and I was brought to term as an embryo with forty other Ministers, but neither the Ministers who share Mara Zhu's genetics nor the Ministers who were raised with me are my relatives. Yes," he said, seeing something in my expression, "I know that my genetics are primarily received from Mara Zhu."

Mara Zhu's last message, her grief-struck face, despairing in the dark. There was something of his ancestor's despair, I realized, in Indigo's mannerisms. I couldn't tell exactly how or why—his expression, certainly, was serene—but it was like hearing snatches of a song in midair; much easier to recognize the song if you'd heard the tune before. Perhaps he was just a melancholy person. Number One had been somber, too; maybe that was what happened when you were several hundred years old, or maybe she'd taught him to be a little bit sad. I said, "But One raised you?"

"Put your flashlight into your pocket," Indigo replied, "and place your other hand on the higher rung."

This time I understood that he would not answer me unless I did as he said. I hesitated, caught on a knife-edge between fear and curiosity, between annoyance that he was treating me like I was weak and gratitude for the help.

By now I trusted Indigo to save my life—as long as our arrangement lasted, of course. I hadn't imagined a scenario between he and I that would require a different kind of trust. The kind of trust that you couldn't negotiate.

It felt like handling one of Lantern-Eyes' grenades for the first time, not sure when it would explode or if it would or how dramatic the consequences would be. I turned the flashlight off like Indigo had told me to, leaving me in no light except for his. And I set my second hand on the ladder rungs.

Indigo said, "We are raised by a sequence of teachers, who teach us everything we need to know. When we are nearly adults, a single Minister takes us under their tutelage and trains us according to their specialties. For me, that was the Minister you know as One."

"What did she teach you?"

"Step onto the ladder."

I did as I was told. So long as I focused on what Indigo was telling me—which was fascinating, secrets of the Ministers that maybe no one knew—it was easier not to think about the tunnel ahead.

I took another step onto the rung without being told and then, carefully, another after that.

"Number One taught me how to protect those who need it," Indigo said, beneath me now, and I heard the sounds of him starting the ascent from below. No: focus on what he was saying, not where he was. Where we were.

"She taught me how to achieve my goals, efficiently and completely, without hesitation or error," Indigo continued. "The second of these being more important than the first. I am a piece of Maria Nova, not a free agent of my own. It's crucial that I achieve my goals swiftly and perfectly."

Wow. He and Tamara had more in common than I'd thought: They'd both been brainwashed.

"Do you have any students of your own?" I asked.

"Several. But none in the past few years."

That was an odd clarification. And he'd volunteered it, too. "Why not?"

"The Ministerial Council and I mutually agreed that it would be for everyone's best benefit."

There was some story hidden in there, I was certain of it. But he hadn't left me anything specific to ask about.

"Climb," Indigo told me.

"I'm not one of your students," I said, though I'd reached out for the ladder when he'd gestured, the metal cold under my palm. Tamara had started climbing again above me. Her boots echoed. I shuddered. "Tell me your name, Indigo."

"You've given me a name."

"Your real name," I said. "You must have an actual name or some sort of designation. Otherwise how would any of you ever talk about each other? There'd be millions of purples and indigoes and blues and greens. It wouldn't make any sense."

"Our names are not for outsiders to know."

"You don't have to say it aloud," I said. "That way I won't accidentally call you by it in front of anyone. You can just show me in Light. Can you even say your name aloud? Or do you only have a name in Light?"

"My name can be spoken aloud," Indigo said. "There is a transliteration system to describe spoken language in Light. Which I will not be teaching you. But I will make you a deal: If you can make it to the end of the ladder with me and Tamara, then I will show you how to speak my name in Light."

I laughed. He was like a dentist offering a child sweets. "Bribery," I said.

"A Minister doesn't bribe," he replied, gravely enough that I thought he was joking.

We climbed.

Each step upward *lifted* me, even as I found myself running into the left-side wall when I tried to climb straight. That was the spinny-force, and I knew it was the spinny-force, but it was hard not to let it disorient and frighten me, like maybe the wall was moving towards me, like maybe the whole space was getting narrower and narrower. Soon I was no longer climbing 'up' so much as I was crawling forward, up and down losing meaning as up and down ceased to exist. No horizon and no gravity. I shut my eyes against the disorientation and set my jaw against the nausea and climbed by feel alone, bracing myself in place with my ankles, pulling myself forward with my hands.

And then my next reach found no rung. I tumbled out into an open space, fumbling for my flashlight, and opened my eyes to the vastness at the center of the ship.

The walkway visibly curved around the central point of the ship—the walkway was a 'ring' around the central point, lined with handholds. Several ladders stuck out of the floor, identical to the one we had climbed up; all the struts of the ship intersected here, at the center of the wagon wheel—and beneath the massive, weirdly-formed monstrosity of the engine.

My flashlight beam glinted off it. An ancient thing,

long dead. Cracks in the metal had been patched over by Dreamer-bots, gleaming like silver lightning against the old and blackened shell. But no heat radiated out at me; that engine had not been functional for a thousand years, ever since Mara Zhu had ensured that her ship would never escape the trap of the supernova she'd put it in. It was awesome, and terrifying. My momentum in tumbling out of the strut had me drifting towards that massive cracked shell, dizzy and awestruck; but my path towards the engine was curving mysteriously away from the center and towards the walkway some distance from where I had emerged; I floundered, baffled, in midair, until a hand caught my heel and dragged me down again.

I bounced off the walkway next to Tamara, flashlight beam flashing around the empty room, until I had the sense to latch on to one of the handholds and stop myself from flying out into empty space again. Indigo was clinging to the wall—floor—whatever a few feet behind Tamara.

We'd made it, I thought, dizzily. We'd made it. Now he could tell me his name.

I opened my mouth to speak to him when Tamara said, "Shh!"

"Why?" I started to ask, and then I saw it.

In the dark of the central engine, lit only by my little flashlight, tiny black shadows flew from place to place. They crawled over the walls, over the ceiling.

The Children were here, too.

CHAPTER FORTY EIGHT: THE CENTER OF IT ALL

"LISTEN UP." TAMARA was speaking very lowly and very quickly. "If we move quickly and quietly, we might be able to get out of here before they decide whether they're going to attack."

I took that to mean there were more than enough of the Children to overwhelm us. I looked around uneasily at those flitting little shadow-shapes, moving gravity-free in weird bending paths through the thin air. If they came at us, would I even be able to tell they were headed our way before they landed in our midst? I clung to the wall.

Tamara was rummaging around in her pack. A moment later she pulled out a ration pack and tossed it out, lightly, towards the central engine. The ration pack rose, then bent, landing against the wall a little bit behind me.

"What are you doing?" I asked. I had to do it in two breaths; the air was so thin here.

"Checking the Coriolis force," she said. "Sean, we've got to get to the other side of the wheel and here's how we're going to do it. We can't go straight through the center because the engine is in the way, so we have to go around. The ship is rotating but as soon as we let go of the wall we're no longer rotating with it. We're going to use that to our advantage. I want you to kick towards the central engine, but very gently; you'll float towards the engine but then your trajectory will curve. Catch onto the walkway when you land back against the wall and do the same thing."

"We're going to hop?" I said incredulously.

"It's faster and easier than crawling," Tamara said. "Come on."

She kicked off, very lightly, tumbled over my head and landed on the wall a few feet away. The fractured curve of the engine loomed overhead; the one place on the ship that was truly zero-g. I shifted to get my heels against the wall and did the same thing as Tamara.

A moment of exhilarating freefall, and then I was landing, very gently, against the wall again. I caught a rung fumblingly and saw Indigo land as light as a bird against the wall behind me. Ahead of me, Tamara tumbled through the air, somersaulting, dark hair drifting like she was underwater. I got my heels under me again and kicked up after her.

It was kind of fun, tumbling like this; pretty funny to see, too, watching Tamara and Indigo do a gymnastics routine in zero-g.

And then my flashlight beam landed on a little face right below me, eyes wide and jaw hanging open, mouth clotted with teeth. My shoulder struck the wall with rattling impact and by the time I looked again the Child wasn't there anymore.

Not visible, but still present. Crouched against the wall I could see them all again, the little darting shadow-children, moving out of the corners of my eyes, hiding from my flashlight beam. I panted in the thin air.

"Sean," Tamara hissed, and I turned to find that she'd stopped, too. We'd reached the other side of the wheel.

"Follow me," she said. She was already half inside the wall, just her head sticking out, the rest of her sticking what would become 'down' once we had gravity again.

There was hardly room for her in that chute. This one seemed even narrower than the first. It was the only way out and I knew it, but my heart started pounding even harder, fighting low oxygen and terror. "I don't—"

"Yes, you can," Tamara said. "Just follow me."

*   *   *

BRIGID HAD NIGHT terrors when she was a little girl. The first time I'd heard her shrieking, it had terrified me. The successive times, it had only annoyed me, because we'd shared a room at that age and each time she would wake me from a sound and peaceful sleep. I was a horrible child, to become indifferent to his little sister's fear.

Eventually, after a week of this, and our parents signing her up for sessions with a therapist and changing her nighttime routine to try to shake the haunting, I'd asked Brigid why she screamed. What was it that frightened her?

There were shadows in the room, Brigid had told me;

shadows that wanted to do her harm. Little shadow people, only as tall as she was, half the height our parents were. They gathered in doorways and crouched beside the dresser, and in the dead of the night they came out and gathered around her bedside like viewers at a funeral while she lay paralyzed.

I'd promised her that I would keep watch, that I wouldn't let the nightmares reach her. She'd been young enough that it had comforted her, but it hadn't been enough. So I'd distracted her every night before she went to bed, teasing and soothing, offering her stories and knowledge like Indigo had bargained with me, guarding her in two ways at once. Her night terrors had ceased.

As for me, I laid awake long nights after that, watching the shadows beside the dresser until I would swear I saw them tremor in the dark, reaching for my sister.

*　　*　　*

THE CHILDREN MOVED around us, like little shadows, closer and closer. But Tamara spoke so calmly I found my own heartbeat slowing down.

"Indigo will have to wait to show you his name," she said. "It'll be safe down below. You can climb down this one, because you just climbed up the other one. I'll be right ahead of you, clearing the space. Put your feet down after me and just take one step at a time. Don't think of anything except the step right below."

Indigo, glowing faintly, knelt in the platform and watched. "You're really good at that," I told her over my shoulder, and focused on one step at a time. It was still hard to breathe, but all I had to do was breathe enough for the next step.

"I practically raised my sisters," Tamara explained, as I descended into the dark of the tunnel after her.

My heartrate immediately tried to speed up. I swallowed, took the next step down, and said, "Yeah?"

"Yeah. My father worked a lot, and my mother wasn't very detail-oriented. She was there all the time, present, but disorganized. I kept the house clean, made sure everyone got to school on time and got their schoolwork done, all that. So they went to me if they needed something as much as they went to mom."

"You were uniquely well-suited for the Republican military," Indigo said from above me, and my ears mustn't have been working very well, because it sounded like he was yanking her chain.

"The military also offered me a chance to get advanced degrees without having to pay for them myself—or worse, take my parents up on their offer to bankrupt themselves and my sisters to pay for me," Tamara said. "We don't get special designated teachers in Terra Nova."

But they did get families, I thought. Indigo had clearly refuted the idea that any of his close associates qualified as a family. It sounded lonely.

Striking out on your own without your family's support, all because you wanted to keep them safe, *also* sounded lonely. "Do you ever regret it?"

"Regret joining the military? Regret coming out here and getting stuck here for five years, knowing that my sisters probably all think I'm dead? There's no point resenting what's already happened; it's done. The only thing to do is make my situation better from here. Watch your step, Sean," she added, and suddenly my next step landed hard on ringing flatness, and palms on my back braced me from stumbling.

I'd reached the end of the ladder, and the top of the spiral staircase for the descent. When I turned and flicked on my flashlight, Tamara stood there, as solid and steady as a stone. Lieutenant Lantern-Eyes was so balanced, like the gravitation scales in a spaceship that, regardless of tilt or acceleration or graviton malfunction, always found their level. It struck me how *sane* she was. I mean, she was neurotic, sure, making me look four times down a hallway and probably counting bullets in her spare time. But all of the sanest people I've ever met were like her, able to find their level no matter where or how they were.

"Move so Indigo can get down," she bade me, and drew me a step away so that Indigo could descend after us, glowing a pale and radiant blue.

When he reached the bottom, he turned to me. He reached up one hand to his collar-light and, slowly and deliberately, dialed out a pattern. A slow brightening like a flower blossoming, followed by a dual throb like a heartbeat. His name.

He lowered his hand. "In this case, the color does not matter," he told me. "My name can be said in any shade."

Fascinating. "So the colors are relative honorific levels, not absolute."

"Precisely," he said. "Blue is generally the default

politeness for strangers. Closer to red is more intimate, or more rude, depending. Violet is more respectful."

"What if you have more than seven people present?" I asked, speaking quickly, before Indigo came to his senses and stopped indulging my curiosity. "Would you—"

"*Shit*," Tamara said, with such meaning that I shut up immediately and turned to see what had so startled her.

Lined up on the stairs below us, just visible now in the beam of my flashlight, gathered and watchful, a crowd of Children stared up at us, forming a wall between us and the exit.

CHAPTER FORTY NINE:
GOD DAMN CHILDREN

"SHIT," I ECHOED, because that about summed it up.

Indigo said nothing.

"How do you say 'shit' in Light?" I asked him, while Tamara drew her club out of the makeshift holder she'd kept strapped to her back.

Indigo shook his head. "My language does not have designated curse words," he said.

Fascinating. "There must be some taboo words, though."

"The word's virtue is in *how* you say the word."

"You should try swearing sometime," Tamara said, her club in front of her and taking a cautious step down the stairs. "It's supposed to relieve pain and anxiety."

"Maybe later," Indigo said, and then pushed past me—shoving me into the wall as he did; the staircase was too narrow—and past Tamara, so that he could get to the front of the line.

Leaving me safely in the back. I peered around Tamara's shoulder. "How are we going to get through?"

Indigo drew his sword.

"Alright, then," I said, and Indigo advanced.

The first round of Children retreated when he advanced, skittering backwards down the stairs, teeth bared, hissing through them. Indigo was a brightness and a blade driving them back, and we went down and down and down the spiral stairs, driving the Children back, until I almost thought we would make it.

Then I looked to the side and found that the walls were pitted here, and the Children were inside, watching us with ink-black eyes. And then I looked back and found that a few of the Children had gotten around us and were crouched on the stairway behind me, watching us go with their cheeks lumpy with teeth.

I glanced over the railing and saw the spiral staircase going down, down, down, platforms and stairs as far as the eye could see. We wouldn't make it.

Almost directly below us there was a platform that protruded pretty far out into the center of the strut. I swung my bag out in front of me and dug around for the rope I knew was there, but the interior of the bag was a mess of random utilities, indistinguishable in the dark. If Number One herself had been curled up inside my bag, I wouldn't have been able to find her.

I gave up. "Hey, Lantern-Eyes," I said. "Do you have any rope in your pack?"

"What do you want rope for?" Tamara asked, but she was already reaching into her pack. It put her into a vulnerable position, head in her bag, but Indigo still stood between us and the Children. One of them, emboldened by his stillness, hissed a rasping breath over its palate and wavered on its feet like it was readying to lunge. When I turned my flashlight back the way we had come, the beam froze two Children in the act of creeping nearer.

Tamara had already found the rope in her perfectly packed bag. She zipped the bag shut and repeated, "What do you want the rope for?"

I took the rope from her hands, unwound it, and dropped one end into the open space over the edge of the railing. It bent with the invisible rotation of the ship— with the *Coriolis force*, as Tamara had been so helpful to remind me—until the end coiled on the platform several levels down.

Tamara's eyes went wide.

"We're not gonna make it through," I explained, even as the first of the Children took another step too close to Indigo, and he had to lash out, cobra-quick, with his sword. The Child retreated, hand bleeding, pitch-black eyes narrowed. I started to tie the rope to the railing.

Tamara smacked my hands away. "Give me that," she said, and took over the knotting, then hauled up some of the length of rope I'd dropped and made some sort of quick loop out of it. "There's more down there," she said, looking over the edge. "I'd better go first."

Indigo jolted forward, driving off another Child. They were getting bolder. "Quickly, if you can," he said.

Lantern-Eyes stared down at the long, long fall. I clapped her on the shoulder.

"Don't worry, Lantern-Eyes," I said, cheerful. "You got this. I'll be right behind you."

She looked at me and then, surprisingly, she laughed. She swung over the railing without another pause, her foot in the loop she'd made, and descended like a professional down and down and down.

I turned around in time to catch a Child reaching out for my pack with grimy fingers. "No," I said, and swung the flashlight at it. I clipped its head and it staggered back.

"Sorry!" I said, horrified; the Child had fallen against the stairs and was blinking up at me dazedly. "God! Sorry—"

The Child lunged. Its teeth closed around my hand, *tight*.

If I wanted to name something with a deadly bite, I would talk about snakes and dogs, something that could really dig in there. But when human teeth close around your skin, you really understand that these are teeth made for splitting flesh and cracking carrots, which incidentally requires about as much jaw strength as breaking a fingerbone. The Child's jaw did not latch on hard enough to crack the bones of my fingers, but I knew as soon as it closed around my skin that those teeth could, and would, split through my flesh and snap my bones.

Someone grabbed my arm, slamming it hard against the railing; the Child hit the railing with a sickening sound, releasing my hand; momentum carried it over the edge, and it fell.

"Oh, God," I said, torn between laughter and horror as the Child tumbled through the air seventeen stories down, striking railings as it fell, nausea roiling as I dragged my maimed hand up to my chest.

"Go down the rope, Sean," Indigo said mildly, standing with his sword out and surrounded.

My hand throbbed. There were indents in my skin where the Child had bit down, and I wasn't sure I could close that hand. But I grabbed the rope, made a loop the way Tamara had done, and stepped out into open space.

My grip on the rope was weak at first and I slid down it, fibers tearing the flesh from my palms, before I got my ankle in a loop and had myself braced. Then I lowered myself as quickly as I could, because Indigo was up there alone and I knew he wouldn't come down until I reached Tamara.

My heels hit the platform with jarring force. "Pull your knife, Sean," Tamara said, and I turned to find her with her club out, facing three Children with their heads held low like snakes. One of them saw me and hissed.

I stepped away from the rope and fumbled to pull my borrowed knife from where I'd tucked it away in my belt. I got it out just as the Children rushed Tamara.

She didn't want to hit them. She kept pulling her blows, flinching back. She didn't want to hit them, and they knew it. They got right in around her, and one of them got in past her reach, and I saw its jaw clamp down on her thigh.

That seemed to trigger something in her. Tamara grabbed the little girl by the hair and dragged her off her, threw her to the ground, and then slammed the club down. The Child hissed up at her in the seconds before the club impacted her face, crushing flesh and bone, breaking it down into red.

Indigo landed like a falling star, took two steps onto the platform, and swung his blade. The other two Children hunting Tamara fell, bleeding, and Indigo stepped into the midst of them, cool and remote and gleaming, a Minister murdering, and nearby a little blonde girl lay on her back with her face caved in.

CHAPTER FIFTY:
THE BODIES OF THE PAST

I WASN'T ON Kystrom. I knew I wasn't on Kystrom, and I knew Indigo hadn't been the one to kill Brigid. I knew that.

"Nice idea with the rope," Tamara panted. She patted me on the shoulder. "Now we need to get out of here."

Indigo, standing between the corpses, looked overhead. I heard the patter of footsteps on the stairs, uneven and intermittent, and when I looked up a hundred little shadows with dark eyes watched us from overhead.

I followed Tamara when she moved, hurrying down the stairs. The stronger gravity as we descended was somehow just as dizzying as the weaker gravity had been on the ascent. It felt like someone had their hands on my shoulders, pushing me down.

Indigo caught up to me several levels down, after we'd left the crowd of watching Children behind. "Are you all right?" he asked me.

A slow brightening, like a flower blossoming. A dual throb like a heartbeat. I knew his name now. And now I knew that he hadn't always been what he was now, cold and brutally efficient. Number One had taught him that. I wonder what he would have been like otherwise.

"Yeah," I meant to say, but instead I said, "My sister's name was Brigid."

His expression changed when I said her name. Like looking at my own face in a mirror. I didn't care how he felt my pain and my grief, or even that it was a Minister who grieved my sister with me. It just mattered that he did. A slow brightening, a dual throb.

"Brigid Wren," Tamara said, and I didn't bother to correct her with the real last name, because when Brigid was alive she and I were Harts, not Wrens. "It's a lovely name. Keep going, Sean. It's all easier from here."

*   *   *

SHE HADN'T BEEN lying. I suspected Lantern-Eyes did not often lie for reassurance; she'd lie, probably, in the line of duty. Maybe she'd lie to all those little sisters of hers about how close they were to their destination on a road trip. But I didn't think she'd lie just to comfort me.

We took another brief rest on the nearest landing, then continued on. Lantern-Eyes had been right—travelling through the center of the ship, as exhausting as it had been, was a lot faster than going around the edges would've been. There were still Children in the strut, but they stuck to the edges, watching us from safe distances.

It was a relief to be where the gravity was as it should be, though I wasn't enthused by the possibility that we might run into manikins again. I thought I saw a little Child-sized shadow dart into a doorway behind us, watchful, following, but I wasn't sure and I didn't mention it to my companions. If we were in danger, Indigo would let us know.

We had not gone far from the exit to the strut when Indigo stopped.

I didn't hear him stop. Indigo walked so quietly that there was very little auditory difference between him following me and him not following me. But I'd become attuned to him somehow, over the course of our time traveling together, and I knew that he was no longer behind me. I stopped, too, and when I turned I found him standing in the middle of the hall, staring through a doorway into a room I couldn't see. His collar-light illuminated his face like a city illuminated the clouds at night, and his expression was stricken, sad and terrible.

He strode through the doorway without a word.

"What's wrong?" Tamara asked, but I didn't answer, hurrying after Indigo.

I found him standing in the middle of that room, surrounded by large cloudy tanks of some forgotten chemical, turning in a slow circle to look at the contents of the room. I turned my flashlight on the nearest tank, to see what he saw.

When my brain finally put together what I was seeing in that clouded water, my heart struck my ribs, a hard and painful beat.

In each of the tanks, suspended, preserved, there was a corpse.

And each of the corpses was a Minister.

CHAPTER FIFTY ONE:
TEST SUBJECTS

IT WAS OBVIOUS even through the clouded water and clouded glass: the angle of their cheekbones, the narrowness of their feet, brushing cheek and ankle against the glass as they floated. Strangely fragile-looking for creatures that could survive the vacuum of space, massive blood loss, and most forms of blunt-force trauma that would cave my ribs in.

Indigo stood before the nearest tank, his collar-light clouding the liquid blue, and took step after step closer, until his nose was inches from the glass. The body inside revolved slightly with unseen currents, turning its cheek to Indigo, like his reflection was turning its face away.

"Successful specimens," Tamara said.

Indigo didn't flinch, but I did. "Is this really the time to be a dick about this?"

"I'm not being a dick." But Lantern-Eyes did glance at Indigo as she spoke. "It's what they are. Why else would they preserve the bodies?"

"I admire your emotional distance from the situation,

Lieutenant Gupta," Indigo said. He was still staring at the turned cheek and shut eyes of the body in the tank in front of him.

"I'm surprised you don't have any," Tamara said. "Isn't that what Ministers are known for?"

Could she get any worse? The man was staring at his dead relative. I flashed my light into Tamara's eyes, then put it under my chin to clearly illuminate me glaring at her.

I should've known she wouldn't be cowed. "He massacred your city," Tamara said to me. "You don't think that implies some emotional distance? I'm not trying to tear you down, Indigo. I'm trying to understand."

"Ministers change, if more slowly than humans," Indigo said. "Some things that have been done should not have been done."

That was cryptic. I turned to share a glance with Tamara and found her already looking at me, mouth parted in surprise, like she had taken something entirely different from Indigo's words than I had.

Meanwhile, Indigo was still watching the corpse, both lit underwater-blue. He looked young for such an ancient creature, young and alone.

"Mara Zhu regretted it," I said, and Indigo's head twitched, just the slightest bit, like he had arrested a turn towards me. "She realized what she'd done in the end and tried to make it better. I mean, I don't think she should've done it the way she did, hiding everything that happened—it should be known. It should be remembered, even though it was terrible. Then everything bad that happened here didn't happen for nothing. But what I'm... what I'm trying to say is—the people who made you, they didn't hate you. They were sorry for what they did."

"I'm not concerned about what Mara Zhu and the other scientists thought of me," Indigo said.

I'd just wanted to comfort him. But I didn't even understand what he was upset about. I was as isolated and alone here with him and Tamara as I ever was on my own aboard the *Nameless*, like we were three islands, separated by the sea.

Islands maybe, but like islands with thin ropes lashed between to make tentative, fragile bridges.

"Mara Zhu shouldn't have tried to hide the truth about what happened here," Tamara commented. "She felt too guilty about her role in it to think about what was owed the dead. But if the Philosopher Stone experiments hadn't been completed, humanity wouldn't exist today. As much as it pains me to admit it, Indigo, it was the Ministers who kept humans alive for the first few centuries of colonization."

As alien as Indigo was, I sometimes thought I understood Lantern-Eyes even less. "So all the horrible things that happened on this ship, they were worth it?"

"They should never have happened," Tamara said. "But they have happened. I can't say I wish they had never happened without knowing for sure what life would be like if the Ministers had never existed. There's no point in dwelling on the past. The only thing we can do is make sure nothing like this ever happens again."

"And what do you predict will happen if the Republic

gains this data, lieutenant?" Indigo had rested his fingertips on the tank, like he was checking the temperature of the glass. "The same thing that happened the first time."

"There's more that can be taken from the data than just how to make a Minister," Tamara said. "I've seen what I've seen on this ship. I know that whatever precisely is in the Philosopher Stone data, we'll be able to use it to cure illnesses, heal wounds, to help people—as well as to guard against your people attacking mine. What will happen if your people get it, Indigo? You haven't said exactly why you want it, but you're going to use it to strengthen yourselves somehow, aren't you? Otherwise why would you come looking? What is the first thing a stronger Maria Nova will do?"

"There are factions among the Ministers, like there are among humans. Not all of my people want war."

"And which faction usually wins out?"

My fingers were aching, so tightly wrapped around my flashlight. Not so long ago, they had been trying to kill one another over this very debate. But now, though Tamara spoke clearly, loudly, she didn't sound angry. And Indigo kept his back towards her, narrow shoulders unshielded.

Indigo said, "Mara Zhu was only wrong because she failed. She should have destroyed both the data and the specimens, but she let the Minister embryos be taken from the ship, and she failed to eliminate every last copy of the Philosopher Stone data aboard the ship. The individuals who suffered and died for this data should be allowed to rest, not have their data picked over by scientists like carrion birds. But my people need this data, so we cannot finish the job our creator started. What she felt for us does not matter, Sean, in the face of what she did and failed to do. I understand the greater purpose of the data, lieutenant, but even knowing, I can't condone the cost."

There was a lot in what he said that I could not understand. Or rather, I could, but to do it would be to sit down and put a shattered stained glass back together—it would result in a picture of symbol and meaning, but I knew I would cut my fingers in the process of putting it back as one. What Indigo had said had brought my memories close to Kystrom.

Indigo took a step back from the glass, squaring his shoulders to it and the body inside. He laid one hand on his collar-light and dialed it to the darkest of violets, then flashed out a pattern of light, rhythmic, hypnotic. In the space between flashes, the corpse in the container revolved; the inconsistency of light lent it some of the life it had lost, like it was turning, willingly, to look Indigo in the eye.

"What was that?" I asked, when the flashes had ceased.

Indigo lowered his hand, his collar-light still glowing dark. "Tradition."

He didn't say *prayer*, but I knew a prayer when I saw one. I thought of the bones I'd blessed, back at the start of this whole disaster, and Indigo kneeling beside me with his palm over mine. "Do you need someone to say it with you?"

His gaze snapped to mine and held there, intense and unreadable. Then he reached out and took my hand that held the flashlight, raising it up to face him. "Like this," he said quietly, and flashed a section of the light-poem at me. I mimicked it as best I could, but knew I was failing to get it precisely. It's difficult to imitate a pattern when you don't know the meaning of the pieces.

He shook his head. "I'll break it down," he said. "This," and he flashed a segment of the light, "means *died*, or *has died*. The pattern at the beginning makes it a noun. Do you see?"

I did, and I slowly flashed the pattern back at him. "*Those who have died*."

He nodded briefly. "The pattern on either end means *addressed to*. Do you see?"

The line started with a dim light that went quickly bright. It ended with the same dim-*flash*, surrounding the noun. Fascinating. The Light language had circumpositions instead of prepositions. "*To those who have died*," I translated.

"The next line is similar," Indigo said, and flashed it at me. "The repeated pattern at the beginning and the end of the phrase means *addressed from*. The noun in the center means *will not die*, or *does not intend to die*. My language has more than one future tense. This future tense expresses intention."

He flashed the phrase at me. I could see the same root verb in both noun phrases, a held darkness between flashes. That must be how to say *to die* in Light. "*From those who will not die*," I translated.

"Or *from I who will not die*," Indigo corrected softly. "It is the same."

He taught me the next two lines as well, walking me

patiently through the syntax until I could remember each phrase. "*Your bodies will stay here,*" I translated—it was a different future tense, a slightly different conjugation of flash and glow, "*but your life will be remembered.*" Future intention, again.

I expected all through the impromptu lesson that Lantern-Eyes would interrupt, remind us that we were surrounded by monsters, that we had to keep moving. But she was silent while Indigo taught me a prayer in his native tongue.

At last Indigo seemed satisfied, and he turned away from me to face the body in the container. I stood shoulder-to-shoulder with him, hand on the dimmer to my flashlight, nerves jittering through my fingers. It was that old anxiety, that a god wouldn't listen to a prayer poorly phrased. I had to get this right.

Indigo started the prayer and I followed him, keeping to his pace, my flashes as precise as I could make them.

"*To you who have died, from we who don't intend to die, your bodies will remain here, but your lives will be remembered,*" Tamara said behind us, her voice rough but clear, falling in cadence with our flashing light.

It was my translation, smoothed out and strung together. Indigo dialed his collar-light back to its customary dark blue.

There was a question I'd been wondering since Indigo had arrived on this ship, that he'd never answered before. I dared to ask him again, in the weird fragile peace of the three of us standing there, surrounded by corpses. "Why do your people need the data so badly?"

Indigo looked at me, one hand still resting on his collar-light. His face was a mask.

"We should find a place to rest for the night," he said. "We've traveled far today."

Just like that, the fragile... *whatever* that had existed in the room between the three of us broke.

CHAPTER FIFTY TWO:
A HOT, PIPING CUP OF COFFEE
WITH A SIDE OF CREEPY CHILDREN

I woke up from a deep sleep full of weird dreams, about Brigid crawling around with a bunch of little ghost children and trying to tell me something important, but I'd forgotten Kystrene so I couldn't understand. The sadness followed me out of the dream and I lay there for some time, letting it sink out of me like water into soil.

Finally I rolled my head around to look for my companions and found Tamara awake, sitting against the wall with the little campstove radiating heat in front of her. She'd led us to another of her saferooms, this one in what seemed to be an old pantry, shelves collapsed, and all the comestibles long gone. Indigo was on the other side of the campstove, curled up knees to chest.

Tamara had been on watch when I'd gone to sleep. Either I hadn't been sleeping long, or she and Indigo had come to a different arrangement regarding the distribution of who would watch when.

I sat up, my head still cloudy with sleep, and cleared my throat. Tamara raised her brows at me, an unspoken dare.

My words died. I cleared my throat of them, and said instead, "I guess you don't have any coffee."

"I," Tamara said, "would kill a man with my eyeteeth for a cup of coffee."

"So, no?"

"So, no."

On the other side of the little campstove, Indigo unfurled himself. I had the odd impression that he had been actually sleeping, instead of closing his eyes and doing whatever passed for sleeping when a Minister expected a knife through the back at any second. He passed one hand over his face, looking very young, then sat up straight, letting his hand drop to his lap and the odd youthfulness vanished.

I sat up too, determined to match my companions' readiness. "So, how close are we?"

"We're on the edge of the labs now." Tamara reached out to the campstove and shut it off; the radiant heat against my arm dimmed. "This is Lab One. The other labs are deeper in."

"We want to go deeper in," I said.

"I'm not as familiar with this part of the ship. My team only made it a little further than here, and then only once." She fussed with the campstove. "This is my last saferoom. We didn't have enough time after this point to establish another... and we didn't find any safe places to establish one, either."

"This is where your team died," I realized.

"Yes. I haven't been back here since; I spent the last few months exploring the less dangerous parts of the ship instead. It's my own damn bad luck that the data's in here somewhere."

The ship so far had been pretty dangerous. Exactly how much worse could it get? "How did you survive last time?"

"We tried to set up defenses," Tamara said. "Traps, deeper in. Didn't do us much good, but it gave me just enough time to escape. I survived because I ran, Sean. Humanity's last hope to get this data; I knew I couldn't die. So I ran away."

I had mistaken Tamara's willingness to move forward for indifference. I'd thought maybe she didn't feel grief. But maybe it was more like the way she'd jumped over the edge of the spiral staircase holding nothing but a rope even though she was afraid of heights, doing what she had to do because it had to be done.

I couldn't imagine ever going back to Itaka, walking the streets where everyone I'd known had died. I wondered if it was something like that for Lantern-Eyes, to return back here.

"Can we use any of the defenses your team left behind?" Indigo asked.

Tamara shook her head tightly. "They won't do us any good now. From here on out we have no more safe rooms, no more supplies, no more resources. I have no more maps, just memories."

"You still know more than we do," I said.

She acknowledged me with a nod, rustling through her

bag for some dry rations, which she passed out to me and Indigo. Moments after she handed Indigo his, he pulled a small bag out of his pocket and tossed it at her.

It landed lightly in her lap. "What's this?" she asked, picking it up and unsealing the top.

Her eyes went round. Even I, a few feet away, could smell the distinctive bitter-sharp of coffee. Tamara reached into the bag and pulled out a few beans. She looked at Indigo, who nodded, then popped one into her mouth and chewed, eyes closing with bliss.

"Are you kidding?" I asked Indigo. "Is that standard issue for Ministers, or are you some sort of addict?"

Incredibly, he smiled. It was fleeting, but I would swear on any God of Terra Nova, Maria Nova, or the independent colonies that he did.

Tamara held out the bag for me to grab some beans for myself. I declined. "That must be really bitter."

"It is," Tamara said, euphoric, and ate another before returning the bag to Indigo.

We hadn't unpacked, so repacking took only a moment. I trailed after Tamara, with Indigo falling into place behind me, as we emerged into a maze of hallways and labs.

"Stop me when you see the right number, Sean," Tamara said.

My heart jolted. "Are we close?"

"You tell me. The labs are suites of labs, not individual rooms. This is Lab 1. This section of the ship contains Labs one through forty-nine, odd numbers only."

I remembered how large the area had been on Tamara's circled map. "And each of the suites are huge."

"Yes. So we have to walk fast," Tamara said. "We wasted a lot of time chasing each other on the other side of the ship."

I'd completely lost track of time. "How long do we have until the star goes nova?"

"Three days, at most," Indigo said. "But if we do not find the Philosopher Stone by day two, we won't have enough time to escape the *Nameless* before the sun goes."

So we had, at most, two days until we had to kill each other.

"Great," I said, and the three of us walked on in silence.

I glimpsed them out of the corner of my eye as we went—the same shadowy little shapes, appearing and disappearing in doorways, always gone before my flashlight could catch them head on. I didn't intend to mention it until I noticed that Tamara, who was leading the way as usual, was walking half-crouched, looking sharply back and forth. Her tangled hair in its ponytail clung to the tattered fabric of her jacket. She'd drawn her club, and held it clenched tightly in one hand.

"Oh, I'm not the only one who sees them," I said.

"Sean, next time, if you notice something creepy, say something," Tamara said.

"You didn't notice them before?"

"Of course I noticed them. But for the future, please."

"They've been following us since the strut." Indigo sounded remarkably casual about the attention of evil ghost Children.

"I was hoping they'd peel off once they realized we weren't easy victims, or that we'd lose them overnight."

Tamara sounded significantly less relaxed.

"What do you suggest?" Indigo asked.

"We need to lose them somehow," Tamara said. "We can't afford to get cornered again; only Sean's trick with the rope got us out last time. Even you can get overwhelmed if there are enough of them, Indigo. And I'm worried that they might make a commotion... that something else might notice. That's how it started with my team. The Children found us first."

I shone my light on the doorways around us. Most of them didn't seem to have doors at all anymore, or never had; one or two had doors visible inside the wall where age had frozen the ancient mechanisms.

The first thing I'd done on this ship, to prove to One that I could read Ameng, had been to open and close a bunch of doors. "Are there any functioning computers around here? We can lock the doors behind us so they can't follow."

"Can't we close doors manually?" Indigo asked.

"No. See?" I shone my flashlight at the nearest doorway. "The Dreamer isn't maintaining any of the purely mechanical doors, so they're rotten. Maybe we'll find a few that we can open and shut but I'll bet that the only doors that still work will be in an area with a functional computer system."

"So we'll trade one monster for another," Tamara said.

"If the computers are working, the Dreamer has no reason to be there," I pointed out.

I knew I'd made a good point by the way she rolled her head to the side. "If we go into the lab suite instead of walking alongside it, there should be more electronics," Tamara said at last. "We might be able to find some functional doors there."

"Someone should stay and stall the Children so they don't realize what's happening and find a way around the blockade before you can set it up," Indigo said. I heard the sound of him drawing his long knife, leaving little doubt about who he thought that 'someone' should be.

I very much did not want to watch Indigo killing Children again, real ones or not. "You have fun with that," I said. "Come on, Tamara. Let's find a working door," and left without looking back at Indigo.

Tamara caught up after a moment. "You're going the wrong way," she told me, and her hand was a solid anchor on my shoulder, turning me in the right direction.

The first few rooms were empty, dust and darkness. I shone my flashlight around in all the corners and saw no electronics. When I examined the doors I found them corroded, rotted into place inside the walls. We moved deeper into the labs. I didn't hear anything from the hall, which meant either the Children had not attacked Indigo, or he was killing them very quietly.

"Every time I think I know your skillset, you show up with a new one," Tamara said.

I glanced away from my examination of the lab door. "What?"

She waved her flashlight at the doorframe I was looking at. "You know Ameng, picked up enough Light language to impress Indigo without even trying, and you know what to look for to tell if these doors are functional."

I couldn't tell what she was asking, if she was asking anything. "It just makes sense," I said. I knew what corroded metal looked like; Benny and I had done our own repairs on our starship for a while. This wasn't all that different.

"On the other hand, you can't throw a punch, are a horrible judge of character, and couldn't navigate yourself out of a paper bag. You know you were going in circles back before the three of us joined up? That's how I found you, probably Indigo too."

"I can throw a punch."

"No," Tamara said, with finality, "you can't."

There seemed to be nothing to say to that. I straightened up. "This door will work," I said. "We just have to find the switch."

She shone her light past me. "Except the room it leads to is a dead end," Lantern-Eyes said, like I'd somehow proved her point. "If we lock the Children out, we'd lock ourselves in."

We kept looking. The next few rooms were dead-ends, or the doors were broken, or there was an easy way around them. We struck gold deep into Lab 1, when we found a room that was larger than the rest, and had the gleam of electronics faintly lighting the dim.

A quick look over the door showed that it was in full working order. The Dreamer-bots had been hard at work here. I passed my flashlight over the room and found something odd to my right: this room was adjoined to a second, much smaller room, separated from this other room by a wall of glass windows. I could see that the adjacent room was small and empty, my flashlight filtering muzzily through the old and misty glass. Beneath the glass windows was a counter that was covered in a complicated array of dials and screens. The source of the computerized glow. That was where we'd find our lock button, then.

I went in to check the console. It gleamed beneath the dust, no rust or mold, and the screens glowing at my touch. Still functional. The Dreamer-bots had been working *overtime* on this. I wondered why.

"Okay," I said, because the self-repair had taken care of the panel's functionality, but had left most of the labels to fade and warp with age. "Look at you. Let me see—"

"Will it work?" Tamara had taken up position at the door, her club upraised. I pictured her panicking and smacking Indigo in the face with it.

Stupid thought; Tamara didn't flail when she panicked, she froze up. "Sure I can do it, but I need a minute. I mean, is the right button labeled? Does it say door, or lock, or close, or what? There's a lot of buttons here."

"So focus," she suggested.

"Talking is how I focus." There really were a lot of switches. And there were even more once I got the screens online. And nothing was helpfully labeled with something like 'lock the front door so that ravenous monster-children won't grind your bones into dust with their excess of molars'.

The main computer screen seemed the best bet. I started flicking through glitchy old menus when a burst of light blinded me.

"Sean?" Tamara said, and I lowered my hand from in

front of my eyes to squint ahead. The light in the adjoining room had come on—it was not particularly bright on its own, but after how many days of no illumination but my flashlight, it was blinding.

In that illumination, I could see that there was a metal panel on the wall in the adjoining room with a little switch on it.

There were too many possibilities, and we'd left Indigo alone to murder a bunch of Children. We had to divide and conquer. "Tamara," I said, and she came over swiftly, club still upraised. "I'm going to check the other room," I said, pointing at the panel visible through the glass. "In the meantime I want you to try these five buttons, okay?"

"Sean, I can't read Ameng."

"Look." I grabbed her hand, held it over the buttons I wanted. "See? This says lock, this says seal, and then these," I brought her hand over to the computer screen, lacy with Ameng's black script. "This menu has something to do with doors. Try these buttons."

Tamara nodded, sharp, and I let go of her bony wrist to hurry into the brightness of the adjoining room, setting my flashlight on the counter beside her hand as I went.

The other room was small, hardly more than a closet. The air smelled stale, like the ship's ventilation hadn't been working in here. It took me barely two strides to reach the panel on the far wall, where there was a little mesh grate over a single button.

The button was labeled 'Talk'. Not useful, then. I turned to go back the way I had come just as a door shot out of where it had been hidden in the wall and sealed the exit to the little windowed room with an aerated hiss.

There was no knob or handle on this side: I rapped on the glass separating me and Tamara, even though she was already staring straight at me, lantern-eyes wide. "Care to let me out?"

She shook her head at me, then mouthed something.

No, not mouthed something—she was saying something, I just couldn't hear her through the glass. So that explained the button, then. I reached back to the wall and the button labeled *Talk*. "Can you hear me?" I asked.

Tamara nodded furiously, but when her mouth moved, I couldn't hear a word.

"Look for another panel like this one; I can't hear you unless you press the button," I said. "It should... No, never mind. Can you press whatever button you just pressed and let me out?"

She gave me a severe look and jabbed two fingers down at the counter.

"Okay, you've been pressing it," I realized. "I'm safer in here than you are right now. Just try those other buttons I said; let's figure out how to get the main door closed before Indigo gets here, then we can let me out."

She nodded, then made some arcane gesture through the glass at the space around me.

"What?" I said.

Her eyes narrowed again. She pointed once, sharply, at me, then turned those jabbing fingers at her own eyes, then pointed at the space around me. Then, for good measure, she mimed looking around, shielding her eyes against the light with one hand like a sailor at sea.

She looked like an idiot.

"There's nothing else in this room but me, but I'll check," I promised, swallowing my grin.

I turned my back on the window and Tamara's bent head to pace around the little room. It was just big enough that I could have laid down on the floor without touching either wall. That meant it was larger than most spaceship rooms, and larger than some apartments in the Republic's capital city. I told myself this several times as I walked around, examining walls and floor and finding nothing. There was a grate in the back of the room, from which emitted a hissing sound paired with an odd little wind; probably the ventilation system sucking up air to clean it of impurities. Nothing else.

A dull knocking from behind me caught my attention; Tamara was rapping on the window. When she got my attention she spread her arms wide and mouthed, *Nothing*.

"No?" I said. "Nothing worked?" I leaned against the window. It was very solid glass; I hadn't realized how thick it was until I was right up against it. Tamara stared at me from the other side, my shadow falling over her face. Some trick of the light made her look worried.

The rest of the room behind Tamara was dimly lit now in the light that filtered through the window and past me. By that light I could see the rest of the big room, a cracked slab of stone in the wall that might have been a chalkboard, the bent and broken plastic of a few ancient chairs behind metal and shattered glass desks.

And, beside the door we'd entered by, almost invisible with age and shadow, another little computer screen.

I hit the talk button on the intercom and said, "Tamara, behind you, at the door we want to close—there's a panel in the wall a little below eye level. Well. A little below my eye level."

That she was shorter than me suddenly struck me as inexplicably funny. Brigid had always been so pissed about that. She'd been tall, too, about as tall as Tamara, but not as tall as me. I could pick up something she wanted and hold it over her head while she jumped for it like an angry little dog.

She'd hated that so much. It had been funny because she'd hated it. I'd done that the morning she died, for no reason except to piss her off. She'd been so mad. That's the last interaction I'd ever had with her. She'd been so furious, and I'd laughed at her.

I didn't like to think about this. I didn't like to remember. The conflict between horrible old shame and my weird hilarity made me nauseous. I doubled over, holding my gut.

Knock-knock. I lifted my head and found Tamara very close to the glass that separated us. "Who's there?" I asked, and laughed.

She mouthed something at me, but trying to read her lips took too much focus. "You should learn sign language," I told her. "Or we should learn Light. Indigo would be mad."

There was something different than usual about her expression. It was hard to put my finger on it, weirdly hard to focus. I felt a little short of breath. Panic attack? The room was pretty small, but no, it was big enough, and

I didn't feel scared. Actually, I felt pretty funny.

She wasn't trying to anticipate me, I realized, insight rising to the forefront of my mind like a bubble popping. Tamara usually looked at me with something like suspicion, trying to stay a foot ahead of me, to plan for whatever I might do next. She wasn't looking at me like that now. She was just... looking.

Very closely and very intensely, too. I smiled at her sheepishly through the glass.

Another thought bubbled up, oddly disparate. "Wait," I said, and my mouth moved a beat slower, it seemed, than I'd wanted it to. "Did the button work? Did it lock the door?"

Tamara gave me a thumb's up. There was a dark bend to her brows—like Indigo, I thought. Indigo always had a little frown.

Where was Indigo? It had been a long time. I wondered what that meant. Was he dead? Or was he systematically lopping off all those little Children's heads, one by one, like plucking dandelions?

The thought was so unbelievably horrible that I laughed again.

Slam. Something struck the glass, harder than before. I looked over to find Tamara leaning hard against the glass, her jack-o-lantern eyes so wide the whites showed all around. She pointed, frantic, down at something on the screen before her.

I leaned into the glass to peer out and onto the screen. There was some sort of diagram there, but it didn't mean anything to me. "I don't know," I said to her. And then

I thought maybe she wanted me to translate, so I took another look. All the letters were upside down, and it was weirdly hard to rotate them in my head.

"It's not a word," I said. "It's just some letters. P-S-I. I don't know what the graph is. Maybe it's a mechanical thing. If it's not grammar I can't do it. I don't know it."

The slam of her palm against the glass, even muffled, jolted my attention back to her. She was mouthing something at me through the glass, frantic, intent. I tried to take a deep breath—surprisingly difficult—and focus.

She was mouthing a word at me in Sister Standard. Of course she was, I mused, thinking about common phonemes, the way Tamara's particular accent affected the shape of her lips and jaw when she spoke. Tamara didn't speak any language other than Sister.

Vacuum, she was mouthing at me. Vacuum.

Vacuum? I thought, and had the odd, irresistible urge to yawn. My jaw clicked, and like that was a signal, for an instant my thoughts were clearer.

Vacuum. The sealed door, the thick glass. My yawning and euphoria, my shortness of breath.

I was in a vacuum chamber, and the air was being sucked out.

CHAPTER FIFTY THREE:
SEAN WREN AND THE INCREDIBLE HYPOXIA

NOW THAT I knew what was going on it was weirdly easier to focus. The vent in the back of the room that I'd thought was removing the air to purify it was just removing the air. One of the 'door' buttons I'd had Tamara push had actually been the symbol to seal the door to this room so that the vacuum chamber could start vacuuming.

The thought made a little giggle bubble up in my throat, but I didn't find it particularly funny anymore. I hadn't died in the vacuum of space; it just wouldn't be right to die in an oversized bell jar. Luckily, Tamara was right there, and if there was a way to start the process, there would be a way to end it, too.

I braced myself against the glass—I was starting to grow lightheaded. "Okay," I said, and remembered a second later to actually reach out and touch the Talk button so she could hear me. "Okay. I want you to look at the screen that got us into this situation. I'm gonna try to read it from up here, and I'll tell you what buttons to push, okay?"

She leaned back, bracing her hands over the screen, and nodded at me.

It was really hard to read. "Okay," I said. "Not that... I think that screen just shows stats, all right."

She waved a hand impatiently at me in a 'go on' manner. Right. If that screen showed, like pressure readout, or whatever, then Tamara was better able to read it than I was. That's probably how she'd known I was in a vacuum chamber to begin with.

Something rapped the glass near my head, and I jolted up. Tamara was staring at me through the glass with weird intensity, like her look—like—like an electric plug, I thought. Like I was a lamp and the only way she could keep me on was by sending me electricity through her eyes, and if she blinked I'd go dark or something.

Maybe I was not concentrating as well as I'd thought.

"Look for something that says stop," I said, then I remembered she couldn't read Ameng. Ameng script was really absurd anyway; the Sister writing system was a lot more coherently phonetic, or at least it had been about fifty years ago, before the Republic won its independence from the Ministers and runaway dialectal expansion had followed, once free of the Ministers' strict control over the official linguistics.

I pulled my brain back to the here and now. "It looks like this," I said, and released the talk key in order to trace out the letters on the glass: S-T-O-P. Then I remembered it was backwards to her and did it again in reverse. My finger felt very heavy.

Tamara nodded at me, a soldier's sharp efficiency, and bent over the screen, scanning it, carefully touching what looked like it was some kind of back button and ending up at a different menu.

There had been a realization growing in my mind ever since Tamara had told me I was in a vacuum chamber. This thought didn't bubble up, bright and quick, like the others. It had risen slowly, thick as molasses. I was standing inside a human-sized vacuum chamber. The vacuum of space was, at nearest, just a few feet away from the inside of this ship; why build a vacuum chamber unless you wished to control exactly how low of a pressure you wished to apply? And why build one large enough for a person to lie down in unless you wished to put a person inside?

The Ministers were very resistant to the vacuum, and to the sudden pressure changes caused by going to and from the vacuum. I'd seen it with Indigo when he'd rescued me, and had been alert and coherent enough to tend to my injuries and keep watch while I passed right out. I'd seen it with Indigo when he'd first come into the ship, passing through straight vacuum and arriving alert and coherent enough to stop our bullets and cut Leah's throat.

The Ministers were designed to be resistant to the vacuum. The scientists who had made them would have had to test that resistance, gather data and develop strategies to improve that resistance. And they would've had to do it with live subjects. I wondered how many people had died in this little room.

If Tamara didn't hurry up, that number might become one more.

Something slammed against the glass again, just as hard as before, but the jolt of adrenaline seemed to rattle me less. I opened my eyes to find Tamara very close to the glass, mouthing something very deliberately and frantically. I stared at the movement of her lips and struggled to shape them into words.

She pointed down at the screen and mouthed, No, over and over. This was simpler, and easier to understand. The computer must not be working perfectly anymore, or Tamara couldn't find the off button, or maybe the sequence to turn off the vacuum was more complicated than the on button had been.

My hand was braced against the glass near my face, and my veins were standing out against my skin, thick and blue. I swear I could see them pulsing quickly. It was revolting, like little blue worms under my skin.

"I don't like my worms," I said.

Tamara tapped against the window. When I looked up at her she contorted her brows in the universal symbol for *What?*

Oh, the Talk button. I reached out and missed the button the first few times.

"I don't like my worms," I said, trying to speak clearly and certain I wasn't succeeding. "I don't like my worms or the tunnels they make in me."

Tamara looked like she regretted asking.

I held up my hand because maybe she didn't know what I was talking about. Lifting my arm was weirdly hard. I let it drop for a minute and stared down at my dangling hand. Then I thought that my arm felt so much better lower down that I might feel better, too. I sat down heavily on the floor.

Something slammed against the glass, hard enough to startle me. When I looked out the window again I saw Tamara with her club upraised, her expression grim. She swung like a batter, the end of the club hitting the glass with tremendous force.

It rebounded, staggering her. She was going to hurt her shoulders doing that. There was no webbing in the glass.

The sound of her beating the glass was weirdly in rhythm with the blood pounding in my head; I let my head drop to my knees, where I panted into the space between my legs and stomach. I couldn't fill my lungs all the way, and behind me, the grate hissed as it sucked more and more air out of the room.

The sudden cessation of pounding had me blearily lifting my head. My skull had gotten heavier, I was sure; made of metal, not bone. I looked through the window on the other side of the room and saw Tamara standing back, expression blank, and aiming her gun at the glass.

Her club hadn't cracked it. Her bullet might pierce the glass; more likely it would ricochet, and hit Tamara, and the crack of a pistol firing would call every monster in this side of the ship to her location. I stared at her through the glass and found that I couldn't even remember the words in any language to tell her not to.

Her expression tightened, mouth going thin; I watched her finger twitch on the trigger—

Then she stopped, turning towards the door. Relief crumpled her expression, so out of character she looked like someone else, and dark blue preceded Indigo into the room.

He looked from Tamara straight at me, and I watched those dark-river eyes go wide. One hand went to his collar light and he flashed a pattern at me in indigo. A quick flutter, a longer hold.

Wait, I remembered muzzily, from his lessons to me in the library. But he'd said it to me in his color, in dark, dark blue.

Politer, then. Not *wait*, but *please hang on*.

Something sizzled, hissed. A loud beep tore through my consciousness like a hand through thin paper. The sucking sound behind me stopped, and my next breath brought air, and a strange painful pressure against my face and ears and eyes.

I panted, each breath agonizing, on the floor of the vacuum chamber without knowing when I'd fallen. Indigo was crouched over me, his sword held awkwardly in one hand, the blade still glowing with heat. He'd cut through the glass. Something was ringing, wailing, or else my ears weren't working right.

"Is he all right?" Tamara called, her voice oddly muffled. I lifted one heavy hand to my ear, thinking to remove whatever cotton was stuffing it.

Indigo caught my wrist and set it back down. "He's fine," he said, and his voice was muffled, too. "Sean. We need to get out of here before the ship's autorepair comes to investigate the damage."

"Oh, Mother of the Redeemer," I heard Tamara say, all on an exhale.

That ringing and wailing. I wasn't imagining it. The lights had gone all funny on the computer—it was flashing red. An alarm—the Dreamer-bots would be here at any minute.

"Right," I said, my mouth oddly sore, and let Indigo pull me up with the hand that wasn't holding the flaming sword. He had to help me out through the hole in the wall, too; the edges of the glass were still glowing with heat.

Tamara waited for us just outside, eyes oddly bright, light flashing red and harsh over her face. She'd shut the exterior door against the Children, just like we'd planned. She said, "I can't believe you got yourself locked in a vacuum chamber."

It hurt to talk. "You pushed the button," I said.

"Hurry," Indigo said, just barely on the edge of my muffled hearing, and dragged me along. So much for us being discreet, and avoiding any attention—we might've gotten rid of the Children, but that sound and flashing lights would call every manikin in a hundred miles.

Lantern-Eyes took the lead from Indigo after a minute, guiding us more confidently through the blackness of the labs. My ears and eyes hurt and the ground seemed unstable underfoot; more than once I found Indigo shoving me upright. His collar-light was a steady glow, but I couldn't seem to keep my flashlight level.

We halted with an abruptness that startled me; Indigo protested something at my side and Tamara said, her voice louder and clearer than his but still fading in and out of my hearing, "We need to stop... To run, we can't have him stumbling... Give me your medical device."

At that point, Indigo pushed me to sit down, and the two of them proceeded to have a brief hissed argument over my head which I only half-heard and less than that understood. I imagined it coming to this, the representatives of the Republic and of Maria Nova, coming to blows over what to do with the Kystrene. How perfectly appropriate.

Tamara must have won the argument, because she crouched down beside me with Indigo's medical device and manhandled my head until she could get to my ears. I could see down the way we had come, partially obscured by Indigo's watchful silhouette. We were far enough from the commotion that I couldn't see the room anymore, but the *Nameless* was so dark that the air was still faintly lightened by the distant lights, a red haze that I could only see out of the corner of my eyes.

Something cool touched my ears and I flinched, but Lieutenant Gupta held me mercilessly still. Then she clapped her hands over my ears and held them there for some time. Indigo was a taut curve against the faint flash of red.

At long last, Tamara took her hands away from my ears. Sound rushed back in, sharp and clear. I blinked. My head still hurt, but I no longer felt as muffled and dizzy.

"Your eardrums ruptured from the pressure," Tamara said beside me, quick and quiet, "which is why you had trouble standing upright. It should be fixed now. God, they weren't kidding when they said Minister technology was better than ours. No wonder we can't get any advantage over them in an open fight."

"More advanced, yes," Indigo said calmly, "but the first aid machine is almost out of uses."

"So nobody else get hurt," I translated. My voice sounded normal to me again, no longer bouncing around weirdly inside my skull.

"If you can stand up straight now, we need to leave," Tamara said. "We've got to get as far from that alarm as possible."

Indigo's voice was so low I wouldn't have been able to hear it before Tamara had fixed my ears. "Get up now," he said. "We're out of time."

Down the hall, the red light had gone dark.

CHAPTER FIFTY FOUR: TRUST ME

PART ONE

EITHER SOMETHING WAS standing between us and the red light, or the Dreamer-bots had arrived and shut down the alarm. Either way, we didn't want to linger here.

I got back up. Whatever Tamara had done to my ears had worked like a charm. I didn't exactly feel like running a marathon, but at least I wasn't going to fall on my face.

Down the hallway, I heard nails scrabbling against metal.

"Okay," Tamara said, "let's go this way," and she took off. I bolted after her, and heard Indigo following.

It was funny; I was almost getting used to running in the dark like this. If I shortened my strides a little bit I'd be more prepared for whatever was on the ground, so I wouldn't go sprawling; I was more attuned to Tamara, too, and better able to follow her sudden sharp turns in the dark without losing track of her. Not a skill I'd expected to gain when I'd first landed on this ship—

I impacted Tamara's back with a *whumph* of breath,

getting hair in my face. Being more attuned to her hadn't stopped me from running straight into her when she'd unexpectedly stopped. "What's wrong?" I asked, catching her when my impact almost knocked her over.

"Dead end," Tamara said tersely, starting back the way we had come.

Tamara had never so much as hesitated, much less made a wrong turn. "Dead end?"

"I've only been to this part of the ship once, Sean!"

Indigo jogged up to meet us, his sword already drawn. "Don't stop," he warned, and far off the way we'd come, I heard nails scratching, metal shrieking against metal.

"Yes," Tamara agreed, taut, and started off again in a new direction. I followed her, thoughts whirling. She'd only been here once, and then her team had died. This might be the part of the ship *where* her team had died.

She still knew more about the ship than me or Indigo. I would've been lost in seconds down the dark halls.

She stopped again some distance from that dead-end, at a split in the hallways. I jogged to a stop, trying to catch my breath. Indigo glowed behind us, sword upraised, facing the way we'd come. The scratching sounds were louder, quiet but intrusive, more disturbing than a louder noise would have been.

"Okay," Tamara said, pushing her hair out of her face, hands to her skull, looking down first one way, then another. I said, "What is it? Which way do we go?"

She flung one hand out to point down the right fork. "That way's not safe. I mean it's closed off. We had to detonate a small explosive—my team and I. The manikins were chasing us, and we collapsed the room to stop them. We can't go that way."

"So what about the other way?" I asked.

She pushed both hands through her hair again. "I don't know."

"What do you mean, you don't know?"

"I mean I never went that way," Tamara said. "If I'd been everywhere on this ship already, I wouldn't need you, Sean!"

"Let's see what we can handle here, then," Indigo said, calmly, just as the first of the manikins appeared in the glow of his collar-light.

I backed up hastily to give him the space to swing his arm without hitting me, and watched him sever the first manikin's reaching hand. Tamara swore and lunged forward, dropping her pack to free her reach and swinging her club at a second manikin, knocking him away from Indigo. I fumbled about my waist for the big knife Tamara had lent me and by the time I'd drawn it, Indigo had one dead manikin at his feet and Tamara was relentlessly beating the one at her feet while it tried to claw at her ankles.

The hallway where it branched was just a little too wide for Indigo's reach to cover it fully, even with Tamara beating things to a pulp nearby, and it wasn't long before one manikin slipped around him and came at me. I raised my knife as it lunged at me, snarling a thousand years of hate, then changed my mind at the last minute and hurled my pack into its face instead. The pack hit it in the face and it stumbled, falling back at the unexpected impact. I slashed at it while it wasn't looking at me.

My aim was decent, and I knew to expect the resistance of skin and muscle, so I kept a tight grip on the hilt of the knife. A long dark line carved through the manikin's midsection and it snarled in pain, fighting to pull my bag off its face. It lashed out at me and I smacked it with the knife, but this time my aim wasn't so good. I got its knuckles with the flat of the blade instead of neatly chopping them off like Indigo was doing.

My companions were trained killers but this kind of fighting was not, how had Tamara put it, my skillset. I needed a different strategy. I turned my flashlight to shine overhead.

The ceiling was just as decayed as the rest of the ship, just as decayed as I'd expected. Old pipes and struts, most of which looked jagged and sharp with broken metal and plastic. I spotted the cleanest handholds and leapt up to grab them just as the manikin freed itself from my pack.

I swung my legs up just in time for the manikin's lunge; it missed, grabbing where I had been a second before. Then it crouched on the floor below me and bared its weird, human teeth. I was significantly taller than it—it couldn't reach up as easily as I had.

I'd solved my immediate problem only to introduce another. I hung from the ceiling and stared upside-down at the calculating eyes of the manikin as it prepared to leap.

I knew what to do right before it jumped. Instead of thinking about what I was about to do, I simply let go of the pipe I'd been holding on to, and let myself fall down onto the manikin just as it reached up to meet me. My weight slammed it into the ground, off-balance, and I used my momentum to jam the knife all the way through its throat. The manikin jolted, spat dark blood, and stopped moving.

That had worked surprisingly well. I looked over to see how my companions were doing and found Tamara beating her last opponent into a bloody pulp while Indigo faced down a particularly large manikin, eyes glinting in the dark blue of Indigo's collar-light and snarling sharpened teeth.

I stood up, found another handhold in the ceiling, and swung up again. It had been a while since I'd swung around on monkey bars, but I'd had to do hull repairs on a starship recently, and that required a lot of crawling around upside-down, too.

My feet crashed into the manikin's face, knocking him away from Indigo, my full weight smashing the monster against the ground. "*Sean—*" said Indigo, and his language might not have any designated swear words but he sure made my name sound like one, and before the manikin I'd stunned could dig its claws through my spine I heard the crunch of Indigo driving his sword through bone.

I rolled off the corpse. "How are we doing?" I asked.

Tamara was panting, leaning on her club, splashed with dark blood. Indigo, untouched, looked past me down the hall—and behind me, I could hear more skitter-scratch of claws. A lot of them.

"So, the left fork, then," I said.

"I think we need to gamble, lieutenant," Indigo agreed

with me.

"I hate gambling," Tamara said, but it was a complaint, not disagreement.

Indigo took the lead down the left fork, since he was a searchlight and first line of defense all in one. I followed, light shining all around us, checking walls and ceiling and floor. It had been a while since I'd gone somewhere on this ship where Tamara hadn't had an idea of what was waiting for us. I hadn't realized how much security that had given me until we were going in blind.

And then the path ended. I swung my flashlight around wildly and found that the hallway should have branched out to our right, but at some point—somehow—the ceiling had collapsed into a mess of metal and debris.

Indigo examined the collapse while Tamara pressed her ear against the far wall, like she was listening to find out what was behind it. I swept my flashlight over the area again, searching for something—anything. We hadn't even passed any doorways on our way here, so there was no point in backtracking.

Tamara lifted her head from the wall. "This is a hull wall," she told us. "We cut through, and we end up in outer space."

Indigo returned to the hall from the mess of the collapsed ceiling. "It's too unstable," he said. "I can't cut through."

A dead end. We'd gambled and lost. "How do you lose poker?" I asked. "Would you say, like, we got a bad card? A pair of ones? Bad roll of the dice?"

"Sean, if the last thing I ever hear is you talking about poker, I'll kill you," Tamara said.

How unlike the logical lieutenant. "If you're dead, you can't kill—"

The metallic clicking of claws on the floor was joined, then, by a high and awful shrieking: the sound of a thousand years of hatred. The manikins burst upon us.

Indigo stepped between the manikins, Tamara and I. I saw the underwater blue of his collar-light shine upon the first row of hateful, rictus faces, and then he was overwhelmed.

We were overwhelmed, too. There were just too many of them. I fell back against the hull wall, the knife useless in my hands, while Tamara swung her club wildly around, searching desperately for space.

A manikin came at me from the side; I saw it in the instant before it hit me. I slashed at it wildly, uselessly, making it recoil but not actually hurting it. Tamara was still beating a manikin to my right, keeping the bulk of them away from me; I glimpsed Indigo in the midst of the crowd of manikins just as one caught him across the ribs.

Indigo staggered, the most graceless he'd ever been. The manikin attacking me lunged, taking advantage of my inattention, and I moved too late: its claws sliced white-hot pain through my jacket, down my back. A switch inside my head that I had not known was there flipped: I turned and sank my knife into its gut. The manikin fell, taking my knife down with it. I watched it go down, watched a living thing die, and felt the heat of its blood soaking my hand.

One of the manikins fighting Tamara grabbed her by the hair. She kicked him away, sending him stumbling, then headbutted the next. That got her just enough space to swing her club again, but she was going to be overwhelmed, and quickly. I lashed out, wildly, uselessly, and missed.

And then the manikin holding Tamara was flung away like the darkness itself had grabbed it, and the stench of cooked meat bloomed in the air in time with the monster's agonized scream. Indigo stood where the manikin had been, his sword glowing with heat and his jumpsuit gleaming wetly in the light. For the barest instant, the space around the three of us was free of manikins.

Indigo was breathing hard. "Do you trust me?" he asked us.

That was surprisingly easy to answer. "Yes."

"Do it," said Tamara.

"Hold on to my waist," he said, "and exhale," and just as I'd grabbed his waist and put my other arm around Tamara, too, he plunged his sword through the hull wall and all the air rushed from the room, taking us and the manikins with it.

CHAPTER FIFTY FIVE: TRUST ME

PART TWO

I LANDED HARD on solid metal and the lumpy shape of my pack, digging into my kidneys. I'd lost my breath as soon as Indigo had carried us into the vacuum of space, and I struggled to gasp it back now that there was air.

In the wall to my right there was a jagged hole cut in the starship hull, oil-slick surface sealing the opening. Blazing orange light shone through the oil-slick from the sun outside. It was the only light I could see. I'd lost my flashlight in the other room.

Something cold touched my neck, right over my carotid. I lashed out at it but it caught my arms instead of slicing my throat, and a shape appeared in my line of sight.

It was Tamara, mouthing words at me. She didn't look too good. Her eyes were bloodshot from her introduction to the vacuum, and there were the beginnings of a massive bruise on one side of her face. Blood was drying in her hair.

Sound warped back into existence, and all of a sudden I could hear her saying, "Stop fighting! Sean, stop fighting! Are you okay?"

I could breathe, and see, and hear. I nodded at her, too breathless still to talk.

She nodded, but the tense expression on her face didn't change. She looked past me. I turned to see what she saw and found Indigo braced on his elbows on the floor, his sword flat on the ground a few feet away. The material of the floor was bubbling around the heated weapon, raising a terrible acrid stench, even as the blade dimmed and cooled.

Indigo pushed himself up off his elbows—and then his arms gave way. He dropped his forehead to rest against the floor. There was a stain spreading beneath him, a peculiarly vibrant violet in the light from outside the hull.

Tamara scrambled over me towards him. It looked like although I'd kept my pack, both my companions had lost theirs. She bent over him, her oversized jacket obscuring my view. My ears were ringing again, but this time not, I thought, from any reaction to the vacuum.

The ringing was not so loud to cover up the sound of scratching nails further down the hall. Wherever Indigo had taken us, it hadn't been far enough.

But maybe he'd taken us back into a part of the ship Tamara had been to, once. I pushed myself up. "Do you know where we are?"

"I think so." Tamara was still bent over Indigo, the curtain of her dark hair hiding his face from me. She stuck her hand out behind herself, towards me. "Pass me the club."

She'd kept a hold of her club even through the decompression and violent reintroduction to the ship. Unbelievable. I found the club on my other side, where she must have landed, and passed it into her waiting hand.

When she stood, I saw that Indigo was conscious, still braced on his elbows and his jaw so tight he must be grinding his teeth. "Are you okay?" I asked.

"Help him up, Sean," Tamara said.

Indigo reached for his sword when I went to pull him up. His hand closed around the hilt, but the sword didn't budge when he tugged it. The blade had melted the floor, and gotten stuck there after it had cooled.

He'd have to reheat the blade to pull it free. Looking at his drawn face, I wasn't sure he could. "Just leave it," I said, as the sound of scratching nails got closer and closer.

He shut his eyes and I recognized defeat. I hauled him up with a troubling wet sound as the fabric of his jumpsuit pulled free of the floor. "You're bleeding a lot," I told him.

"Let's go," Tamara warned us, already backing up, and I pulled Indigo away from the sound of scrabbling nails.

He couldn't quite find his footing at first, stumbling and slow. His collar-light was the only light we had and I tried to spot some sort of pathway to escape in the dim blue glow. With Tamara guarding our backs, I was suddenly the guide.

I knew the manikins had caught up to us when I heard the solid *thunk* of Tamara's club impacting something's skull. I pulled Indigo to a wobbling stop and turned to see what our pursuit was.

They were spread out all down the hall, glinting eyes and glinting claws, plasticky flesh and corpselike limbs. "We have to find a way out of here," I said.

Tamara slammed her club into an advancing manikin's reaching arm. "I'm open to ideas, Sean!"

There was a manikin on the edges of Tamara's reach, creeping around her, its eyes fixed on Indigo and me. I fumbled at my belt and realized I'd lost my knife with the flashlight. "Do you remember this part of the ship? Is there another room where we can lock the door?"

"I don't know, and we don't have time to look for one!" She shouted as she brought her club down on the head of another manikin. It staggered, blood streaking blackly down its features.

The manikin approaching Indigo and I was too close for comfort, and I didn't have a weapon. I grabbed Indigo, ready to haul him back and curl around him, provide some shield from the monster, but he shoved me away instead with surprising strength.

I landed hard on the ground, Indigo between me and the manikin. "Tamara!" Indigo gritted out, and she glanced over her shoulder, then tossed him her club. He caught it in midair and she turned back to the manikin lunging at her, drawing a knife from her belt in the same motion. Indigo slammed the club into the manikin's skull with inhuman strength, hard enough to split bone. The manikin fell, dead, but Indigo dropped to his knees as well.

"Tamara," he said again, more gravelly than before; she extended one hand to catch the club he tossed back at her, and flipped the knife over her shoulder towards him. He caught it but didn't try to stand. The manikins were drawing back a little, regrouping, watching Tamara and her swinging club with calculating eyes. A moment's reprieve. But when I crawled to Indigo's side I saw more open emotion on his face than I had ever seen before—sadness. An apology.

He expected to die. And when I looked back at Tamara I saw her expression hard, determined, utterly devoid of hope. They both expected to die here.

No. No, not again.

And then I remembered something else I'd found on this ship. "Tamara, you said that you survived here last time because your crew set up defenses before they died," I said. "Are there any left? Any at all? Or are there any of those gas traps around here? I found one in the labs on the other side of the ship; it was a gas trap that knocked out the manikins who went inside."

Tamara's shoulders stiffened. Indigo said, "What?"

"There's another gas trap not far from here," Tamara said. "Get him up."

"What trap?" Indigo asked sharply as I hauled him up, putting one arm over my shoulders. It was awkward, him being shorter than me, but he wasn't going to stay upright on his own.

"If I lead, can you get him running?" Tamara asked me.

I'd just pick him up and carry him. "Yeah."

"Ready," Tamara said, "*go!*"

I didn't warn Indigo before I hauled him up into my arms. He let out a sharp breath between his teeth, from annoyance or pain or both, but there was no time to protest and he didn't. I ran after Tamara with warm dampness spreading down my shirt where Indigo's torso pressed against mine. The manikins chased after us; I heard their scratching claws, the soft huffs of their breath. I wished they made more noise than that; it would've been less frightening if they shouted or howled or something, less frightening than this awful whispering and scratching. Indigo's free arm slung around my neck, the hilt of Tamara's knife in his fist bumping against my spine. I wondered if he planned to fight off the manikins by hanging off my neck.

He was bleeding a lot. It had already soaked my shirt.

There was no time for caution. I ran flat-out after Tamara, my only light the pale glow of Indigo's collar-light shining out from near my own neck, praying I didn't stumble or fall. Hopefully the gas trap was close by. I wasn't sure how long I could keep the pace going, carrying both Indigo and the pack.

Running flat-out, Tamara and I were faster than the manikins. The sound of their nails receded into the distance, not far enough to escape them, but enough to get some breathing room.

I nearly ran past Tamara when she stopped short in front of an open doorway, winding down to a slow stop and nearly dropping Indigo when I did. It was only when his arms slipped around my neck that I thought to brace him, letting his legs down so that he could try to stand up on his own. His blood was all down my front.

Tamara was breathing so hard she almost couldn't speak. "This is it," she gasped. "Listen, when we go in,

Indigo, the gas will affect you too. It won't hurt you, but it will knock you out."

"What is this?" Indigo's voice was ragged. "What *trap?*"

"I'll explain everything later," Tamara said. "Trust me."

"There shouldn't be a trap on this ship that would work on a Minister," Indigo said. He was shaking under my arm and I really didn't understand how there was any blood left in his body. The manikins' scratching was getting louder; catching up. "There weren't any Ministers on board when Mara Zhu tried to destroy the Stone, so there shouldn't be any traps that work on a Minister unless they have been added recently. What *trap*, Tamara? Why is it here?"

Lantern-Eyes looked at us, still breathing fast, but that old familiar hardness settling back into the bones of her face. She said, "Because I was ordered to catch a Minister alive."

CHAPTER FIFTY SIX:
TRUST ME

PART THREE

"My mission wasn't just to find the Philosopher Stone," Lieutenant Gupta said. "It was also to capture a Minister alive. The Ministers were supposed to find this ship. But the years passed, and my team died, and you still didn't show up. If the Ministers saw Republican military arrive to rescue me, they would've finally noticed this ship—but they would've been on their guard. So I didn't call for rescue. I set off the SOS instead, to lure you in."

The SOS. That's why the SOS had gone off, why the ship had only been found now, after a thousand years. Lantern-Eyes' lure hadn't just caught the Ministers. It had caught me.

"And now you have me," Indigo said.

"No," Tamara said. "This isn't a trap, Indigo, this is the *only way we can survive*—"

"What will I be used for," Indigo rasped, speaking over her, "a test subject? Like Mara Zhu? You—"

"You think you can say something I haven't thought already, after all this? I swear to you, Indigo," Tamara said, and breathless as she was it came out harsh and hard, "that if you go into this room now, and we all survive, no Minister will be caught by me or my traps, I swear it."

Indigo sagged against me. I adjusted my grip on him and found Tamara gazing appeal at me.

I thought about Lieutenant Gupta's bare-bones pragmatism, the dispassionate way she'd spoken of the ancients' choice to commit human experimentation on this ship. That, however indirectly, it was her fault I had been sent here.

The scratching of manikin claws was closer, and I could just see them down the hall, eyes glimmering. "I stay with Indigo," I said.

"So you'll die together," Tamara said, but she said it to Indigo, not to me.

"We go into the room," Indigo said, just as harsh as Tamara, and I had to move with him or risk his collapse.

There was no chance to question his sudden about-face. We were already in the room, and the manikins' nails scrabbled down the hall, closer with every second that passed.

"Get to the back," Tamara directed us, hard. She was backing into the room behind us, club upraised. "It will take some time for the gas to take effect. If we're too close to the door, they'll still be able to kill us."

I could hear a hissing sound from some unseen vent. The trap had been triggered.

Indigo staggered suddenly, and when I braced him, he

refused to move. We weren't even halfway across the room yet. "Come on," I said, and I could've dragged him, but I was afraid of hurting him worse than he already was. "Indigo, come—"

"The Ministers are dying," Indigo said, through gritted teeth. "Sean. Tamara. The Ministers are dying."

If this was some sort of metaphor, it was badly timed. "You're gonna be all right. We have to get deeper in the room."

"The Ministers are dying," he insisted, but he moved when I did this time. I could smell that weird metallic tang now, stinging my nose. "There's something wrong in our genetic code."

Like an electric shock, it hit me. Mara Zhu saying: *I sabotaged the shipment.*

She'd meant the Ministers.

Mara Zhu had poisoned her own creation.

CHAPTER FIFTY SEVEN:
THE SHEDDING OF BLOOD

INDIGO WAS HEAVY against my side, a physical reminder of his mother's crime.

"We need the data to save ourselves," he said. Indigo's voice was fading in and out; he couldn't quite find his footing. "We need the Philosopher Stone."

I glanced back at Tamara but saw only her hunched shoulders, guarding the door.

"We need the data," Indigo told me, and I finally understood what he was asking.

"You'll get the data yourself," I told him, instead of the promise he wanted, and then the first of the manikins came through the door.

Tamara shouted behind me, but it was rage and not pain, so I didn't look back. Indigo was heavy under my arm and the air smelled like sour metal and we were still not quite at the back wall when he folded.

I carried him the last few steps. He was gasping like a beached fish, eyes glazed over. "Tamara—"

She had backed up to stand over us, facing the manikins

that were still coming into the room. "Put pressure on his stomach."

The ground was dirty; I didn't want to put his head down. I looked around wildly for something to put beneath him, one palm under his skull, reaching out to his stomach.

There was not one wound there, there were several. Claw marks that had scored home. When I pressed down against them, lacerated flesh shifted wetly under my hand. Behind me, I heard Tamara shout.

"Do you need help?" I asked. My own voice sounded weirdly far away.

"Stay with him," Tamara said. "Make sure he keeps breathing."

She'd said the gas would only knock him unconscious! "Is stopping a possibility?!"

"He's bleeding out and drugged on top of it! Make sure he's breathing, and put pressure on that wound," Tamara said, and drove another staggering, hissing manikin away from us.

I crouched awkwardly, one palm beneath his head, the other reaching out to where the blood had soaked through his clothing and was spilling over onto the floor. I could see bone through the four deep claw-marks in his side—

Thoughts clicked off in my brain, the same way they had back on Kystrom, turning over Brigid's body. I knew even as it happened that I would never clearly remember the sight of Indigo's wound. Instead I pressed my free hand over his side, like Tamara had told me to, and stayed.

Some time later, I realized the noise of fighting and the

hiss of gas both had stopped. Awkwardly, without losing my grip either on Indigo's head or his side, I craned my neck around to see what Tamara was doing. The floor was covered with manikins lying unconscious, and she stood in the midst of them with her club. "Should I—"

"Stay with him," Tamara said, in the same hard calm voice, and lifted her club.

The ground was splotched with thick black blood by the time she finished, and I crouched just outside the reach of those puddles and counted the space between Indigo's breaths.

Tamara said, "Is he breathing?"

"Yes." My voice came out unsteady.

"Pick him up."

I picked him up. I tried to nudge his head up onto my shoulder but I couldn't get it to stay; his head lolled back, eyes shut. I couldn't keep pressure on his side while I was holding him but I tried, shrugging his torso up higher so I could curl my hand around his ribs. Tamara led us down the hallway through a series of turns my brain couldn't commit to memory, checking doors as she went. None of the rooms we passed seemed to satisfy her. Our journey took us through another server room. I tensed as we passed through, looking around for signs of Dreamer-bots. What we'd done in the past hour or two, crushing Dreamer-bots and cutting holes in the ship—I couldn't imagine the AI was happy about it.

At the far end of the server room there was another door. It led to a smaller room that had two exits, and was totally empty. Tamara gestured for me to put Indigo down.

The floor in this room was a little cleaner. I lowered Indigo carefully.

Tamara locked the door behind us. I noted, with a type of awareness that was becoming habitual, that the door could be locked on both sides—within the little room Tamara had picked as a temporary safe haven, and from the adjoining server room as well.

She said, "Is he alive?"

Indigo's blood wasn't red anymore. It had gone a deep dark blue, almost a match to his collar-light. He had run out of blood in his iron-based circulatory system, I realized. His body had switched to copper. "He's still bleeding," I said.

Tamara knelt beside us. Her hands were steady, quick and decisive. She reached into the pocket attached to his belt and pulled out Indigo's medical device.

"Wipe away the blood and hold the fabric of his shirt away from the wound," Tamara said, and I obeyed without thinking. Indigo's skin was cold. Tamara looked at his side, then at the machine, then she knelt down and braced one hand against his sternum and with the other she held the device over the deep gashes in his side.

Bit by bit, artificial flesh closed the wounds. It looked plasticky, oddly pinkish against Indigo's blue-white pallor. She moved his skin too soon once, and the wound tore open against the sim flesh again, and she had to do it all over.

At long last, all four gouges had been filled. Indigo lay deeply unconscious and covered in three types of drying blood between us. He didn't react when I patted his cheek and called his name.

Tamara asked again, "Is he breathing?"

He was, lightly. I could feel it against my wrist. "Yeah," I said.

She set the medical device aside. It rattled emptily. *Nobody else get injured*, I remembered saying, right before the manikins had started chasing us.

"Are you okay?" Lantern-Eyes asked. A strand of her hair was clinging to her bony jaw with dried black blood.

"Yeah. I'm okay."

"Okay," Tamara said, then, in a voice that shook, "Okay."

She pulled up her knees, wrapped her arms around them, then hid her face in her arms.

I shrugged off my pack. I'd forgotten I was wearing it, but as soon as it was free, ignored pain sprung up in both shoulders. Aside from that ache, and some bruising, though, I was uninjured. Tamara was bleeding, bruised all down one side of her face, and Indigo was unconscious with hardly any blood left in his body, but I was fine.

"Did you mean it?" I asked. "When you promised him not to catch a Minister?"

She lifted her head and wiped at her cheeks with one dirty hand. "Yeah," she said, and the word came out wet and unsteady.

I found that the last thing in the world I wanted at that moment was to see iron-lady Lantern-Eyes cry. I dug the last flashlight out of my pack, and stood up.

"We probably left a blood trail leading right here," I said. "I'm going to clean it up so nothing follows us in."

She nodded, and I unlocked the door and left.

I shrugged off my jacket, which had been sliced open in the back by a manikin's claws anyway, and used it to mop up the trail of Indigo's blood. That same blood was drying down my front, on my shirt and down my pants, stiffening as I walked.

I followed the blood trail across the empty server room and back out to the hall, and followed our path back down the hall a little bit as well, just to be sure. And because I didn't want to return, just yet, to Indigo half-dead and Lantern-Eyes grieving, the horrible sinking pit in my gut that knew we couldn't kill each other when the time came, but that we would have to anyway.

I hadn't gone too far down the hall, though, before I heard it. The manikins were dead, Lantern-Eyes had seen to that, and we'd left the Children far behind. But a machine could not die, and we'd left a trail of physical destruction across its ship—and nothing left alive between us and the machine to satisfy its need to kill.

I heard the hum of the Dreamer-bots coming our way.

CHAPTER FIFTY EIGHT:
LAB 17

I KNELT IN the hallway, over the drying spots of Indigo's blood, for some time after I heard that sound.

I didn't want to die. I never had, not even after Kystrom; life was a gift from the God Who Shed His Blood For Us, and I was angry that lives I cared for had been taken away. I never wanted mine gone with them. But I was exhausted, there in the hallway, exhausted down to bone, and so I did not move.

We could not run. I knew that. That is to say, we had a way out—our temporary hiding-place had two exits, which was likely why Tamara had chosen it. We could seal one door and go out the other, carrying Indigo. But the Dreamer-bots were the computer, and whatever I did to electronically lock the door they would be able to undo—and whatever I did to mechanically seal the door, they could break.

Even given that, we could not run. Tamara and I were exhausted. And if we moved Indigo so soon, the sim-skin would tear open again, as it had when Tamara had shifted him too far on the floor. There was no more sim-skin left. We didn't even have any bandages.

We could not outrun the Dreamer, even if we could get Indigo moving. We could not move quickly enough to escape it. The only thing that could stop the Dreamer's relentless hunt would be a sacrifice. We'd let the machine search out a manikin to kill the last time we'd encountered the AI; here and now, there were no more manikins left. We'd killed everything in this part of the ship.

There was nothing to sacrifice except ourselves.

I thought of Indigo, always stepping between me and danger, telling me secrets of his people to distract me from my fear. I thought of Tamara, stalwart and strong, guiding me and warning me, willing to fire her last bullet to save me even knowing she'd fail.

I got back to my feet and walked back down the hallway and into the server room, and stopped at the doorway to the little room. While I'd been gone, Tamara had shrugged off that oversized uniform jacket she always wore. In just her tanktop, I could see that there was nothing left of her bare shoulders but skin and bone. The Republican soldier jacket was draped over Indigo.

Maybe seeing that decided it for me.

"Tamara," I said, and she looked up, her jack-o-lantern eyes reddened but clear. I reached out to the door controls on the server side of the door.

"The Philosopher Stone is in Lab 17," I said, and before she could speak, I shut the door. It sealed shut, and I locked it. Then, for good measure, I grabbed a bit of debris from the floor and slammed it against the controls until they shattered. It would take her longer to break through the door that way, but I knew she wouldn't try. Lieutenant Lantern-Eyes was clearheaded and pragmatic, and she had Indigo to care for. She wouldn't waste three lives failing to save one.

Then I went and sat in the center of the room, cross-legged, eyes shut. No point in running, or in hiding. All I had to do now was wait.

The humming sound got louder and louder, approaching as relentless as rain, as inexorable as... well, as Death. I'd have a great story to tell Brigid when I saw her again. She'd be astonished by all the wild things I'd seen. Or maybe she'd be mad, that I died saving a Minister and a Republican soldier, the very two monsters that had murdered her—

The first of the Dreamer-bots landed on my spine, a light touch I barely felt through my shirt. Then the rest descended, a humming, glittering swarm, crawling over my neck and into my mouth and my eyes.

CHAPTER FIFTY NINE:
SOMETHING IN MY EYE

I JOLTED AWAKE like I'd been shocked back to life, gasping for breath on a cold hard floor.

Voices warped the air, familiar but scarcely recognizable. "Is he awake? Is he all right? *Sean!*"

I blinked and blinked again. My eyes felt dry and gritty, and my vision was weird; colors and overlapping patterns with no obvious point of reference. I swallowed and blinked and blinked, and then the space before me settled, colors wiping away like water down a drain, and I found myself staring up at the Indigo Minister.

He was about as pale as he'd been when I'd last seen him, a troubling blue-white. His expression was set and hard, and he stared down at me as unblinking as an owl. I reached up one hand for him, half-expecting my fingers to pass through his skin like a mirage, but as soon as my fingertips brushed his cheek something weirder happened.

My vision *glitched*. There was no other way to describe it. In the weird mosaic that was Indigo I thought I saw

One, and Kystrom, and bodies in the streets.

Indigo's fingers curled around my wrist, removing my hand from his face. The patterns slipped away again, like a puddle of water soaking into a towel. Indigo looked normal again, though pale. My mouth was dry.

"Sean?" said the familiar voice again. Tamara. Suddenly she crowded beside Indigo. "Mother of… Are you okay?"

She was weirdly hard to understand, like she was speaking a language I wasn't very familiar with. When had speaking Sister gotten so difficult? "I'm fine," I said, then admitted, "I can't see right."

Tamara shouldered Indigo further out of the way to bend over me, her worried face filling my whole field of vision. She pressed her fingers to my face, turning my head this way and that, examining my ears, making me open my jaw. Then she spread one palm over my head and pressed the other to my cheek and peeled my eyes open as wide as I would go.

It was uncomfortable, and I tugged my head free. "Indigo," I said, and tried not to worry what it meant that it was as difficult to speak as it was to understand. "Are you okay?" Last I'd seen him, he'd been unconscious with massive blood loss and a huge gaping hole in his abdomen.

"He's fine," Tamara told me. "Ministers are hardy. And that sim-skin did its job."

Indigo watched me over her shoulder. He did seem to be okay.

Tamara peeled my eyelids back again. "Ow," I said.

"You've got something in your eye," she said.

I stopped resisting her cold, bony fingers. "What? What is it?"

She released my skull. "I don't know. I'm afraid to touch it. This isn't exactly hygienic—you should be in a coma!"

"Sorry I'm not?"

"Don't joke. Is anything else wrong, or is it just your vision?"

I had a headache, but it was surprisingly mild. It was secondary to my real concern. "It's difficult to speak, and to understand what you're saying. Like I'm trying to translate in my head instead of talking fluently."

She frowned. "Say something in your native language, then. Say something in Kystrene."

In Kystrene, I said, "I'm glad you two are okay."

To my relief, the words came out easily, the syllables natural. It wasn't speaking that I was struggling with, just speaking to them.

"Good." Tamara seemed less relieved than her word choice would allow. "Your language processing abilities can't be too damaged, if you can speak Kystrene without problem. Assuming that you were actually speaking Kystrene and not Kystrene-sounding word salad."

I'd had no trouble speaking Kystrene, I wanted to reassure her, and then I realized that Indigo could understand Kystrene. I would've picked something different to say if I'd remembered that, something a little less honestly embarrassing.

But Indigo was only watching us with a cold, set expression, giving no sign that he had understood what I'd said. Come to think of it, I wasn't sure why I'd thought he could understand Kystrene anyway. I couldn't remember whether he'd actually spoken it in front of me, or only spoken it to me in a dream.

The implication of Tamara's words chose that moment to sink in to my conscious processing. "Wait, can't be *too damaged*? Are you telling me I might be brain damaged?"

"You had a swarm of Dreamers in your skull," Tamara told me. "If you're not a little bit brain damaged, I'll be shocked."

"Oh, God."

"I'm sure it's only minor brain damage," Tamara added hastily, apparently under the misconception that her words were comforting. "You're conscious, coherent, and tracking really well—"

"We should keep going." It was the first words I'd heard Indigo speak since before he'd passed out. The contrast between his shaken, desperate plea then and his icy calm now unsettled me.

It seemed to settle Tamara. "Right," she said, and offered her hand to me. "The sooner we find what we're looking for, the sooner we can get you a doctor."

Indigo had already risen. I saw the scratches on his jaw as he looked out towards the hall.

In the instant Tamara's hand closed around my wrist, hauling me up, my vision warped again. The room in front of me—the same room where I'd passed out, server room with a working computer not far from where I lay—became an odd mosaic of disparate pieces. Indigo was feathers, talons, manikin claws and blood on the sidewalk. Tamara was a swirl of Mara Zhu's horror-struck face and the photographs of the smiling scientists, in weird tessellation with the Republican ships in the clear blue sky leaving Kystrom behind. My eyes struggled to recognize Tamara and Indigo's now-familiar forms in the noise.

Just as suddenly as it had started, it stopped. I blinked black dots out of my vision from the sudden change in elevation, and pressed my palm against my pounding skull.

Tamara patted my back. "Okay? Anything else wrong?"

I lowered my hand. "I'm fine."

"Okay. Now, if you can walk a straight line, I'm ready to tell you that there's no brain damage at all."

She steered me towards the little room. The door was open. I thought I saw the lock panel intact, but when I blinked my gritty eyes, it was still broken—smashed, like I'd done before the Dreamer-bots had arrived. I wondered how Tamara had gotten the door open.

There was a stain of dried blood on the floor of the little room where Indigo had lain. When I blinked, that violet blood became red, not on the floor of the *Nameless* but on the floor of my parents' kitchen back on Kystrom, a trail leading deeper into the house.

Then I blinked, and it was just a dark stain on the floor of the *Nameless* again. Whatever was wrong with my vision was starting to freak me out.

"Here we are," Tamara said, and stopped at the far end of the little room, where the second door was located. I blinked until my vision cleared, looking at the door, and realized that inscribed upon the front was the Ameng words LAB 17.

"No way," I said. "It was right there all along?"

The center of the labyrinth. The one thing everyone on this ship was looking for, that we were all fighting to get; the thing Mara Zhu had died trying to destroy and the other scientists had died trying to protect—and we'd stumbled there by accident, looking for a temporary haven. Tamara, Indigo, and I had almost died on the doorstep of immortality.

It was curiously unreal to be here at last. Getting here had been hard—almost fatally difficult, in fact, for all of us. And yet it seemed abrupt that we should be here, with no final obstacles to clear. Nothing but us and the Stone.

"Some good luck at last," Tamara said.

And then she pushed open the door.

Lab 17 was... not what I'd expected, insofar as I'd expected anything. On my first step into the room behind Tamara, my vision warped again. I saw... fragments, little repeated fragments of things I'd seen before. I recognized the three solid tomb-like doors I'd seen on the other side of the ship, and there was a huddled shape in the middle of the room, distorted but still, blonde hair and *BRIGID*—

I blinked and the weird distortion was gone again, leaving my heart pounding in its wake. Instead, I was standing in a medium-sized room, dark and empty, except for a table in the center of the room upon which sat a stone.

The ancients had stored their data in crystals, I remembered, gazing at that filmy white stone in the middle of the room. How ironic that their Philosopher Stone was, in fact, a literal stone.

There was no dust on the table. "Careful," I said to my companions. I couldn't shake my uneasy feeling, like this was all far too simple. "There might be traps."

"The scientists who hid the Stone wanted it to be found," said Tamara. She was hidden in the shadows. "The Stone wants to be taken."

Indigo passed into the room behind me, a shadow and a wind.

I opened my mouth to say something else when Indigo moved, swift and decisive, hurling something that glinted through the air. It buried itself in Tamara's throat and her hands came up around it, red spilling out over her collarbones, beneath her thick dark hair. The gun she had half-drawn flew out of her hand, skidding over the floor to rest at my feet.

Indigo had thrown the knife Tamara had given him, and with it split her throat.

Tamara dropped to her knees, choking around metal and blood in her windpipe, then collapsed to her side to bleed beside the table that held the Philosopher Stone. My head was pounding, brutal. This couldn't be real. Indigo hadn't just murdered Tamara. It had to be, it had to be fake—

I saw, suddenly, with my damaged eyes, the first thing I had ever seen of Indigo. On the ground with Leah beside me, his expression cold as he drew his knife through her throat. My knees hit the floor with an impact that rattled me while Indigo, serene, stepped up to the center table and picked the Philosopher Stone up in one hand.

This was all too simple, I'd thought. No final obstacles. How could I have forgotten that the last and worst obstacle the three of us would face was each other?

Tamara's gun was cold under my palm, but light when I lifted it. Only one bullet, I remembered her telling me. Indigo, holding the Stone, gazed down at me over the barrel.

"You want this Stone," he said, with the flat calm that characterized a Minister, the absolute indifference to a human life.

Tamara had tried to warn me about the monster he was. I'd known from the moment I'd met him what kind of monster he was. I'd seen him and his people destroy my planet, slaughter millions.

"Why'd you do it?" I asked, over Lantern-Eyes' body.

"That was our bargain," Indigo said. He was unmoving, watching me with the calculating, hungry eyes of a bird of prey. "If you kill me, the Stone will be yours."

I could. It would be easy. Not even Indigo could outrun a bullet, and it would be justice, even, for Lieutenant Gupta's murder.

My arms were shaking, and the gun had gotten very heavy at some point between when I'd picked it up and now. I lowered it to my lap. "I don't want it," I told Indigo. "I don't want it."

When he did not kill me, I looked up again. He watched me over the table, the Stone in his hand.

He said, "You have something in your eye."

A weird horror climbed its way up my spine, like a thousand little needle-sharp feet marching under my skin.

"What?"

"You have something in your eye," Indigo repeated.

Blinding pain hit me in the back of my skull, right below the implant. The world went black.

CHAPTER SIXTY: EYE FOR AN EYE

I OPENED MY eyes to the Indigo Minister bending over me, a worried expression on his bloodless face. I recoiled into hard metal at my back. The floor, I was lying on the floor.

"Is he awake?" Tamara Gupta's voice echoed, out of sight. "Is he all right?"

Hard to speak with a knife through your throat. "What?" I said, and my voice came out hoarse and dry.

Indigo sat back. The open worry on his face had vanished, leaving expressionless impassivity behind. I regarded that calm mistrustfully. I'd last seen him standing over me with the Philosopher Stone in his hand, and Lieutenant Gupta's blood underfoot.

Tamara Gupta herself shouldered her way into my line of sight, shoving Indigo back. Beyond her head I could see the ceiling of the server room. I wasn't in Lab 17. I was in the server room, where I'd already woken up. Where I'd dreamed I'd woken up?

"Hey," Tamara said. "Sean. Can you understand me?"

It was still weirdly hard to understand what she was

saying, like she was speaking an unfamiliar language. That wasn't nearly as weird, though, as speaking to someone who a minute ago had had cold steel driven directly through her windpipe.

A thought jolted me. "Do I have anything in my eye? Tamara, look!"

"Okay, okay!" She pressed me down with a hand on my collar and used the other to peel my eyelids back. It was exactly as uncomfortable as it had been before. Had seemed before? I'd already been here and done this. What was going on?

She released me. "I can't see anything. Why do you think there's something in your eye?"

I'd watched you die. "Because I saw... I—"

"You did get attacked by the Dreamers, I guess there could still be traces in your eyes," she worried.

It was difficult to breathe. Maybe there were Dreamers in my lungs? "Could they cause visions?" I asked. "Could they make me see things?"

"What? What are you talking about?"

Indigo pushed past her suddenly, close to me—too close. I tried to flinch back again, unable to shake the image of him expressionless and cold with the Stone in his hand. His palm laid over my eyes, cool and solid. I exhaled and tried to control my instinctive need to flee.

He withdrew his hand. "No nanomachines," he reported, and I saw that his palm was empty.

If there had been Dreamer-bots in my eyes, they would've flocked to him. *You have something in your eye.* There was nothing in my eyes.

It was suddenly impossible to just keep lying there. I pushed myself up and found myself caught by two separate sets of hands.

"Rest for a minute," Indigo told me. A trick of the light made his dark eyes warm.

"You were dead just a minute ago," Tamara said, sounding angry. "Not comatose, Sean, not unconscious, not sick, *dead*. We revived you but no one just comes back from that. So sit still a minute."

Dead.

But I hadn't been. I'd seen things—no, I'd lived things. I'd felt and smelled and heard things. But I couldn't have. Tamara was alive in front of me, and there was no Philosopher Stone.

In a sick way, it made sense. The Dreamer-bots had killed every human they'd come in contact with, at least as far as Tamara had seen. They must have killed me and then flown off, leaving my body behind for Lantern-Eyes and Indigo to find and revive. But then what was it that I'd seen while I'd been dead? A nightmare? Dead men didn't dream.

But dead men might glimpse what came after death, if they believed they could remember it on waking. I said, "Do either of you believe in Heaven or Hell?"

There was a terrible little pause.

Carefully, Tamara said, "Sometimes, in extreme moments, the brain... hallucinates. That's what near-death experiences are. If you... saw something, Sean, it was just your brain firing unrelated synapses."

That would explain the weird, surreal vision warps;

seeing Brigid's body lying dead where the Stone sat. And yet so much of what I had seen felt horribly real, and horribly true. "You don't think it meant anything?"

"Maybe your dying subconscious put together a pattern that you hadn't consciously recognized," Tamara said. "But was it a message from beyond? No."

Indigo watched me over her shoulder, impassive inhuman face.

"Okay, up you get," Tamara said. "I think the sooner we find what we're looking for, the sooner we can get you out of here and into medical care."

Her words rang through my mind like an ominous bell, tolling through my body. She didn't seem to notice, and as soon as she had helped me up, she walked off, leading the way again, out of the server room and into the little room nearby. Indigo lingered.

My imp prodded me with a devil's pitchfork. "What do you think, Indigo?" I asked. "Do Heaven or Hell exist?"

He gazed back at me with his dark-water eyes, currents flowing beneath I couldn't recognize. And I'd thought he'd been so transparent to me when he'd been dying.

"I believe I will never know," Indigo said at last.

It was too hard to keep looking at him directly, and seeing overlaid my vision of him cold and cruel, murderer holding the Stone. I turned away and followed Tamara.

A divine warning or my brain putting together a pattern in my dying moments. Was there a meaning to it? I'd been wrong to trust a Minister; my sympathy had been taken advantage of, but just because he'd been in pain didn't mean he was on my side. Tamara had been taken in by it, too, but I wouldn't let that trust cause her death. I'd watch Indigo now, more closely than I had before.

I was so lost in my thoughts I didn't immediately realize why Tamara had stopped. She'd led me across the little room and to the far door, where she had stopped.

"Lab 17," Tamara said.

The door was the same one I had seen in my dream. I went cold.

Something wasn't right. "That's written in Ameng," I said to Tamara. "How did you read that?"

"I'm not a total idiot. Half the doors in this ship are labeled Lab Something, and the numbers are easy to learn," Tamara said. She was gazing at the door with a strange, rhapsodic expression. "Come on. It's right through this door."

Before I could stop her—before I could summon a reason to stop her—she gripped the handle and slid the door into the wall.

The room beyond was similar to the one I'd seen in my dream, though not quite the same. It was medium-sized and dark, but the shape of the walls was different—different, yet somehow familiar. There was a little alcove in the back, draped in shadows. The size and layout of the room reminded me, weirdly, of Brigid's bedroom back on Kystrom.

In the center of the room, covered in dust on a rotting old table, there sat a crystal. The Philosopher Stone.

The déjà vu was making me nauseous. How had I dreamed this? Had I dreamed it, or was this the brain damage from the nanomachines making me think I had dreamed it before? I would swear I had seen this room, seen that crystal, before.

But the crystal now was dull, covered in thick dust, the way it should be. The room had more details, corners and odd edges, not a shapeless shadowy space.

Indigo paced in behind me, silent and dark, a shadow and a wind.

I turned to watch him. I'd been distracted before, in my nightmare, or my vision. I'd been distracted and I'd missed the moment until it was too late and Lantern-Eyes was dead. I wasn't going to miss it this time, if there was going to be a *this time*. I was going to stop—

The *crack* of gunfire split the air and Indigo's head jolted back on his neck before his whole body went limp and collapsed to the floor, dark-blue blood spreading in the light of his glowing collar-stone.

I looked over his corpse and found Lieutenant Gupta lowering her one-shot gun.

"Good thing I saved that last bullet," she remarked, and tucked her empty gun away.

I didn't know what to feel. I didn't feel anything. But it wasn't the absence of feeling, it was the moment before the train car hits; nothing but the wind and the sight of solid metal coming towards you down the tracks.

"You shot him," I said.

Tamara Gupta strode over to the table, plucked the Philosopher Stone out of its nest of dust. She blew on it, sending an ancient cloud drifting through the air. The Stone gleamed clean. "What did you expect me to do?"

The lieutenant turned the Stone over in her hand,

admiring its facets. Admiring the data stored inside the crystalline structure.

The Republic was just as bad as the Ministers, I remembered, breathing out in the space before that freight train of grief reached me, inexorable and inescapable and absolutely crushing. They'd summoned the Ministers to Kystrom like Tamara had summoned the Ministers to the *Nameless*, and both times me and mine had gotten caught in between.

"You made him a promise," I reminded her. Her aim had been precise. Indigo's body had a neat little hole between his brows.

"I kept my promise," Tamara said. "No Minister will be taken alive. Other than that, Sean, it was me or him. What's done is done. No point in regret." She lowered the Stone and stepped towards me, walking towards the door.

I moved, without thinking, to block her.

She stopped short, gazed up at me with a wary eye. She was a soldier trained to kill whose instincts had been honed by five years alone on this ship, as merciless and efficient as Indigo had been. But all that seemed to matter right now was that I was taller than her, broader. I knew, somehow, that if I attacked her, I would win.

Lieutenant Gupta said, "So you want the Stone."

I'd almost forgotten the Stone was there. "No. I want... Why did you kill him? Enough people have died already!"

"Toughen up, kid," Lantern-Eyes said. "The worlds are at war."

"I can't keep watching people die," I begged her.

"You can. You will. You can't stop it—unless you have

the Stone."

She held out her hand, palm-up, between us. The Philosopher Stone was a milky crystal between her face and mine.

"With the Stone, you could become immortal, and make the people you love immortal, too," Tamara told me.

Indigo had been immortal. It hadn't stopped Tamara from putting a bullet through his head. And taking the Stone now wouldn't take that bullet back out, or reassemble Brigid's skull.

"I don't want it," I said.

Tamara said, "You've got something in your eye."

It was at that moment, and that moment only, that I realized she and I had been speaking to each other in Ameng this whole time.

"What?" I said.

CHAPTER SIXTY ONE:
WHAT MUST BE SEEN

I WOKE SUDDENLY and panicked on a hard floor.

"Calm down, Sean, calm down!" Tamara shouted at me, in Ameng, while Indigo pressed my shoulders to the floor, worry in his dark eyes. "Sean! It's all right!"

"It's not all right!" I shouted at her, but now that I knew I was speaking Ameng it was harder to speak, and the words came out translated wrong.

"Brain damage?" Tamara wondered to Indigo. He met her gaze with equal concern.

"I'm not brain damaged," I tried to tell them. "There's something wrong with *you*."

Tamara's palm landed over my mouth. "The Dreamer is gone, but if you keep shouting like that, they might come back."

I licked her palm to get her to recoil. She *tasted* normal, salty and a little sour with sweat and whatever else she'd gotten on her hands. But she sure as hell wasn't acting normal. Lantern-Eyes couldn't speak Ameng, so why was she speaking Ameng now? And how the hell were both she and Indigo sitting in front of me when I had watched Indigo kill her, and then her kill Indigo, and now here I was waking up again?

"What's in my eyes?" I asked her, asked Indigo. "Is there anything in my eyes?"

"There is nothing in your eyes," Tamara soothed me.

She hadn't even looked. "Check my eyes," I said. "Indigo, put your hand over my eyes. Is there anything in there? Dreamer-bots? Anything?"

He laid his palm over my eyes. I waited for something—itching, or crawling, or pain; anything. Nothing happened. When he pulled his hand back, his palm was clean.

"There's nothing in your eyes," Tamara said. "Are you having trouble seeing?"

"No," I said. "No, no. There must be something."

"Okay," Tamara said, but not to me, to Indigo. "Let's get him up and get the Stone and get out. The sooner the better. He needs a doctor."

"You have to be joking," I said.

"Not about medical care. Up, up!"

Indigo hauled me up this time. I did nothing to help him; frankly, I'd rather stay lying on that floor for a little bit longer. I'd already lived this twice before, and it had ended badly both times.

Indigo dragged me forward. Having carried him in the recent past, I knew how light he was compared to me, but his strength was terrifying. There was absolutely no resisting him.

We entered the little room and stopped at the far end where, as in the past two times I had had this nightmare, the door was clearly marked LAB 17.

"You can read that," I told Tamara. "You can read that because apparently you can speak Ameng now."

She glanced at Indigo. "Brain damage?" she asked again, in an undertone. He nodded somberly.

"I don't have brain damage! Listen, Lantern-Eyes, don't open that door!"

Lieutenant Tamara Gupta, Lantern-Eyes, that Republican son-of-a-bitch, slid the door into the wall.

Lab 17 looked much the same as it had the last two times I had been here, only this time it looked even more like Brigid's bedroom. If I wasn't looking directly at where the wall met the ceiling, I could see rafters.

"This is fucked up," I said, but they were both ignoring me. "Something's wrong. This isn't right."

The first time I'd been here, Indigo had killed Lantern-Eyes. The second time, Lantern-Eyes had killed Indigo. Someone had died both times I'd been in here, but I didn't know anymore who to protect from whom. Tamara stalked through the shadows, eying the dusty Stone on its little pedestal. Indigo drifted around to the other side of the table, quiet as a night breeze.

"Guys, please," I begged, but it was like they did not hear me. Lantern-Eyes drew her gun as Indigo drew his knife, and the crack of her gunshot was followed by the sick wet sound of the knife going into her neck. She choked wetly, grabbing at her throat; on the other side of the table Indigo fell to the ground, hemorrhaging blood he couldn't afford to lose from a hole in his chest.

They were too far apart for me to go to them both.

Indigo bled to death on my left while Lantern-Eyes suffocated on my right, blue blood and red blood spreading over the floor on either side.

On the table, untouched and free for the taking, the Philosopher Stone shone, uncanny.

I wasn't holding a flashlight or anything. Nobody was; just Indigo with his collar-light. Yet I'd never had any trouble seeing anything in the hallway or the room without a source of light.

This wasn't real. None of this was real.

I sat in that room between their bodies, feeling half-removed from mine, until the uncanny light from the Philosopher Stone dimmed and went black.

CHAPTER SIXTY TWO:
THIRD EYE

THE FOURTH TIME I awoke it became clear to me that there were two distinct possibilities. The first was that I had died and been sent to a very specific, possibly ironic version of Purgatory. The second was that infection by Dreamer-bots had some effects that Tamara Gupta hadn't been aware of. Like detailed, wild hallucinations in the hours before death. Given the aching in my skull, which seemed particularly physical and therefore unlikely to exist in some kind of afterlife, I was leaning towards option two.

I opened my eyes to Number One bending over me, owl-eyes cold, collar-light gleaming a cruel violet. "Oh, this is new," I said.

"Get up, Mr. Wren," One said, and leaned back away.

I sat up. My head was *killing* me, the low-grade ache that had been present in the last three... nightmares... fast on its way to a full-blown migraine. Surrounding me in the server room was not just Number One, but numbers Three through Seven, and Benny and Quint huddled together in the back like the world's sulkiest captives.

"I don't suppose you know where Indigo and Tamara are," I said.

"We found Number Two and a Republican soldier dead a few rooms away," One told me. "It appeared that Two had bled out from a wound in his abdomen, and the Republican had been savaged by some sort of beast. Her throat had been bitten out. If you're hoping for rescue, give up your hope."

I'd watched Indigo and Tamara die twice each now, and I was pretty solidly convinced that this hallucination was about as real as the last three had been. Still, grief hit me, all the more powerful for being unexpected. I could imagine them travelling around the door I'd sealed, trying to get to me; being attacked by something and Indigo tearing open his wound trying to protect Tamara but them both dying anyway.

I wanted to tell myself it was better than them killing each other, but any scenario that ended with them dead was ranking low on desirable to me. Weird how once you've given up your life for a pair of people, their survival becomes so significant.

"It is fortunate for you that we found you here, Mr. Wren," One said. "You would have died without our aid. And we still need you for your translating abilities."

If I hadn't already known I was dreaming, that would have confirmed it. I looked up at her and laughed. "To translate Ameng? Don't you know you're speaking it?"

The corners of One's eyes tightened. "Four," she said, and the Green Minister came over, dark ringlets around her face. She knelt in front of me and pulled out a medical scanner.

"Not speaking in the Light language, huh?" I asked her sympathetically, while she ran the scanner over my head and torso. "Probably because the AI doesn't know it." Which would explain why I could speak Kystrene, but my hallucinatory Indigo couldn't.

The scanner beeped, and Green read aloud off the screen. "Severe brain damage in his auditory and visual cortex."

"Meaning?" said Number One.

"He might see things that aren't there, and hear things differently than they are."

"A dream will say anything to stay plausible, won't it?" I remarked to One.

"We don't have time for this," she decided. "Stand him up."

Red pulled me upright. I let him do it, because honestly, at this point, why not? "Where to now? Lab 17?"

Even in a nightmare, One's stare was piercing. "Lab 17," she agreed.

There was no surprise in her voice. The real Number One had been hellbound for Mara Zhu's office, but this dream of Ultraviolet knew everything that I knew, including the location of the Stone. As a group, we moved through the server room and directly to the little room where Indigo and Tamara had hidden. There was an ache in the back of my skull now, to go with the gritty itching of my eyes.

"So is this it?" I asked my hallucination of Number One as we walked through the little room—no bloodstains this time! The AI was slacking—and towards the door marked LAB 17. "The lesson the universe was trying to teach me?

About how I should give up and I'm alone and everybody is terrible?"

One turned and looked at me. My vision *warped*, the way it had the first time I'd opened my eyes since the Dreamer had infected me, and instead of One's lovely inhuman face I saw fathomless black eyes like the Children had, and gnashing metal teeth like Dreamer-bots in formation, humming out of a human mouth.

Then it was just One again, looking more human than usual out of sheer contrast with the nightmare visage I'd seen. She gave me a remote mountain-top look, and said nothing.

Lab 17 was exactly where I'd left it the last few times. Red slid the door into the wall and in we went. Benny and Quint got shoved to the side as soon as we entered, and I got summarily tossed in with them.

I landed hard on the floor next to Benny. He had his handbrace on and was rubbing the skin beneath it.

"Do me a favor, will you," I said to Benny, who gave me a narrow look. "Take a look. Would you say there's something in my eye?"

"What the fuck?" Benny said.

The table was where I'd left it, and the Stone in the center. The room around the Stone looked distinctly more like Brigid's bedroom, but done in darkness and steel, decay rotting metal. If I squinted, I could almost make out where her bed had been.

One reached the center of the room. She plucked the Stone from the table and held it before her eyes, pale Stone, pale face, glimmering.

And then the back door to the room that hadn't been there before burst open, and the manikins came snarling in.

They didn't bother with me, or Benny, or Quint. They went straight for the Ministers. There was an equal number of them, six Ministers to six manikins, and when they fought their movements matched, like they were fighting their own reflections.

Matched *exactly*, in fact. The Dreamer was getting lazy.

The stench of blood and viscera was real enough. It filled the room when all the Ministers and manikins had killed each other, and black and violet blood ran over the floor. The Philosopher Stone had fallen near One's corpse, and her blood running under cast it a vibrant violet.

"Sean," said Benny, "grab the Stone."

"Not you too," I said, trying to speak as little as possible around the nauseating scents of death.

"It's the only way we'll make it back alive," Quint added, her voice high with fear.

Somewhere in this dream, Indigo and Tamara lay dead on the *Nameless*. I could only hope that wasn't true in reality. If I had to be stuck forever in this Purgatory nightmare, the least the universe could do in return was make sure the two of them survived.

"Sean," Benny said.

"You've got legs," I told him. "If you want it, you take it."

Quint said, "You don't want it, then?"

"I don't want it," I told her.

She stood, Benny a beat behind, and plucked the Stone

out of the carnage. It dripped violet.

The two of them paused at the door. "Last chance to change your mind," Benny said. He didn't sound like himself at all.

"No, thank you," I said.

Some long minutes after they were gone, the corpse on the floor that looked like Number One opened her eyes. They were fathomless and black.

"Let me guess," I said to that body. "I've got something in my eye."

Blood rippled beneath her cheek when she spoke. "And something in your spine," the corpse told me.

CHAPTER SIXTY THREE: HINDSIGHT

I OPENED MY eyes to sunlight and cheeping birds and a scent in the air I hadn't smelled for eight long years. Kystrene wood and dried flowers. Through the crack in my bedroom door, I heard voices downstairs, talking and laughing.

I lay in my childhood bed, sinking into the sheets. Wrapped up in the familiar sounds, and scents, and feel of the space, so real and absolute, I knew that everything that had come before had been a miserable dream. I'd dreamt Kystrom destroyed and my family dead and myself alone. I'd dreamt a strange starship and an ancient secret. But it had just been dreams.

Downstairs, I heard Brigid's voice raised with playful indignation, counterpoint to the lower tones of my father teasing and my mother laughing.

But no. To forget was the cruelest thing. My mother, my father, Brigid, all of Itaka. They were dead, and I remembered.

Downstairs, the talking ceased. A dark light fell on the

room, dimming the sun to silver. I pushed aside the covers and set feet on silent floorboards.

With a nightmare's certitude, my feet carried me to where I needed to go. I moved like a train on a track, no stopping, returning, diversions possible. I walked across the hall of my parents' old house and halted before the door to Brigid's bedroom.

LAB 17, it said on the door, scrawled in artful, girlish calligraphy on a piece of paper that I remembered saying "*Brigid*".

That was funny. If this whole thing hadn't been horrifying beyond measure, I might be able to laugh at the AI's weird failure to integrate memory and dream. LAB 17 written in swirls and curlicues using sparkly pink pen. Honestly.

I pushed open the door.

Brigid lay where I had seen her last, a sprawl across the floorboards, facing the far wall as if she'd been running through the door when she'd died, fleeing whoever killed her. Her blonde hair was a spill around her head, soaked through with red like veins in an egg. I moved towards her body as I had moved towards her body almost ten years ago, and though I wanted desperately to do anything but this, I could not stop myself from crouching at her side and rolling her body over.

But when she rolled over her face was intact, whole and untouched. She blinked at me out of clear blue eyes and when I sat back she sat up.

I stared at my sister's face for a long time, trying to make it make sense in my head. But I could not remember all her features precisely any longer, and I remembered her being the same age as me. But Brigid had been sixteen when she died, and I was twenty-five; she should look like a child in my eyes, and I could not make memory and reason match.

Brigid said, "What's that in your spine?"

"It's an implant," I told her. "A leash."

"It's not supposed to be there?"

I shook my head. "It's the only reason I went looking for the Philosopher Stone on this cursed ship."

She raised her brows. That wasn't Brigid's mannerism, though. It was Lieutenant Gupta's. "You could use the Stone to save me."

"I don't think it works that way."

She tilted her head in acknowledgement. Again, not my sister's mannerism; that one was stolen from the Indigo Minister. "But if you took it," Brigid said, "then neither of the two people who killed me would get it."

The sunlight was silver and misty. Like light through a filmy quartz.

"It still wouldn't bring you back," I said.

There was blood on her temple again. I was suddenly terrified I would watch her face crumple in, all her features shattered until they were unrecognizable, and it could've been any girl's corpse on the floor there, nothing left of my Brigid. But the light around me was dimming, too, the dream starting to fade.

I spoke quickly, before it could. Just in case this wasn't an AI's dream in the minutes before I died, but real, and really Brigid. "You know I love you, right? You know I miss you every day?"

"You didn't love me until after I died," Brigid said, and the dream winked out.

CHAPTER SIXTY FOUR: EYE ON THE PRIZE

BY THE TIME I woke for the—fifth? Sixth?—time, I was sick of the AI's shit. Why couldn't it just kill me outright, like everything else on this stupid ship? Why did it have to play with its food?

I opened my eyes this time, again, to see Indigo and Tamara bent over me, matching expressions of concern on their faces.

"Oh, come on," I said. "This again?"

"Brain damage?" Tamara said to Indigo, worried. He nodded somberly.

I pointed at her. "Spot on."

My head was aching something fierce. My eyes were gritty, and the implant was a nub of pain in the back of my skull.

"We should get him to a doctor," Tamara said to Indigo, and the two of them got me under the arms and hauled me up.

"You're not very imaginative, you know," I told Tamara. "I mean, you've said the same thing in like three different dreams."

"Okay, Sean," said Tamara.

"And you know what," I said, "I think you need to see a doctor, too. But a head doctor. All this counting bullets and making plans on top of plans on top of plans and freezing up when something changes? I don't know if that's you or if that's, like, some sort of PTSD, but it's definitely not a healthy thing."

The two of them, together, were dragging me towards the little room, just like the past few dreams. Indigo patted my arm in what seemed to be reassurance.

"Don't get me started on you," I told him. "I can't even tell what you want from me but I feel like you want to cry half the time."

"It's going to be okay, Sean," Tamara reassured me, kindly. "Everything is going to be just fine. Here we go."

We'd reached, as anticipated, the far door. Neatly marked LAB 17. There was one difference from the prior times we'd visited the LAB 17 door—this time, the inscription was written in Brigid's sprawling pink pen. I laughed.

Indigo pushed the door into the wall this time, for a change of pace, and then we emerged into the room. Lab 17. It didn't look like Brigid's bedroom this time; there was something sullen about its determined blandness, as if to say *see, we can generate a convincing habitat for you.* Which I would've believed more if it hadn't been for the giveaway writing on the door.

In the center of the room, dust-free, the Philosopher Stone gleamed.

"There it is," Lantern-Eyes breathed.

"The Stone," Indigo rasped.

"Which of you is going to kill the other this time?" I asked. "Because you've already traded off once, and then killed each other at the same time. There's not really any more permutations of that conflict, unless you start repeating yourself. Or maybe you start making out furiously, and I'm supposed to take the Stone and run while you're distracted." That mental image was somehow both disturbing and weirdly fascinating.

"I couldn't kill Indigo," Tamara declared, gazing off into the corner of the room, dramatic.

"I would rather harm myself than do harm to either of you," Indigo said softly, but with feeling. "You've saved my life."

"And you've saved mine," Tamara said.

"Of all the... of all the different versions you've made me watch go down, this is definitely the least believable," I said. "Hey, Tamara, have you got your gun? Maybe I'll shoot myself for a change of pace."

"You should take it," Tamara said to me.

I hadn't expected her to actually agree. "What, the gun?"

"The *Stone*."

I took a minute to try and track her logic, and found nothing to track. "Um. Why?"

"Because you sacrificed your life for ours." Indigo had crossed to the other side of the table, and the light of the Stone shone with faint rapture over his face. "Consider this our payment for the debt."

"You also tried to sacrifice yourself for me a couple of times, you know," I pointed out.

"He didn't succeed," Tamara said.

They both stared at me expectantly over the table. Side-by-side, there was a certain similarity to them: soldierly stance, dark hair, a completely unnerving and absolutely out of character adoration for me shining brightly from their two loving faces.

I sighed.

"Okay," I said. "Let's just cut the crap. This is obviously a test of character, right? You're asking me the same question every time and tempting me to answer it in a particular way."

They gazed at me in weird twin adoration for a little while longer, and then Tamara said, "Do you want the Stone?"

"Seriously?" I said. "I mean, seriously? What is it with you and the stupid Stone? Would you leave off about it for *five* seconds; you're clearly a sophisticated AI; you've got to realize I can't do anything with the data while I'm trapped in the mind of a computer, Dreaming myself to death—"

But that was it, wasn't it? The Philosopher Stone was data—data in a computer. And I was inside the computer.

I eyed my companions warily. Tamara and Indigo were thin skins over running code, nothing more than programs. Hell, the whole room was. Tamara and Indigo weren't any more real than the walls or the floor. If you could peel off the skin, you'd find the same abstract code behind; they were indistinct from their surroundings, just different textures projected on a wall.

Still, I couldn't stop myself from meeting their eyes

when they spoke, from trying to read their expressions. "You keep asking me about the Stone," I said, wary of the implications, but slowly beginning to understand, "as, what—a sort of password prompt?"

The avatars of the AI smiled at me benevolently. "The Dreamer cannot give you the data until after you enter the correct password," Tamara said.

"And the correct password is...?"

"Do you want the Stone?" Tamara asked, and gestured down at the pristine crystal, gleaming on the table between us.

I stared down at the crystal. "It can't be that simple."

"It's that simple," Indigo said. He was still smiling at me, *beaming*, showing all his teeth.

It was surprisingly unsettling. "I, uh, I'm not sure I understand why everyone else has been dying," I said, eying those teeth with suspicion. "This seems like a really simple test."

But it wasn't, I realized. It was only simple if you could understand the question being asked of you. There was an ache in my head that had grown steadily worse and worse with each cycle of dreaming; I could see how that ache could grow until it killed me. If the only way to break the cycle was to give the AI the correct answer—well, you'd have to understand Ameng to understand what question was being asked.

Aside from Tamara's translator, none of her teammates had spoken Ameng. Her translator, probably, had been killed by a different monster—or had given the wrong password.

And yet, the ache in my head was powerful enough to almost blind me. It was centered around the implant at the base of my skull. I didn't know how long I'd been here, on this ship. For all I knew the world outside was on the verge of destruction in a dying star.

I'd given up on the Philosopher Stone already. Maybe I could get it through the computer, by answering the password prompt correctly. But the data would be stored in a physical location somewhere on the ship, and that place was Lab 17. Indigo and Tamara had already headed there. One of them, or both of them, would get the data they needed.

The *real* Indigo and Tamara had, anyway. These photorealistic shells were here with me. I wasn't sure I wanted to let that comfort me, but the strange thing was that it could.

I'd made my peace with what would happen to me the moment I shut the door on Tamara. It was done. At least in dying, it wouldn't seem like I was alone.

"I don't want it," I told them.

The vision of my two companions blinked at me. "Don't want it?" Tamara echoed.

"Think of the power it would give you," Indigo reminded me.

"I don't want it."

"Think of all the good you can do," Tamara said earnestly, and she had the same hungry eyes as the scientists in the photo.

It was like the Senator all over again, insisting I take his generous offer. "But what's the cost?"

CHAPTER SIXTY FIVE:
THE LAST WORDS OF MARA ZHU
PART TWO

"The only excuse I can offer future generations is that the human race was going extinct," said Mara Zhu.

I did not wake up on the floor of the server room this time. I opened my eyes to a small bedroom, lit only by a computer screen in one corner of the room, the light of it partially blocked by a woman's figure.

"They might still kill us, but I don't think so," Mara Zhu said, seated in front of the computer, recording her final words. I walked carefully around the shadowed edges of her bed until I could stand beside the desk and watch the side of her face as she recorded the very video I'd watched several days ago.

She looked more like Indigo in person, or maybe she only looked more like Indigo because now I knew what Indigo looked like when he was dying.

"What happened here was evil," Mara Zhu said. There was a handgun resting on the desk beside her hand, out of the view of the computer's camera. "It must be forgotten, it can never happen again. I've done what I can. I've sabotaged the embryos," and that was it, that was why the Ministers had come here, that was the darkness in Number One's eyes, "I took this ship as close to a supernova as I could before the others stalled the engine," and that was why here and now, a thousand years later, I waited on the edge of extinction.

"I can't fly us into the sun, but they can't fly us out," Mara Zhu said. "Sooner or later the sun will explode and turn all this to dust."

"Later," I said, but the hallucination, or recording, or whatever, she didn't react. "Much later."

"The others are holed up in Lab 17 with the data," she said. "I can't get in to them, but they can't get out with it. I've guaranteed it. If you find this ship, or if the star doesn't go nova soon and you find this log, I beg you. Leave the ghosts here in peace."

My head was pounding, a pain so deep it stopped feeling like pain. There were claws in the base of my skull.

"The final log of Doctor Mara Zhu," Mara Zhu whispered, and shut the camera off.

The light in the room dimmed, but the hallucination did not end. Instead, Mara Zhu stood up from her desk chair, picked her pistol up from the desk, and walked back around to her bed. I pressed a hand to my skull and tried to track her progress through the lightless flashes in my eyes.

She sat down on the bed, lifted the gun smoothly and calmly, pressed the barrel to her temple—

And stopped.

Across a thousand years, through a dreaming machine, Mara Zhu looked at me. "You have something in your eye," she said.

And soon, I was sure, my eye would burst. "I know," I managed.

"The others all died."

"I know. Did you program the nanomachines to do that?"

Mara Zhu spoke calmly, the barrel of the gun still held directly to her temple. "Yes. We deserve to die for what we've done. We all deserve to die."

"Nobody deserves to die," I said. Nausea was rising in my throat, and my skin felt hot. It was hard to speak, to speak Ameng, to speak clearly. "What happened here was evil. But you're still hurting people even after you're dead. How is that helping?"

"You want to take the data," Mara Zhu said.

My head was cracking open. Like Brigid, I thought. Splitting down the skull.

"I don't want anything to do with your data," I said.

I was going to die here. I'd known I was going to die the minute I faced down the Dreamer-bots, but it was taking longer than I'd hoped. I was going to die here. I could feel my head splitting.

Mara Zhu's voice cut through the agony not like a sound heard, but like a thought.

"You have something in your spine," she said.

I blinked open half-blind eyes to see her sitting on the bed, a little above me now—at some point, I had fallen to my knees. The barrel of the gun was still pressed to her temple, and an instant after I blinked my eyes clear she pulled the trigger. The side of her face shattered, blood and brains and torn ragged flesh. Like Brigid, I thought.

Like Brigid.

Her body fell to the bed like a puppet, limp limbs; the gun fell to the floor and rolled beneath the bed. Somehow I knew she'd had only one bullet in that gun.

A thousand years passed by in an instant as I watched, my brain spinning feverish. Mara Zhu's body bloated and blackened and rotted, from skin to bones until it was nothing left but a stain on the wires of the rotted bed, and the Ministers standing around it solemn and radiant like angels of death. Number One and her followers had survived the destruction of the hull, then. They'd reached Mara Zhu's office—and found nothing inside.

And then the humming got louder and louder, in my ears, my eyes, my skull. Something was burning inside my head, seizing through my face, melting my bones. Brain damage? I wondered, Tamara's voice in my head, and I would have laughed but I was too busy gagging up chunks of my own insides.

I came to face down on the floor of the server room with a ringing head and a solid ache in the back of my neck, radiating down shoulders and over the top of my skull. There was something sticky on my face and ears, and when I reached up to find out what it was, my hand came away red. I'd bled from my ears, my mouth and eyes.

I reached down to push myself up, though my limbs felt remote, cold and shaky. Before I could do more than place my palm on the floor, a familiar voice said, "Don't try to move."

My scrambled brain could not place the voice, only knew that I knew it. I let myself lie back down, cheek to the floor, sticky with my blood.

A flashlight flared; the speaker stepped over me and crouched down so that I could see his face. Lying sideways, still blinking agony out of my eyes, I did not at first recognize him. Then my brain pieced together all the features, wiped away the unrecognizable covering of dirt and blood.

"Good," Benny said, when he saw me staring. "You're awake."

CHAPTER SIXTY SIX:
AN OLD FRIEND

IF THIS WAS another dream, it was a lot more uncomfortable than the last few. I swallowed blood and said, "What?"

Benny grimaced. He reached out of my narrow field of vision and when he returned, he was holding a water bottle, dented and half-empty. "Think you can sit up?"

He was speaking Sister. I'd never been so glad to hear Sister in my life.

Benny helped me sit up, drink some of the water. I felt weak all over, shaky. There was no telling how long I had been unconscious, but my blood had dried in stages on the floor, so it looked like I had been bleeding for most of that time. Lucky I hadn't fallen on my back, or I would've probably choked to death on a nosebleed. There was no sign of the Dreamer-bots at all.

Indigo and Lantern-Eyes. I twisted around until I could see the door to the little room, dimly lit by Benny's flashlight. It was shut, but the Dreamer-bots had repaired the locking mechanism I'd shattered. "Hey," Benny said sharply when I pushed myself upright, struggling against unsteady limbs, and quickly unlocked the door.

The door slid into the room, exposing the little room, and the emptiness inside.

There was a bloodstain on the floor where I'd set Indigo down, but no body. No pack, either—Tamara and Indigo had left under their own power, with enough time to take supplies with them.

They'd left some supplies behind, though. Just a few packages, neatly stacked.

Indigo had probably convinced Tamara to leave them behind for me, I imagined. She wasn't sentimental enough to leave behind food for a dead man in case he came back to life, but Indigo, I thought, might. Unless this sad small pile of food constituted some sort of Ministerial offering to the dead. *To you who have died, from I who shall not.*

I took a step or two into the room and sat down heavily beside the dried blood.

"Hey, nice." Benny's voice echoed overhead. He'd followed me in and was now examining the little pile of supplies, knocking them out of order as he sorted through for something he liked. I let my head drop back against the wall while I caught my breath.

A twinge from the back of my neck felt like a rubber band snapping. I winced and lifted my hand to rub the base of my spine, around where the implant was. The skin felt swollen and hard.

"Are you hungry?" Benny asked. He was peeling open one of Tamara's rations, wrapper crinkling.

I let my hand drop. "That one doesn't taste good unless you warm it up. Is Quint around?"

"We can't exactly make a campfire."

"Where's Quint?"

"Dead."

Dead. I hadn't liked Quint, exactly, and she hadn't cared about me one way or the other, but I'd still known her. Thinking about her dead added another ache to the collection of pains that made up my physical form. "How'd she die?"

Benny finished unwrapping the ration, looking at it instead of at me. I wondered how long it had been since he'd eaten. "Ship's full of monsters. Some of them got Quint."

I wondered which monsters it had been. If it had been the manikins, swift and efficient, or if little Quint with the fussy hair and the frightened eyes had been torn apart slowly by a horde of black-eyed Children.

"What the hell happened to you?" Benny asked. "You were just lying there when I found you, bleeding. And what looks like something else's blood down your front."

I glanced down when he gestured and realized that I did, still, have a dark stain down my front from Indigo's blood. It was smeared all over where he'd leaned against me, and spread in drips and streaks down from there.

I *was* alive, though. And conscious. I'd been infected by the Dreamer; there was no doubt about that. And Tamara had said that no one she knew of had survived.

"I'm not sure," I admitted, looking down at my hands. There was blood flaking off them, too—I was a mess. "I thought I was dead. I was travelling with Lantern-Ey... with that woman who appeared out of the wall when we first arrived, remember? Turns out she's a Republican officer... And with the Indigo Minister."

"How the hell did you swing that?"

"We needed each other," I admitted. "There are monsters on this ship."

My hand twinged, in the same sharp rubber-band way as my spine. I rubbed at the skin—and stopped cold.

Beneath my palm, something was moving.

I lifted my hand quickly, holding it before my face. Maybe it was the poor light, but I couldn't *see* anything on my skin. Just a myriad of little cuts accumulated on my journey through the *Nameless*.

Benny spoke around a mouthful of Tamara's rations. He didn't seem to have noticed my panic. "So they tried to kill you, left you for dead?"

I pressed my fingertips to the back of my hand. Nothing, nothing. "Uh, no. I stayed behind to fight off some monsters. Indigo was hurt."

Then: *there*. Beneath my fingertips, under the skin of my hand, something moved. Something very, very small.

Out of habit, I turned to look at the second door in Tamara's saferoom. In all my dreams, it had read LAB 17 on its front. In reality, there was no inscription at all.

I was alive, all right. And I was awake. But I was still infected by the Dreamer-bots. Every person Tamara had seen infected had died—I wondered how long until the infection would kill me.

Benny sat across from me, alive against all odds. I was dead, implant or not, but he still had a chance to survive.

"I know where the Philosopher Stone is," I said. "It's in

Lab 17."

His brows lifted, then he nodded, grim and satisfied. "I know where that must be; the numbers increase in that direction." He gestured vaguely off to the side. "Soon as you can stand, let's go."

"Indigo and the lieutenant know the data's there, too." The thought made me uneasy, but what else had I expected? Aside from the aberration with the Dreamer-bots, I'd always expected to end up in competition with them again.

"Then stand up now." Benny set the empty ration box aside. There were still traces of food in the crevices of the plastic, and I thought of Lantern-Eyes swirling water around in her bowl to clean it, wasting nothing. "We don't have long, either way. We've only got a day until the sun's radiation starts to tear the ship apart."

"Only a day?" I echoed. I'd lost track of time long before I'd fallen into a machine coma, but I still hadn't imagined we were so close to destruction.

"Quint had a timepiece on her." Benny's words were clipped.

He didn't want to talk about Quint, and I couldn't blame him. I stood. My legs were shaky, but they would hold me for a little while longer, at least. "Lead the way."

CHAPTER SIXTY SEVEN: THE WALL

BENNY HAD THE only flashlight. I trailed behind him through dark, inaccessible hallways, and trusted he knew where he was going.

Benny had everything, in fact. I hadn't been in as pathetic a situation, supply-wise, since the hull wall had decompressed and Indigo had hauled me back inside. And even then, I'd had Indigo, who was better than a backpack full of supplies. Now I had the shirt on my back, torn in places and soaked in blood, and—oh, and I had Lantern-Eyes' tablet. It was in my pocket and ominously dark, which could mean either it needed a charge or I'd broken it by landing on it.

As we walked, it struck me, all that Benny did not know. "I know what the Philosopher Stone is, Benny. It's the data on the experiment that made the Ministers."

"Yeah, I know. Quint told me."

"*Quint* told you?"

"Yeah. Turns out she, and her boss, knew a lot more than they'd told us. She even knew what quadrant of the ship the data was probably hidden in. If the Ministers hadn't arrived so fast, she would've directed us there. She was very chatty, before the end."

The only way Quint could have known that was if her boss had known it, and the only way the Senator could have known that is if he had known about Lantern-Eyes. But if the Senator had known Lieutenant Gupta was here, why had he bothered to send us at all?

It didn't matter anymore. The odds were good I'd be dead before ever finding out. "What happened after the hull blew out? How did you survive?" And, too, "How did you find me?"

"The Ministers thought the data was in Mara Zhu's office, but the last thing I wanted was to run into any of them. Besides, I had a theory. Remember that blocked-off tunnel we crawled through? Well, there's more things like that. Some barriers are still up, some have fallen apart, but I figured whoever made the blockages was trying to protect something important. So Quint and I followed the barriers backwards for a while. She was adamant we get the Philosopher Stone at first."

He paused for a moment, nothing but the sound of his crunching footsteps to fill his silence. My head was throbbing, centered around the implant. I didn't dare reach back to touch the back of my skull, afraid of what kind of swollen mess I would find.

"After the first time we ran into those things that look like children," Benny said at last, "she changed her tune. Wanted to go back, promised to justify it to her boss. We were pretty far from the *Viper* but by then we'd made it to the bridge. So we stopped there, figuring we could radio for help, or find a way back to the *Viper* that didn't take us through all the monsters. The bridge had this big window out to space... When we looked out, we saw that the Ministers' ship was gone. So was the *Viper*."

"Wait, gone? As in they left?" Impossible. One wouldn't abandon a mission as important as this.

"Not gone," said Benny. "Moved. They went back and moved their ship and took ours, too, so that we couldn't escape. Parked them both somewhere near here. Must've been faster to fly than walk through this maze. So I knew the Philosopher Stone must be over here. I came over here, and ran into you."

"I thought you and Quint decided not to get the Philosopher Stone, and just to leave," I said.

"We got to talking more and it came out that Quint didn't have a good chance of convincing her boss that us leaving was justified. And now she's dead, so."

So he was stuck—or he had been stuck, before he'd found me. I firmed my heart. I would get Benny out of this, one way or another, no matter what the residual Dreamer infection did to me.

"Hey, there's one bright side about the Ministers moving the *Viper*," I said. "Now it's close by. We can definitely escape with the Philosopher Stone before the sun goes nova."

He hummed, without reply. The underside of my arm itched. I rubbed at it, and felt something move beneath my skin, in unison with the throbbing at the back of my skull.

The beam of Benny's flashlight abruptly terminated at a solid wall. He stopped short. "Sean. What is this?"

"It's a wall, Benny."

"I know what a wall is, asshole. Why is there a wall in a hallway?"

He swept his flashlight left and right, revealing the walls of the hallway we'd been following, which terminated abruptly into the solid mass of the wall ahead. I pushed past him to touch the wall. It was surprisingly solid, but rang hollowly when I knocked on it.

"Maybe there's an opening further down," I said, and backed up down the hallway until I found another branch. I stood aside for Benny to take the lead, and we followed the passage until a door opened up to our left.

Inside, we found that the room had been sealed off as well, a doorway visible on the opposite wall, but filled up with a sheet of some kind of craggy metal or plastic. "Interesting," I said.

Benny led me further down the hallway, into a particularly large room, flooring uneven with rubble, that appeared to be some sort of lecture hall or schmooze space rather than a functional lab. Across the back of this room, too, someone had built a wall.

I laid my palm over the ancient wall, which carved through rooms and hallways so adamantly. It was distinctive by being no one particular thing; the wall looked as if it had been put together out of pieces of whatever else was in the room, rather than being an intentional part of the décor. It had been assembled very solidly, too, or else the monsters on this ship had avoided it the same way they'd avoided some of the labs elsewhere on the ship. When I knocked on the craggy, uneven surface, it tolled hollowly.

The pounding in my head resounded in unison with the echoes from the solid wall. I reached up to rub the base of my skull, then thought the better of it.

"I bet Lab 17 is inside," I said. "Someone built this wall. Maybe Mara Zhu, to keep the other scientists inside. Or maybe the scientists built it, so that none of those monsters could get through." I stepped back from the wall and sighed. "Bad news for us, good news for the Ministers. They'll be able to cut right through."

"Maybe not." Benny's voice was muffled; he'd pulled his shirt up over his mouth and nose and was bracing his flashlight between cheek and shoulder. He'd managed to pry open one of the rotten old panels on the wall, and was shining the light inside. "Take a look at this."

I peered in over his shoulder and saw a mesh of wires and solid lumps of something unidentifiable, like swollen mushrooms, wedged between the oddly sized pieces of wall. "What am I looking at?"

Benny pointed at the wires without touching them. "These are live. I bet they're wired right into the ship. There's a lot of voltage going through them, too—if you put your hand close you'll feel it. Don't touch."

I reached out carefully, my hand beside his. The skin on my arm prickled.

"These," Benny continued, still muffled through his shirt, but now pointing at the weird lumps of material, "are bombs. I don't know if they'll still go off after so long, but I'm pretty sure there's some sort of radioactive material packed in and around them too. Plutonium, I think."

"Why do you think?" I couldn't see anything distinctive about those lumps.

He pulled his hand back, holding up his handbrace for us both to see. He tapped one of the bars. From this close, I could hear it vibrating slightly against his skin. A miniature Geiger counter.

He'd always been a great inventor. "Brilliant," I said.

He drew his hand away, shrugged his shirt higher up on his nose. "Plutonium has a half-life of something like six, seven thousand years. There's still plenty of it left in there. It's safe enough, unless you eat or inhale it." Very carefully, he pushed the wall panel back into place.

"Dirty bombs," I realized.

He nodded. "And if you cut through that wall, you'll electrocute yourself, or trigger one of those bombs." He lowered his shirt from his face. "How close do you think we are to the actual Philosopher Stone?"

"The data itself? Probably pretty far away," I said. "The lab complexes are huge. And I don't think they'd set up bombs close enough to the data to destroy it—plus, if that would work, Mara Zhu would've just blown up the data a thousand years ago. They *really* didn't want anything to get through this wall."

Benny nodded slowly, flashlight back in hand, trained on the solid wall before us.

Something scratched from far away, back the way we had come. I had grown so attuned to that particular sound that I picked it up out of a thousand other small sounds, the quiet groans of a dying spaceship.

Next to me, Benny flicked his flashlight off, and we

were thrown into dark.

In that dark, I heard another scuff, a scratch, from down the distant hall. "Benny," I said. "Do you have any weapons?"

He shifted beside me in the dark. "I have a rusted old scalpel I looted out of one of these creepy labs."

That was... the phrase 'bringing a knife to a gun fight' came to mind, but that was worse. It was like bringing nail clippers to fight a pack of wolves. "Come this way, quiet. Let's hide."

I drew him aside, moving through the darkness with an ease that would have made Lantern-Eyes proud. We clambered over a pile of debris at the very far end of the room, and there I drew him down, behind that sheltering mound, and we crouched small and silent in the dark.

The light came in first. A pale blue underwater-glow, as familiar to me now as a friend's voice.

On the other side of the room, glowing faintly, Indigo and Tamara stepped in together.

CHAPTER SIXTY EIGHT: SEAN WREN'S SPECIAL NEW SKILL

INDIGO STILL WORE Tamara's jacket. It fit him even worse than it fit her; at least when Tamara had been healthy and not half-starved, that jacket had been her size. It hung off Indigo's shoulders like a too-narrow hanger. In the blue of his light, the faded red was further softened to a dark violet. Tamara herself seemed particularly agitated, club swinging, circling Indigo twice as she scoped out the room. She was holding a little flashlight, probably the extra from my old pack, which was now slung over her shoulder.

Benny touched my shoulder. I leaned towards him so that he could whisper, close to my ear: "Is that them?"

I didn't dare to speak. I nodded.

The collar of Tamara's jacket stood up taller than I was used to seeing Indigo wear, so that the glow from his collar-light was directed like a lighthouse. Right now that light was directed away from us.

I could stand up. That's all it would take; I could stand up and they'd notice me. Maybe I'd have to shout their names.

But they'd see me, they'd notice me, they'd come over. I could speak to them, so that the last words we ever said to each other weren't full of fear and pain. Maybe wipe away the dreams the AI had given me of them lying dead.

But I was dead, sooner or later, from that Dreamer. And I could see perfectly well from here that they were alive and safe. Indigo was moving cautiously, but he was upright and walking—Ministers were all but unkillable.

And if I caught their attention, spoke to them, then I would lose the little advantage that I had. Because now, no matter what, I had to reach the Philosopher Stone first—or Benny would die.

I tapped Benny's shoulder, rose to a low crouch, and started to pick my way across the room to where I knew there was a door.

"What was that?" I heard Tamara say sharply, but by the time her flashlight gleamed our way, we were out the door and out of sight. I heard her footsteps start in our direction, Indigo's a beat behind. If only I could seal the door behind us, lock it, we might gain a little time to escape—

Something hurt in my hand, sharp and painful, like something crawling out from inside my skin.

Behind me, without my touching it, the door we'd left through came out of the wall and sealed itself shut.

There was no time to gape, not if we wanted to escape. We had ended up in another suite of rooms—offices, or lecture halls. Not the lab. "Come on, quick," I urged Benny, and we ran through the maze of small rooms, weaving through rotten debris and climbing through holes in the scarred walls. We kept close to the curve of the wall surrounding Lab 17.

At last I judged we were far enough from Tamara and Indigo that they wouldn't immediately catch up. Benny slowed next to me, and we stood there for a minute, panting, before he flicked his light on. The wall surrounding Lab 17 was still solid to our left, bisecting rooms and sealing up doorways with mosaicked debris.

"How'd they find us?" Benny demanded.

"They know where the data is," I said. "They're going the same way we are."

"Or they're looking for you."

As far as they were concerned, I was dead. "Maybe. It doesn't matter. We have to get through this wall."

"We can't do it with them breathing down the back of our necks. You said the Minister was hurt. How badly? Can we kill it?"

"Whoa!" I spread my hands, stepping between Benny and the path back just in case he had some wild idea about going off already. "There's no need to kill anybody."

"That's what you said about that cop," Benny said. "Back on Parnasse. You said there was no need to kill anybody, and guess what? That cop turned around and arrested us."

"That cop was just a kid," I said.

"Just a kid or not, he arrested us, and that's how we ended up here!"

"And how are you gonna kill the Minister, Benny?" I demanded. "What, run at him with your tiny little scalpel? He's still a *Minister*. And that woman with him is a Republican commando; she's survived here for five years on her own. You'd be dead before you got within five feet of them."

I thought Benny would take a swing at me. He'd done that a lot, in the early days, when we were both too raw with grief to stand each other. He hadn't done it for ages, replacing the hot anger with a certain dull indifference. We all scarred differently, I supposed.

Instead, Benny said, "Fine. It doesn't matter anymore."

"Fine," I repeated, rubbing at the raised scars on the side of my hand. My fingertip touched something wet as it did, and I glanced down to see that one of the cuts on my hand had opened back up, blood beading at the mouth of it.

I rubbed the skin of my hand, and felt nanomachines skitter beneath my skin.

Benny pressed his hands to the wall, his ear to the metal.

"What are you looking for?" I asked.

"A gap."

"In the wall?"

"In the defenses." The fingertips of his braced hand trailed over the surface. "I don't care how well-made it was, or how many redundancies, or if the AI has been repairing the defenses this whole time. It's been a thousand years. There will be a gap in the defenses, probably more than one. We can get through that gap."

He seemed to know what to look for. Unless part of finding the gap involved conjugating a verb tense, I was pretty much useless. I trailed after him and his flashlight as he followed the wall from room to room, rubbing the skin of my neck below where the throbbing pain was centered. The ache was a deep and frightening thing that seemed to go straight through into my bone. Maybe the Dreamer-bots wouldn't kill me. Maybe they'd accidentally detonate the implant, and that would be the thing that killed me.

The thought brought a chill through all parts of me except the back of my skull, which felt achingly hot. I dropped my hand again and watched Benny as he touched and rapped on the wall, examined the machinery hidden in his handbrace, and paced methodically from room to room. He reminded me of one of my neighbors on Kystrom, a veterinarian. Doctor Marco had been a retired exobiologist who was always delighted to see something new. Brigid and I had brought any number of injured wildlife to his door, often with Brigid's friend Liza trailing behind, too squeamish to touch the animal. Doctor Marco had always taken the wounded thing and examined it much like Benny examined the wall, fingers firm but cautious, feeling for gaps and broken places.

"Do you remember Doctor Marco?" I asked Benny.

He didn't pause his examination of the wall. "Who?"

"On Kystrom. The veterinarian."

Benny sighed. "I never met him, Sean."

That's right. Benny had lived on the other side of the town; Doctor Marco had mostly kept to himself. Certainly Benny had never gone with me and Brigid and Liza to the doctor's doorstep, carrying a new alien species in need of aid.

It occurred to me that I didn't know if Benny had ever had pets, on Kystrom. My memory was hazy—he'd had a dog, hadn't he? Maybe a little yappy dog. Here I was, dying from nanomachines burrowing their way into my skull, and I didn't even know if Benny had ever had a dog.

I opened my mouth to ask when a flare of blue light caught my attention. I jolted, turning back the way we had come, and saw Tamara and Indigo several rooms away, staring at us through the open doors.

Tamara said, "Sean!"

"Oh, shit," I said, and to Benny, "Run!"

CHAPTER SIXTY NINE:
LAST ONE THERE LOSES

"WHAT THE—" I heard Tamara say, distinctly, and then, "*Sean!*" A moment later boots pounded on the ground in pursuit.

Benny's flashlight bounced wildly over the walls and floor as he ran. "I've got the scalpel," he reminded me, breathless, and I saw the flash of metal in his hand.

"No!" I said. "No, no, no. Look, they're after me. Split up and I'll lose them. Meet up further down the wall."

He nodded briefly, short of breath already. I'd always been a better runner than Benny. The next room we entered, I went right and he went left.

"Hey, Lantern-Eyes!" I shouted, and waited until she'd burst through the door behind me, a stormy look on her face, to peel off running again.

Tamara was *fast*. I'd known that because I'd run alongside her just recently, but it was one thing to run with her and a whole other thing to have all that ferocious attention and dedicated speed chasing you down through the halls of an abandoned spaceship. I was almost scared.

My only light was her flashlight beam, and my steps were obscured by my own shadow, a long-legged man-shape stretching out over floor and walls.

She was gonna catch up. I'd been the subject of one of her take-downs before, back in the farmlands, and I wasn't keen to have that brutal efficiency smashing my face into the metal floor. I found what I was looking for and slowed to a stop, standing just inside a doorway.

Tamara jogged to a stop a few feet away. "What the fuck, Sean?"

"Where's Indigo?" I asked.

"He's following us at a walk, because he has a fucking *hole* in his stomach. What the hell are you doing? Why are you running? How did you find your friend?"

"Sorry, Tamara," I said, and raised one hand beside the doorframe. I had a theory to test.

She took another step towards me. "I don't like apologies. You'd better have a damn good explanation."

"No, sorry for this," I explained, and *willed* the door to close. There was a bright spark of pain in my palm as another of those little cuts in my skin was pushed open from the inside, and a tiny little machine emerged, smaller than my fingernail, barely a glint of light in the beam of Tamara's flashlight. It vanished into the darkness of the wall where the door was hidden.

A moment later, the door slammed shut, cutting off my view of Lieutenant Gupta's shocked expression.

I stood there a minute, staring at the shut door, inches from my nose. It was a very ordinary door, for the *Nameless*. Decaying man-made materials. No markings.

A blank slate, right before my eyes, easy for my brain to project the image of Lieutenant Gupta's face onto.

If I stared at that memory too long, I might see the betrayal in her expression. Why was she looking at me like that? This was what we'd said we'd do, all those days ago. I was just leaving in a way that didn't get anyone killed.

I had to find my way back to Benny. If my sense of direction was correct, and I was pretty sure it was, I wanted to go thataway. I turned thataway and started walking, feeling my way through the dark. I wasn't particularly worried about running into a manikin or one of the Children or whatever else was around; this zone seemed pretty abandoned and I bet every monster with a working brain—or single brain cell, or whatever the coral had—had realized very quickly that the wall was more dangerous than it was worth.

Several rooms later, my foot caught on something and I pitched forward, hard, to the ground. A bright bar of pain sliced along my thigh, just above my knee. I hadn't been worried about the monsters, but it turned out I should have been worried about my own clumsiness. I sat for a second, examining the cut by feel. It was pretty deep, and bleeding enthusiastically. In a perfect world I'd say I needed stitches.

The pain of the gash didn't compare to the solid aching of my skull. I probably wouldn't live long enough to make stitches matter.

As I crouched there, examining my leg by feel, a pale glow trickled into the room like the first grey fingers of dawn. I went very still, as if that light hadn't already heard me, as if its bearer didn't already know where I was.

Indigo entered the room through the far door, serene and glowing, still wearing Tamara Gupta's Republican Lieutenant's jacket. He must have gone around, I thought numbly. While Tamara was chasing me directly, Indigo had figured out where I was headed and had gone to cut me off.

There was no hoping he hadn't seen me. I was crouched out in the open, and he was staring right at me. We looked at each other in silence for a time, and then he reached out one hand towards me.

The simplicity of the appeal shook me. I'd expected Lantern-Eyes' rational demands—she *would* want a detailed explanation—but I didn't feel that I ever knew, really, what to expect from Indigo. Now here he stood, asking nothing more of me than the offer of his outstretched hand.

Nanomachines squirmed beneath the skin of my leg, hot around my bleeding gash. I realized abruptly that I did not know what the Dreamer-bots inside me would do if I brought them near to Indigo.

"I'm not falling for that," I said to him, and knowing that he could not run with his abdomen torn open and barely held intact, I stood up and walked away.

CHAPTER SEVENTY: SYMPATHY FOR THE DEVILS

I FOUND BENNY when he nearly stabbed me in the face.

"Whoa, whoa!" I shouted, leaping back, a rusty scalpel slicing through the air inches from my nose.

Benny's flashlight clicked on a second later, revealing him standing in front of a rugged section of the Lab 17 wall. "Sean," he said.

"That was pathetic," I told him. "You couldn't even stab me; you'd better not try to take on Indigo or Tamara."

His glance kept bouncing past me. "Where are they?"

"Where do you think? I lost them some while back." Lost Tamara looking shocked, abandoned on the wrong side of a locked door, and lost Indigo alone and gleaming with one hand outstretched in mute appeal. Guilt roiled in my gut, stupid and inappropriate. We'd always known we would part ways when we reached the Stone.

"Are they looking for you or for the Philosopher Stone?" Benny demanded.

The question jolted me, like a wheel going over a stone. "The Stone. They just care about the Stone."

Tamara needed the data as leverage against the Ministers, to protect the Republic. Indigo needed the data because his people were sick, and the Philosopher Stone was the only hope of saving them. Billions of people in the Republic, billions of Ministers. Billions of lives on either side.

I was just trying to save one.

My leg ached. I reached down to rub at the skin above the cut, feeling suddenly very tired. The ache in my head surged, almost enough to blind me. Maybe that was why I spoke without thinking. "I left them behind to kill each other."

"So?" Benny had already turned away.

So when I'd seen them, Indigo had been wearing Tamara's uniform jacket. "I feel bad," I admitted.

"The Republic and the Ministers *fucked* us, Sean. Why would you feel sorry for them?"

"I don't control who I feel sorry for or not," I said, annoyed. He was always like this, yelling at me about not agreeing with him exactly all the time.

"You need to face the real world," he snapped at me. "If someone fucks you over, the only thing to do is to fuck them back."

"All right, forget it," I snapped back. "Let them stab each other; who cares? We'll get the data, we'll get out of here and we'll screw over that Senator somehow, happy?"

Benny didn't answer. My leg ached and itched, much like the lump of pain in the back of my skull. I rubbed at my thigh above the gash, and when I looked back up, Benny was walking away, following the bend of the Lab 17 wall.

Several rooms later, I had to stop. I crouched down to examine my leg while Benny continued on, feeling around the wall for some weakness we could exploit. My fingers probed the gash I'd seen briefly in the light of Indigo's collar. It stung, as I'd expected, but weirdly, it wasn't bleeding.

Benny's light was receding fast. He didn't seem to have noticed that he'd lost me. I couldn't see anything anymore, much less what kind of damage I'd done to my leg. I stood up, wobbling on my injured leg, and took a step towards Benny, opening my mouth to call his name—and then a solid bar of something caught me around the throat, stopping my breath in my lungs, and a moment later everything went black.

CHAPTER SEVENTY ONE: A FRIGHTENINGLY EFFICIENT KIDNAPPING

I WOKE UP the captive of a very annoyed Republican lieutenant and an icily composed Minister.

That takedown had been terrifyingly efficient. There was no telling who had actually rendered me unconscious so swiftly; the silence and speed suggested Indigo, but the bruise to my larynx implied Tamara. Maybe they'd both done it together. Whoever had done it had somehow managed to cure my headache, though. Instead of an all-encompassing throbbing, all I felt now was a vague ache. I guess a good knock on the head did cure some things.

It was a good thing their alliance wouldn't last much longer. The world probably wouldn't be able to handle the two of them working in concert for long.

"Hey, guys," I said, from flat on my back, while Tamara crouched at my side, hands dangling between her knees and flashlight on the floor and Indigo watched me from a height, dark-water gleaming. I smiled disarmingly.

Tamara was not disarmed. Actually, I don't think she ever went unarmed. "You got that explanation ready?" she asked.

"Uh, explanation of what?"

"Of what the hell happened, Sean." She was speaking with deliberate patience. Not a good sign. "I heard the Dreamer coming before you shut the door. Then I couldn't get through. But when Indigo and I made it the long way around the door, you weren't in the server room anymore. What happened?"

"This and that," I replied, and nodded at Indigo. "Is he Good Cop?"

Indigo gazed down his nose at me and did not speak.

"Hey." Tamara patted my cheek to pull my attention back to her. "Why'd you run? What's going on?"

"I just thought I'd get the drop on you when it came to ending the arrangement," I said. "I mean, you can both kill me with your bare hands. We're close to Lab 17 now, and I was a little bit worried you might try to winnow down the competition, you know? Thin the herd? Make things easier for yourselves."

"Really," Tamara said flatly.

"Are you going to choke me out again if I sit up?"

Her glance flickered. Then she sat back a little, giving me the space to sit up.

And sit up I did. A quick glance around the room showed that Tamara had dragged me into a closet. There was no way out, unless I suddenly gained the hand-to-hand combat skills necessary to bludgeon Indigo and Tamara both into unconsciousness. There was very little subtlety in the way Indigo stood in front of the only door.

"So that's it, then?" I asked, eying the blocked door. "I didn't think I'd be the first one down."

"God damn it, Sean, we didn't drag you here to execute you," Tamara said. "And if you expect me to believe that you threw away your only advantage by telling us the location of the Philosopher Stone, then stood between us and certain death because you wanted to end the arrangement and beat us to the Philosopher Stone because all of this has been one big fuck-you, then—"

She caught herself, jaw working. She almost could believe it, I realized. She almost could believe the story I was trying to sell her, and that frightened Lieutenant Lantern-Eyes, who wasn't scared of anything.

Indigo's steady regard bore through my defenses by the sheer weight of it.

"We thought you were dead, Sean," Tamara said, and somehow her being so matter-of-fact about it made her words drive into me more deeply than any emotional confession could have done.

My paper-thin resistance to their presence crumbled like, well, paper.

"I am dead," I admitted.

CHAPTER SEVENTY TWO:
THE WHOLE TRUTH

"Explain," Indigo said.

It was the first word I'd heard him speak since he'd lay dying, discounting the nightmare versions of him the Dreamer had made me hallucinate. His voice was rough, dry. Massive blood loss would dehydrate you, I reflected.

"After we got you to the saferoom, I went out to clean up the blood trail," I explained. Tamara nodded; she knew this part. "I didn't want something to follow us in. While I was in the hallway I heard the Dreamer-bots. I knew we couldn't run... you were unconscious," I said to Indigo. "If they didn't find someone in the server room, they'd keep looking, and they'd find you. But if they found someone in the server room, I gambled they'd stop. So I let the Dreamer-bots find me."

"But you're not dead," Tamara said.

"Not yet. They're still inside me."

Tamara recoiled; Indigo stepped forward, hand outstretched towards me and pain on his face.

"Don't." I didn't recognize my own voice when I spoke,

but Indigo did stop. "Don't touch me, Indigo."

He blinked and pulled back, lowering his hand to his side.

Tamara spoke to the floor between her knees. "I don't understand how you're conscious."

That was Lantern-Eyes, rigorously hammering the details out of my story. "The Dreamer-bots induce vivid hallucinations. The only way out of them is to convince the AI you don't have any interest in taking the Philosopher Stone. None of the prior infectees could do this, because the AI only knows Ameng and none of your crew spoke Ameng. I convinced the AI to let me go, but the nanomachines are still inside me. I don't know how long before they kill me."

"How do you know they'll kill you?" Indigo asked.

I felt almost embarrassed to admit it. "My head's been killing me, Indigo."

I saw Tamara's jaw flex. Indigo sank down, until he was sitting with us on the floor. "It's a horrible perversion of something that was designed to protect and repair," he said, "that instead, they've been made to kill."

"Benny found me after I woke up," I continued. "You've both met him, but you don't know... Benny is the only other survivor from my town on Kystrom. He's the only one left. He's the closest thing to family I have—I had to go with him."

Indigo looked stricken. It was a strange reaction to have, and I was on the verge of asking him why he should look so horrified when Tamara lifted her head and said, "And that's why the two of you are out to find the Stone? So you can get rich together?"

Those jack-o-lantern eyes of hers were unfriendly. I glared back. "I didn't sell the two of you out for money, Tamara."

"So why did you run away? Explain it to me, Sean. We want to understand."

"Benny and I made each other a promise," I said. "Like the arrangement the three of us had, but forever... We had nothing after Kystrom. No family, no friends, no money, nothing. We promised to be each other's family, to keep each other alive, to always put the other person first. You understand," I said, and Tamara nodded curtly.

I took a breath, and continued. "Benny and I made our money by smuggling," I said. "We were a good team. I could speak the language of whoever we needed to speak to, and Benny could rig up new ways to avoid Republican scanners. And since we weren't citizens, we weren't people to the Republic—we were a lot harder to track, and there was nowhere to extradite us to, if we did get caught. So sometimes the authorities didn't want to put in the effort.

"On our last job, we almost got caught. There were cops chasing us, and one of them followed to this old house on Parnasse... Benny wanted to kill him, so they wouldn't pick up our trail again, but the cop was just a kid. Younger than us. You understand?"

Tamara didn't speak.

Indigo said, "I understand."

It was more of a relief to hear that than I could've expected. I'd known I'd made the right choice, done the right thing; I knew that, if I did it again, I would make the same choice even knowing what would come of it. I couldn't live with myself if I'd let Benny kill that boy. But I'd spent so long suffering the consequences of it, listening to Benny berate me for it, hearing Quint speak of my choice as a moment of weakness. Indigo's understanding came as a relief after all that.

"So I let the guy go," I said. "And he came back, faster than I expected, before we could get away. And they arrested us. I think the cop was some politician's son. They were going to charge us with smuggling, theft, and attempted murder, because of how much Benny had talked about killing him."

"You never went to trial," Tamara said. She sounded, somehow, like she knew the ending of this story.

"No. While we were waiting to be tried, someone approached us with an offer. He was a Senator, but I never met him and he never told us his name. If we stole the Philosopher Stone, he'd clear our names and let us go."

"You're here to steal on commission," Tamara said.

"I told him no."

She looked at me for the first time since I'd told her that the Dreamer-bots were still inside me. She and Indigo were both so terrifying, in such different ways. When Indigo looked at me, it was all veiled, dark-water currents, powerful and unseen. When Tamara looked at me it was as bare as bones in a desert, sand-scoured and painfully open.

"He didn't take no for an answer," I told them. "He put an implant in our skulls—mine, and Benny's, and Leah's. It can't be removed or deactivated, and if we don't do what he said, he'd kill us."

My hands were shaking for no good reason; I clasped them in my lap.

"I don't want the Philosopher Stone," I told Tamara and Indigo. "And I'm dead anyway, with or without the implant. But if I don't find the data, Benny will be dead, too."

CHAPTER SEVENTY THREE: THE BREAKING OF THE FELLOWSHIP

TAMARA GUPTA SAID, "You're only telling us this *now?*"

"Excuse me?" I said, baffled.

"I could find this Senator—I have contacts, in the military, in the government. If you offered to help the Republic—the real Republic, not that Senator—to find the Philosopher Stone data, you could *name* your reward. My superiors would remove your implant as soon as they learned of it, and they'd have no problem wiping your record clean. Sean. Why didn't you ask me for *help?!*"

She ceased, breathing hard, glaring at me with those jack-o-lantern eyes on fire.

As if it could've been that simple. "What did you expect me to do, Tamara? Trust you? You're the same people who got me into this situation to begin with!"

"I could've—"

"Could've *what?* You can't perform surgery on me here. The Senator would probably detonate my skull by the time you could get me to a doctor who could figure out how to get that thing out of my skull—if it could even be done. Who's got more power in the Republic, Tamara? A lieutenant who's been away from home for five years, or a Senator with something to hide?"

She sat back hard against the wall, her expression mulish and angry. Emotional, I realized. Pragmatic Lieutenant Gupta was reacting from pure emotion.

Softness, for her and her metal-boned strength, hit me like a wave. I said, as gently as I could, "I know you don't like to hear this, but this is something you can't control."

She laced her bony fingers in her lap, squeezed them tight.

Indigo was still watching us, glowing softly. I said to him, "I don't guess you could tell me that the Ministers could get this thing out of my head."

"We have the technology," Indigo told me. "Better technology than the Republic. But we do not carry that kind of technology with us. If what the Senator told you is true, you would be dead before my people could save you."

Weirdly, that hit me harder than Tamara's plea. I'd already known there was no help for me from the Republic; Tamara's offer was treading familiar ground. But Indigo was a step removed from magic. So long as he was in the room with me, I was safe from anything else; the Ministers, too, had technology that I didn't know of and could barely imagine. So if Indigo said I could not be saved, I knew that there was no known technology in the Sister Systems that could save me and Benny from the bombs inside our skulls.

"You see why I left," I told them.

"Two lives instead of billions," Tamara said, bitter. She was still staring down at her clasped hands.

"Is that what the Republic thought when they gave up Kystrom to the Ministers?" I snapped. "Just a few million lives instead of a billion? Watch how you tally it up, Tamara."

She glowered down at her palms. I turned to Indigo. "What about you? Have you got anything to say? Disappointed I'm just a selfish, ordinary smuggler?"

My voice broke, horrifyingly, on the last word. Neither of my companions reacted, but I swallowed like I could force the cracked edges of my voice back down into my lungs, cutting my windpipe like metal splinters as they went.

Indigo said, "One of the reasons I stayed with you, and not my own people, when your Benny blew out the hull was because I had seen that you were kind." Indigo was as calm as if Tamara and I hadn't spent the last few minutes lashing out at each other with the broken-bottle edges of hurt. "I trust your heart. I have to do what I have to do, regardless of whether it is right or wrong, but I believe that if you believe what you are doing is right, then it must be so."

I'd never heard anything like that spoken aloud, certainly not to me. The words almost didn't seem to make sense in that combination, echoing around in the enormity of their meaning while Indigo looked at me like living as long as he had had eroded his ability to feel embarrassment.

Tamara said, "God damn, Indigo."

Her incredulity punched a laugh out of me, shaken up from deep in my sternum. I pressed the heel of my hand to one eye, then the other, until my laughter had shaken itself away.

Tamara was looking at me again, her fingers still clasped but expression no longer stormy. "If you truly believe in what you're doing, with no reservations, then I respect that," she said to me. "I have to do what I have to do, but I wish you the best of luck, I really do."

It struck me then that she, and Indigo a moment before, was saying goodbye. It seemed rather sudden—yes, our arrangement had to end; yes, I'd rushed to its end, skipping past the negotiation and the speeches, but now that they'd caught me, surely the whole thing should take a little longer to dissolve?

And what would happen once it had? I couldn't help but remember the nightmares the Dreamer had shown me. "What now?"

"Indigo and I talked about it already. We're going to split up." Tamara shifted, straightening her spine, a little more soldierly and familiar. "He's gotten back into contact with the Ministers, who have re-docked their ship not far from here."

Re-docked their ship, and re-docked the *Viper* with it, according to Benny. Indigo had told me once that his collar-light could function as a radio somehow, but only over very short ranges. The Ministers must be quite close—and the *Viper*, too. I squirreled that fact away in my skull. That was Benny's way out.

"As for me, the Republic will arrive within the hour." Tamara's fingers flexed against her leg, then relaxed, deliberate. "I'll rendezvous with them."

So they would send each other off to opposite ends of Lab 17. "And after that?"

"What do you want to happen after that, Sean?" Tamara asked, and her question scored me down to the bone.

It wasn't as if I could ask them not to kill each other. That was the way things had been from the start, and we'd all known it. And I'd gone off with Benny, after all. I was as much their enemy as they were each other's. I had no say in their choices, and at some point in the next day, it was just as likely that I would find myself at the end of Tamara's gun or Indigo's knife, or that I would have to decide whether or not to let Benny use that rusty little scalpel.

"The wall's booby-trapped," I warned them. Indigo took off Tamara's jacket and shook it out, the deep red of it dirty and faded. "Watch out."

"We know, Sean," Tamara said, and shrugged her jacket back on.

I couldn't let them leave. Not with things ending this way; not when there was a chance we might all have to kill each other in a few hours. "Maybe we can figure something out," I started to say, but Tamara lifted a hand.

"There's something you should know," Tamara said. No apology, just explanation. That was Lantern-Eyes. "What the Senator did to you is inexcusable. Coercion isn't acceptable to the Republic, and attempting to hire you to steal the Philosopher Stone out from under the

Republic's nose is reprehensible. The details of how and why you were chosen and sent weren't known to my superiors, I can guarantee that. But the Republic did know that someone was being sent here."

That was a hell of a disclaimer. It was hard to see around it. "What?"

"That Senator," Tamara said, "had strict instructions to find some civilians willing to undertake a risky trip for their government. *Willing* civilians—volunteers. These volunteers would fly a civilian vessel to this ship, they would land, and they would leave again once the Ministers had noticed their presence."

There was a pounding in my ears and that was why, I was sure, I was having such trouble understanding her. "What are you saying?"

"My team set a trap," Tamara said calmly. "But the Ministers were taking too long to spring it. We were running out of time before the sun went nova—*I* was running out of time," she clarified, only the barest flicker in her expression that might hint at grief. "The others were all dead by then. I'd set off the SOS, but the Ministers weren't taking that bait, either. They were too cautious. I couldn't let them be cautious. I couldn't let them realize it was a trap. I needed them to panic and rush here, quick and unguarded."

She took a shaky breath, and when she started to speak again, her voice was steady and measured. "I could've called for extraction," she said. "But if the Ministers had seen Republican military come to this ship, they would've arrived guns blazing, expecting resistance, expecting a trap. Like on Kystrom. But if the Ministers saw a *civilian* vessel discovering this ship... they would still panic, because they couldn't let humanity take the Philosopher Stone instead of them. But they wouldn't send an army. They would send a full spectrum, nothing more. And they would walk in here expecting no resistance. Which is what happened."

Indigo wasn't reacting. Either she'd told him this already, or he'd guessed it long ago.

"I knew I could prepare a trap that could handle seven Ministers," Tamara said, still unnaturally calm. "So I advised the Republic to send a civilian ship here."

She'd shown up as soon as we docked the *Viper* on the *Nameless*. Tamara Gupta had climbed out of the wall and looked at us, and we'd stared at her, shocked by her unexpected appearance. By our very shock, she must've realized that something had gone wrong. And then she'd screamed and the others had all assumed she was crazy, so Lantern-Eyes had sat back and listened. Our conversation after she'd appeared would've told her everything she'd needed to know about whether the Republic had sent us there or not, and whether her cover was blown. And then Indigo had arrived, the Ministers taking the bait Tamara had dangled before them, but our ignorance had spoiled whatever trap she'd planned to spring upon their arrival. We'd wasted too much time talking, and the Ministers had gotten the jump on us, and from there everything had spiraled out of control.

The Senator was the one who had chosen me, trying to weight the scales in his favor. Probably that was why

Quint had told us to kill Lantern-Eyes upon her arrival. But it was Tamara Gupta's request that had brought me here.

Tamara was buttoning up her uniform jacket, neat and precise. I looked at Indigo, because he was the one her trap would have caught if it had been sprung correctly, and he would understand how I felt for having been a victim of Lantern-Eyes' machinations.

Indigo met my gaze and said, simply, "I was the general in charge of capturing Kystrom."

CHAPTER SEVENTY FOUR: PERVERSION OF POTENTIAL

THE POUNDING IN my ears rose to a roar. Indigo and Tamara left the room together, then parted outside the door. Tamara left her flashlight lying at my feet, but took her pack away with her. Indigo dialed down his light once he was outside, to just the palest wisp of blue. Five minutes ago I might have followed after them, called their names, chased them down and tried to bring them back. Now I sat on the floor of a closet in the *Nameless*, Tamara's flashlight illuminating one empty corner, and drowned in the white noise.

I felt an urge to pray, but I had no words to say. I rubbed my thumb over the scars travelling down from pinky to forearm on my right hand. The last time I'd felt this numbed and alone, I'd been in Benny's ship flying away from Kystrom for the very last time. If I'd had a knife, or even Benny's little scalpel, I would've added two more scars to the collection, an offering to the God of Blood, if I even lived long enough to scarify.

There was still the wound on my leg. It had stopped

bleeding somehow, but when I'd looked at it earlier, the wound had been deep enough to scar. I could get my nails in, open it up. Not traditional, but what was tradition about scarring yourself for a Republican soldier and the Minister who had killed your family? It would be a long, deep scar—

My fingertip brushed the edges of the wound. It hurt, a bright sharp warning pain, my body telling me in no uncertain words to STOP MESSING WITH THAT, IDIOT. But I touched it again, tracing my finger along the length of the wound despite the pain, because I could not quite believe what I was feeling.

The gash had been sizable. I could still feel blood drying on my pants from when it had been bleeding. And then I'd walked on that leg, run on that leg, and that alone should've kept the cut open. But I wasn't bleeding anymore. In fact, the wound had somehow closed up. Not healed—it felt too raw, too sharp to be healed—but somehow, it had closed up.

I grabbed for Tamara's flashlight and missed it the first two times. The beam of light wavered when I picked it up, shaking in my shaking hand. I trained that unsteady light on my leg and found no gaping wound, no scab, but a red line where the wound was. Like it had been stitched up, but there were no stitches on the outside.

No stitches on the outside, but I had nanomachines inside me, with tiny little legs that could function almost like sutures.

Nausea rose in my throat. A horrible perversion of something designed to protect and repair, Indigo had said.

Something designed *to repair*.

I fumbled for my arm in the half-light. There was a scabbed up cut over my forearm where a manikin had scratched it while we fled. I got my fingernails on either side of the cut and dug them beneath the scab. The scab peeled off, taking fresh flesh with it, and blood welled up in its place. Not enough. I got my nail into the slit in my skin, and pried it open. Then I sat back and watched blood well up and curve over my arm—watched the cut close up on its own, and seal as if sutured from the inside.

The nanomachines weren't killing me.

They were repairing me.

In the dreams, the AI had asked about the implant. *There's something in your skull.* And I'd told it—I'd told it that the implant wasn't supposed to be there—

It had been some time, I realized, since I'd had any pain in the base of my skull.

I raised one hand, fingers trembling, to hover over the back of my neck. When I touched my skin I'd feel it there, I told myself, heart pounding. When I touched my skin I'd feel the swollen lump I'd felt earlier, or if that was gone, I would feel the implant as small and hard as a pea nestled right up next to my skull. The headaches being gone didn't mean anything. The implant was certainly still there.

Carefully, expecting pain, I laid my fingertips over the back of my spine. The skin was cool and flat, no fever, no swelling. I ran my fingers up and down my nape and felt nothing but smooth flat skin, taut to my spine. I pressed my fingertips down hard and felt nothing but my own muscle and bone.

The implant was gone.

CHAPTER SEVENTY FIVE: BENNY

I FOLLOWED THE wall surrounding Lab 17 until I found Benny, kneeling at a corner of the wall, inspecting the fragile covering. It was possible, I realized abstractly, that I might not have found Benny. That he could've gone a different way, and I might have wandered alongside the wall for ages without running into him. But I hadn't even doubted that I would. There had been no room in my mind for anything other than what had filled it—Lieutenant Gupta's trap and Indigo's crimes and the smooth skin at the nape of my neck.

"Oh," said Benny, lowering his flashlight and the scalpel I saw he had been using to scrape along the edges of the wall, "it's you."

"Benny," I said, because in all the noise in my head, the one word I could remember was his name.

"What happened? Were you followed?"

He was shining his flashlight past me, into the dark, like there might be someone there. The idea was impossible. They were gone; Tamara and Indigo had severed their connections to me and left.

And the ship itself had severed my connection to the Senator. "I'm okay," I told him. "We parted. Parted for good."

"You make it sound like a breakup," Benny muttered, and turned his attention back to the wall.

I stared at his shoulder, the side of his head, the place where, if his hair were parted a little at the back, the implant would be. Where the implant still was, on him.

"Benny," I said, while his scalpel *scratch-scratched* on the wall. "My implant is gone. They repaired me. The nanomachines weren't killing me, they were repairing me."

"What are you talking about?"

"The Senator can't kill me anymore. Benny, we don't have to steal the Philosopher Stone."

"Sean," said Benny, "what are you talking about?"

He knelt, flashlight on the floor, scalpel in his good hand, dirty face. Familiar face, the last one from my hometown Itaka. I felt a surge of fondness for that Kystrene face. "We can leave."

He studied me. "Have you lost it?"

"I'm not crazy. Listen." I sat down beside him, crosslegged, and held out my arm. And then I *willed* a Dreamer-bot to emerge, to fly to the wall Benny had been examining, to repair his little scritch-scratches.

A tiny cut on my hand bulged, split. A miniscule glint of metal emerged, glimmering with wings. It flew through the light of my flashlight away from my hand and to the wall, where it landed on the scratchmarks Benny had made on the metal.

Benny threw himself backwards, shoving himself across the floor away from the wall, the machine, from me. "God of Blood," he gasped.

I closed my hand into a fist, hiding the dot of blood in my palm. "I was infected by the ship's self-repair system," I explained to Benny. "It's happened to other people before, but they all died. But I didn't. I thought it was killing me as we went, but it wasn't. It was *repairing* me. And that meant it was dismantling the implant in my spine."

Benny stared at me, chest heaving, something like horror in his eyes.

"They can repair you too," I explained. "You'll hallucinate a little bit, first—I'll walk you through how to pass that test, teach you some Ameng. And once you've passed it, the nanomachines will repair you, too. The implant will be gone. We can leave the Philosopher Stone, get the *Viper* and go."

"The Ministers have the *Viper*," Benny said, numb. He was still staring at me like I was something frightening and strange.

"You think we can't steal it out from under their noses? Come on, Benny." I grinned at him and flexed my wrist. The cut in my hand had already closed back up. "We've got to get to the *Viper* anyway, or we'll get stuck. How were you planning on getting off this ship anyway?"

I had spent so long preparing for a worst-case scenario I'd forgotten what it was like to hope for the best. An unexpected aid had come to us, and we were free. We could get off this ship, get some revenge on the Senator maybe, but it didn't matter, because we were *free*.

"Have you lost your *fucking* mind?" Benny said.

The shards of a future I was assembling in my mind—get the implant out of Benny, get on the *Viper*, get off the *Nameless* and find out where the Senator banked his money then cheat him out of a couple million terraques—blew apart like leaves in a gale. "I—"

"You've got *things* inside you, you don't know what they're doing, and you want me to do the same thing?" Benny said.

How couldn't he see it? "I'm trying to save your life! Why the hell else would I suggest it? Do you think it was comfortable, having a swarm of little robots crawl into my eyes? I don't want to hurt you, I want to help—like we promised, Benny!"

"Like we promised," Benny repeated, cold and sharp, like metal splinters left outside in the snow. "All you've done for the past few years is make it hard for me to survive."

"What the hell is that supposed to mean?"

"You promised to put my life first. But every chance you've gotten, you've put other people's lives ahead of mine. Sometimes it didn't matter and I could ignore it, because what other choice did I have?" Benny said. "My family and my friends are dead. All that was left was you."

"It's the same for me," I said, but he didn't seem to be listening. "What are you talking about? When did I put anyone ahead of you?"

"And sometimes it's like that cop," Benny said. He looked at me harder, colder than Indigo had ever looked at me, even when Indigo had been about to kill me. "We could've gotten away. We could've lived. But you put that cop's life ahead of ours, ahead of mine, and here we are."

He couldn't mean that by sparing the cop I had chosen the cop over him. If there had been a gun to that cop's head and a gun to Benny's and I could only save one, of course I'd pick Benny. But I couldn't just let him kill a man because that man might make our lives harder in the future. How could Benny think I could've seen this coming, with the Senator and the implant and the magic data on an abandoned spaceship?

"You got us killed, Sean," Benny said. "You telling me you kept your promise?"

"You don't really think I should've let that cop die—"

"Yeah," said Benny. "And everyone else you've risked your neck and mine trying to help, when it wasn't our fault or our problem to do it."

Now and again when Benny and I traveled, I'd taken the time to help people we passed who needed help. Sometimes little things, like we came across a ship that needed a part to get to dock safely. Or sometimes riskier things, like that girl on Reyka who had been running from someone, stepfather or boyfriend, determined to show her what. Of course I helped them. Benny and I needed help all the time, though we didn't always get it. And service was as much a sacrifice to the God Who Shed His Blood For Us as blood of our own. No one else was going to help them, like no one else was going to help us, so I always did. Even if we were short of parts ourselves, or that stepfather/boyfriend had a gun. Benny couldn't imagine that was me putting other people's lives ahead of his. It made our lives harder from time to time, but he couldn't think it was the same.

"You said you didn't mind," I said. "You said we should help people—"

"No, I said we should get our affairs in order first, then help people," Benny said. "How could you give away things we needed? And when you did, after I told you not to, whose job was it to make sure we didn't starve or get shot? It was mine, because you don't realize there's a problem until it's already happening."

I felt helpless. "We were doing the right thing."

"According to *you*, Sean! Why should you get to decide?"

There had been a sapling in my parents' backyard. One summer, when I'd been about nine and Brigid eight, we'd peeled the bark off the trunk. Sapling bark was more supple than a grown tree's bark, and we could bend and shape it into little plates and bowls and teacups. My mother had seen the stripped wood of the tree and our misshapen menagerie of kitchenware and she'd scolded us. I hadn't understood why she'd been so angry—the tree had looked fine, only a little naked, but the leaves still green and firm. But over the weeks that passed, the leaves had shriveled and gone brown, the branches brittle, and, before autumn, the sapling had fallen. The tree had died on the day Brigid and I had torn the bark off, but it hadn't shown the damage until weeks later. My relationship with Benny had ended long ago, only I hadn't seen it until now.

The strangest thing was that it didn't really hurt, not like hearing the truth from Indigo and Tamara had hurt, not like watching them walk away had caused me pain. Benny's anger hurt the way the loss of Kystrom hurt: a low, dull ache. The pain of an old scar, not a nanomachine-sutured wound.

"So what will you do," I asked, "if you won't let me help you?"

"I'm going to destroy the Stone."

"Why?"

"Because the Ministers and the Republic want it," Benny told me. He sounded strangely calm, for someone with such a pinched expression. "I'm going to make sure neither gets what they want."

The Philosopher Stone had medical data that could help millions of people, even leaving aside that the Republic intended to use it as a shield and the Ministers as an antidote. It had been made out of suffering and horror and death, sure, but it was going to be used for *good*. Benny wanted to destroy it?

"Spite?" I said. "That's your grand plan? That's what's worth dying for to you?"

"What else do I have left? The Ministers killed our families, Sean. I'd die before I let them get what they want."

"It doesn't have to be your problem," I told him.

"It isn't your problem either way," he told me.

I ran my hand through my hair, tugged at the strands. I wanted to shake him, but I didn't think he'd let me touch him. "This ship will be destroyed in a matter of hours anyway!"

"But your friends back there might reach the Stone

before the sun goes."

"It's not worth dying for! Benny, we can still get off this ship! *You* can still get off this ship!"

"You know what Quint told me before she died?" Benny said, and he said it strangely, like he was telling it to the air, and not to me.

"What?"

"The Senator was going to kill us anyway, even if we got the Philosopher Stone. And it was going to be Quint who pushed the button."

Words faltered in my throat. I could remember Quint so clearly, how indifferent she had been to me, neither care nor hate. Had that been a deliberate indifference? The attitude of the farmer to the meat cow?

And then another troubling thought came to me, a quiet seed of suspicion grown to fruition by the odd way Benny held his scalpel. "Benny," I said, "what happened to Quint?"

"She died."

"How did she die?"

He looked at me finally, bringing his attention away from whatever phantom he was seeing in the empty air. "Does it matter?"

"Yeah," I told him, my heart filling my throat. "It matters."

Benny shrugged.

My image of Quint changed. I no longer imagined little Quint lying limp in the corner of a ship, Children's bite-marks on her leg and cheek, but I saw Quint lying discarded with a throat slit by a rusty little scalpel, murdered by someone she'd known. I hadn't even known if Quint had been a first or a last name.

Perhaps Benny and I had never been family, never even been friends. Perhaps after this we would go our separate ways and never speak again. But we had lived in each other's pockets for almost a decade. That had to mean something, if only because in looking back at my life, there would always be a part of it that was defined by him. Maybe we had no affection between the two of us, but we had to have *something*. So many years couldn't pass unmarked. No matter what he thought. No matter what he'd done.

"Benny," I said. "Please trust me this once. Let me make up for everything. I can get us out of here."

"I don't care what you do, Sean. But I'm going to the Philosopher Stone, and I'm going to destroy it." He turned his back on me.

There was a buzzing in my skull, like a thousand bees, or Dreamer-bots swarming. Did Benny really think I could stand here and watch him die? It was my fault that our friendship had failed, by spending years doing what I thought was right regardless of what he wanted. I saw that now. It was too late to apologize—but it wasn't too late to save him.

Since whatever we'd once had was already lost, there was no reason for me not to do what I thought was right, one last time. No matter what he wanted.

"Benny," I said, while that humming and swarming filled my ears, my eyes, my hollow chest, "Remember this word: *No*. That is how you say 'no' in Ameng. If anyone asks you if you want the *Philosopher Stone*, or if they ask you something in Ameng, or if they offer you a stone or a gem or a rock, you say *No.*"

The buzzing was humming down my arms through my veins, crawling up through my skin, little splinter pricks from the inside out.

"Can you remember that?" I asked Benny, over the roar of machinery. "The answer to every question, no matter what you see or hear, is *No.*"

He turned just before the first of the machines could claw free of my skin. I don't know what he saw, but his eyes went round with horror. And then he charged at me, body striking mine, driving me down to the floor.

My concentration was shot; the stinging inside-out needle-pricks receded, but the humming stayed in my skull. Benny landed on top of me, pinning me down, and his face was twisted into a snarl of hate.

He could hate me all he wanted, as long as he was alive to do it. "I just want to help," I told him.

"That's your fucking problem," Benny said. "You can't help everyone. You have to pick a goddamn side."

And then he grabbed me by the hair with one hand, pulling my head back, and slashed my throat with the other.

CHAPTER SEVENTY SIX: SEAN WREN, UNKILLABLE MACHINE MAN

I'D SPENT A few days in the company of Lieutenant Gupta and the Indigo Minister. My reflexes should have been better than they were. Benny telegraphed every movement; I knew enough now to recognize that, and to know it early enough that I could've stopped it. But my arms didn't move to defend me, as if my body did not believe he would do what he did. It was only after the little scalpel went through my throat, like it must have gone through Quint's, that I could move my hands up to clutch at my neck. I felt air bubble up through my hands, and my next breath came in thick and wet.

The last thing I saw of Benny was him walking away, fingers trailing along the wall, before he moved into the next room and was gone out of sight.

* * *

I WOKE UP on a hard floor, something sticky beneath my cheek. I was absolutely certain in the moments after I returned to dim consciousness that I was still in the Dreamer, that I'd woken up after another dream gone wrong, and that I was, if it was the last thing I ever did, going to find the AI and destroy its every last circuit.

My next breath disturbed the fluid in my lungs and I started coughing, and coughed and coughed for a long time, liquid coming up my throat and stopping the passage of air. I gasped and drowned on the dry floor until at last I'd coughed out the worst of the wetness and could manage to take a few sore damp breaths that got actual air into my lungs.

There was a terrifyingly large puddle of blood on the floor beneath me, visible in the light of my flashlight. I touched my throat and found it sticky, damp—and a thin line of vibrant pain bisecting my skin, neatly and tightly sealed up as if sutured from the inside.

I wasn't in a dream. I'd woken up on the floor where Benny had left me to bleed out, and the nanomachines had closed up my throat.

I should've gotten myself infected by the Dreamer *days* ago. I was unkillable. Sean Wren, unstoppable machine god-man.

I sat up, careful not to move my head too much just in case the nanomachine sutures didn't hold. Sitting upright all the blood left in my body rushed from my head and I nearly faceplanted in my own blood. I caught myself and waited, breathing hard, until my blood pressure stabilized.

A good portion of my total arterial volume was puddled

on the floor. I doubted the nanomachines had any way of accounting for that. I'd just have to move very carefully—what mattered was that I was *alive*.

Alive, and as free as I'd ever been in my life. Indigo and Lantern-Eyes had severed their connections to me with the end of our arrangement, and gone their separate ways. Benny had severed our connection when he'd attempted to sever my head. The *Nameless*'s AI had cut the leash connecting me to the Senator when it had destroyed the implant. I was the perfect free agent, owing nothing to nobody. And I knew that the *Viper* was nearby. I could take the ship and leave. It wasn't like I wanted the Philosopher Stone for myself.

And what would happen on the ship after I left? A miniature of the war going on at large; the Ministers versus the Republic, a bloody war on this ancient ship. And maybe a last-minute suicide attack by Benny, destroying the Ministers' last hope for survival and the Republic's last hope for a successful defense.

Billions of people on either side, Tamara had said. But I could walk away from all that. It wasn't my problem. What was I going to do, pick a side? That had been Benny's last words to me. *You can't help everyone. You have to pick a goddamn side.*

Alright, then. Fuck you, Benjamin.

I picked myself up off the floor, head still spinning. I was now covered in my own blood in addition to Indigo's. There was no part of my front that wasn't stained. If anyone saw me they'd probably think me a ghost, a dead man lost on this ship for a thousand years. If I spoke

Ameng to them they'd be sure of it.

I flexed my hand, palm up. I wasn't exactly sure of the limits of my ability to command the nanomachines still crawling through my veins, but I was about to find out. First things first: I *willed* a few nanomachines to leave me and head off, giving them a spitefully simple directive: Whatever Benny is trying to do, stop him.

A few of the cuts on my hand jolted painfully, splitting open from the inside. A tiny glimmering handful of machines hovered over my palm, then split off, dispersing into the dark.

Step two, easier than the first. I *willed* the machines to shut down all the defenses in the Lab 17 wall directly in front of me.

Another glimmering cloud hummed out from inside my hand, beaded red with blood. These drifted over to the wall and settled on it, sinking into the cracks like water into soil. I waited.

When I was pretty sure they'd done what they could, I reached out and began to break off the wall covering. It came off in flaking panels, metal splinters and dust on my palms. I looked in at the exposed wire mesh, then, carefully, held my palm close to the mesh. No static raised the hair on my arms. I set my hand on the mesh and did not get immediately electrocuted, so I cracked the wires and peeled them aside, forcing an opening.

When I was done, I'd managed to make a very tiny opening in the wall, scarcely large enough for me to get my shoulders into. But through that hole, I could see the other side: the suite of labs that made up Lab 17.

I'd been through smaller tunnels in my time on this ship. I reached into the wall and crawled through.

CHAPTER SEVENTY SEVEN: THE REPUBLIC

NOTHING HAD COME through this wall in a thousand years. The silence in Lab 17 was the silence of the grave, and the dust was as thick as snowfall on the ground.

And there was no telling how big this suite of labs was. It was time to try something new. I held out one hand, cut palm up, and *willed* some Dreamer-bots out.

They hummed free, tiny and glimmering, and then dispersed to the four corners of the world. Fly, my pretties, fly. I kicked some dust around until I'd cleared off a little spot of floor, and then I sat down and waited.

It was a while before they returned, long enough that I started to get worried my plan had failed, and considered getting up and looking around the old-fashioned way. But those little glimmering machines came humming back towards me, and I had to hold myself very still, eyes wide, while they landed on my skin and crawled into my eyes.

Images flashed over my retinas. I dreamt, briefly but vividly, of the layout of the Lab 17 suite, just as I'd directed the nanomachines to record.

At the very center of the maze, guarded behind doors locked and barred and sealed, there was a room. And in that room, there was an empty space, a void the nanomachines couldn't see or understand. The scientists had guarded the Philosopher Stone even from the AI. That void, I knew, was the data we all so badly wanted.

I also saw, through my dreaming machines, that Benny was at the far end of the outer wall slowly breaking through, having shaken the machines I'd sent to inconvenience him. The Ministers had broken through the outer wall not too far from Benny, and the ancient-eyed Ultraviolet stood in snowy dust up to her shins. Indigo was a somber shadow at her back, glowing underwater-blue. He'd gotten a new sword from his old comrades, slung across his back in the place of the old one. A group of Republican soldiers had come through the outer wall between me and the Ministers, and were already working their way through the labyrinth, Tamara directing them with sharp, decisive gestures, her uniform jacket closed up to her collar and her gun now holstered openly on her hip.

The Republic was also, I noted, about two rooms away from triggering a particularly resilient trap that had stood the test of ages and would easily wipe them all out. Assuming that they survived that trap, in another two rooms after that their route and the Ministers' would intersect.

I stood up, smacking dust off my bloody trousers. I held my hand out again, palm up, and sent a little army of nanomachines out to inconvenience Benny a little longer. I sent a few more out to unlock all the sealed doors on the path between me and the Republic, and then I sent another group off to the Ministers to lock a couple of doors on them and slow their progress just enough.

When I was done, I staggered, a little woozy. The first few times I'd used the Dreamer-bots, I hadn't felt any ill-effects; this last time it took some effort to set them free. There must be a finite number of nanomachines in my body, and none of the ones I'd sent out on tasks had returned—barring the scouts, who had come back to climb over my open eyes. But even those scouts, once they'd shown me their dreams, had climbed out of my eyes and hummed away into the dark. Perhaps the act of using the nanomachines ended the programming that bound them to me. If that was the case, then I would, eventually, run out.

I had only a few hours left before we all died in an explosion. After that, it wouldn't matter whether I had any nanomachines running through my veins or not.

I stuck my hands in my pockets—the fabric crackled, stiff with dried blood—and whistled a cheerful little tune as I walked down the path I'd opened up for myself, through opened doors and winding around collapsed ceilings. I was off-key and the whistle echoed weirdly, sharp off the metal ceiling and muffled off the dusty walls, but all that mattered was that the Republic heard me coming. It seemed likely that my dwindling number of Dreamer-bots could save me from a bullet wound, unless it was to the skull, but I wasn't keen on testing it. And Lantern-Eyes struck me as a crack shot.

I emerged into the room where the Republic was waiting

just before they attempted to break through the door that was trapped, I knew, with a set of very well-designed explosives that would kill at least the twenty people or so who were clustered closest to that wall. I saw Lantern-Eyes in that group, almost unrecognizable with her hair pulled neatly back and her jacket buttoned up.

When I entered the room, hands spread to show I was unarmed, I stepped into a circle of light from their portable lanterns and a half-circle of soldiers all with their guns cocked and trained directly on me.

I stopped whistling and I stopped walking. The soldiers stared at me in shock, which was a pretty understandable reaction, I thought, to a man covered in blood emerging from the bowels of an allegedly abandoned spacecraft.

From the back of the crowd, standing near the door, Tamara Gupta saw me and her eyes went round.

"Mind if I offer my assistance?" I asked the crowd.

CHAPTER SEVENTY EIGHT: SISTER

THE MISSION'S CAPTAIN, or commander, or whatever the hell rank, was named Jack Carson.

"I want to know who the hell you are and why the hell you're on this ship," he commanded, one of his... under-officers, or whatever, holding a gun menacingly to my head. Behind them both, Tamara Gupta attempted alternately to telekinetically alter the angle of the gun pointing at my temple, and kill me herself with the power of her glare.

At least my arrival had temporarily halted the suicidal mission to force open the door, which had been the goal all along. I smiled up at Mister/Officer/Commander Carson. Captain? General? General seemed too high. I'd consider Lieutenant but he seemed to outrank Tamara.

"I was sent here by the Republic to precede your arrival," I told Carson. "Didn't your superiors inform you?"

He exchanged a glance with the soldier holding a gun to my skull. "For what purpose?"

"To lure the Ministers in," I said. "Something that

worked a little bit too well. And to provide back-up to Lieutenant Gupta. I can speak Ameng. Isn't that right, lieutenant?"

Carson turned around to look at Tamara. Several of the soldiers around us, grimly listening in, turned to look at Tamara. I was pretty sure the would-be executioner holding his gun to my head turned to look at Tamara. "Is that true, lieutenant?" Carson asked.

Lantern-Eyes looked at me hard, like she could see past my face into the machinery of my mind, like she could pick out my intentions from the clockwork. Certainty shook through me, ice-cold, that she would not confirm my cover story—that she'd expose me to this Captain-Commander-General-Whatever Carson, and I'd have a lot more verbal dancing to do to prevent that friendly soldier from shooting me in the head.

"It's true, sir," Lieutenant Gupta said.

There was no time to indulge in surprise or gratitude. "We were attacked on our way in here," I explained, as Carson turned back to look at me with slightly less suspicion than before. "The monsters got the better of me, and then chased off Lieutenant Gupta. I believe she thought I was dead."

I gestured to the vivid mark splitting my throat, still streaked with blood even though it was closed up now.

A little stiffly, and with murder hidden in the consonants, Tamara said, "Seeing you here is something of a *surprise*, Mr. Wren."

"Mister?" Carson questioned.

"I'm a civilian consultant," I said quickly. "What's

important is that I can get you through to the Philosopher Stone safely."

Carson exchanged another glance with the soldier holding his gun to my head. His second-in-command, I guessed. I had no idea what rank that made my executioner. Maybe I should call them Violet and Indigo, just for old time's sake. "And how would you do that?" Carson asked.

"There's a lot of data on this ship, if you know where to find it and you know how to read it. I know where to go and how to get around. I'm sure you've realized that this lab, Lab 17, is heavily trapped against intruders. Well, I know where those traps are, and how to disarm them."

Carson's military mask did not perfectly conceal his pleasure at the idea that there was someone here to make his impossible job achievable. Tamara, if anything, looked warier than before.

"May I?" I asked, and Carson nodded at the soldier holding me captive, and the gun was lowered from my temple. "Thanks," I said, and walked over to the trapped door.

The door itself was locked and sealed, creating the impression that the only obstruction to passing through it was the door itself. If you opened it, though, it would complete a five-thousand-year-old circuit, faithfully maintained by the AI, that would trigger a small and precise detonation. "The data I read said there's a little bomb hidden in the wall, right about here," I told Carson, patting the wall above where the nanomachines had told me there was a bomb.

He shouted someone over, who appeared carrying some sort of scanning device, which he waved over the surface of the wall where I'd indicated. At first he seemed to find nothing, then he frowned deeply and knelt beside the wall, tapping at the old metal while examining the readings on his device. Tamara stood in the back, shifting her weight from foot to foot, her glance darting between the wall and me.

"There's a nugget back there," the technician reported at last. "Solid, superficially resembles the Ministerial ball bombs. Maybe a very early version of that design."

"Is it live?" Carson asked.

The technician nodded.

Carson looked at me. "Then we have you to thank, Mr. Wren," he said, and called for someone to come disarm the bomb blocking the door. I stepped aside to let them through and, very discreetly, turned my palm to the wall. The skin of one of the cuts split, bright needle-pain, and a nanomachine drifted lazily and invisibly out to vanish into the wall and short the circuit, just in case.

The entire group split their focus, some guarding the rear exits from the room, others focused on disarming and unsealing the door. I could've told the soldiers guarding the rear exits that there was no point in watching those; there was nothing that way but dust. The only threat to them in Lab 17 lay ahead of them, on the other side of that sealed door—a threat I didn't intend to let them face, and a bloodshed I wouldn't allow to happen.

The others' distraction gave Tamara Gupta the chance to corner me she'd been waiting for. She came up to me while

I stood apart from the others, in a relatively private corner of the room. Her hair was tidied back into a braided bun and her expression was dark.

"Hey, sister," I greeted her when she came near enough to speak. "You clean up nice."

She spoke in a low and cutting whisper. "Why are you here?"

"To help out."

She glanced back over her shoulder, a brisk, nervous movement. She really didn't handle surprises very well, did Lantern-Eyes. "Last we spoke you were planning to get the data for yourself."

"The implant's gone. The Dreamer-bots, they were designed to repair." I pressed my hand to the back of my neck, the smooth, implant-free back of my skull. "I think they realized the implant wasn't supposed to be there, and broke it down. I'm not after the Stone for me anymore."

"So you're here to help the Republic get it?"

"That's right."

"Bullshit," said Tamara.

So harsh. "You're hurting my feelings."

"Sean, listen," Tamara said, "there's only so far I can protect you here. If they find out... If they even *suspect* that you might take enemy action, they will put a bullet through your head before you can open your big mouth. If you are up to something, this is not the time or the place to try to pull a fast one. I can distract them and get you out of here, if you need to, but the closer we get to the Stone—"

"Mr. Wren," Carson called across the room, and Tamara

flinched like he'd laid a hand on her shoulder. "Is the next room safe to proceed?"

Sure it was, and it would be safe—if my sense of timing was correct—for another two minutes or so. I could see over Tamara's shoulder that the soldiers had gotten the door unsealed.

"Sure is," I said, brightly. Tamara looked frightened, so I clapped her on the shoulder. "Don't worry so much, Lantern-Eyes," I said, and walked off to join Carson and the first wave of soldiers as they advanced into the next room.

The next room had been some kind of break room. A massive hollowed-out rectangle, fallen onto its side like a coffin left lying out, that had been a refrigerator. The rest of the room was in eerily good repair, consequence of no monsters in this part of the ship around to destroy what was left. Tables stood, hunched and sagging, where they had been left a thousand years ago. Some of the chairs had been pulled out and left there after their occupants had gone, no one left to put them away. And the dust was ankle-deep, thick and soft. It muffled our steps.

On the other side of the room, past the fallen bulk of the refrigerator, I saw the locked exit door. I moved through the crowd towards that door as quickly as I dared. I had to get over there first, and quickly, if I wanted to pull this off without any bloodshed. Tamara tried to stick to me like a burr, but halfway through my path another soldier called her name, asking some technical question about room layout, and she was forced to linger behind. I picked up the pace. I'd thrown up a dozen roadblocks, but the

Ministers could cut through walls; it wouldn't take them long to—

At the far end of the break room, the door clicked open. A many-colored glow spilled through the opened door, preceding the people who bore the lights like the dawn breaking on the pitch-black starship.

I hadn't been fast enough. The Ministers had arrived.

CHAPTER SEVENTY NINE:
THE MINISTERS

"MINISTERS!" SOMEONE SHOUTED, Republican accent thick with loathing and fear. I dropped to crouch behind the nearby table as the ancient break room shattered into prismatic light.

The Ministers entered like fragments of stars, gleaming eerie, inhuman and terrifying. I couldn't track them individually as they flickered into the room, unnatural-fast and certain. One unlucky Republican soldier was felled almost immediately by a shadow who glowed magma-crack red, blood gleaming redder in that light.

A beat later, the Republican started firing. I crouched low to the ground, hopefully beneath the line of fire, and thought about how *pissed* One must be about these people firing guns on a spaceship.

Through the deafening percussion of gunfire, I heard someone scream. Clamping my hands over my ears, I peered around my scant cover to see a chaos of light and shadow. The Ministers had turned their collar-lights up high, not as bright as they could go, but still blazing.

Instead of the increased light making them easier to see, the strobing brightness as they moved disoriented the eye and concealed their motions. Lights of many colors flickered wildly, and combined with the pounding rhythm of gunfire, began slowly to separate my mind from my senses.

The Republicans had hunkered down behind the scant cover of the tables, some of them retreating back to the previous room. And they *were* retreating—the Ministers were advancing, flashing and slicing, moving so fast I wasn't sure that any of the Republic's bullets were hitting home. There were already bodies on the floor, all in the dark crimson uniforms of the Republic, visible only in glimpses during the flashing light. The dust, disturbed by the quick motion through it, was rising into the air like a mist, diffusing the light and shadow still further.

I hadn't wanted this. I hadn't been quick enough to prevent it. The Republic and the Ministers, slaughtering each other, this was *exactly* what I was trying to prevent—

Tamara was still alive. I spotted her in the back of the room, near enough to the far door to allow a retreat, hunkered grimly down. Not firing wildly, not like the rest of the soldiers, who were giving away their position.

A deep blue underwater-light, familiar to me now as a friend's face, gleamed in from the far door. I looked in time to see the Indigo Minister enter the room. He'd gotten a new sword, presumably from the other Ministers. It wasn't quite the same shape and size as his first one, but he held it with the same certitude.

Indigo and Tamara were both in the battle, and on

opposite sides. Blood was already running over the floor. I had to stop this *now*.

My original plan—to get through the far door first, lock it against the Republicans, and lure the Ministers away— was shot. Time to improvise. I took a deep breath and held out my hand, palm-up. Forcing some nanomachines from under my skin was difficult this time, like squeezing the last bit of toothpaste from the tube. I wasn't totally out, not yet, but I was running low.

Protect me, I willed, and, hoping that the little Dreamer-bots could turn aside a bullet, I stood up from my sheltered spot and strode towards the door that had admitted the Ministers.

When I'd crossed the threshold of the door, mouth dry and coated with the dust that floated around the flashing, gunsmoke-reeking air, I turned back around.

"NUMBER ONE!" I shouted, as loudly as I could.

In the midst of the smoke and dust, gleaming a violet so dark it was nearly black, the Ultraviolet Minister turned around and saw me.

Time for stage two of the new, improvised plan, which was, simply, *run like hell*.

I ran.

"SEAN!" I thought I heard someone scream over the gunpowder and shouting, sounding equal parts frightened and furious. Goodbye, Lantern-Eyes.

They caught up with me two rooms away. I was almost surprised it was not a blade that caught me, but a hand, grabbing me around the arm and spinning me to the floor. I landed hard on my back and saw Green standing over me, curly hair shading a face lit verdant by her collar light.

Hidden beneath my back, I opened my palm. "There's a bomb about to go off at that far door," I warned her, as nanomachines crawled out of my palm like ants.

Indigo arrived at Green's side in time to hear me speak. He sucked in a breath, then turned back around and bellowed, "BOMB! *At the far door!*"

Weird to hear him shouting aloud instead of in Light, but perhaps it was too chaotic in the battle for a message in Light to be seen and clearly understood. I heard the shout taken up in the far room, by Republican voices; heard the clamor of retreat.

An eternity later, my little Dreamer-bots reconnected the bomb that they and the Republic had disarmed. The explosion, after the thunder and lightning of the battle in the break room, was curiously small. I'd instructed my nanomachines to control it as much as they could. I wanted the door turned into an impenetrable mass of rubble, not the soldiers wiped out, but at this point I was afraid that nothing short of collapsing the ceiling was going to separate the two warring armies.

Green didn't even flinch at the explosion, preternaturally serene face gazing down at me. Indigo looked down at me over her shoulder, and his expression was afraid.

General on Kystrom, huh? I wondered if he'd been afraid at all then. Certainly Brigid had been afraid, before he'd killed her. My parents too.

A whisper of movement, lights shifting. Green dropped her gaze and stepped to the side. Black-violet light filled the spot where she had stood, and a slender, androgynous figure stepped forward to gaze down at me with owl-eyes. "Hello again, Mr. Wren," Number One said.

CHAPTER EIGHTY:
NUMBER ONE

IT WAS JUST as unsettling as I remembered, being the subject of her indifferent predator gaze. I smiled up at her as brightly as I could. "Long time no see."

"You have something you want," One said. "Speak."

God bless the patience of an immortal. A human would've probably killed me by now. "Well, I had a long thought while I was taking a walk through this ship," I said. "You know, thinking about life, the universe, surviving, all that. And what I realized, especially after seeing you guys in the other room—really impressive, by the way, are any of you even hurt?—what I realized was that if I want to survive this ship, I need to be on your side."

She just looked at me, patient, unspeaking.

Okay, I was going to have to hold her hand as I brought her to my point. "I want to help you find the Philosopher Stone," I said. "I've read Mara Zhu's notes; I understand why you need it. And I've read Mara Zhu's notes, so I know where it is and how to get to it. Keep me alive, and I'll help you."

I smiled up at her while she gazed down at me, ultraviolet and silent.

Then she descended, swooping down to crouch before me on the ground, and the cold strong fingers of one hand closed around my chin claw-like. I was held, inescapable, for her intent perusal of my face.

She said, "You've changed."

I was uneasily certain that she could see the Dreamer-bots crawling around beneath my skin, gathering in the corner of my eyes like tears. I tried to smile again but found her nails in the way. "I've learned that lesson you told me about," I said, and prayed she did not see through me. "I'm alone. I need to look after myself first."

"You've only learned half the lesson," One said, and released my face. She stood up again, and she was not tall, but with me on the floor she towered. "You think you are cleverer than you are, Mr. Wren. I believe you have some mad plan now."

I wasn't going to have the rest of this conversation on the floor. I shifted to stand, and beneath the thick layer of dust my knuckles brushed something solid. I glanced over to see what I had touched and found myself frozen.

Eye sockets black, head-dome colored sunset-orange by the nearness of the Orange Minister to my right, there was a skull on the floor.

It was not the only bone on the floor: fading into invisibility beneath the dust, outside of the light of the Ministers' collars, I saw the color-stained arcs of other bones still lying in the same order they'd been in when their bearer had died. There had been nothing alive in Lab

17 to disturb their order, after all.

When I looked around I saw other bodies, skulls grinning and ribs curving, lying on the ground beneath the shroud of dust, lined up in neat rows as far back into the room as I could see. It was a somber room, doors at all four walls, and empty except for the bones. So this was where the other scientists had died. When I'd run into this room and Green had caught me, she'd thrown me to the floor between the bodies.

I said to One, "What do you know about Mara Zhu?"

"Only what is necessary."

"She felt terrible about what she'd done," I said, looking down at Mara Zhu's last victims, her colleagues and probably her friends, too. "She... uh, she despaired about it. She killed herself, you know, all alone in her office. You told me once that I was trapped in the moment I'd lost everything. I've left that moment behind now. So I will help your people. I will help you get the Philosopher Stone."

I remembered that photograph of the scientist who looked like Number One—her genetic ancestor, I was certain. That great-grandfather of hers had had dimples when he smiled. That was genetic, wasn't it? I wondered if One would have dimples, if she ever smiled. I wondered if One's ancestor was among the bones in this room, if his daughter stepped between his ribs on immortal, indifferent feet.

Number One said, "You have not left that moment."

She reached to her side as she spoke, where she kept sheathed her slender flight-feather knives.

"You will never leave that moment," One said, with glacial sympathy, that could feel pity and yet not be moved. She raised one of her graceful little knives, and I watched the line of violet light that gleamed on the edge of her knife. Perhaps my nanomachines could stop a blade, or sew up my throat when she slit it again, but I somehow did not believe that anything could stop the Ultraviolet Minister's killing blow, death herself—

Metal rang against metal, resoundingly loud in the catacomb-room. Another sword had stopped One's long knife. I followed the line of metal, hand, wrist, arm, back to the underwater-blue glow of a familiar collar-light.

CHAPTER EIGHTY ONE: BROTHER

ONE FACED INDIGO over their crossed swords, shock and a question in her eyes. Indigo shoved her back; she staggered, and his hand grabbed me under the arm. "Sean, go!"

I got up, stumbled backwards when he dragged me. One watched us as Indigo dragged me back out of the room through the far door. I did not like the look in her eyes.

Indigo slammed the door shut. "Can you lock this?"

I *willed* it locked, and glittering machines tore through the skin of my palm, shedding blood in drops, and vanished into the darkness between door and frame.

"What was that?" Indigo demanded.

I lowered my hand. I'd lost my breath somewhere between One going to kill me and locking the door. "The nanomachines. There's not many left in my body but I can sort of control the ones that are left. What the hell did you do out there? What the hell were you thinking?"

"What was *I* thinking? What were *you* thinking? You knew she would kill you!"

"I, uh, actually thought I could talk myself out of that,"

I admitted.

He stepped closer to me, anger clouding around him. "Is it because you're dying? Is that why you're throwing your life away?"

"I'm actually not dying; you were right about the nanomachines, they're repairing me—but wait, if you thought I was dying what the hell were *you* doing? Talk about throwing your life away—"

"Explain why you're not dying," Indigo said.

"The nanomachines aren't killing me. They're repairing me; they got rid of the implant, they closed up my throat after Benny." I made a slicing gesture to demonstrate and something weird happened to Indigo's expression; he turned his back on me, pacing into the dark of the room we'd retreated to, taking his light with him. "I don't know what'll happen when I run out of them, but I'm fine now."

I could not tell Indigo's thoughts from his silhouette. That was the thing, though, wasn't it? I'd never been able to tell what Indigo was thinking, not really. If I had, maybe I would've realized who he was far earlier. I didn't know how the murderer of my people could have hidden himself from me so long. Surely I should have known him on sight, seen him marked, like Cain.

Indigo's voice was as calm as usual when he spoke again, no sign of whatever thoughts I couldn't read. "I assume you came here with a plan."

I took in a breath. I hadn't told anyone my reason for coming here instead of leaving on the *Viper*, not even Lantern-Eyes. Honestly, I hadn't even said it to myself because I was a little worried that the stupidity of my plan might be more obvious when spoken aloud.

Lieutenant Gupta would have tried to stop me, if she'd known. But Indigo had defended me, taken us both away from his own people, and now stood beside me alone.

So I told him the truth: "I'm going to get the data for both the Republic and the Ministers."

"Both?" he repeated.

You can't help everyone, Benny had said. *You have to pick a goddamn side.*

The thing about the Philosopher Stone, I'd realized, kneeling in my own blood while nanomachines repaired the wound Benny had given me, was that everyone wanted it *independently*. Tamara Gupta's reasons for needing the Stone didn't preclude Indigo from getting the Stone, and vice versa. The Republic could still defend themselves with the data if the Ministers used the data to heal themselves. The Ministers could still heal themselves with the data if the Republic used the data as a guard against them. Win-win. The only reason each side didn't want the other to get the data too was spite.

I have to pick a side? I can't help everyone? Watch me, Benny. "Yeah," I said. "Both."

"Number One was my second teacher," Indigo said. "I watched my first teacher die before I reached my first century in age. One day I found her staring out the window at the Marian sun, and her eyes and gums were bleeding. She was alive but she was not moving, the blood seeping out of her. She'd lost the ability to speak a week before she began bleeding. At about the same time she'd developed difficulty swallowing. A few months before, she'd lost the ability to sleep. She lost her sanity before she lost consciousness.

"Mara Zhu was subtle in how she murdered us," Indigo continued. He faced away from me as he spoke, nothing but profile, like he could not stand to look at me directly. "The disease does not manifest until later in life, and never at a set time. A Minister may die at nine hundred years, or ninety. There is no predicting when. The first symptom is the dreams—we lose the ability to enter slow-wave sleep first, and our sleep is restless and full of dreams. Then we lose the ability to sleep at all. We have no way of curing it—some misfolded protein kills us, no virus or cancer. Our own body creates the protein. We poison ourselves. Only this data can tell us which gene Mara Zhu altered so that it creates the fatal disease. You wondered why the Ministers didn't send anyone who could speak Ameng. That is because any Minister who remembered how to speak Ameng has already died."

And died horribly, from the sound of it. I asked myself, in the depths of my heart, if this was a death I could wish on my worst enemy. The answer came quick, and simple: No. I couldn't wish that kind of suffering on anyone, not even the people who had taken my family from me.

"I'm still going to give you the data," I said.

"You will give the Republic the data, too. You would allow them the ability to kill my people."

That was rich. "Would you have attacked Kystrom, if you'd known we could defend ourselves?"

All that I could see of Indigo's profile was expressionless: smooth cheek and the straight brushstrokes of his brow and eye. "I can't allow you to give the Philosopher Stone to the Republic."

"What are you going to do, then?" I demanded. "Kill me? Benny's already tried. He wants to destroy the data, you know. I don't. I just want to help everyone, and I don't care that you and One and Tamara all think that's stupid. I'm not going to stop and if you want me to stop, you have to kill me."

He turned around then to look at me directly, the same dark remoteness as I'd seen when he'd first arrived on the ship, a killing shadow.

"Come on, Indigo," I said, my good old imp of the perverse telling me to push, push, push until it snaps. "You didn't have any trouble killing everyone else on Kystrom. Do you think sparing one Kystrene now would make up for what you did to the rest?"

The way he looked at me was something worse than I'd ever seen him look, even dying on a dirty floor. Indigo looked at me like an open wound, the bandage torn off, and the flesh exposed sore and weeping and open down to bone. Indigo looked at me like his mother, Mara Zhu, gazing angry despair into a thousand-year-old recording.

But even with all that killing terror written all over his face, Indigo did not draw his sword, made no move against me.

The last time he'd threatened me seriously, I remembered, had been after he'd rescued me from Benny's explosion; he'd held his knife to my throat while I struggled for breath to defend myself. And I'd watched his expression change, and then he'd taken his sword away and saved my life. I thought maybe that was the last chance he had to kill me. I thought maybe that, even if I pushed him as far as I could, he would not be capable of killing me now.

I didn't forgive him. I couldn't. But some of my black anger drained away.

"You told me that you trusted what I decided to do would be right," I said to the man who had murdered my people, who now looked at me like I had the power to tear him apart and he intended to let me. "This is what I've decided. You can decide whether you're going to kill me later. Right now, we're almost at the Philosopher Stone, but we're not the only people looking for it. Let's go find it, yeah?"

He took a breath, short and sharp, like he had not been breathing before. "You know the way."

"I don't," I admitted, "but I know who does," and I held my hand palm-up in the air. Nanomachines pulled themselves free of my skin, glinting in the glow of Indigo's collar-light before vanishing into the shadows like sparks going out. Indigo watched their progress with an expression on his face I still could not name, but felt closer to understanding now than I had before.

The Dreamer-bots returned a moment later, crawling over my eyes, between my lids, before lazily drifting away to return to their home with the AI. I opened my eyes to meet Indigo's gaze.

"We're only a few rooms away," I told him, and couldn't stop my smile because this was it, the center of the maze, the end of it all. He followed when I led.

A few minutes later, I pushed open the door to the center of Lab 17.

CHAPTER EIGHTY TWO: THE PHILOSOPHER STONE

THE CENTER OF Lab 17 looked nothing like the setting the Dreamer had constructed for me. Indigo's blue light diffused into the thickness of dust like a flashlight underwater, and in that weird sunken-ship light I saw that someone had erected a fragile barricade of desks and lab equipment, ancient glass filmy, stacked atop the rotten bones of old desks and metal bars. Wordlessly, we cleared this final barricade away, putting the pieces to the side.

The rest of the room was square, larger than I'd expected but not oversized. At the back of the room, weirdly connected to the wall through a sequence of wires like moss hanging off a tree, there was a box balanced precariously on a scaffold of metal that had maybe once been a desk.

The box had a screen on one of its faces, filmy with dust but visible. Indigo said, "That's a portable computer."

"I've never seen one that shape," I said.

"We have a few in Maria Nova." He walked over to the box and wiped his hand over the top. Then he brushed the dust off the rest of it, between the wires that had been hooked up to the back and cracked through the cover. Then he laid his hands on either side of the box, his fingers finding precise spots in the sides, and miraculously the screen flickered.

Curious, I sent a nanomachine out towards the box. Just one—it probably wasn't wise to expend the things that were keeping me alive on curiosity, but it wasn't like I was going to leave my curiosity unindulged.

When the nanomachine came back to my skin, it reported something strange. "The Dreamer doesn't know that computer's there," I said. There was a blank space in the nanomachine's vision, like a gap in reality.

"If it had known, it would have wiped the data," Indigo pointed out.

"But the computer's hooked up to the ship."

Indigo looked up from the screen to frown at the wires connecting the little box to the ship at large. He touched one of the wires carefully, rolling it between its fingers.

"I believe," he said, "that the scientists connected the hardware to the AI in such a way that the AI would provide power to this computer and keep it in good repair without being aware of its existence or what data was kept inside."

"So can we disconnect it and leave?"

"I am concerned that the hard-wired connection is the only reason this computer is still functional," Indigo told me.

Yikes. No disconnecting that, then. I crouched down next to the slightly glowing little computer. "So how do we get the data?"

"Perhaps we can broadcast it," Indigo said. "I can't read the text."

"Oh! Right." I leaned into his space to see the screen, which was of course written in Ameng. The screen was cracked, the image unsteady. Even with assistance from the Dreamer AI, this little computer was on the verge of failure.

"Put your hands on either side," Indigo instructed. "There should be indents for your fingers to slide into. You can type that way. And the top is a touchscreen."

There were indents, just about the right size for my hands. I rested my fingertips in those indents, the way a dying scientist must have done a thousand years prior. "Okay, here we go."

The computer was slow. I was afraid of sending it into a failure, so I had to baby it, waiting for it to load, changing course slowly, taking my time to read the Ameng so I didn't click the wrong thing.

It was harder to concentrate than I'd anticipated. "How long until the sun goes?"

Indigo was somewhere behind me, quietly pacing the empty space from the sound of it. "A few hours."

"How many?"

"It's impossible to say precisely," he reminded me. "The radiation is constantly increasing; it's a gradual process. After a point it will become lethal for us to remain here."

"Estimate for me," I said.

He sighed. "We should be gone in three hours."

That cut it rather fine. "How far away is the *Viper* from here?"

"If you wish to make it safely, you should leave within the next hour," he told me.

"The Minister ship is docked right next to the *Viper*. One way or another, you'll have to leave at the same time as me."

The screen finally loaded. I leaned over the little box like proximity could make translation easier, and began to parse through the sentences.

"We can broadcast," I said at last. "But not very far; the *Nameless* itself is shielded against radiation. But the three ships docked on the *Nameless*—the Minister ship, the Republican ship, and the *Viper*—they should be able to pick up the data if we broadcast it to them."

The sound of Indigo's pacing didn't pause. "Are you certain this is the correct data?"

"I'd feel pretty stupid if it wasn't," I agreed, and left that screen behind for a moment to go look at the files preserved on the computer. The screen shivered, resistant to change.

"I've seen many humans die," Indigo said suddenly, while I tried to cajole the computer into letting me leave the broadcast screen.

My fingers faltered. Was this his prelude to killing me? Some sort of slow, immortal apology?

"I am over three hundred years old," Indigo continued. The slow sound of his steps was almost hypnotic. "You vanish like sparks. After a while, it stops meaning to us what it means to you. We struck hard and fast on Kystrom. The goal was to prevent prolonged bloodshed, and it worked: the planet folded after your city fell. An unconditional surrender. A brief strike, not a drawn-out war."

The screen in front of me had finally, sullenly, loaded, but the letters blurred in front of my eyes. I could not have translated Ameng then, not even if Indigo had put his knife to my throat.

"We believed the Republic had a more significant foothold on the planet than they did," Indigo said. "We believed the only way to excise the Republic was to strike decisively, and we anticipated resistance nonetheless. But there was no resistance. I did not destroy your planet—there was no need to; it fell after one battle that was more a slaughter than a fight. The rest of Kystrom lives still, mostly unchanged, under Ministerial control. But I wiped out your city, thinking I was carving out a tumor and instead carving healthy flesh. The planet fell. The Republic lost its advantage, one way or another. I see the greater purpose, but I can't condone the cost."

The screen had loaded. Blindly, I opened the first document I saw, but I didn't read what was before my eyes. I could *feel* Indigo behind me like a light on my back, a trial and a test. Eight years ago, all my suffering, all my grief, all the suffering and the fear and pain of those I'd loved—that had been him who had caused it, *him*, this person in the room alone with me. There was no forgiveness for that. There couldn't be. Even if I somehow forgave him, which I could not, I couldn't forgive him on behalf of Brigid, or my mother, or my father, or Liza or Kenny or any of my old friends who now lay dead in the fields and houses where we'd lived and played.

I wanted him dead. I should want him dead. I had the

power, at my fingertips, to deny him the thing he needed most; to make him watch his own people die, helpless, the way I'd watched mine. Benny had been right; to destroy this Philosopher Stone would be justice. The ghost of Mara Zhu would be satisfied; even Indigo would accept it as his due, though he might kill me for it after.

Probably that was why he was telling me this now: to give me that choice.

My fingers relaxed on either side of the computer. I hadn't realized how tightly I'd been gripping it until I'd let it go.

"There's at least one Kystrene left," I said, and turned around so that I could look at Indigo. I tried smiling at him; I could not quite manage it, not now, not after all this, but I tried. And it must have worked, at least a little bit, because something lightened around those dark-water eyes.

Metal sizzled and cracked. Beyond Indigo's shoulder, at the far wall, I watched a glowing blade push itself through the wall.

Indigo was suddenly in front of me, crowding me back. He drew his own borrowed long knife, placing it and himself between me and the Philosopher Stone.

The glowing knife stuck through the wall curved as it carved, acrid metal sizzling. I watched a circle cut in the wall, edges glowing, and then that circle was kicked out to land solidly in the middle of the room, the wind of its landing blowing the dust aside to the far corners.

Number One stepped through the hole in the wall, collar-light blazing black, furious.

CHAPTER EIGHTY THREE: CENTER OF THE COMPASS

ONE DIDN'T EVEN spare me a glance, all of her thousand-year attention on Indigo. "Have you come to your senses yet, Shay?"

Indigo freed one hand from the hilt of his sword to tap out a response on his collar-light quickly, in ultraviolet.

"Speak aloud," One said, grimly. She held only one of her two swords, and it was still glowing with heat. "I want the Kystrene to hear." She did look at me, then, and her glance was venomous.

"Hey," I said, "I understand more of the Light language than you think."

"Sean, be quiet," Indigo said.

"Did you teach him our language?" One asked. "Why; because he is Kystrene? I knew you were compromised on Kystrom and I hid it from the Ministerial Council for you. These things can take time to process. But here you are, compromised by a Kystrene boy."

"I am helping our people," Indigo said. "I will make sure they get the data."

"And what is the cost?" One demanded, taking one step closer, her blade still glowing, her collar-light still brilliant black. "Don't tell me this boy doesn't demand a cost."

Oh, don't tell her, Indigo, I thought, but Indigo said, "The Republic gets a copy of the data as well."

She shut her eyes for a moment. She was less terrifying with them closed, more human, tired. "This is your last chance, Shay," she said. Shay, I realized: the transcription of the slow blossoming light and the dual throb like a heartbeat. Indigo's real name. "I came alone because I wanted to persuade you back. We have known each other for hundreds of years; I trained you, I *raised* you."

Indigo stood in front of me; I couldn't see his face, but his spine bent like a great weight had been placed across it.

"Come back," One commanded, collar-light glowing like a void.

He laid his hand on his collar-light and flashed a word at her, two sharp spikes of ultraviolet black, like the two blades she wore. "Kora," Indigo said, softly, her name; spoken like a word in another language that meant *no*.

Their poised stillness shattered like a lightning strike; One's other blade leapt into her free hand and Indigo shoved me back and down. "Stay by the Stone!" he commanded, and shifted his weight just in time to meet her swift hard swing.

Number One wouldn't dare to risk damaging the Philosopher Stone, I realized; so long as I was near the computer, I was sheltered. A nice safe corner for me to hide in.

I looked around for something, anything, to use as a weapon, just as I saw a figure step into the doorway Indigo and I had used, barely illuminated by a thin flashlight beam.

I'd know that way of walking anywhere. It was Benny.

"Benny, not now," I warned him, as he took in the battling Ministers trapped in their own little world, and then the Philosopher Stone and me, unarmed, sitting beside it.

He walked towards me.

"God *damn* it," I said, and stood up between him and the Philosopher Stone.

Metal crashed on the other side of the room, swords shrieking across the walls, and Benny said, "Get out of my way, Sean."

"Not a chance," I said, and when he swung the little scalpel at me I made Tamara Gupta proud and *dodged*.

Metal crashed and light flashed on the other side of the room as I ducked under Benny's arm, then surged forward to knock him off his feet, carrying us both to the floor. He slammed the little blade into my back; it hurt like a *bitch* but the blade itself wasn't long enough to do real damage, and I felt the nanomachines stirring in my blood anyway. I wasn't sure how many of them I had left, though, and I couldn't exactly let Benny stab me with impunity, so I twisted on top of him to grab at his arm, wrestling him for control of the knife. I was taller than he was but he'd always been a better fighter, and he twisted beneath me, driving a knee hard into my gut.

My breath left me and I fell onto my side, releasing

him from beneath me. That little knife of his stabbed into my side, stopped on my ribs. The pain roused me from my breathlessness and I slapped at him, driving him back a little, and then surged forward as crashing sounds resounded from the battle on the other side of the room.

I managed to pin his wrist, the knife pressed uselessly against the ground, and got my knee up onto his hip. "Benny, stop!" I shouted at him, and had to rear my head back when he tried to headbutt me.

More crashing behind me, and someone cried out in pain. Indigo.

I spun around, leaving Benny lying against the wall, and saw Indigo on his knees on the floor, holding a bloodied wrist to his chest. His sword was on the floor, out of his reach, and Number One had one of her slender flight-feather blades held to his throat.

He looked up at her while she removed the blade from his throat, raising it up to her shoulder level—drawing it back for a fatal blow. I shouted, rising to my feet and lunging for them even knowing that I'd never make it across the room before One completed the swing.

A *crack* split the air, deafening me, ringing through the dust-thick air. Number One jerked, a red splash appearing on the wall beside her head. Then she folded, to her knees and to the floor, owl-eyes staring sightlessly out and collar-light still glowing a rich dark ultraviolet.

Lieutenant Tamara Gupta stood in the open doorway, gun still held up, the muzzle still aimed in the direction of the two Ministers.

A shadow pushed past me. I turned dumbly to follow

it, ears ringing, and realized it was Benny, running for the computer that held the Philosopher Stone.

He would destroy it, destroy it easily. I reached out one hand after him, useless, and *willed* him stopped.

Pinpricks bit my hand, skin splitting, as a swarm of nanomachines drew themselves out of my veins and spun in a glittering cloud to swirl around Benny's face. He stopped a few steps from the Stone, hands flying up over his eyes, lashing out wildly at the swarm. I stepped forward as he collapsed onto his back, hands grabbing uselessly at his eyes.

It was just an infestation, I told myself; he'd come out of it in a few hours with the implant gone; really, I had saved Benny's life. But when I stood over him, when I saw his face in the dimly reflected glow of the flashlight he'd dropped, I saw red between the roiling glitter of the nanomachines over his eyes.

No, I thought, but I couldn't move, standing over Benny as he opened his mouth and made a horrible choked sound that was maybe a scream, muffled by the nanomachines that I could see crawling into his open jaw. There was blood coming from his ears where the nanomachines had burrowed in.

The ground struck my knees with jarring force. Benny twisted, mouth open in soundless agony, while the nanomachines burrowed through his skin and into his brain. Not like this, I wanted to say. Not like this.

The blood from his face had spread across the floor as far as my knees by the time he stopped seizing, and the only other survivor of my home and my past died.

CHAPTER EIGHTY FOUR: SEAN, TAMARA, AND SHAY

I SHOULD'VE LET him destroy the Stone, I thought. I'd killed him instead.

My world broadened from Benny's corpse as I turned around to see Indigo still on his knees, One's body in front of him, and Tamara in One's place with her gun held to Indigo's head.

Her one-bullet gun, I remembered, thoughts slow and stunned. Hadn't her gun had only one bullet? She'd just shot One.

And where were the other soldiers? "Where are the others?" I asked.

"I lied to them about where I was going and left them behind," Tamara replied, without taking her gaze or her gun off Indigo.

"Why?"

"So that they wouldn't *execute you as a traitor to humanity*, Sean. What, Minister? Still not scared of me?"

"Should I be?" Indigo asked, his voice more gravelly than usual, on his knees next to One's corpse.

Tamara sighed. When the air had left all her lungs, she dropped her arm, flicking the safety back on the pistol one-handed. "Fuck it," she said, and then turned a beady look on me. "I assume your plan is to get the data and give it to both factions."

I hadn't told her, had I? No—she must've figured it out herself. I shouldn't be surprised. Lantern-Eyes was intelligent and methodical; she'd probably realized it as soon as I'd ditched the Republic for the Minister side. "That's right."

"Then we don't have much time." Tamara tucked her gun into its holster at her side. "The Republic will come after me sooner or later, and I'm guessing the rest of the Ministers will do the same. How are we getting this data out?"

I stood up. My pants fabric was sticky and damp at the knees. "Come here."

I led her to the ancient computer and showed her the screen. "I can read you what this says," I told her, "but I don't know anything about the science. Can you confirm it's the data?"

"You don't need to read it, I recognize that diagram," Tamara said, hovering one finger lightly over the screen. "So this is an ancient computer. Interesting design."

"We can't detach it from the *Nameless* without frying it. I'm going to transmit the data to the Republican ship, the Minister ship, and the *Viper*—Benny's ship. That way we'll have a copy in case either of the other two groups misses a part."

She nodded. "Understood. We've got to make sure we're

not interrupted, though. I'll radio my people, tell them that I have the data but they should return to the ship to receive it. Indigo, can you do the same?"

"Yes," Indigo said. When I glanced back I saw that he had turned One onto her back, hands crossed over her chest, and he was removing her collar-light. Without the dim glow, she was just a slight figure in the dark, indistinguishable from human.

"Right." Tamara stood up, pulled a little black handheld radio from her pocket. "Sean, you get to work starting the transmission."

"Yes, ma'am," I said automatically, and she stepped away to speak into her radio.

The ancient computer loaded slowly and painfully while the others turned aside our remaining pursuit. Tamara spoke quickly and clearly, clipped, into her radio. Indigo pressed the sides of One's removed collar-light in a deliberate and rhythmic fashion. I remembered that the collar-lights could be used in short-distance not line-of-sight communication as well. I wondered how the absence of visual reception was interpreted. Vibrations against the skin maybe? I wondered if Indigo would explain it to me.

I managed to start the transmission at last, and glanced back at Indigo and Tamara to confirm it was working. Tamara listened to her radio then flashed me a thumb's up; Indigo nodded his confirmation.

Beneath my hands, the computer buzzed and flashed an error.

My heart stopped, then pounded back again when I read the Ameng: *Connection weak*, the message warned.

Continue?

Continue, I instructed, and the transmission resumed.

A few minutes later, the error popped up again.

Tamara crouched down next to me just as I clicked *continue*. "What's wrong?"

"I think the program freezes every time the connection to one of the three ships goes below a certain threshold," I said. "It starts up again no problem, but it's slow and it needs babysitting."

"Probably a safeguard to prevent the data from being scrambled," Tamara observed. "I bet there'll be gaps in the data transmitted. It's a good thing we're sending it to three different places; we might need the three copies to compare and figure out the gaps and errors."

"That sounds like you're expecting cooperation, lieutenant," I said.

"Your optimism is catching." She looked a little pinched, but she smiled at me.

I lowered my voice to say, "Your gun was empty, right? You used your last bullet on One. You were bluffing with Indigo."

The smile vanished. "Sean," Tamara said, patiently, "I was just with the Republic. I got more ammunition from them. My gun is definitely not empty."

She really could've shot Indigo. "Oh."

"But I chose not to use it," she said, pointedly.

"Oh," I said again, and she gave me a tired look and walked away.

The transmission proceeded with agonizing slowness, glitching out every few minutes and requiring confirmation from me to continue on. I started to wonder, a little worriedly, exactly how much longer this was going to take.

Indigo came up to stand behind me, silent warmth at my shoulder. "It's taking too long," he said.

"What's our exit plan?" Tamara asked.

"You return to the Republic," Indigo told her. "Sean and I will manage from here."

My unsteady heart jolted sideways in my chest. I didn't want Lantern-Eyes to leave. But Indigo was right; the Republic didn't know exactly what she'd done, so she still had a way out. She'd spent years here alone; she'd suffered enough.

"And spend the rest of my career covering up a lie?" Tamara said. "I'm not interested. The Republic will figure out what I've done soon anyway, if they haven't caught on already. I don't do things halfway, Indigo. I thought through the consequences and I'm here anyway. So what's our exit plan?"

The transmission had paused out again at some point during Tamara's speech and I hadn't noticed. I pressed *Continue* again. The transmission resumed. "The *Viper* is our escape plan," I said.

"It's docked near the Minister ship," Indigo explained. "I trust you know where that is."

"Yeah, it's close but not exactly next door," Tamara said. "If we're going to get out of here before the ship starts peeling apart, we need to leave soon."

"The transmission isn't done," I pointed out.

"So one person stays behind and monitors it while the

others get the ship," Tamara said. "We dock as close as we dare—I assume the *Viper* can force dock?"

"Yeah, we've got gripping arms and a chute," I confirmed.

"Do we have a way around the traps on the hull? The Republic told me that the hull around here is rigged with explosives, just like the walls."

"I can shut down those traps the same way I remotely disabled and re-enabled that bomb in the door earlier."

Tamara didn't ask me how. I don't think I realized until just then exactly how much she trusted me. "So we have a way to shut down the bombs," she said. "One person stays behind. Two others get the *Viper*, dock as close as we dare, and whoever's monitoring the transmission can stay with it to the last minute, then get on the ship."

"Lantern-Eyes," I said, pleased. "With the plans."

"Thanks," she said.

"The explosion of the sun is not precisely timed," Indigo said. "It could happen sooner than anticipated. It's possible that the team going to get the *Viper* won't make it back before the radiation becomes too strong for a human to stand. I'll remain behind."

"I'm the one who can read Ameng," I told him.

"And I'm the one who can survive a solar flare," Indigo answered. "You're the one who knows how to fly the *Viper*. And Tamara is the only one who knows the *Nameless* well enough to get to the *Viper* quickly."

"Don't look at me, he's right," Tamara said, when I turned to look at her.

"You know we're not just going to leave you behind,

right?" I said, while Indigo began to undo the straps holding his ever-present gauntlet to his wrist. "We're going to come back."

"I know." Indigo handed the gauntlet to Tamara. "In case of emergency: this produces the hull seal. Press that button there, and aim from that nozzle."

She nodded, studying the shape of it. Indigo placed it on her forearm and started to close the buckles for her.

The computer in front of me beeped plaintively, and I had to turn back to press *Continue* again. "Do you think we'll need that?"

"Take these also," Indigo said, addressing not me but Tamara, and when I looked back around he was pressing One's two slender knives into her hands. "I don't recommend using the heated function, but if you need to, you must tap this pattern against the handle. There will be a pinch in your palm as the blade connects with your bloodstream; this is normal, it is drawing metabolic energy. It will exhaust you quickly, so be ready. Sean."

"What now?" I asked, but Indigo was already holding out Number One's removed collar-light to me.

It still glowed, separate from her body. I remembered Indigo telling me that a collar-light would illuminate for some time after the wearer's death—seven days or a few hours depending on brightness, right? One's corpse was dark and unrecognizable without her gleaming violet collar.

"Take it," Indigo said. "On the top there is a hidden switch; press it, and the light can be used as a communicator even if we're not in sight of each other. Messages will be felt as vibrations against the skin. We can communicate that way, if anything goes wrong."

The collar-light dangled, ghostly violet.

"Take it," Indigo insisted.

I took it. "What are you leaving for yourself?" I asked. Tamara looked strange, half-alien, with a Minister's gauntlet strapped over the sleeve of her Republican jacket and two Minister blades in her hands. One's collar-light was warm and heavy in my palm.

"I have my knife," Indigo said, and knelt beside me. "Is this the error message?"

Continue? The computer asked again, plaintive and confused. I quickly hit *Continue* and the transmission started up again.

"Yeah, you hit the button I just pressed whenever it shows up," I said. "Indigo, we'll be back soon."

"I know." He lifted my hands from the sides of the box to place his hands there instead. "Go quickly, or you may not make it to the *Viper* in time."

"Let's go, Sean," Tamara said. She'd tucked the two knives into her belt, one on either side.

I lingered at the door, despite her urging. I'd taken Benny's flashlight, and the absence of the narrow beam meant the only light in the room was Indigo's collar light.

"Shay," I named him, and at the same time I flashed out Indigo's true name with One's collar-light, a slow blossoming brightness and a heartbeat-pulse.

He turned to me with an expression like a riverbed exposed to the sun.

I couldn't forgive him if he was dead. "Promise me you'll

be alive when we get back," I said to Indigo. "Don't tell me about odds and likelihood and when the sun might nova. Just promise me."

Indigo's eyes reflected the blue glow of his collar light. "I promise."

"Promise me in Kystrene," I said.

"I promise," Shay said, in the language of my people, the language spoken in Itaka, whose people he and I together had made extinct.

"We'll be back," I promised, and I left Lab 17 with Lantern-Eyes.

CHAPTER EIGHTY FIVE: MEMORY

"Okay, it's not far, but we've got to be fast," Tamara said.

"Preaching to the choir," I said. One's collar-stone felt heavy at the base of my throat while I fumbled through fastening it. I wasn't used to wearing necklaces, but it seemed to feel extra heavy, like I was carrying the weight of its bearer and not just her jewelry.

"We're near a vent," Tamara said, looking around the room. "There should be a chimney sticking out the hull near here. Once we're in the *Viper*, we can use that chimney as a landmark."

I finally got the necklace fastened. "Great, let's go."

She grabbed at my arm. "Not that way. Follow me."

Right. I wasn't on my own anymore. I followed Tamara when she went to the left. Even in the hidden lab, she knew how to get around.

We wove through maze-like rooms, kicking up dust with our feet, and following the trail of other people's footsteps through the decay. As we went I held my hand out, palm-up, letting nanomachines spill out of it like smoke from a quenched wick. Each nanomachine I sent out through my palm had one simple directive: disable the bombs in the hull nearby Indigo's location.

At last Tamara and I ended up at a hole in the wall, carved through, where the footprints stopped.

"We're going back into the main ship now," Tamara told me, sticking her head through the gap in the wall. "Which means monsters. Keep a sharp eye out."

"Yes, ma'am," I said.

"Stop ma'aming me. I'm a deserter now."

"You're still a ma'am to me," I said.

I thought about that as I followed no-longer-Lieutenant Gupta through the hallways of the *Nameless*. I hadn't asked her to desert her post, or Indigo to turn on his own people. But they had done it, both of them, because they trusted me.

No matter that Tamara had lured me and Benny here as bait, or that Indigo had led the army that attacked my planet. I wasn't going to lose either of them here on this ship. Not like I had lost Benny. Or Brigid.

We were walking together down a dark and narrow hall when I said, "The last thing I said to my sister before she died was that I wished I was an only child."

Tamara's steps did not falter, nor the alert sweep of her head, checking for monsters. "Did the two of you fight often?"

The memory came free bitterly, like pulling a stone free of tar. "Yeah. We were really close in age, so I think that's why we... we fought a lot."

"If you were close in age you must've played together a

lot, too."

"All the time. I mostly played with my sister, when I was a kid."

"Brigid, right?" Tamara asked. "Sean, I have six siblings. I've fought with all of them at some point in our lives, sometimes fought with them continuously. Sometimes I said or did things to them, or vice versa, that as an adult I would never stand from a stranger. It sounds to me like you and Brigid had a pretty normal relationship. If the Ministers hadn't attacked Kystrom, you would've grown out of your fights. Or maybe you wouldn't have. Either way would've been normal. Did you love her?"

Not until after she died, I almost said, the echo of the Dreamer's interpretation of my deepest nightmare, but I swallowed the words back and thought about it: Brigid, annoyed, posting signs on her door to keep me out; Brigid, calling me down for dinner, her voice a high playful taunt; Brigid, smiling at me conspiratorial at night while our parents bustled on, assuming we'd both been successfully put to bed.

"Yeah," I said.

"Did she know that?"

The last thing I'd said to her had been *I wish I was an only child*, cruel and stupid, and I would've forgotten about it if it hadn't been unintentional prophecy. I'd probably said things like it before, only I couldn't remember, because none of them had resulted in me being an only child scarcely eight hours later.

And yet I'd felt bad about it even after I'd said it, because Brigid had looked so hurt. She hadn't cried, but her eyes had been bright. I'd remembered that after I'd left her to go to school.

But that wasn't the only time we ever interacted. It wouldn't have even been a significant one, if it hadn't been the last. Brigid had been sixteen when she died. I'd known her since the moment she was born. Sixteen years, the entirety of her life. We had been all but inseparable as children, though we'd started to grow apart after we'd become teenagers.

When she'd died, that would've been her last memory of me, but not her only memory. I had never doubted that my sister loved me. I had known my sister too well to doubt that she knew I'd loved her, too.

"Yeah," I said to Tamara as we walked through the abandoned spaceship, and couldn't say anything more.

"Then you have no reason to feel guilty," Tamara said, and I was glad she was leading the way, so she could not see that I had to swipe my palm across my eyes.

We'd walked a little further through the dark, following turns only Tamara knew, before she said suddenly, "Lashana Pecking. Raphael Warren. Lian Wu. Jacob Tarver. Pelle Takgaard. Sara Boccanegra. David Etten. Jen Primrose. Evan Colgate. Evan Gallagher. Christian Glaceau."

"Who were they?" I asked.

"The people who came with me on this ship," Tamara said. "My team, the ones who died."

She'd told me once that she hadn't remembered their names. Yet she'd recited them for me like they'd been waiting on her tongue all this time.

"I didn't like to think about them," Tamara said. "I had to focus everything I had on staying alive. But sometimes something will remind me of them and it'll hit me, who they are and what they sound like and look like and what they smelled like, even. All so real it's like I'm back there, not here and now. So I tried to put that away, to keep myself alive."

I brought out my memories of Brigid and Kystrom so often that they were starting to fray from the overuse, the way a piece of cloth will grow thin and fragile if you rub it with your thumb for too long.

Suddenly Tamara's arm came up and struck me in the chest, forcing me to a stop. She grabbed the flashlight from my hand and flicked it off, turning as she did to press her finger to her lips, the whites of her eyes gleaming in the moment before the flashlight died. I lifted my hand to Ultraviolet's collar-light and dialed it down to black.

In the stillness, I heard what Tamara had heard: movement several rooms away, footsteps. Sound did travel further than light in this ship. There was someone, or something, directly in our path.

Tamara's hand landed lightly on my arm, drawing me forward. We crept through the blackness and the blackness brightened around us, a strange, colorless light.

Not a colorless light, I realized, as we peered around the last corner that separated us from that glow. A light of many colors, glowing softly together.

The Ministers were between us and the *Viper*.

CHAPTER EIGHTY SIX: IMPROVISATIONAL LINGUISTICS

WE'D TURNED OFF our lights as we approached, so they hadn't seen us; Tamara, so attuned to the ways of the *Nameless*, had detected their presence before they'd heard ours, so they hadn't heard us either. They were waiting in the room before us, some standing still, some pacing. There were only three of them present: Green, Orange, and Red. A fiery orange light flickered up from a portal in the floor where they'd cut through the hull and sealed the opening off with the oil-slick; their starship must be docked just outside. The Blue Minister was probably in the spaceship. Yellow and Ultraviolet were dead, and Indigo was on my side now; of the seven Ministers who had come aboard, only four were left.

If it had been just a matter of their presence, we could have retreated and snuck around them. But not far away from the oil-slick hole in the floor I could see a familiar shape sticking up out of the floor: the *Viper*'s docking chute. They'd force-docked the *Viper* to the *Nameless* in this very room.

There was no way we could sneak into the *Viper* without being seen.

I felt Tamara move next to me in the dark and knew, even without seeing, that she was reaching for her gun. I put my hand on hers to stop her. She was a good shot, I knew that. She had enough bullets now to take them all out. But I had seen the way the Ministers moved in battle before; I did not think even someone as good a shot as Tamara Gupta could take them all out at once.

And if she could—even if she killed only one of them—I did not know if either of us could face Indigo knowing that she had. Somewhere, somehow, the bloodshed had to stop.

I stood up slowly, lifting my hand to my borrowed collar.

The movement, or the sound of my clothes rustling, caught the Ministers' attention. The Green Minister, who seemed to be the ranking color, ceased her pacing and snapped out something sharply in white collar-light aimed at our direction.

I didn't know precisely what she said, but I knew it was a question. There was one question a human would ask in this situation, and that question was: *Who goes there?*

And the Ministers were human, after all.

I crouched down a little, from standing at my full height to standing at a height closer to what Number One's height had been. Then I lifted my hand to my collar-light and flashed out my answer to Green's question: two sharp flashes of ultraviolet light, like the twin blades Number One had worn. Who goes there? *Kora.*

It was too dim with only the collar-lights for us to see

each other's faces, and the room where the Ministers had docked was fairly large. Even so, I saw Green's shoulders relax. She flashed out some other question at me, this time addressing me in ultraviolet light. The only word I recognized was a slow blossoming of light followed by a dual throb: *Shay*. She was asking about Indigo.

My vocabulary in the Light language was limited, my grammar even more so, restricted to the odds and ends I'd picked up while the Ministers' captive, and the bits and pieces that Indigo had taught me. I could recite a prayer for the dead, but I didn't know how to tell the other Ministers to *please leave, get on the ship and go, don't wait for me*—which was a shame, because the Ministers were so strictly hierarchical that they would probably obey my order, if only I could find the vocabulary to give it. I was half-guessing what Green was saying, but I had to guess quickly; any lack of fluency would cause Green to doubt.

But I was good at languages, and better at improvising.

Shay is dead, I flashed back, in white light, to the whole group.

What about Kora? Green asked.

What about Kora? Kora was lying dead on the floor next to the man who'd killed her, bereft of weapons, armor, and light. Kora had come on her own to find Indigo and bring him home, like Tamara had done for me. The difference was, Tamara had held her fire, and Kora had not restrained her knife.

But she *had* gone back for him. *I've known you hundreds of years*, she'd said. She'd covered for him with the

Ministerial Council. She'd loved him, in her own snowy fashion, and as far as these Ministers knew, she'd killed him. Because of Benny, I knew what that felt like.

Number One had once told me that a traumatized person was trapped in their moment of trauma. That they do not leave, that they cannot leave. As far as these Ministers knew, Kora had just accomplished her mission, and murdered her student.

I used the future intention tense, just like Indigo had taught me, and flashed out my response to Green: *Kora will stay.*

Or, translated another way: *Kora intends to stay.* I had barely known One, and I'd recognized the melancholy in her. I trusted that these Ministers, who had known her far better, would understand why she might refuse to leave this place and this moment.

Green was silent, collar-light dark, for a long, long time. Then she flashed, *Kora will die.*

Yes, I said, and trusted that they would not dare to question One any further.

Again Green was silent, her light dark; Red and Orange flanked her, their lights as dim as distant stars.

Pity struck me like a blow to the chest. I touched the collar-light and dialed out another word Indigo had taught me, a slow brighten and a slow dim: *It's okay.*

Green straightened her spine, the movement graceful, half-seen in the darkness. She flashed out a pattern to me that I recognized as the last line of Indigo's poem: *Your life will be remembered.*

Then she turned and gestured at the other two, and

Red, then Orange, slipped out of the hull through the hole they'd cut into it, vanishing through the oil-slick. Green was the last to go. She paused before slipping out through the portal, looking back, and for a terrible instant I was certain she had seen *me*, Sean Wren, not the Ultraviolet Minister. But she had only seen the glow of my stolen collar-light: feet-first, she slipped out of the *Nameless* and into the sunlight beyond.

Tamara and I waited a beat after she'd vanished, but none of the Ministers resurfaced from outside. My breath rushed out of me. I flicked the flashlight beam back on, drowning out the eerie corpse-glow of the collar-light I'd used to impersonate the dead.

"Well done," Tamara said, sounding just as breathless as I felt.

We rushed into the now-empty room together, heading for the docking chute in the floor. All we had to do was step into the hole in the floor and climb down into the *Viper* below and—

And something was wrong. Instead of an opening, I found nothing but smooth metal.

Tamara crouched beside me. "This looks like it was welded shut."

I felt along the edges, near where her fingers were probing. It had been welded shut, the metal ruined, melted into a solid hunk.

"The Ministers didn't want anyone to be able to get into the *Viper* from the *Nameless*," I realized. "If they needed to use the *Viper*, they could still get into it by traveling through the vacuum, and then just cut the docking chute off."

"I can cut the docking chute off," Tamara said, a little dubiously, and I found that she had one of One's swords in her hand, the white metal of the blade gleaming in the flashlight beam. "But what happens then?"

Then the only way to securely connect the *Viper* to the *Nameless* would be a severed hunk of metal sticking to the side of the *Nameless* a mile away from where we needed. "We'll have to improvise," I said.

Tamara Gupta looked miserable at the thought.

We'd survived crazed monsters, a murderous AI, uncountable booby-traps, and the combined might of both the Ministers and the Republican military. The *Viper* didn't stand a chance. Lantern-Eyes cut through the seal with One's heated sword, and then we climbed into the chute. Once we were inside the chute she fumbled with Indigo's gauntlet until she managed to produce an oil-slick seal, then she stuck her arm out through the seal, charged One's blade again, and cut the docking chute off from the *Nameless*. The oil-slick seal held the air inside the *Viper*, even as that room on the *Nameless* was decompressed; I climbed down the last few ladder steps and went into the *Viper* proper while Tamara lay flat on her back and caught her breath.

"Come on, Lantern-Eyes," I said, while I started up the *Viper*'s engines for a speedy escape, "it can't be that bad."

"Indigo wasn't exaggerating," she gasped.

I glanced out the cockpit window as the engines came to life. The *Nameless* was revolving, and I wanted to keep a close eye on where I was on the ship's surface, so I came down as near to Indigo as possible.

Between spokes of the great wheel, the dying sun glowed, brighter and brighter still. The cockpit windows began to dim themselves automatically against the radiance, but the sun was still so bright it was almost unbearable, the glow of it swallowing up the shadow of the *Nameless*.

"Tamara," I said quietly, and heard her get to her feet and press herself beside me in the narrow piloting cradle.

We watched as, a thousand years coming, the star began to explode.

CHAPTER EIGHTY SEVEN:
THE DREAMER

QUICKLY, QUICKLY, QUICKLY. I flew the *Viper* as close to the *Nameless*'s hull as I dared. "Is this it?"

"Slow down; it's hard for me to tell," Tamara said. "I'm used to looking at the ship from the inside."

The light of the solar radiance spilled around the edges of the wheel. The ancient metal starting to peel. It was lucky we were in the shadow. "*Hurry*, Tamara!"

"There," Tamara said, pointing, "there, I think. Do you see that outcropping? That's the exhaust chute in Lab 17 that we saw on our way out."

"Good." I aimed for it.

"What are you going to do?" she asked me. "The docking equipment doesn't work."

"I'm going to improvise," I said, got myself situated over the hull near the exhaust chute, and then rammed the *Nameless*.

Tamara shouted in surprise, the jolt slamming her into my chair and out of the pilot's cradle. It rattled my teeth, even in my seat. But when I peered up out of the cockpit about where the *Viper*'s broken docking chute extended, I saw that I hadn't quite penetrated the hull.

"Get ready," I warned Tamara, backing off a bit, and then *ramming* the other ship once more.

I felt the pop as the docking chute punched through. Immediately I extended the gripper arms, slamming into the ship, preventing us from bouncing back out.

Tamara was already on her feet. "The impact will have caused a decompression," she warned me. "I'm going to go seal it off," and she waved Indigo's gauntlet at me.

"Be careful," I said.

"I'll be back with Indigo," she said.

"Wait!" I said, and fumbled with the collar fastened around my neck. It was warm in my hand with my own body heat. I passed it over to Tamara. "Take this in case there's any problems. See that switch at the top? You two can use that to communicate if there are any problems."

She took it gingerly. "I can't speak Light."

"Then use it as a proximity sensor. It doesn't have a long range. The *Viper* won't move, but if something happened, Indigo might have."

She nodded tersely, fastening the collar around her own throat far more quickly than I'd managed around mine. "See you soon," she said, and climbed up the ladder through the chute so quickly I didn't have time for another word.

We'd need to get out of here fast. I waited, bent over the cockpit controls, ready to retract the gripper arms and key in the launch sequence as soon as Indigo and Tamara cleared the hull. I waited, and I waited, muscles twitching from being held so taut and still for so long.

Where were they? It wasn't that far to Lab 17 from here, or it shouldn't be. Had Tamara been wrong? Had we landed in the wrong part of the ship?

Had something happened?

The light outside the cockpit window was getting brighter and brighter as the sun swelled, waves of radiation blasting off its surface in a massive explosion. This was just the vanguard of the supernova. In who knew how long, maybe as little as seconds, the shockwave would ignite us. The sun-side of the *Nameless* was probably already starting to burn.

Maybe the Republican soldiers hadn't obeyed Tamara's orders, and sent someone to Lab 17 to find out what was going on. Maybe the other Ministers hadn't believed my pretense, and had returned to Lab 17. Maybe Indigo was dead, and Tamara was finishing the broadcast; maybe both were dead, lying side-by-side on the floor of Lab 17, just like the Dreamer's nightmares had shown me.

I left the cockpit, went to stand under the docking chute. The oilslick seal gleamed on the other end, but I couldn't see Tamara or Indigo. I climbed up the ladder and stuck my head out and found that I had punctured through in one of the empty rooms I'd already walked through an hour or two ago, which meant we really had landed quite close to the center of Lab 17. There were torn places in the hull around where I'd punched the docking chute through, but they were sealed off with more oilslick surfaces, keeping the *Nameless* airtight.

Distance shouldn't be a problem. Tamara and Indigo

should be back by now. Why weren't they back yet?

If I went to find them and I got lost or they came back before I did, then they might come looking for me, and we'd all be stuck here. I had to wait. But if I waited too long the crash of the sun's explosion would strike the *Nameless* and the attached *Viper*, and then we'd all be dead too.

I held out my hand, scratched palm up. And then I *willed* every last one of the nanomachines still in my body, every last tiny Dreamer-bot still crawling through my veins or holding little cuts and bruises shut, to leave through my skin. Find Tamara and Indigo, I willed them, find them, and clear a path for them, to make it quickly and easily back here. Bring them back.

It ached, like I was drawing all my blood from my body and leaving my veins collapsed behind; it ached, but I pushed. And one by one the glittering things came up through my skin and hummed off into the ship, swarming, until although I *willed*, nothing more came free of my skin.

I let myself sag, tired, hanging half-in and half-out through the oilslick sealing the *Viper*'s docking chute. As an afterthought I reached up to my split throat, which the nanomachines had been helpfully holding shut for me. I met a thick ridge of half-healed flesh: they'd closed up my throat before they'd left.

There was nothing else I could do but wait, as much as I hated to wait. I had no control over this situation, as little as I liked to admit that—Tamara and I, I supposed, had that in common.

There was nothing for me to do but wait and trust them

to come back.

I turned my hand palm-down so that the blood could drip onto the floor, small but sincere offering to the God Who Shed His Blood For Us. Let them come back, I prayed to the God of Kystrene. Let them come back. I have no more room for scars on my arm.

A crash across the room caught my attention and I looked up in time to see Tamara and Indigo burst through, looking slightly worse for the wear, but both upright and alive. "What are you doing?" Tamara demanded when she saw me. "Get back in that ship!"

I didn't even bother to use the ladder. I just stepped off and let myself fall the six feet back to the floor of the *Viper*, landing hard and going immediately for the cockpit.

Tamara and Indigo landed behind me just as I roused the engines again. The light outside was so bright I couldn't even see the background stars, and the side of the *Nameless*, even in shadow, was lit up clearly in all its rotten and scarred glory.

"We're in, go!" Tamara shouted, and I gunned it, tearing carelessly free of the *Nameless*, because in a few minutes it wouldn't matter anymore if part of the ship had lost atmosphere. The whole ship was about to be destroyed.

I felt a pang at the thought of all the things living on that ship, the tortured things Mara Zhu had made and abandoned. I couldn't have saved them now, and if I had tried, they would have killed me for it. But it was hardly fair that they should be left behind to die. In my head and my heart, I offered a brief prayer for whatever souls they might have.

I had Tamara and Indigo, at least. "What happened?" I asked, as I tried to outrun a shockwave of light and superheated matter.

"I must've triggered something in the ship's computer," Indigo explained, terse. "Dreamer nanomachines started to appear. I sealed the room against them to finish broadcasting the data, but even after the broadcast was done, they were trying to get in."

"Then they all just stopped," Tamara seamlessly took up the narrative. "No cause that I could see. Maybe the sun fried the Dreamer."

Or maybe my nanomachines had shut them down. "I'm glad you made it back," I said.

"So are we," Tamara said.

I glanced back once, as soon as the *Viper* had gathered enough speed to clear the stellar explosion. Where the *Nameless* once had been, I saw nothing but light.

CHAPTER EIGHTY EIGHT: A LETTER FROM THE DEAD

"IT WAS A solid plan until I thought about it," Tamara said.

"Well, I didn't see you coming up with a better one," I replied, annoyed.

There were seats on the *Viper* but somehow we'd all ended up sitting in a circle on the floor, crosslegged. The *Viper* didn't need active piloting while it was in open space like this. I'd just set it on a vague course towards the Republic, because I'd known that, eventually, we would need food and fuel and other supplies. The Republic was less effectively policed than Maria Nova.

Tamara had her hands wrapped covetously around a mug full of coffee, looking a lot less spectral now that she'd had a proper shower and was wearing a clean T-shirt, one of Benny's. "I'm not saying it was a bad plan. Obviously I stand behind it, or I wouldn't have deserted my country for a Minister and a cheap pirate."

"Hey," I said, but without heat; I'd caught Indigo hiding a smile behind his own mug of coffee. He'd showered and changed too, into a robe that had belonged to Quint, and he'd turned his light collar off: no eerie blue illuminated him from beneath, and the collar itself could've been just an ordinary piece of jewelry. In human clothes, with his hair still damp and a bruise showing blue on his jaw, he looked nothing like the nightmare personified he'd appeared when he'd first carved his way onto the *Nameless*.

They both looked relaxed. They were comfortable.

I was comfortable, too. And the shower had been nice.

"The problem is logistics," Tamara continued, gesturing sharply with the hand not holding the mug. "Everybody's got a copy, but nobody knows the other people have a copy. And judging from our copy, no one's copy is entirely complete. We'd need to compare all three copies to get the complete data—but no one knows they can share, or would share if they did know."

"Cooperation seems unlikely," Indigo agreed.

Tamara nodded. "Someone high up would have to be willing to take the first step."

A crazy idea sidled sideways into my mind, dragged there by a chuckling imp that could not believe its mischievous luck. It was crazy. It wasn't detailed or clearly worked out, but with Tamara's logic and Indigo's insight, it might just be transformed into a crazy idea that could work.

"Guys," I said, already grinning at the thought, "I might have an idea."

*　　*　　*

PARNASSE WAS *EXACTLY* how I remembered it: sunny, blue

skies. Senator Todd Ketel's office was only a few floors up from the shady little room where I'd met Quint. It was decorated sort of similarly, too. He had the same kind of clock—the man must have a thing for antique clocks.

Todd Ketel. Ketel, Todd. Senator Ketel. *Todd.* He wasn't just "the Senator" anymore. I knew his name now, the bastard.

I picked up that clock while I waited and began to dismantle it on his desk.

Ketel burst in after I'd only been in his office for about ten minutes or so, red-faced, looking winded. He looked exactly like he did on the vidscreen, a man who'd aged out of his good looks but kept the lantern jaw. He stared at me for a minute like a frightened deer, breathing hard in the doorway to his own office.

And then, to give Senator Ketel some credit, he took a slightly deeper breath, straightened his spine, and fixed his tie. He shut the door precisely behind him, then walked around to sit on the other side of the desk from me. He said, "Mr. Wren."

Enchanting. "You probably have *no idea* what happened, do you?" I said.

To the Senator's credit, he didn't try to dissemble or lie. Presumably my appearance in his office one sunny afternoon without an implant in my skull was enough proof that I'd figured out who he was. "No," he admitted, sitting back in his chair and watching me from wary eyes, "after Alicia—"

I stopped messing with the clock. "Alicia?"

"Alicia Quint, your contact."

So Quint had been a last name. "Right. After she died…"

"She's dead?" the Senator asked, searching my face like I might give something away.

"They're all dead. Quint, Leah, Benny. Just me left. And I have the Philosopher Stone. Of course, so does your country, now."

A calculating gleam entered his eyes, imperfectly hidden by his relaxed lean. "The Republic's copy of the data has a few gaps. I'd be interested in negotiating a price for your copy of the data, assuming that it is more complete than ours."

"Not more complete, maybe, but it fills in some gaps where yours doesn't," I said. "And I'm very willing to negotiate a price for my copy of the data."

"Name it."

I tossed a few gears from the back of the clock onto his desk, ringing like coins. "You'll share both copies of the data with the Ministers."

He was silent while he absorbed that blow. I smiled to myself, and pulled a few more gears from the clock. Then the Senator burst out laughing.

"I can't do that," he said. "Are you insane? We're at war."

"Sure you are and sure I am, but you're still going to do it," I told him cheerfully. "Let me describe a scenario for you: you open a détente with Maria Nova. As a gesture of goodwill, you offer them this piece of mutual history, the data from the Philosopher Stone experiments. See, what you didn't know—what nobody knew, really, except the people who have seen the data themselves—is that humanity *created* the Ministers. That the Ministers, really, are just humans too. We're all one big family. We shouldn't be fighting, and this is the first step to a universe free of war. That's a good spin for a politician, isn't it? A hero for peace?"

"Or a traitor to his country," Ketel replied. "The Republic isn't gaining anything from this bargain, just vague suggestions that maybe a peace could be possible."

"Right, there's one thing I didn't mention, that nobody but you and I know," I said, and turned the clock upside-down to shake out the last few remaining gears. "The Ministers also have a copy of the data."

Across his desk, the Senator went still.

"I'm guessing that the only way we'll find out anything close to the complete set of data from the Philosopher Stone is by comparing all three sets of data." I stuck my finger in the clock to jostle loose any remaining pieces. "And if you offer your set of the data on the condition that they share theirs, then both sides gain something they need, as well as establishing the grounds for future diplomacy."

"The Ministers won't refuse?"

"The Ministers need that data more than you do." I set the empty clock down. I sat back in my chair and beamed at him. "What do you think?"

He tapped his fingers on the arm of his chair, studying me. Cautious son-of-a-bitch. I dearly hoped he'd challenge me.

He lifted his head like a bull raising his horns. There was the challenge! "We still have sufficient data to put to use medically, and against the Ministers," he said. "The complete data would be preferable but the Republic won't fail if we don't have it. I'm not interested in a risky gamble, Mr. Wren."

"Right," I said. "I forgot to mention; you'll do what I say or I'll expose you."

"You have no proof of any wrongdoing."

"Senator Ketel," I said. "*Todd*. After Quint died, I inherited all her things. You two have a lot of interesting correspondence about very illegal activities. Some bank accounts, some files, some secret offices... No point in shutting any of those down now, I've already gathered my proof," I added. "I have this one friend who knows a lot about the Republican legal system, and this other friend who thinks Republican technological security is laughably outdated."

He leaned onto his desk, hands steepled over the pile of gears from his disassembled clock. If he hadn't been a murdering piece of shit, I might've almost felt bad for him.

I reached over the desk to clap him on the shoulder, firm and friendly grip. "You think it over," I told him kindly. "Just remember, there's every reason to say yes, and no reason to refuse. You can contact me via this," and I placed a little communicator on his desk that Benny had made and Indigo had improved, "when you've come to terms with what you need to do. I promise I won't even stick an implant in your skull."

I left on my own, letting him process that alongside the wreckage of his gorgeous vintage clock.

The *Viper* was parked where I'd left it, on the outskirts of a spaceport, landed neatly on a concrete landing zone beneath a broad empty blue sky. I was really good at getting past Republican security, after all, and it wasn't like Senator Ketel had been able to report the existence of the ship to any authorities. Tamara and Indigo were waiting for me by the airlock door. She had her face tilted up to the sun, beatific, her jack-o-lantern eyes crinkled at the corners. Indigo watched me advance and when I was near, he gave me a smile as soft as a gentle night breeze. In casual human clothes, he could pass for human from a distance.

"Did it work?" he asked.

"Exactly like we expected," I said. Tamara stopped luxuriating in the sun long enough to smirk. "Where do we want to go? We should probably clear out of town, just in case he decides to try something."

"I don't care where we go, as long as we can get food," Tamara said. "And Sean, you got a message from someone. I think it was addressed to you, anyway. It was written in Kystrene."

"It was addressed to you," Indigo confirmed.

There were a few other expats in the Republic, though none from Itaka. Still, we'd made contact with them, and had a fragile network of communication set up. "Was it important?"

"I didn't read it," Indigo said.

We left the sunlight behind, but parted ways within the *Viper*. "You guys pick where we go," I said. "I'm going to check that message."

Tamara lifted a hand in acknowledgement, then headed up to the piloting area with Indigo, while I walked over to the living areas.

There was a message waiting for me in my room, just like Tamara had said. It was addressed to me in Kystrene.

I sat down in front of the screen, in case this message was long, and opened up the attachment.

Dear Sean, it read:

I hope this message reaches you. I hope what I've heard is true, and you're still alive. Please forgive me for not trying to find you sooner—I thought you were dead. Why are you going by a different last name these days?

If you are alive, and this does reach you, then the group of Kystrene refugees who received this message will know where to send an answer.

Please, please reply as soon as you can—I need your help.

All my love,
Brigid

ACKNOWLEDGEMENTS

THERE'S A NOTE on my desk that says, "Thank Jenny for the worms."

I'm not (just) thanking my friend Jenny. I'm thanking Jenny's husband, and Jenny's husband's friend, who once made a comment in passing that the veins in the back of his hand pulsing blood looked like little worms moving around. Exactly why he said something so unsettling has been lost to history, but the comment itself was passed on to Jenny's husband, then to Jenny, and then finally to me, when a determined-looking Jenny approached me at work to tell me, "You need to hear this."

I did. And now a hypoxic Sean compares the veins in the back of his hand to horrible little worms, because that delightfully awful image never left my head.

One person may write a novel, but the people around her give her the encouragement, the space, the energy, and the terrible venous imagery she needs to complete it. I'm grateful to all those friends who inspired me, who encouraged me, who listened to me bitch and moan for months on end, and whose pleasant company I enjoyed with or without the presence of a manuscript hanging over us.

Especially I am grateful to my readers, all of them talented writers on their own: my mother, Sarah, and Cornelia. They've been with me for every manuscript I've written, and I admire their red pens as much as I fear them. I am grateful to my agent, Hannah, who supported me through the long miserable process of publishing, encouraged me when I needed it, and caught me when I made major errors in my physics (curse you, centripetal force). I am grateful to both my editors, Kate and Jim, who improved this book every time they looked at it.

And finally, thank you to my Michelle, for being everything.

FIND US ONLINE!

www.rebellionpublishing.com

/rebellionpub /rebellionpublishing /rebellionpublishing

SIGN UP TO OUR NEWSLETTER!

rebellionpublishing.com/newsletter

YOUR REVIEWS MATTER!

Enjoy this book? Got something to say?

Leave a review on Amazon, GoodReads or with your
favourite bookseller and let the world know!